The Third Act
of Theo Gruene

Also by Talya Tate Boerner:

The Accidental Salvation of Gracie Lee

Gene, Everywhere

Bernice Runs Away

The Third Act
of Theo Gruene

Talya Tate Boerner

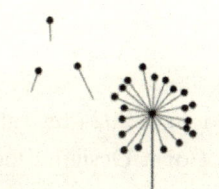

One Mississippi Press

One Mississippi Press LLC
Fayetteville, Arkansas 72701

All rights reserved. No part of this publication may be reproduced, stored in a retrieval system, or transmitted in any form or by any means, electronic, mechanical, photocopying, recording, scanning or otherwise, without the prior written permission of One Mississippi Press LLC. Excerpts may be used for review purposes. Thank you for your support of the author's rights.

This is a work of fiction. Names, characters, places, and events that occur either are the products of the author's imagination or are used fictitiously. Any resemblance to actual persons, places, or events is purely coincidental.

The contents and opinions expressed in this book do not necessarily reflect the views and opinions of One Mississippi Press LLC, nor does the mention of brands or trade names constitute endorsement.

ISBN-13: 978-1-951418-10-6 Hardback
ISBN-13: 978-1-951418-11-3 Trade Paperback
ISBN-13: 978-1-951418-12-0 ePUB

Copyright © 2024 by Talya Tate Boerner
Front Cover Design: One Mississippi Press LLC

Printed in the United States of America
First Edition 2025

To those who look for magic
in the ordinary—this book is for you.

One

It was an inconvenient time for a visitor, so Theo ignored the person knocking at his front door. Using stainless steel tweezers, he lifted the edges of the plant specimen and centered it over the mounting paper. Once he placed the brittle stem onto the glue, that would be that; there would be no shifting the delicate seed pod. The specimen would be preserved where he placed it for eternity. Concentration was a necessary skill.

Again, the knocking.

A storm had been building all morning so Theo told himself the howling wind was to blame for the noise. He placed the native columbine specimen onto the glue and then pressed it into place using the tip of the tweezer. Collected twenty years before his birth, it was in remarkable shape, with its pistils and stamens still intact. He read the tag that came packaged with it—*West Mountain, Washington County, Dr. Demaree, February 1930.*

Three more raps on the door—*rat-tat-tat*—rattled his mind. "Coming, coming!" Whoever was there wasn't planning to leave. He would see to the uninvited caller and send them away.

Theo suspected it was Nita Johnson, who lived two doors down. Her husband had died several years ago, and since then, she'd made it her mission to check on him occasionally. "Just making sure you are alive in there," she would say. Sometimes he invited her inside for a glass of iced tea or a cold beer. Theo wasn't altogether unfriendly (or at least didn't mean to be), but given the choice, he preferred solitude.

He opened the door with a flourish, fully prepared to explain his busyness to Nita, but instead of his neighbor, he was surprised to find a young girl standing there. She wore an oversized lime green raincoat, and her dark, luminous eyes appeared enormous through the lenses of her eyeglasses. She looked like a spring grasshopper.

"Well, now, what have we here?" Theo said, finding his voice.

The girl blinked but said nothing. Theo thought of the plant specimens waiting for him, the mounting glue thickening in the jar on his dining room table. He glanced along the sidewalk in front of his house, expecting to see the girl's mother waiting nearby, urging her to *go on, speak up,* as she attempted to sell the World's Finest chocolate bars, or raffle tickets for an Easter ham, or whatever Lafayette Elementary School was promoting for its next fundraiser. But there was no one else around.

He crossed his arms and continued taking in the child from head to toe. The hem of her raincoat dripped water onto his doormat.

"Can I help you with something? Are you lost?" She *looked* lost. Or confused.

"Actually, I'm a who, not a what."

"Come again?" It was his turn to look confused.

"When you opened the door, you said, 'What have we here?' But I'm a person, not a thing. And the proper interrogative word for a person is *who,* not *what.*"

Theo frowned. *Was this kid for real?*

Again, his eyes swept the sidewalk and street in front of his house, but no one else was out on such a stormy morning. He thought of the television show *What Would You Do?* He watched it occasionally when he happened upon it, and it always left him wondering what his reaction might be to certain circumstances. This could be one of those situations. His first inclination was to shoo the smart-mouthed girl away, but in case John Quiñones was hiding in the hydrangeas growing around his front porch, he decided to play along. "Pardon me. I stand corrected. *Who* have we here?" Despite his eagerness to return to the plant specimens, Theo maintained a calm voice. By now, he was curious.

"The truth is, I missed my school bus by two measly minutes, and I can't get back inside our house. I forgot my key, and it's storming, and I don't want to be struck by lightning."

Theo had to listen carefully to keep up with her rapid-fire words.

"Would it be okay if I come inside and stay with you for a while?"

"Me? Well, no, I don't—"

"My mom gets off work just before noon today, and I'll go home then." She swiped at her glasses with wet fingertips, further smearing the lenses. "I won't bother you. I promise."

Too late for that, he thought.

Shallow pools of water shimmered on the sidewalk leading from his front steps to the street. The fern he had successfully overwintered before returning to its porch hook just yesterday began spinning in the wind, its fronds whipping all around. Overnight, the March winds had blown in alright, bringing quite the quandary. He couldn't invite a strange urchin child into his house. She could be a pickpocket or a scammer of some sort. But what if she wasn't? He couldn't leave her outside in such awful weather, hidden camera or not. "Well, I guess you better come inside. Let's see if we can't sort this out."

The girl stepped into the foyer and slipped off her shoes. Her sockless feet looked cold, and her pale skin was tinged purple. When she noticed him frowning at the chipped blue polish on her toenails, she covered her feet with the rainbow-colored backpack she removed from her shoulders.

"Let's start with your name," Theo said, his interest in the child and her circumstances growing.

"Can we start with the restroom? I really need to pee. Like really, *really* bad." She began to squirm, dancing almost, crossing one leg over the other, as though the urge had hit her so suddenly she might not be able to walk another step without having an accident.

Good grief. What had he gotten himself into? "Right this way." Theo rushed the girl through the family room toward the half-bath, just off the kitchen. After she disappeared behind the door, he heard nothing but the grumble of thunder rolling over his rooftop. Theo had not been expecting a morning thunderstorm any more than he had expected to find a young girl on his doorstep. Work had consumed him since the latest package of specimens had arrived from the university. Even the local newspaper and the weather forecast had fallen by the wayside. He had barely eaten during the past two weeks.

Soon, the toilet flushed, and he heard a rush of water from the faucet. Finally, the bathroom door opened. Having shed the green raincoat, she looked different, smaller if that was possible, a bit daintier.

She smiled. "Thank you. I feel loads better. I hope it's okay that I left my raincoat on the hook behind the bathroom door. It's drippy. Also, I used a hand towel to dry myself off a little bit." She sounded relieved.

Theo nodded. "That's fine. Now, how about we have a little visit?" He motioned toward the kitchen. She scampered to a chair and hopped into it.

"Could I possibly borrow some socks? Your floors feel completely frozen," she said, staring at him with those huge bug-like eyes.

Theo sighed, looked at the girl's naked toes, and then the oak floorboards running the length of the kitchen. Even though he was wearing his favorite old sneakers (as well as socks, thank you very much), he knew his floors were indeed cold. When he worked on herbarium specimens, he kept the downstairs temperature at precisely sixty-five degrees. Cooler temperatures helped preserve ancient plants.

"Wait here. I'll be right back." Theo went to fetch a pair of white athletic socks from the clean pile he'd dumped on top of the dryer but had never gotten around to folding. "They'll swallow your feet but should warm you right up," he said, handing her the socks while experiencing the oddest out-of-body sensation. Something about the girl seemed familiar to him.

The girl thanked him and began pulling a sock over her left foot, her entire shin and knee disappearing underneath the stretchy fabric. She laughed at this, and he wondered about her age. She looked awfully young.

"Okay. How about I make you a nice cup of hot chocolate while we figure out what to do? Should we call your mother and let her know you missed the bus?" Theo disliked having his work interrupted, but relished having a problem to solve.

"Do you have any green tea instead?"

Green tea? What kid preferred green tea to hot chocolate? "I can probably rustle up a bag of Lipton, but it won't be green."

She pushed her glasses up on her petite nose. "That would be perfect, Mr. Gruene."

The sound of his name coming from the girl's mouth stopped him cold. He had never met this child—he was sure of it. He'd never purchased a box of Thin Mints from her, or seen her riding bikes with the other neighborhood kids. "How do you know my name?"

"It's right there on that envelope." She giggled and pointed at the stack of unopened mail collected on the kitchen table.

"Oh. Of course." It was an obvious explanation; one he would have guessed if he'd not been completely thrown by her sudden presence. Now feeling antsy about a whole host of things—a precocious child at his kitchen table; the way her eyes had quickly scanned his mail; the fact that she was now wearing an article of his clothing—he pulled the stack of envelopes toward himself protectively, and straightened it. He didn't yet know the girl's name or age, but he knew she had no difficulty reading. She had even pronounced his German-derived surname correctly; *Green*, like her preferred tea.

Theo put the kettle on and then sat across from her. "Okay. Go ahead."

"What would you like to know?" The girl's feet didn't quite reach the floor, and when she swung her legs back and forth, the toes of the athletic socks flopped against the braided rug.

He inhaled slowly, trying to sooth his nerves. "First off, your name. I think that would be a good place to start. Don't you?"

"Yes, sir. I failed to introduce myself because I was dying to go to the bathroom. I'm sure you know what that's like. It's hard to concentrate under such desperate circumstances."

"Well…I guess that's—"

"Oh, you might be interested to know you're almost out of toilet paper. I only used two squares, and you have fourteen squares left."

He stared into the girl's gleaming eyes. Like a withered plant needing a deep soaking, she was rejuvenating before him, her cheeks flushing rosy now that her feet had warmed.

"I have more toilet paper under the sink," Theo said, although he had no idea why he was telling her. Good lord, he needed to get this girl back to her mother so he could return to work. With less than three weeks until the herbarium closed for spring break, he still had over fifty specimens to mount and log into the system.

The girl grinned as though a spare roll of toilet paper was the best news she had received in some time. "I thought you might have more, but I didn't look. My mom says you should never ever open someone else's bathroom cabinets."

"Your mom sounds like a wise woman. How about we call her?"

"Oh, she is *very* wise, but I'm not allowed to call her at work. Not except in the case of a dire emergency," she said, each word spoken slowly and wrapped in awe.

Theo scratched his eyebrow and thought about what to do next. He had the strangest feeling the girl would never leave. And he still didn't know her name! When the kettle whistled, he welcomed the distraction of fetching her tea.

"Alrighty, young lady, here's your tea. It's very hot." He placed the cup and saucer on the table in front of her. "Now you wait here while it cools. I'll be right back. I need to check something."

The dining room was his favorite room in the house; the oyster gray paint on the walls created a calm environment for working. He stirred the glue brush and was relieved the adhesive had not hardened in the jar. He allowed himself a quick moment to admire his earlier work. The columbine specimen was incredible. Theo peeked at the next specimen waiting in the stack of old newspapers. It was another wild columbine, perfectly unspoiled, with a mass of tiny, hair-like roots still attached to the plant's stem.

"Mr. Gruene, are you doing arts and crafts?" The girl stood so near him he could smell the fresh aroma of strawberry shampoo emanating from her rain-dampened hair. She leaned over the walnut table and peered at the fragile specimen.

"Please don't touch anything."

"What are you planning to do with this dead weed?"

Theo swallowed the impatience building in his throat. "This isn't a dead weed. It's a dried native plant specimen. My job is to preserve it for future generations."

"Oooohhh. I've read about the global seed vault in the Arctic Circle, you know, the place where all the seeds from the earth's plants are stored in case civilization is completely wiped out by a cannibal galaxy or catastrophic climate change or a humongous asteroid, and we need to start over. But I didn't know people like you store entire plants, roots and all."

"I thought you were drinking your tea." Theo folded the newspaper back over the specimen, feeling like their entire conversation had taken a Ray Bradbury turn.

"No, I'm letting it cool off. You made it too hot. Remember?"

Theo sighed. He'd specifically instructed the child to wait in the kitchen while her tea cooled, but evidently, she couldn't follow the simplest directive. The clock on the antique sideboard began chiming. It was only nine o'clock, yet his day had already been derailed in an extremely weird way.

"Oh, cool. It's a secret, isn't it?"

He stared at the child, still confused about the turn his morning had taken. What was she talking about? "What do you mean?"

"This project." She waved her hand over the stack of newspapers. "You're working on a top-secret assignment that involves the survival of plant life in the event Doomsday happens."

Theo chuckled. What a wild imagination this kid had! For a fleeting moment, he thought of his wife. Annie had been wildly imaginative too, and deeply concerned about the planet. Years ago, during an unseasonably hot summer, she had coordinated a neighborhood carpooling program in hopes of reducing carbon dioxide, or at least not adding to the problem of a depleting ozone layer. Even though Theo still knew very little about the girl who was studying the supplies arranged on his dining room table, he knew Annie would have taken to her instantly. The thought brought with it a familiar pang of loss. "I'm afraid my project is nothing quite so intriguing. I volunteer for the University of Arkansas, helping the herbarium preserve plants for future study." He thought of the serene campus workspace and wished he was there, alone, his mind fully engaged in his work.

She cut her eyes at him. "If you say so."

Theo led the girl back to the kitchen. He placed an ice cube in her still-steaming cup of tea and then went to the pantry to root out something for her to eat. She might be more forthcoming with information if he made the conversation more like school story time.

"Now then, why don't we have a snack while you tell me your name and explain what stroke of luck brought you to my front door." He placed a possibly stale package of peanut butter crackers in front of her and tried to remember when he had eaten last. Perhaps the entire morning was a hallucination brought on by a lack of protein.

The clock in the dining room chimed the quarter hour. Time was slipping away.

"Okay, I can do that." She sat with a very straight back, flattened her hands on the table on either side of the teacup, and drew in a long breath, as though preparing to deliver important news. In the short time she had been inside, her hair had begun to dry to a rich auburn shade, curling and spiraling along her shoulders like a mass of vermicelli noodles. Again, he thought of the columbine waiting on his dining room table, its roots a tangled knot.

"Well, sir, my first name is Penelope." She paused as though waiting for him to comment. When he said nothing, she continued. "I know what you're thinking." Again, she paused and stared at him, her eyes flashing.

"I doubt it," he said. Despite the girl's wide grin and charming dimples, the disruption of Theo's morning was ballooning into a case of indigestion. Why wouldn't the girl explain herself? He suddenly felt weary and wondered if he was missing something that should be obvious.

"You're funny."

"Not in the least."

"Well, I can tell you have a contemplative side, but yes, you are decidedly funny. You may not realize it."

Contemplative? Decidedly? Theo had never heard such large words come from a young person's mouth. Perhaps she was older than she appeared.

"Anyway, you're thinking, *my, what an old-fashioned name for such a modern girl*, right?" She opened the package of peanut butter crackers and scooted one across the table to him.

"Not really, but it is old-fashioned. I'll give you that." He didn't think he'd ever met anyone named Penelope, but he liked the name. It seemed to fit her. Theo ate half of the cracker in one bite, the saltiness waking his taste buds.

"I've been told I was named after my great-grandmother, but I believe I was named after Odysseus's incredibly patient wife. She was queen of Ithaca, you know."

"Well—"

"Mr. Gruene, do you remember Queen Penelope? She waited twenty years for her husband to return from the Trojan War. The war lasted ten years, and her king, who evidently was terrible with directions, took ten long years to get home. In the meantime, Queen Penelope resisted over a hundred suitors! Can you imagine?"

He knew she was waiting for him to respond to this soliloquy, but all he could say was, "No, I cannot."

She nodded. "Me neither. But she was definitely a faithful person." Penelope rested her elbows on the table, her chin on her hands, and dreamily blinked her eyes. Then, jerking upright, she added, "Names are super important, don't you think?"

Since his retirement ten years ago, Theo's life has been reassuringly predictable, each day unfolding much like the one before. And he liked it that way. He spent time on his herbarium work, ate lunch at Hugo's every Friday with his buddy, Winn, and if there was a Razorback game on (his favorites being baseball, basketball, and football, in that order), he watched it on television. Sometimes, he even attended a game in person. But that morning was certainly turning out to be unlike any he'd experienced in recent memory. He never would have imagined such a strange conversation transpiring in his kitchen. Theo reckoned he was completely losing it. He shut his eyes and waited for insanity to fully claim him.

Penelope signaled her continuing presence by abruptly clearing her throat.

She was still there.

"Anyway, I live on Josephine Street, just behind your house." She pointed to Theo's backyard, where, beyond his privacy fence, Josephine Street ran parallel to his.

This news instantly refocused him. "Right back there?" He stabbed the air with his finger. Through the canopy of the massive white oak tree growing in the center of his backyard, he could see the slate roof of the house behind his.

"Uh-huh. I mean, yes, sir."

There was no way this girl lived in that house. The enormous house behind him belonged to Gloria Rice. Theo should have listened to his gut from the beginning! He held his tongue and refrained from disputing the girl's information. She had finally begun talking, and he was determined to get to the reason for her visit.

"In two weeks, I will be eight-and-a-half years old—my birthday is September fourteenth. I'm in the fourth grade at Lafayette Elementary. I was allowed to skip third grade because I tested off the charts in math." Penelope recited all this information as though she were repeating lines memorized for a school play. When she blinked her gigantic eyes, her long lashes practically brushed against the lenses of her glasses.

"Penelope, I'm curious. Do you have a last name?"

She laughed. "Of course. Everyone has a last name. Even famous people like Lizzo and Zendaya have last names."

For a split second, he thought she had begun speaking in a foreign tongue. Then he realized she was likely referencing two people famous in her world, but not his. He would not let this quick-talking child distract him from the situation.

"Okay, so what is it?"

"Palmer. P-a-l-m-e-r. Palmer." She answered as though participating in a spelling bee.

"Well, Penelope P-a-l-m-e-r, I may seem like a very ancient man to you, slow on the uptake and all, but I happen to know Gloria Rice owns the house behind me. That's been her property for at least fifty years. And, unless you are Ms. Rice's long-lost granddaughter or something, I highly doubt you live in the mansion behind me." Theo wasn't friends with Ms. Rice, but he had lived in the neighborhood long enough to know a thing or two about the homeowners immediately surrounding him. Especially someone like Gloria Rice, who frequently made the news for her philanthropic endeavors.

Penelope giggled.

"Now listen, I don't know what sort of—"

"Mr. Gruene, I wouldn't classify you as ancient! The Egyptian pyramids are ancient. Scribes used those clay tablets back in the olden days of Mesopotamia—now those are ancient. Can you imagine carrying a clay tablet to school in your backpack?" Her eyes glittered, and he realized she was waiting for him to respond.

"No...um...that would be heavy coursework."

"Seriously." She offered him another peanut butter cracker, and he took it. "So, regarding Ms. Rice, she's in Aspen. She goes there this time of year and stays through the summer. And no, I'm not related to her, and I don't live in her mansion, but I sure wish both things were true. Don't you?"

"Well, not—"

"My mom and I live in the guest house over the garage. We moved there on Valentine's Day. It's small, but it's such a very nice place to live." Penelope's lips formed a perfect circle as she blew a stream of breath across her tea.

This news unsettled Theo. Even though he didn't partake in gossip and rarely attended the occasional neighborhood get-together, he couldn't believe he would have overlooked new neighbors living only yards behind his back fence. Last year, an artist from Spain had lived there while teaching a course at the university. He had been a quiet fellow, who kept to himself, but still, Theo had known he was there.

"Have you ever visited Aspen? It's in Colorado, by the way."

"Yes, I know where Aspen is, and no, I've never been to that particular city."

"Well, I am planning to go there. I want to travel all over the world." She flung her arms wide as though holding an enormous globe. "I'm going to be rich and have my own airplane, just like Cardi B. I'll jet around anywhere I want, any time I want. People will say, 'Where's Penelope off to now?' and everyone everywhere will be extremely jealous. My plane will have a cool name too, although I haven't thought what it will be yet."

Theo stared at her but had no idea what to say to any of this, so he responded with the question at the forefront of his mind. "What exactly is a Cardi B?"

"Hellll-loooo? You're killing me, Mr. Gruene. Cardi B is a famous internet sensation. An influencer with millions of viewers."

"I see." He didn't see, nor did he care to see. He was confused just thinking about it. "So tell me again, why can't we call your mother?"

"Because she's a nurse, well, *almost* a nurse. Technically, she's a certified nurse's assistant. She has to leave her phone in her locker during her shift. That's why. Anyway, it's very nice to officially meet you, neighbor." Penelope offered her tiny hand and grinned like she had saved that line for just the right moment.

"Well, yes. Welcome to the neighborhood, Penelope." He wasn't sure he meant the sentiment, given how she'd shaken up his morning like a cheap snow globe, but he shook anyway. Such a tiny little thing, her hand was as soft and slight as a ragdoll's.

"Oh, and Mr. Gruene? You can have all these crackers." She slid the remainder of the package across the table to him. "I have a peanut allergy, so I can't eat them."

He should have figured as much. It seemed the whole world was allergic to a host of foods he'd had no problem eating as a child.

Theo placed his empty teacup in the sink and stared out the window past his backyard to the apartment where the girl lived with her mother. The rain seemed to have already blown over, but even so, he couldn't ask the child to return home. She had no way of getting inside. Also, wasn't she too young to be home alone anyway?

When no other solutions came to mind, he suggested Penelope settle herself at the kitchen table and do some schoolwork. She nodded and ran to get her backpack, pulling out a textbook, an iPad, and a fistful of pens and pencils bound with a thick rubber band. She arranged everything in a neat row.

Theo returned to his plant specimens in the dining room. At first, he remained aware of Penelope in the kitchen, as she turned pages in a school book or adjusted her position in her chair, but after a while, she went stone silent, and he forgot she was there. Theo worked without interruption, completely losing track of time.

Eventually, a clear voice rang out, startling him back to the present. "It's almost noon. My mother will be home soon, so I'm leaving now. I can let myself out."

"Alright. I'll help you collect your things." Theo had forgotten about the girl, but he was still relieved to know she was leaving. By the time he walked into the kitchen, Penelope was already standing in the foyer.

"Thanks for letting me stay awhile. I'll bring your socks back later if that's okay. And don't worry, I'll take excellent care of them while they're in my possession."

Theo had plenty of socks and was about to tell her to keep them, but he lost his train of thought when he saw how ridiculous she looked. She wore the hood of her raincoat draped over her head, the legs of her jeans tucked tightly into the white athletic socks, and the socks pulled over her knees. He would credit her for one thing—she didn't concern herself with her appearance, and he admired that.

"Maybe I can come back again when it hasn't been raining," she continued. "I'd like to play with your dog sometime."

His dog? The dog had not been around all morning. "How do you—"

"SeeyalaterdearMisterGruene." Before he could reply to Penelope's mouthful of chirpy, blurred-together words, she was out the door and down the front porch steps, her green raincoat flapping in the early March wind. Amused, Theo waved a tired goodbye and watched her skip along the still-damp sidewalk until she was out of his eyesight. Overhead, a sapphire sky offered no trace of the earlier storm.

Two

Several days passed while Theo worked through the university specimens. He had barely done anything else, getting only a few hours of sleep each night (he no longer required much sleep) and eating when his empty stomach demanded sustenance. Being on schedule to meet his mid-March deadline felt remarkably satisfying. He had all but forgotten Penelope Palmer when she knocked on his front door a second time.

"Well, hello again," he said, pleasantly surprised to see her. This time, the girl's visit was not a bother. He was at a good stopping place with his work.

"Hi, Mr. Gruene. I brought your socks back. They're clean, and they smell amazing. I washed them using a few drops of my mother's lavender hand soap."

"Well, okay...thank you for—"

"Go ahead, you can sniff them if you'd like."

He chuckled. "Oh, that won't be necessary. I believe you."

"They really do smell like a lavender field in Provence. Did you know lavender is a calming herb? You might find it helpful."

Provence? He decided to play along, holding the tightly balled-up socks to his nose and deeply inhaling. "Oh, yes, very calming. So, exactly when did you travel to Provence?"

Penelope smiled banana-wide. "Most recently, last night. I was walking barefoot through a lavender field, and the smell was quite aromatic. There were bees all around, but they weren't the stinging kind. Somehow, I knew that. You know how dreams can be that way."

Theo understood the omniscient power of a dream, but he wondered how Penelope could know so much about the qualities of lavender, or that it grew in the south of France. Perhaps kids today were simply more worldly than he realized; technology did make information easily accessible. Still, Penelope's intellect seemed to exist on a level deeper than could be explained by facts memorized from the internet.

"I know what you're thinking, Mr. Gruene. I've only traveled to Europe virtually, and that doesn't count. But I believe traveling virtually is better than not going at all. And, it will have to suffice until I can visit in person." With this, Penelope did a rather graceful pirouette, her lime green raincoat flapping around her.

"Well, that's good. To have goals, I mean. I was planning to stop by and check on you, but it slipped my mind." Theo said this more to scold himself, than to point out his lack of follow-through. It was true, though, he had intended to stop by and introduce himself to Penelope's mother, to ensure she knew where her daughter had got to that stormy morning.

"It's okay. I've been busy, too." She pushed her glasses up on her nose. Her smile seemed wobbly around the edges.

A stretch of silence spread between them until he finally said, "Well, kiddo, thanks for stopping by." Penelope was possibly the most charming person he'd met in some time, but that didn't mean he wanted to encourage these impromptu visits.

"Wait. That's it? You aren't going to invite me to come inside again?"

"Do you *want* to come in?" He squeezed the balled socks between his fingers. He truly could smell lavender.

"Sure, I guess I can. But I can only stay a little while." Penelope slipped past him and waltzed right into the house. By the time Theo closed the front door, she was peering into his backyard through the sliding glass doors leading onto the back deck.

"Would you like another cup of tea?"

"Can I play with your dog instead? It's not raining, so it seems like a good day for it."

"Sure. If she's out there. She comes and goes."

"I bet she's sleeping back there behind your thinking tree." Penelope yanked on the door, but discovered the ornery latch. She couldn't open it.

"My what?" Theo reached around and gave it a firm tug.

"Your thinking tree." She pointed to the oak tree growing in the center of his backyard.

Theo felt suddenly naked, his thoughts and emotions stripped bare in the presence of this curious young girl. "What are you, some sort of tiny enchantress or something? Can you read minds?" The tree, with its furrowed bark and massive canopy, was what he loved most about his backyard. And Penelope was right. He did some of his best thinking while sitting on the wooden bench underneath it.

She made a little clicking noise with her tongue. "Hardly. I'm just a girl named Penelope Pie Palmer."

"Penelope what?"

"My full name is Penelope Pie Palmer."

"Pie? Like a tart?"

"Yes, although technically, a pie is not a tart. My middle name is Pie, spelled *p-i-e*, not *p-i*, like the mathematical constant. You might be interested to know that Pi Day is my half birthday."

"Well, Penelope Pie, shouldn't you be in school today?" Theo rubbed his forehead, but it didn't stop his mind spinning from this onslaught of facts.

Penelope laughed, her expression incredulous. "I *was* at school, but it's almost five o'clock! Anyway, Pie was my great-grandmother's last name. It's English. And to answer your prior question..."—she paused to give him time to remember his question (which he had, indeed, forgotten)—"no, I'm not an enchantress, although that would be incredible. I'm just observant. And since I live so close, I can see your backyard easily from the window. You sit out there with your dog almost every night at sunset. Often, your eyes are closed, like you are praying. If you opened your eyes, you would see things too."

Wait just a minute. He saw plenty of things! Had he just been insulted by a not-quite nine-year-old named Penelope Pie? "Has anyone ever—"

"Do you pray, Mr. Gruene?"

Before he had a chance to say, *That's a little personal, don't you think?* the dog came bounding over from behind his garden shed.

"There she is!" Penelope stepped onto the deck, tentatively, as though suddenly remembering she had a fear of dogs. But the dog began sniffing her hand, which made her giggle. "Oh my goodness, she's so sweet. And her coat is the color of melted caramel. What's her name?"

"She doesn't have one. She's just a stray." The dog had showed up a while back, wearing a frayed collar with no tags. Against his better judgment, he had given her a bowl of shredded chicken and tucked several old flannel blankets underneath the deck chair for bedding. A week later, after no response to the missing dog notice he'd posted on the neighborhood website, Theo had taken her to a nearby veterinary clinic. Some responsibilities seemed to fall into a person's lap, and the doe-eyed dog, likely a Labrador-Terrier mix, had temporarily become his. Although he still intended to drop her off at a rescue facility at some point, Theo had paid for neutering, purchased a bag of kibble from Ozark Natural Foods, and let her stay in his backyard. But he hadn't given her a name. A name seemed too permanent.

Penelope glared at him with disbelieving eyes, then looked down at the stray, carefully rubbing between its expressive ears. "Don't listen to him—of course, you have a name. He just doesn't know what it is yet." Soon, they were rolling around together in the grass and playing fetch, Penelope's green raincoat relegated to the wooden bench.

For some time, Theo watched from the sideline, enjoying Penelope's bubbly laughter. He heard the exact moment when the spring peepers added their high-pitched chorus to oncoming evening. It seemed Mother Nature had flipped a switch in Theo's backyard. Spring's promise was beckoning.

When the dog went to get a drink from her water bowl, Penelope draped the raincoat over her shoulders, and announced she'd better get home. "Oh, I almost forgot. Is it okay if I give your dog a treat?" Before he could answer (it seemed she was always one step ahead of him, in thought and action), she pulled a napkin from the pocket of her raincoat and unwrapped a dog biscuit. "There was a small bag of dog treats at the Little Free Pantry this week, so I got some for your dog. If I bring one every time I come, she'll like me better."

Theo was stirred by her sweet gesture, but the slight desperation in her voice dismayed him. "You don't need to bring treats to make her like you. You're instant buddies." Watching them play together had warmed Theo. Every dog needed a kid to romp with. He resolved to spend more time with it.

Penelope commanded, "Sit," and the dog sat, her eyes trained on the treat. "Did you see? She knows how to sit!"

"She's smart, like you," he said, the easy-flowing compliment a surprise to him even as he said it.

Nose to muzzle, Penelope stared into the dog's eyes for several seconds as though trying to read her mind. The dog stared right back. One of her ears permanently stood at attention, making her appear attentive and ready to play. Theo realized that it was those ears of hers—one pointy and one floppy—that had endeared him to the dog from the minute she'd shown up.

"Alice. I think her name is Alice," Penelope said. Then, in a quieter voice, she spoke directly to the dog. "You're lucky I'm here now. Mr. Gruene didn't even think to give you a name."

Once again, Theo shook his head, intrigued by Penelope's keen observations. Her words seemed to cut straight to the heart of every issue.

"What do you think? Can we call her Alice?"

It seemed a strange name for a dog, but he didn't see why not.

Three

Theo couldn't remember the last time he had been inside a pet store. He pushed his cart up and down several aisles, marveling at the sea of product selections. When it came to making a nametag, he contemplated the designs offered at the store's engraving kiosk, deciding the star shape was the obvious choice for such a smart dog. The circle shape was too plain, the heart too presumptuous, and the bone shape a complete cliché. The simple act of typing *her* name and *his* phone number into the machine felt like a giant step for him. Besides Ralph, the shepherd mix his dad had brought home from work when Theo was a kid, he had never owned a dog.

Two hundred dollars later, Theo headed home with his purchases: a raspberry-colored collar and matching leash; a twenty-pound bag of Science Diet; a package of bacon-flavored treats; and a sleeve of neon orange tennis balls. He smiled. If Annie could see him now. Early in their relationship she'd asked him, quite seriously, if he was a cat person or a dog person. Theo had been relieved she'd not asked about his religious or political beliefs, or whether he wanted children someday. When he'd said he liked cats and dogs equally, she didn't believe him. According to her, nobody liked them equally; everyone had a preference. He could still hear her saying, "You either prefer cats or dogs. That's just the way it is." Theo didn't think her theory was true, but because of her cats, Daisy and Finch, he had become a full-time cat person too.

God, how he missed her.

When Theo got home, he found Alice waiting for him outside the kitchen door, her tail gently waving like a flag, her nose not quite touching the glass. Theo had never let the dog inside the house, and he didn't plan to start, no matter how earnest her eyes or polite her demeanor. It wasn't that he was worried over the cleanliness of his home—he wasn't all that adept or concerned about housekeeping—it was just that a dog, any dog, couldn't possibly coexist with the fragile plant specimens spread across his dining room table.

"I picked up some things for you," he said, feeling self-conscious under her intense stare and wondering if she was judging his pet store selections. Through the glass, she kept watching him as he unpacked the sack and fastened her nametag to the collar. "Alice? What do you think of that name?" It being Sunday afternoon, Theo was not working. His rule about not doing any work on Sunday wasn't because of religion—he was spiritual, but not particularly religious—but he'd learned the value of taking time off to rest and observe the simple things. So once he had gone outside to attach the collar, he and Alice set off on their first official walk around the wooded neighborhood, her gleaming nametag jingling with each step.

At first, Alice strained against the leash, pulling him along the sidewalk while he yanked her back, pleading for her to slow down. Then, right in front of Nita Johnson's house, she planted her haunches, gazed up at him with limpid eyes, and refused to take another step. They stood in a mid-block standoff, each waiting for the other to do something.

Theo tugged on the leash. "Look, I don't have time for this. You need to show me if I'm doing it wrong." Still, the dog didn't budge. Had she never been leash-walked before? It appeared Alice was a stubborn girl. Well, stubbornness was something Theo understood. With each passing year, it seemed his habits became more ingrained, the ability to mellow practically non-existent. Bottom line, he would not be outdone by a young dog. "Alice, I'm in charge here. This is intended to be pleasurable. And it's called walking for a reason. One paw in front of the other." He gave her leash another tug, and she rose to her feet. It was awkward going at first, but by the time they reached the end of the block, man and dog had settled into a companionable stride. Theo was pleased by their progress.

"That's much better," he praised her as they reached the intersection. "Let's go find Penelope Pie, shall we?"

Alice replied with a single swift, "Owff."

It seemed Theo had become a man who not only had a dog but also conversed with her. What an amusing turn of events, he thought, chuckling. They turned the corner, and he began naming the plants they strolled past—*Narcissus, Helleborus, Iberis sempervirens*. If Alice was going to live with him, she may as well learn which perennials would thrive in growing zone 7a.

Up ahead, he spied Nita Johnson walking in his direction. He groaned. After finally developing a good pace, they would be forced to stop and talk. Theo began power-walking, allowing quick-trotting Alice to take control. There was no avoiding Nita, so he might as well get it over with.

She started waving like a maniac.

Once they were within steps of one another, he tugged on Alice's leash and said, "stay," having no idea if she knew the command. She stopped instantly and looked up at Nita with soulful eyes.

"Oh, I see the puppy has decided to keep you." Nita's broad smile seemed forced, and he sensed sarcasm in her voice, which instantly set his teeth on edge. The woman always rubbed him the wrong way. Some people were simply not meant to be friends.

"Hello Nita. Yes. Actually, technically, she isn't a pup—"

"What's her name?"

"Alice."

"Alice? Like *Alice in Wonderland*?" She leaned down and offered Alice the back of her hand to sniff.

Theo had not thought to ask Penelope about the source of Alice's name, but he figured that particular protagonist was as good as any. "Sure. Why not? Alice in Wonderland."

Nita started stroking Alice's coat and making a fuss, cooing in a baby voice. "We're going to be good friends, Alice. I hope you'll come to see me any time. I have lots of squirrels you can chase." She straightened up, pushing her shoulder-length yellow-white hair behind her ears. "Theo, I'm glad to see you've committed to something. Enjoy the rest of your stroll." With that, Nita continued walking before he could say anything else. Not that he had anything else to say. Theo confessed to Alice that he was relieved about the brevity of their exchange.

Soon, Theo and Alice were standing in front of Gloria Rice's house. Compared to his humble hundred-year-old clapboard, hers was a veritable manor. He had been inside only once, years ago, when the entire neighborhood had been invited to a fundraiser for a city council candidate. Although Theo had strong political views, he was not an activist, and had attended primarily to find out the candidate's position on a nearby high-rise development. It had been a struggle for him to mingle with folks he didn't know. Thinking back on that afternoon, he realized it was likely the last neighborhood event he had attended.

Theo opened the front iron gate and guided Alice around the side of the Rice house, keeping to the stone pathway, feeling somewhat like an intruder. The boxwood topiaries on either side of the walkway were so perfectly shaped, he touched one to confirm it was real. He was impressed, not only by the expertly sculpted foliage, but by the overall lushness of the plants. Theo saw no visible evidence of disease despite the excessively wet winter they'd had. Passing the south side of the property, he noticed shades had been drawn over all the windows. They looked like rows of heavy-lidded eyes. He wondered if the furniture inside was covered with white cotton sheets. Wasn't that what wealthy people did when they closed up a house for the season? Theo couldn't remember anything about the inside of Ms. Rice's home other than it was stark, with minimal furnishings. When he got around to the back of the house, he whistled slowly. The expansive back veranda was decorated with black iron furniture and large potted plants that had somehow survived winter. It looked like something from a travel magazine. How incredible, that a space like this existed just beyond his so-ordinary garden fence. Even the air seemed fresher, the slight fragrance of late-winter jasmine swirling in the breeze.

He couldn't imagine having Gloria Rice's sort of money. Theo had grown up in a small, comfortable house, with kindhearted parents who were always worried about the next Great Depression. His father, a supervisor at the local parts company in Midland, taught him to love baseball and read the newspaper daily. His mother had been the real glue of the family. She was a master at whipping up family meals from vegetables she grew in the dusty garden patch. She had been a saver too, tucking away a dollar or two each month in a coffee can she kept in her pie safe; her crackerjack fund, she'd called it. But Theo never saw her use that money for herself. Instead, she would dip into it to make a meal for an ailing neighbor, or in support of a church fundraiser. On rare days, she bought boxes of Cracker Jacks for Theo and his brother. What a treat those had been! All these years later, he still marveled at the self-restrain his parents showed. Even after inheriting money from the sale of Grandpa Gruene's farm, his father only tapped into the savings account once, to buy a like-new car.

Eventually Theo reached the four-car garage that backed onto his lot and part of his neighbor's. He had never viewed the Rice garage from the front, and the change of view brought a completely different perspective. It was indeed massive; it seemed excessive to Theo. Did Gloria Rice really need so much space? Did she own four vehicles? Along the side of the garage, a stairwell led to the guest property where Penelope and her mother lived. Theo guided Alice to the first stair but its open tread seemed to confuse her. She sat on her haunches and refused to budge.

"Fine then, you wait here." Theo looped the handle of the leash around the iron banister. The dog did as she was told while he proceeded cautiously up the stairs and knocked on the door.

He saw some movement in the nearby window. Seconds later, the door swung wide open, and Penelope popped into the doorway, cheering, "It's you!"

"It's both of us. Alice is waiting downstairs. Evidently, she's afraid of stairs like this."

The stairwell vibrated as Penelope raced down and threw herself on the dog, hugging her around the neck and talking to her in a low voice.

"You got her a collar and a nametag and everything," she said, as Theo returned to ground level. "Alice." She beamed as she read the nametag. "Such a virtuous girl."

Virtuous? Again, Penelope's vocabulary impressed him. He imagined she must read books at a level much higher than was typical for her age. He wondered if she worked at it, kept a list of interesting words and used them intentionally.

"Is your mother home? I was hoping to meet her."

"No, she's at work." Penelope was scratching Alice's ears.

"She's working on Sunday?"

"She works at the VA hospital. Mr. Theo, sickness knows no day of the week."

Had Penelope mentioned her mother worked at the VA hospital? Surely, he would have remembered that detail. Since the hospital was practically adjacent to his neighborhood, he drove by it almost daily. He'd always admired the property's expansive green space. "So you are home alone?"

"Just for a little while. I'm very responsible, and I'm used to it. Mostly, my mom works when I'm at school. Today, she got an extra half-shift, and we can't turn that down, you know?"

"And there's no one in the big house?"

"No. I'm pretty sure I told you that Ms. Rice is in Aspen. Are you having memory problems, Mr. Theo?"

He chuckled. "No, no. I just worry how safe it is for a young girl to be alone here."

"Oh, I never open the door to strangers. If someone knocks, I peep through the side window, and if it's someone I don't know, I stay real quiet until they leave. Not that that's ever happened. No one comes back here other than the gardeners on Saturday morning. Except now you have!"

Penelope invited him to see the apartment, but Theo wasn't comfortable going inside when her mother wasn't home. "Maybe next time," he said as he wrote his cell phone number on the pet store receipt he pulled from his back pocket. "If you have any trouble or get scared, you call me. I can be right over." He heard the words leaving his mouth, and knew his offer would surely interrupt the reliable and peaceful daily routine he treasured. But as a retired educator, he couldn't help himself.

She grinned. "It's a deal, Mr. Theo. And you can call me too. Or FaceTime me. Unless it's near the end of the month and we've run out of data on our phone plan. In that case, it won't work."

He stared blankly at her. Theo had never FaceTimed anyone and didn't see the need for it. He was a simple man with basic needs, preferring phone calls to text messages and books to movies. He didn't like to waste money or time.

"Will you tell your mother I came by? I'd like to meet her." He didn't *really* want to meet her, not in the way he wanted the Razorback baseball team to win the College World Series, or the way he wanted to see the threatened plant *Geocarpon minimum* blooming with his own eyes, but with Penelope having shown up on his doorstep, he thought meeting her mother was necessary. Transparency. Wasn't that what today's culture demanded?

Penelope nodded as she continued lavishing her attention on Alice. "I will. She doesn't work tomorrow, so we'll come over after I get done with school."

She said 'done' as though school was a chore to be checked off, like cleaning the toilet.

"By the way, I'm curious how you came up with the name Alice. Is our girl here named after Alice in Wonderland?" *Our girl here?* Such strange phrasing had slipped from his mouth! Still, and he had to admit it was odd, he seemed to feel an invisible energy connecting him to the girl and the dog.

"Nooooo! She's named after Alice Paul, of course."

"Of course." Theo smacked a hand against his forehead as though this should have been obvious. In reality, he had never heard of Alice Paul and wondered who she was.

"I can tell you are making fun of me, and that's okay. I'm very accustomed to that type of behavior. Hey, I have an idea. Maybe I could walk Alice for you after school. I could be your official dog-walker, and you could pay me? Not a lot, though, like two dollars a walk? I've been trying to find ways to earn money, and now it's completely obvious. Whatdoyouthink?" Her last question gushed out as one long, enthusiastic word.

"Well, I don't know. Alice is very strong, and you are a tiny thing." At the beginning of their walk, the dog had practically pulled Theo's arm from its socket.

She laughed. "I may be tiny, but I'm awfully mighty," she said. "Just like Alice Paul. She was a brilliant suffragist and an important women's rights activist. In fact, her tireless work on the Nineteenth Amendment ensures my right to vote in ten years."

"Is that so?" Theo registered the passion in her eyes. This child was unbelievable! The scope of her knowledge was certainly beyond what his former seventh grade students had displayed, or even the college freshmen who had taken his beginning botany class at the university throughout the years!

"Yes. Cross my heart, it's one-hundred zillion percent so."

"Well, mighty Penelope, I appreciate the mini-history lesson," he said. He fully intended to read up on Alice Paul when he got home.

Four

Delivering his most recent specimen work to the herbarium provided Theo with a sense of accomplishment, but it also left a hollow feeling in his belly. Until he received another delivery, he would be at loose ends, walking into the dining room each morning with anticipation, ready to see which species awaited him—perhaps a delicate wood lily or a native sunchoke collected decades earlier—before remembering his table was vacant of work, his tools put away. Botany had consumed much of his adult life, and volunteering at the herbarium connected Theo to the university even after retirement. But with campus soon closing for spring break, more specimens wouldn't be delivered until mid-April.

Mid-April was nearly a month away.

As he drove the short distance home, Theo considered all the long-ignored projects crying out for attention around the house: the gutters needed unclogging; the exterior could use a good power-washing; a few of the front porch floorboards had begun to crumble around the edges and needed replacing. Values were soaring in the historic district, but Theo's house was definitely the tired one on the block. Perhaps his friend Winn had the right idea. Winn and his wife Julie had moved to Sequoyah Trail Village three years ago, and they often encouraged him to do the same. But as Theo saw his home come into view beyond the dogwood trees lining the parkway, he was glad he didn't live in a homogenous community like Sequoyah. No sir, Theo Gruene didn't care that his kitchen had not been renovated since he bought the house in 1989, nor that his roof was at the midpoint of its thirty-year warranty. He simply needed the house to last as long as he did.

If only Annie were still alive. Everything would look different if breast cancer hadn't slipped into their lives and snuffed out their future together. When Annie's cancer had been diagnosed, she had only been forty years old. Theo would have gladly changed places with her, invited the disease to wrack his body instead of hers. She had not deserved the hollow-eyed weakness and late-night vomiting, the rotten, unavoidable end of days. Annie, who'd had a talent for finding magic in plain vanilla days, should have flourished into old age. She would have been more fruitful with her time than he had been.

He couldn't believe she had been gone twenty years.

Theo pulled into his driveway so deep in thought and longing, it took him a few seconds to notice Penelope sitting cross-legged on the porch beside Alice. Why was she back again? And why was she always wearing that silly lime green raincoat? He shoved away the gloomy mood threatening to drown him and stepped from the truck.

"Well, if it isn't Mighty Penelope Pie and Alice the Virtuous," he said, walking toward them, his sciatica screaming after sitting too long that morning.

"Hello, Mr. Theo. Is something the matter with your leg?"

"Nah. Just a twinge from being sedentary. Nothing to concern yourself over. So tell me, are you expecting rain?"

Penelope cast her face to the bright sun, scrunched her dark brows, and said, "Nope. Not a drop of rain today. Just clear sailing." She jumped to her feet, holding a small paper sack he'd not noticed. "I brought you something."

"Oh, you did, did you?" Theo couldn't imagine what she might have brought him but was heartened by it. Curious, he watched as she unfolded the bag and peeped inside as though making sure whatever it was had not escaped.

"Yes, sir. It's a cherry hand pie."

The pie was nestled inside a paper napkin, and when Penelope reached inside, Theo's belly growled with surprising intensity. Breakfast had only been two slices of buttered toast, eaten hours ago.

"I'll warn you now, you'll probably lose your mind when you taste it. My mom is the best baker in the whole wide world. I thought we could share it."

Theo was impressed at how considerate Penelope was. At the mention of her mother, he recalled their conversation on Sunday afternoon. She had failed to bring her mother by after school the next day. He was beginning to wonder if she really existed, although the hand pie was quite convincing evidence. "Where *is* your mother? Weren't you going to bring her over?" They settled into the porch swing, the pie still cradled in Penelope's hands. "And what's her name? I don't think you've ever told me."

"You're awfully inquisitive today, Mr. Theo." She broke the pie into two pieces and offered him the larger half. "Her name is Ivy. Ivy Lillian Palmer. And by the way, we did come to your house Monday afternoon, but you weren't home."

"Oh, I'm sorry I missed you." Theo thought back and realized they must have come by while he had been walking Alice. The weather had been unseasonably warm all week, and they had begun regularly exploring the trails on Mount Sequoyah. While Alice was learning not to strain at the sight of every scampering squirrel, he hunted for spring ephemerals just beginning to unfurl in the understory.

"It's okay. Anyway, right now, she's at home catching up on her sleep. She's been working lots of shifts lately because we need the money. We are what is called a single-parent family living below the poverty line."

Theo's heart twisted at Penelope's words. Not only did he find her reality distressing, but the idea that such a young child was well-acquainted with poverty terminology seemed particularly cruel. "What about your father? Where's he?" There weren't many things that riled up Theo more than men who didn't take responsibility for their children. He suspected that might be the case for Penelope's father.

"Mr. Theo, could you please stop talking and enjoy your fried pie? I didn't come here to discuss the lack of parenting in my life."

For a moment, he had forgotten about the sweet in his hand. And since he had no retort to Penelope's rebuke, he filled his mouth with a sizable bite. "Oh my lord, this is marvelous."

"Told you." Penelope beamed.

A bit of cherry filling slipped from inside the pastry, but Theo caught it and slurped it from the side of his hand.

"Baking cherry pies is my mom's superpower," she said as she gobbled down her smaller portion in two bites. "I told her all about how you rescued me the day I missed the bus, and she wants you to come for dinner at six o'clock. Can you, please? She's making spaghetti, and there will be more cherry pie, too. We're celebrating. Today's Pi Day, you know." She dusted her hands together, and powdered sugar drifted through a shimmering slant of sunshine.

"And Pi Day is your half-birthday," he added, glad he remembered that detail from their first crammed-packed conversation.

"Yes!" Penelope's grin revealed her snaggletooth smile.

Theo thought there was nothing so endearing as permanent teeth half-grown between the spaces left by lost baby teeth.

"So, can you come?"

If he accepted a dinner invitation, he would become even more entangled with this child. And something told him that the more entangled he became, the less serene his life would be. But as he thought about how to gracefully decline, he heard himself say, "Kiddo, I would be honored to attend your half-birthday party."

A gleeful "Oh, yay!" escaped Penelope's lips. She clasped her hands together as though she couldn't believe her good fortune. For a fleeting second, Theo thought he glimpsed her very soul, fragile but indomitable, behind eyes as dark as currants.

IVY PALMER TURNED out to be nothing like he expected, not that he'd had any real idea what to expect. She looked like a teenager who should be excited about her looming high school graduation, rather than the mother of a fourth grader with all the accompanying responsibilities. With each passing year, Theo grew older, while the world seemed younger and younger.

"I'm glad you could come, Mr. Gruene." She offered her hand. So much could be revealed by a person's handshake; Ivy's held just the right amount of firmness.

"Penelope is quite the young lady."

"Thank you. I think so too." Ivy had a long mane of wavy auburn hair and eyes like a pale blue moon on a clear night. She was stunning, in a natural way, with a smattering of tiny freckles on her nose and arched eyebrows that lent a playful expression to her heart-shaped face. For a moment, Theo forgot he was a seventy-year-old man who preferred solitude to the company of people.

"Please, *please* tell me there's chocolate candy in that beauuuutiful gold box," Penelope pleaded.

"Oh, yes." He had almost forgotten about the box in his hand. Theo's mother had taught him years ago that arriving empty-handed to dinner simply wasn't done. "Chocolate *without* nuts. Happy half-birthday, kiddo."

"It's for me?"

"It's for you and your mother."

Ivy took the box, reminding Penelope, "No candy until after dinner." Turning to him, she said, "Mr. Gruene, Pea's been talking about you and your dog non-stop. Thanks for letting her barge in on you that morning. I know she can be a handful." Ivy tossed her head back, shifting her hair from where it had fallen over her eyes.

"I am *not* a handful. Where's Alice? I wanted you to bring her."

Theo had never heard Penelope whine before. It reminded him how young she actually was. "Oh, no. Alice is at home, where she belongs." Theo thumbed toward the back apartment wall, to the window where Penelope *(or Pea?)* had a bird's eye view of his backyard activities.

"Oh yeah, I forgot, she doesn't like the outside stairs. Would you like a tour of our apartment, Mr. Theo?" Penelope tugged his hand and pulled him further into the small space.

In the thirty-plus years he'd shared a back fence with Gloria Rice, he had never been inside her garage apartment. He was surprised at how tiny it was.

"This is obviously the main room," Penelope explained solemnly. Bookcases lined portions of two walls, empty but for *National Geographic* magazines arranged in yellow horizontal stacks here and there. "These built-in bookcases are a nice feature, don't you think?"

"I do, but you need some books. Are those your magazines?"

"No. They came with the place. But I totally agree with you. I can only read books from the library, but when I have my own house, bookcases will fill every room, floor-to-ceiling, like the Morgan Library in New York."

He wondered if she'd learned about the Morgan Library in school or if she had, in fact, visited there. Before he could ask, she squeezed his hand and pointed to the tiny lavatory barely visible behind a half-opened door.

"There's the bathroom, in case you need to use it. FYI, two extra rolls of toilet paper are under the sink." Penelope winked at him, and he chuckled, thinking how strange it was that they already shared a private joke. "We sleep right there on the sofa; it turns into a bed. And here's our closet." A rolling rack held what must have been all of Ivy and Penelope's clothing. He noticed the lime-green raincoat hanging there, and a jumble of shoes beneath it. "The kitchen is over there." The galley kitchen was separated from the rest of the apartment by a bar-height countertop. In the corner by the bar, notebooks and papers covered a small circular table.

"That's pretty much it. Cool, right?" Penelope dropped his hand and gazed at him.

Theo sensed she was waiting for a favorable reaction to the apartment, so he commented on the coziness of the space, calling it minimalist. He thought that was popular these days.

"Pea, maybe you should give Mr. Theo a chance to catch his breath," Ivy said as she pulled a baking sheet from the tiny oven and placed it on the stovetop.

"No, he's good, aren't you, Mr. Theo? He knows how I am," she said, flashing her snaggletooth smile again.

"I'm just glad to be here," he said, even though so much chatter overwhelmed him, and the size of the place was slightly claustrophobic. He couldn't remember the last time someone had held his hand.

Finally, Ivy announced, "We'll eat soon," and asked if he would like a glass of tea. "I meant to get a bottle of wine but didn't have time."

"He loves tea. Don'tchaMisterTheo?"

Theo nodded, happy that Penelope had answered for him. The rich aroma of garlic and tomatoes drifting from beneath a lidded pot on the stove reached him and suddenly he was no longer standing in Gloria Rice's small garage apartment. Instead, he had traveled back in time. His mother cooking spaghetti for New Year's Eve dinner. His father listening to the radio. Playing gin rummy with his little brother and talking about the exciting things they would do when they were older…

"Pea, I asked you to clean off the table. Do it now, please," Ivy said as she poured tea into glasses.

Theo blinked away the memories of his childhood and glanced at the table piled with books. "Looks like you had a lot of homework today," he said, squeezing his hands together and concentrating on the present.

She shrugged and began gathering books and papers into a stack. "Not really. My class is just starting on decimals," she said, rolling her eyes, "but I'm working on probability and pre-algebra with the sixth graders. Miss Markum lets me go to math with the sixth-grade class, so my mind stays engaged, and I don't get bored. I get bored anyway though."

Theo considered this, wondering if Penelope had been tested in some way beyond the standard school tests. She seemed brighter than most adults he knew.

A timer began ringing, the sound of it resonating through the sparsely furnished space. Ivy silenced it and then started filling plates with noodles and sauce, working quickly, as though dinner was merely something to check off an over-full schedule. Theo offered to help but was relieved when she said everything was under control.

They sat down to eat as soon as dinner was on the table; Ivy had made a basic green salad and a plate of buttered garlic toast to go with the spaghetti. Theo had not enjoyed a meal at someone else's home since his annual New Year's Day lunch at Winn and Julie's. For a while, he just ate. Penelope filled all the quiet spaces with talk of school.

Eventually, he asked, "How do you like living here? It's small, isn't it? Almost like those tiny houses people go mad over on television." The place reminded Theo of an efficiency apartment he'd rented years ago in Hell's Kitchen. He tried to blink away memories of that time, but still felt a twinge of sorrow. He had been a different person then, a young man drowning in tragedy and struggling just to survive. He took a bite of bread and barely tasted it.

"It's waaaaaay better than the last place we—" Penelope had answered Theo immediately, but then stopped herself from continuing.

"We like it fine," Ivy said. "Finding affordable housing is difficult, especially in this neighborhood."

"Yeah, you're super lucky! Your house is humongous!" Penelope chimed in, her overly enthusiastic voice a ripple around the table. Ivy shot Penelope a swift glance, and Theo recognized the universal signal of *take it down a notch right this minute*. "Sorry. Sometimes I get excited," she added and picked up her fork.

"Housing *is* expensive. I bought my house over three decades ago, but I couldn't afford to re-purchase it in today's market." Back then, home ownership was within reach for the ordinary person, and with the money he had inherited from his family, Theo had been able to purchase his house outright. Now, the appraisal district valued his lot at five times the original purchase price of the structure.

"We're saving up for a bigger place. And someday we're going to buy a house, right Mom?" Penelope slurped noodles into her mouth, smiling and talking throughout the process. Her serving contained no meat sauce; she ate only noodles and butter.

"That's the plan. Please don't talk with your mouth full, and use your napkin." Ivy glanced at Theo and for the briefest moment their eyes met. She smiled stiffly, looking quite uncomfortable with the amount of personal information Penelope was disclosing.

During the meal, Theo discovered more snippets of information about Ivy. Not only was she a nurse's aide at the Veteran's Hospital, but she was also slowly completing her nursing degree, taking a class here and there when funds allowed.

"My mom will clean your house or run errands for you too, if you need help in that area, Mr. Theo. She sometimes does that for extra money."

"Thank you, Pea, but I don't need you to find jobs for me."

Penelope shrugged.

"How does Penelope's father fit into the picture?" Theo blurted out, knowing instantly he shouldn't have asked such a private thing. And sure enough, the energy in the room drained as though a plug in the floor had been yanked free.

Ivy placed her fork on the side of her plate and looked directly at him, a tired yet defiant expression on her youthful face.

"I apologize, please forget I asked. You'll have to ignore me—I spend most of my time with ancient plants and a stray dog. My social skills are non-existent." Theo reached for another piece of garlic toast and stuffed half of it in his mouth.

"No worries. It's a story for another time," Ivy said, offering a strained smile.

"I don't have a dad," Penelope interjected matter-of-factly as she loaded her fork with another twist of noodles and raised it to her lips.

"Pea..."

"Well, that's the truth of it." Penelope crammed the bite into her mouth and continued speaking while chewing. "My mom was a teenager when she had me, and her mom, who would be my grandmother, not that I ever knew her, got short-changed in the mothering gene department. Anyway, I don't remember much about my dad; he died when I was little. We're survivors, right, Mom? All for one and one for all."

Theo's face warmed. Penelope's revelations provided much to absorb. He swirled the ice cubes in his glass, then took a sip of tea, wishing it was something stronger.

"I'm Pea's mom and dad. We'll just leave it at that," Ivy said calmly, before adding in a hushed tone, "Penelope, remember what we talked about?"

Penelope's face fell flat, but she nodded.

Theo searched for something to say, a neutral topic to fill the sudden silence. He settled on the virus that had been spreading across the globe. The day before, it had been declared a national emergency in the United States. "Ivy, what's your take on this coronavirus? Has it affected your work?"

Ivy's eyes flashed first at Penelope and then at him. Her words were carefully measured. "Yes. Hopefully, we'll have a vaccination sooner rather than later."

Of course, it would affect her work. She was a nurse's aide, for Pete's sake!

"It's gonna be like Ebola. That's what I think," Penelope said, her sparkling eyes wide with excitement. "You know, that monkey disease, Mr. Theo, the one that makes your skin blister and your insides hemorrhage something awful?" She made a disgusted face and shuddered.

"Well, I don't think that will happen." Theo grimaced at both Penelope's description of Ebola and his idiocy for having introduced coronavirus as a viable topic in the first place.

Ivy stood abruptly. "Who wants dessert? Everyone?"

"Yes, everyone! Yes, yes, yes!" Penelope cheered and jabbed her fist overhead three times.

Theo was beginning to wish he'd never agreed to this dinner. His entire left thigh was on fire—a common occurrence when he sat too long—and the talk of hemorrhages had made his belly queasy. Would it be rude to ask for his pie to go? He could say he wasn't feeling well; feeling bone-tired after seven p.m. *was* usual for him. Just as Theo was mentally compiling a list of possible excuses to leave—*I need to feed Alice, my leg hurts like a son of a bitch, I've had all the social time I can endure for one evening*—Ivy opened the door of the oven, releasing the aroma of sweet cherries, sugar, and cinnamon. Theo closed his eyes and, for the second time that evening, was flooded with long-ago memories of his childhood.

Penelope touched him lightly on the arm. "Did you fall asleep, Mr. Theo? Your ice cream is melting all around your cherry pie. It would be unfortunate for the crust to get soggy."

It was as though time had both stood still and passed in a blur. He had forgotten his whereabouts. Suddenly, Theo was so tired and blue that he thought he might cry. He spooned an enormous bite of dessert into his mouth, wondering how long he had zoned out. "Ivy," he said, with a full mouth, "you might want to consider abandoning the nursing profession and jumping full-time into pie-making."

"That's what I always say, but she never listens to me!" Penelope bounced in her chair, her lips as crimson as the cherry pie filling.

"Oh, I do love to bake, but it's just a hobby for me, a good way to de-stress after a long day at work."

"Well, you excel at your hobby. And if you ever need a taste-tester, I'm at your service." Theo had never been comfortable in social settings and thought he was probably talking too much, but the pie merited high praise. He took another bite. If heaven had a flavor, it would be this.

Once dessert was eaten and the plates stacked in the sink, Theo thanked Ivy for the delicious meal and stood to leave, wincing at the intensified flare of pain in his leg. The evening had been eye-opening, enjoyable even, but he was thankful it was over. There was something to be said for a quiet house with no obligatory conversation.

The moon illuminated Theo's short walk home. Hanging like a lantern over the treetops, it was precisely where he knew it would be, a dependable companion through the years. As a kid in West Texas, the moon had enthralled him so much that he'd tracked the lunar phases in his science notebook. Then, several years later, during the darkest time of his life, the moon had provided much-needed strength to him. Despite the waxing and waning of his life, Theo knew it would eventually be there, back in the night sky, lighting it up. He steered his mind back to the present, and his new neighbors. What must it be like to live in such a cramped space behind Gloria Rice's huge house? Penelope seemed happy, despite her circumstances, but he wasn't sure about Ivy. She was so young, and had to juggle so many responsibilities, and, no doubt, a secret or two. Theo suspected everyone had at least one secret closeted away like a scratchy, ill-fitting sports coat.

Five

The morning sun journeyed higher in the sky as Theo moved the hand sander along the porch floor. Spiffing up the porch would require more prep work than he'd initially expected. After sanding a rough board in one area, he noticed soft boards in another. He both congratulated himself for tackling the work and lambasted himself for allowing the porch to fall into such disrepair in the first place.

The fingers on Theo's right hand were beginning to cramp from the repetitive sanding motion and his lower back ached. As he stood and stretched, he noticed a bright yellow flyer poking from his mailbox. Junk mail of some sort, he guessed, advertising new window installations or solar panels. No doubt the road to hell was paved with junk mail.

We buy houses at appraised value. As-Is! No repairs needed!

Theo folded the flyer and shoved it into the back pocket of his jeans, returning to work wondering what 'as-is' meant to the bottom line of a sale price.

"Grruggg!" A section of flooring had given way beneath the sander. Repairing the porch properly would mean prying up and replacing several boards. As Theo began to estimate both the time it would take to do the job, and the expense of new lumber, his wrap-around porch suddenly seemed larger than he'd ever realized. Still, tackling such a large project might be just what he needed. Perhaps a full porch renovation would be the impetus he needed to tackle *all* the projects that demanded his attention. Maybe it would light a fire under his ass. He snorted as one of his father's favorite phrases came to him. When had he become so disinterested in the upkeep of his home?

"Mr. Gruene, do you have a minute?"

What now? Theo had already been interrupted once that morning by Nita Johnson, who'd come to ask if he wanted to catch a movie that afternoon (he had not.)

He peered over the top of the hydrangeas surrounding his porch but saw no one.

"Hello? Who's there?" he said, his voice sounding surly even to his own ears. Perhaps he *would* call the number on that junk mail flyer. Perhaps, in today's implausibly hot real estate market, he would sell his house, disrepair and all, and still recognize enough profit to buy a couple of acres deep in the Ozark Mountains. Moving to a smaller house surrounded by nature was sounding great to him about now.

"Mr. Gruene, it's me, Ivy. Over here." She waved from the driveway side of his porch and began walking toward the front steps, her auburn hair springing all around her head like party ribbons.

Theo gave her a nod, dusted his hands together, and stood up, feeling every minute of his seventy years knotted in his lower back. He'd certainly not expected to see Ivy again so soon. Dinner the night before had been a bit uncomfortable, but he'd already shelved the experience in a corner of his mind he rarely visited. Theo had a talent for compartmentalizing his life; detaching was his superpower.

"Is Penelope okay?" Instantly, he'd forgotten the floorboards that needed sanding and the ache in his lower back; he worried something might have happened to the kid. She had certainly managed to wriggle underneath his skin in the two weeks since he'd met her.

A gust of wind whipped Ivy's hair across her face before she could answer. "Goodness. This wind is something else." She laughed and brushed it away. "Yes, Pea is fine. She's at school. But that's what I want to talk to you about. Is it okay if I come up on the porch and escape this wind?"

"Oh, of course, just be careful. I'm attempting some repairs." He was relieved to know Penelope was okay, but still, he wondered why Ivy had come.

"Mr. Gruene, last night when you asked me about coronavirus, I didn't want to talk about it in front of Penelope." She paused; the wind had whipped her hair across her face again. She attempted to tame it, gathering it and holding it to the side.

Had Ivy come to admonish him for mentioning a subject he'd not known was off-limits at her kitchen table? He'd only been trying to keep the conversation flowing. Theo gazed at the serviceberry in his front yard. It was nearly in full bloom.

"But that's not why I'm here," she added, when he said nothing.

Theo wished she would get to the point. "Well, that's good. I expected you were here to scold me. It's hard to know what to say about anything these days."

"Oh, no, it's all good." She laughed, sounding young, and what, nervous? For a protracted moment, they stood facing one another, Theo itching to get back to work, Ivy shifting her weight slightly from foot to foot while looking at him.

"The thing is," she finally continued, "Pea's school is closing because of coronavirus. The whole Fayetteville school system is moving to virtual learning. It was just announced this morning."

"Yeah, I heard something about it on the radio. That will sure be strange for the teachers." Theo rarely watched television news anymore, not since every possible topic, ranging from minimum wage to the weather, had become politicized. Instead, he limited his news intake to that provided by the local newspaper and his preferred public radio channel, KUAF. Still, even without a regular stream of television, he knew the virus had recently held a group of vacationers hostage on a cruise ship off the coast of California. Cruise ships were Petri dishes of bacteria anyway, so the fact that a virus had spread through such a place did not surprise him in the least.

"Students won't be returning to school until after spring break, so that's not for another two weeks." She held up two fingers, and instantly, his mind went to his brother. He and Michael had always flashed the peace sign in the school hallway whenever they spotted one another.

"I bet most kids will love an unexpected longer break from school. I sure would have at Penelope's age." Theo chuckled, attempting to lighten the conversation while keeping it flowing to its eventual (and hopefully fast approaching) conclusion.

"This is a big deal, Mr. Gruene. Governor Hutchison has closed public schools all over the state. You should wear a mask when you go to the grocery store."

Theo's neck grew warm above the collar of his work shirt. If this very young woman was going to stand on his porch and lecture him on a public health issue, he would speak his mind too. "How old are you?"

he asked.

"I'm twenty-four, not that—"

"Well, I'm seventy. And believe me when I say I understand the widespread problems of a pandemic. Lest you've forgotten, I've spent a lifetime studying the environment." He couldn't remember if his career as a botanist had come up during dinner, but her patronizing tone prickled his skin like a wool blanket. "Frankly, I'm surprised something like this hasn't happened already," he added. Again, his eyes found the serviceberry tree he had planted the spring before Annie died. Underneath it, a robin hopped along the grass, his red breast a bright spot in an otherwise deteriorating morning. Was it too much to want to be left alone?

"The virus is in central Arkansas now," she said. "And if I had to guess, I'd say it's already here too."

Theo knew several cases had recently been identified in Pine Bluff. And like Ivy, he suspected it was only a matter of time before coronavirus spread into northwest Arkansas. He was concerned, of course, but he imagined his risk of infection was low, since he kept to himself the majority of the time. Or he would, if neighbors didn't keep seeking him out.

Ivy continued describing what she knew about the virus, how it was transmitted from person to person, and her concern over the lack of a vaccination. Eventually, she stopped talking.

"Thanks for letting me know. I should probably pay better attention, maybe turn on the evening news occasionally." He laughed, hoping to end Ivy's unexpected visit on a positive note.

"Well..." She paused, suddenly looking unsure of herself. "I'm here because I have a favor to ask." She pressed her lips together, almost grimacing.

"Well, go on then. I really do have things to do." A gusty wind sent an eddy of fallen leaves swirling onto the porch, and Theo's gaze followed their path. Valuable work time was slipping away. He needed to finish sanding, and get to Lowe's for lumber and stain before the afternoon traffic became heavy. Theo scuffed the toe of his boot across a spot near the edge of the porch where the stain had faded entirely, and the board crumbled. He sighed. So much rotted wood to replace! Again, he thought of the real estate flyer in his back pocket, picturing a 'For Sale' sign in his front yard and imagining a slew of offers to consider. In today's seller's market, it might be like winning the lottery.

"...so, what do you think, Mr. Gruene? Will you do me this one small favor?" Ivy chewed on her lip and stared at him with her full-moon eyes.

Theo chided himself silently. Once again his brain had tuned out what it saw as irrelevant chatter. Was this a survival technique that came with aging? He thought so. Turning seventy had brought not only clarity, but also less willingness for nonsense. He needed to wrap up this meandering conversation. "Sorry, Ivy. I didn't quite catch that."

"I thought Penelope might do her virtual learning with you."

"Come again?" Surely he had misheard.

She inhaled slowly before clarifying. "I'm hoping Pea can come to your house when I'm at work. While school is closed. She has nowhere to go during the day, and I thought you could help her. Help *me*."

The fog of confusion dissipating, Theo grasped what she was asking. *A favor?* A favor was moving Nita Johnson's fiddle leaf fig inside for the winter. Or giving Winn a ride to C & C Auto when the repairs on his Chevy were finished.

"You want me to *teach* your daughter? In my home?"

She nodded, smiling. Her eyebrows lifted in anticipation of his answer.

He shook his head and took a step back. "Oh no. I'm no teacher."

"But I thought you *were* a teacher. A retired professor."

Theo had spent decades as an educator, but in that tongue-tied moment, he completely discounted his career. Three years teaching seventh graders in Texas and twenty years as a botany professor at the University of Arkansas seemed inconsequential when faced with educating a young child.

"That was a lifetime ago. I don't know anything about teaching spelling to little girls."

"Sure you do! I think you are the perfect person for the job!"

"You don't even know me. I could be a complete lunatic."

"Mr. Gruene," she said, staring intently at him and never losing focus, "I can't leave my young daughter home alone all day every day, and I can't quit my job. I *need* my job. Desperately." In the late morning sunlight, her silvery-blue eyes were somber and pleading. "We are barely scraping by as it is, so I can't hire a babysitter. And I can't pay you, either."

The idea that he might be viewed as a paid babysitter struck him the wrong way. "I would never accept money for spending time with Penelope. But surely you have family or friends who can help?"

She shook her head and gulped, "No," in such a dejected tone that Theo's heart lurched. Theo could sympathize with having no family. But no friends either?

"I'm not trying to pry, but what happened to Penelope's dad?"

"An amoeba killed him," she said bluntly. "He got a form of meningitis from swimming in stagnant water. The lake was closed, but he dove right on in anyway. It was a stupid thing to do, because signs were posted and there had been warnings all summer. Penelope was only three when it happened."

Theo cringed at his insensitivity. "I apologize for asking."

Ivy shrugged. "He wasn't a very nice person."

"Still, it must have been terrible."

"The point is, I can't be in two places at once, and there's no one to help me. I think you'll agree that Penelope is smart and self-sufficient for someone her age. And yes, sometimes she stays home alone an hour or two, but *still*, she's only eight." Ivy crossed her arms. She looked as though she was hugging herself.

Eight and a half, he thought.

"We were lucky to find Ms. Rice's place. When the apartment we lived in before was sold to developers—we were living in a one-bedroom off Leverett—well, I thought I would have to switch Pea's school. I really didn't want to do that to her. We actually lived in our car for two weeks before moving into Ms. Rice's apartment."

An involuntary tremble ran through Theo, a hairline crack that began to split his resolve. Once upon a time, he had slept in some pretty awful places too.

"Listen, I would like to help but—"

"How about we try it for one week and see how it goes? I know it will be a huge inconvenience, but I'll make it up to you somehow. We've not had the easiest time of things lately, and for whatever reason, Penelope trusts you, and she *really* likes you."

For whatever reason? If Ivy's immediate plan was to filibuster until he agreed with her request, it wouldn't work. *Pull it together, Theo. End this conversation.*

"I have work to do for the university." He had no plant specimens to process right then, but it didn't matter. As much as he liked Penelope, Theo couldn't be responsible for her, having her around every day. "I need to finish this porch. And I like to hike around the woods looking for rare species." Everything he said was true; but, even to his ears, his reasons sounded like weak excuses.

She frowned. With the persistence of a black fly, she repeated, "Just. One. Week."

He huffed. "Why on earth are you asking *me*?"

"Because you are obviously a nice guy. You're a dog person, and dog people are overwhelmingly good. And, like I said, Penelope really likes you. *Pull-ease?*" She stretched out please until the word nearly snapped.

"Starting when?" He shook his head even while asking the question.

"Tomorrow morning? Eight o'clock?"

"Well..."

"You're a lifesaver, Mr. Theo. You really are." She grabbed his hands and grasped them tightly, seeming reluctant to let go.

Theo didn't particularly like being touched; he broke from her clasp and took a step back. "Okay, okay, we'll take it one day at a time. No promises."

Ivy nodded, her head bobbing quickly, her curls wild in the gusty March wind. "I guess I should probably ask you, though, for the record...*are* you a complete lunatic?"

He laughed. "No more than the next person."

AS SOON AS IVY LEFT, Theo abandoned his front porch project and planted himself in front of the television to learn more about coronavirus. Facts, figures, and statistics provided a guiding light for Theo's actions and beliefs and so, for the remainder of the afternoon, he rotated among the various cable news channels so that he might get a better overall picture of the current situation. At five o'clock, he watched the local news and learned that things were indeed changing rapidly. Effective immediately, only essential workers were to report to city jobs. University of Arkansas students would not return to campus after spring break. Instead, they would pivot to virtual classes for the remainder of the semester.

Pivot to virtual classes? Thank goodness he was ten years retired.

Theo went out back to clear his head, and for the first time since Alice had shown up at his house, she wasn't there to greet him on the back deck. His stomach sank. He should have known this would happen. As soon as he grew attached to the dog, buying her a collar and giving her a proper name, she'd upped and vanished.

But disappointment quickly gave way to relief as Alice came bouncing over from the far corner of the yard. "There you are. I was worried." He stroked her, then walked to his thinking tree, Alice following. It was the time of year when dusk came on quickly, and the temperature dropped with the sun. Theo sat beneath the oak's broad canopy on the bench he had built years ago for Annie. She had adored the bench, often saying it was the best gift he'd ever given her. The first few months after she died, he had spent countless early mornings sitting there alone, watching the sunrise, hoping to feel her lingering presence. Sometimes he believed he had. All these years later, the bench was a quiet spot for remembering. He rubbed Alice's ears until her eyes closed, and she rested her head against his thigh.

As a scientist, Theo didn't believe in magic, luck, or divine destiny, but he did believe in the power of nature. He listened to the serene sound of an owl hooting in the distance. He was no longer thinking about porch repairs, and despite his research that afternoon, he wasn't worried about the mysterious new virus spreading across the country. Theo was simply enjoying a restful moment of contentment.

He had no idea that his life would soon become completely unrecognizable.

Six

Theo's first two days as Penelope's virtual teacher passed uneventfully. In fact, other than eating lunch with her at exactly eleven-thirty, which she preferred, his routine was barely altered. He continued with the front porch repairs, stripping and sanding boards, while Penelope worked on her school assignments at his dining room table, books and spirals spread open, her fingers tapping on her iPad. On the morning of day three, Theo was stretching a roll of yellow caution tape across his front steps when Penelope announced, "I've finished my work. What should I do next?"

Theo checked the time on his wristwatch. It was ten-fifteen, and the morning was beginning to warm up nicely. With such ideal weather, he expected to make significant headway on the porch. "How about you do tomorrow's assignments? It's good to work ahead." He couldn't imagine how prolonged virtual learning could be successful, having to email lessons and assignments. The day before, he had heard Penelope talking to her teacher about equalities and inequalities, and he didn't think she was referring to the Bill of Rights.

"No, I mean, I've finished *everything*. I've done all the work Miss Markum assigned us for the foreseeable future."

The foreseeable future? Theo's foreseeable future was going to be...interesting. The girl was whip-smart; that was the truth, and he felt as dull as a broken pencil lead standing there unrolling caution tape. He tied off the tape while Penelope watched intently, her hands on her hips.

"Well, Miss Penelope Pie, I suppose you'll become my assistant. Ever built a porch?"

"No, but I find the idea intriguing. And it seems you could use some help. Your porch doesn't look so safe right now, especially over there." Penelope pointed to the far corner, where he had pried up a rectangular section that had begun disintegrating around the railing.

Her words had a way of both entertaining him and getting under his skin. "Come with me, Grasshopper," he said, recalling *Kung Fu*, the television show he had always watched on Thursday nights, during his years as a seventh grade teacher. It had been a favorite of his Mount Pleasant class, especially the boys, and being able to discuss it on Friday mornings became a way for a young teacher to connect to his class.

"I'm not a grasshopper," she protested with a snort.

"Oh, but maybe you *are* a grasshopper, and you don't know it. Not everything in this world is literal, Penelope Pie."

"Hmm. I'll have to think about that." Her dark eyes were uncertain. Theo was pleased to have given Penelope something to ponder.

The unlikely construction team began counting replacement boards and making a list of supplies to buy at Lowe's. Although Penelope wanted to use her iPad for list-making, Theo claimed there was nothing virtual about their project and insisted she use a pad of paper and the mechanical pencil he pulled from his shirt pocket. Despite already knowing the dimensions of his porch, he produced a tape measure from his back pocket and instructed her to calculate the length and width of the space.

Her eyes glinted as she extended the tape and began measuring her arm from shoulder to fingertips.

"No, no, no. Measure the porch, Pie girl, not your arm. Today's lesson is very important, so write this down and underline it." He paused for emphasis. "Always measure twice, so you only have to cut once." Hearing his father's words automatically flowing from his mouth reminded Theo of the pride he felt in having learned handyman skills from him.

Penelope began writing. Until that moment, Theo hadn't realized she was a left-hander. He noted how she held the pencil and printed small round letters. Perhaps her handwriting was the only thing about her at grade level.

Since Theo hadn't gotten around to buying lumber or paint earlier in the week, they drove across town and spent an inordinate amount of time walking the aisles of Lowe's, searching for everything on their list. Until their venture to Lowe's, Penelope had seemed overly mature for her age, an old soul trapped in a youngster's body; at the store, however, she seemed an alien child, overly-inquisitive about everything she saw. It was as though she had been dropped on earth and told to discover as much as she could as quickly as possible.

"If you don't stop touching everything, you'll have to sit in the truck." Theo's nerves were fraying. It didn't help that he was unable to find an employee to help him.

"I really like your red truck, but I'd rather stay with you." Penelope continued running her fingertips along the display of brightly colored paint sample strips, each one containing four gradations of a color. When a particular shade caught her attention, she plucked the sample strip from the shelf and pointed to the square she liked. "Someday, when I get my own bedroom, I'll paint the walls this bright green color—Good Luck. What a perfect name for a bedroom wall color. Just imagine being surrounded by good luck all the time. Wouldn't that be amazing?"

Theo would need lots of good luck to get out of the store and back home without completely losing his mind. Not that he believed in luck, per se. "Kiddo, I believe in cause and effect. Work is what leads to results. Let's get what we came for, and get back to it."

Penelope sighed and went to return the sample strip and, for a split second, he felt terrible for squashing her enthusiasm. "You can keep that, you know."

Her eyes widened with disbelief. "You mean *all* of these are free? Like *totally* free?"

How could she be so bright, yet so unfamiliar with commonplace things? "Yes, that's what they're for, so customers can take them home and consider various colors before committing."

"Oh. That's so smart." Her words were dreamy and pillow-soft.

Finally, after making his stain selection, buying replacement boards, and paying at one of the self-check kiosks (because the manned check-out counters were unmanned), they returned to Theo's truck.

"That was exhilarating!" Penelope said, her tiny body practically levitating from her excess energy.

"That was the opposite of exhilarating." Theo collapsed behind the wheel; his energy had drained out back on Aisle 22.

"Tiresome? Dull? Unexciting?"

"More like exhausting." As he backed from the parking place, he thought even the motor of his old Silverado sounded weary.

Penelope rolled her eyes and then returned to admiring the paint sample in her hand. "Good Luck. That name practically guarantees fame and fortune. Don't you agree? I wonder who gets to name paint colors. Wouldn't that be a fun job?"

Theo wasn't sure he could drive home safely with such a distracting level of chatter in his ears, but he couldn't let her go on believing such nonsensical things. "I'm sure I don't know who names colors, but that sounds like an odd way to make a buck, and a complete waste of your obvious talents. Nothing guarantees fame and fortune, especially not a paint color. Those internet people you consider so famous are putting on a show. You don't really know them. Underneath the masks they wear, they have wrinkles and junk drawers and can't remember where they put their car keys the minute they lay them down."

She shook her head. "That's gross and untrue. They have *money*. And with money, they pay people to smooth wrinkles and organize junk drawers and drive them around in shiny black cars. I refuse to let your shriveled-up imagination affect me negatively. No way."

He shook his head. His dander was stirred, probably more than it should have been. "Penelope, I have no idea what you want to be when you grow up, but I hope you do something more stimulating than naming paint colors."

"Oh, I've not decided on my career path, but I have lots of thoughts on the matter."

Of course you do. "No rush. You have plenty of time."

"I might be a cultural immersion enthusiast."

He said nothing, having no idea what she was talking about.

"Or an opera singer. I'd like to sing at the Met in New York City. Did you know there is already a famous mezzo-soprano named Penelope Palmer? She was born in nineteen forty-four and has performed in some of the most famous opera houses in the world."

He wished he'd never engaged with her over the topic of career.

"I wonder if it wouldn't be better for me to choose a different profession, since there is already a famous opera singer with my exact same name. You know? Like maybe the world can't really handle two of us?"

"I'm not sure the world can handle one of you." Theo tried to remain focused on the road, but he could feel her eyes boring into the side of his face. "Pea, isn't that what your mom calls you?"

"Yes."

"Tell me something. Can you even sing?"

"Of course, I can sing. Everyone can sing."

"No, everyone most certainly *cannot* sing. I come from a long line of folks who are practically tone-deaf." He thought of his mother, warbling along with the radio while rolling out biscuit dough in their stifling West Texas kitchen. She had belted out hymns from their pew at Polk Street Methodist, her voice so bad it must have made congregants repent their every sin.

For much of the drive back home, Penelope explained her belief that anything was learnable, even singing opera. Theo admired her enthusiasm, but suggested she might want to explore careers in science or math. "The world needs more women in these fields. Lots of scholarship money goes unused because there aren't enough girls who want to study those areas. Did you know there's a prestigious high school in Hot Springs that specializes in science and math?"

"Mr. Theo, what were you like when you were a kid? Did you always aspire to be a savior of dead plants?"

He felt a jolt at her word choice. "I'm no savior of anything. Not by any stretch of the imagination. I'm a preserver of plants, but no, when I was a kid, I never imagined being a botanist."

"So, what did you want to be?"

There had been a time when he had imagined being a journalist for a major newspaper, like the *Fort Worth Star-Telegram*. It was a paper his father read daily, beginning with the oil and gas news, then the sports page, and ending with the comics. Or, as he sat with his family, glued to the reporting on Vietnam, he aspired to be a reporter like Walter Cronkite, always the respected voice of reason.

"How about we not talk for a while." Theo's head was reeling from so much conversation. He was having difficulty concentrating on his driving.

She snickered. "Why would we do that when we have this perfect time for discussing things? Really, Mr. Theo, I hear you saying you don't want to discuss your childhood. But if I'm correct in my assumption, that's exactly what you *should* talk about. Face your problems head-on by talking things out. That's what I like to do." She smiled and nodded encouragingly.

He shook his head and clenched his jaw. She wanted him to spill his guts right there in the cab of his old truck! If he was around Penelope much longer, he'd have to look into getting one of those night guards for teeth grinding. Only he'd need to wear his during the day.

"Well, let me know when you're ready. I'm here for you. By the way, what's the name of the paint color you got for the porch?"

The girl must have a mental list of questions running like a ticker tape. Theo dug deep, excavating a few more words from his near-parched well of language. "I bought stain, not paint. It's called driftwood."

"Driftwood? *Driftwood?*"

Theo glanced over to see his passenger slumping over dramatically and taking her head in her hands. "With a bazillion paint colors, you couldn't choose something more exciting than a boring stain named after washed-up and bleached-out shore debris?"

He sighed. "It matches what's been on the porch since I bought the house." There were only a few color choices available in exterior non-slip stain, and driftwood would complement the dark gray paint of his house.

"That is the pitifulest thing I've ever heard. A color change might provide more excitement than you realize. Mr. Theo, you should hire me to be your life coach. I could guide you in matters of inspiration."

The things she thought to say. If he wasn't so bushed, he might find her comments humorous. "First of all, pitifulest is not a word. Second, Missy, I've survived quite well for seven decades without a life coach." His voice trailed off as he remembered quite a few times when he had not only needed help, but had asked for help and gratefully taken it. Theo turned on the radio to provide distraction. KUAF was reporting on new state-wide measures to curb the spread of coronavirus in Arkansas. *All restaurants and bars have been closed for in-person service. Virtual school has been extended to April 17.*

April 17? That was a month away! Theo quickly silenced the radio and hoped Penelope had not picked up on the dire news of the day. But how strange, to hear of such extreme measures being taken. All around him, everyone was going about their normal business. Certainly, nothing had changed at Lowe's; the place had been bustling for a weekday.

Theo glanced at Penelope, but he needn't have worried. She did not appear to be listening, and for the moment, she wasn't talking. She seemed to be mesmerized by the paint sample in her hand. A breathy tune flowed from Penelope's lips as she ran her finger along the shades of green paint, admiring it like it was a free ticket to the moon.

Seven

As the sky lightened in the east, Theo sipped his coffee, enjoying nature's early morning symphony: the call of a cardinal, the twitter of a chickadee, the distant drumming of a woodpecker. Alice joined him beneath the white oak, gazing at him knowingly. Grandpa Gruene, who had never ventured more than a few hundred miles from his Iowa farm, had believed in the power of good soil and a beautiful sunrise. Theo liked to imagine certain ancestral beliefs were handed down from generation to generation, encoded in DNA, because the natural world was vital to him, too. Whether he was digging out nut grass from around his heirloom peonies, watching morning chase away a dark night, or helping to preserve plants for future research, nature helped ground him in a way nothing else did.

"Today's our last day with Penelope Pie," Theo said, stroking Alice's soft coat. "I wonder if she's aware," he added, feeling a slight hitch in his stomach. The child had been a handful at times, but not an actual bother. Still, after four days of constant questions and chatter, he was craving a return to normalcy.

The single window in Gloria Rice's garage apartment glowed faintly. He imagined Penelope still sleeping while Ivy prepared her daughter's lunch. Each day, Penelope brought the same thing; the plainest cheese sandwich he'd ever seen, just a slice of American cheese between two slices of white bread or in a hot dog bun, and a large bag of potato chips. She would eat only a handful before re-sealing the bag with a clothespin at the end of their lunch break. Theo worried Penelope wasn't getting enough to eat. He suspected her small portions were intentional; that the child knew the large bag had to last until her mother's next paycheck. Theo always offered her something to go with her sparse meal, some carrot sticks or apple slices, and once he'd even offered his personal favorite snack, microwaved popcorn, but she always declined.

When Ivy had come to pick Penelope up the day before, while Penelope was in the dining room packing her things to go home, Theo had acknowledged how positive the experience had been for him. "I'm glad you persuaded me to keep Penelope for the week. I've enjoyed my time with her despite the fact I had to put some things off." With another collection of herbarium specimens waiting, he was eager to return to work. He even thought he might go camping, maybe drive to Jasper and hike to a waterfall.

Ivy had flushed and stared at him in silence a minute, before croaking out a flat, "Oh. Well...I was hoping she could stay on with you next week too." She wore a weary expression, her face as pale as her cloud-colored scrubs.

Theo frowned. "We said it would be one week. Anyway, since next week is spring break, I'm sure you have something fun planned." As a former educator, Theo knew spring break was scheduled well in advance on every school calendar, elementary through college. Not only that, living in a college town meant being mindful of the school calendar, even at his age. The city moved with a different vibe when school was in session.

Ivy nodded, rather unconvincingly. Exhaustion seemed to cloud her normally bright eyes, and she placed a hand on the door as though it was the only thing keeping her from fainting dead away.

"Are you okay?" he asked, and then mentally scolded himself for asking the question. Of course, she wasn't okay! She had been working double shifts during unprecedented times and under stressful circumstances.

Now, as Theo went back inside to wait for Penelope, the memory of yesterday's conversation filled him with ambivalence. He was elated to be reclaiming his time, but dismayed by his ease at brushing aside the troublesome reality—no matter what plans Ivy had made for spring break, he knew Penelope's school would be closed at least until mid-April. That was four weeks away. Their arrangement had only been meant to be for one week, but he realized Ivy would probably still need help even after spring break.

Guilt and relief were mighty strange bedfellows.

AT PRECISELY EIGHT O'CLOCK, Theo heard the three little raps he had come to expect. Penelope Pie was at his door. Like the first time she had appeared on his front porch, like every time, in fact, she wore her lime green raincoat.

"Happy Friday, Mr. Theo."

It was indeed.

"It's time to feed Alice!" She skipped past him, tossing her backpack on the kitchen table and shedding her raincoat across the chair. Penelope had taken over Alice's morning feeding for the past three days. Even though it involved nothing more than pouring a cup of kibble into a dish and refilling her water bowl, she loved doing it.

"Can I ask you a question, Penelope?"

"Sure thing, Mr. Theo."

"Why do you wear that raincoat every day? Even when there's no rain in the forecast."

"Why do you wear the same shirt every day?"

Confused, he looked down and pressed a hand against his chest. "I don't. This isn't the same shirt I had on yesterday."

"Are you sure? All your clothes look identical to me, like a uniform. A neutral shirt, like gray or tan, and khaki pants or jeans. Do you have something against happy colors?"

Goodness, the kid was a character! "Of course I have nothing against color. I really don't think about it. I buy multiples of shirts and pants I find comfortable, especially when they are on sale. Just because they look the same, doesn't mean they are." Why was he justifying his shopping habits to this tiny tyrant?

She shook her head.

"What?"

"Oh, nothing." She reached her thin arm into the large bag of Science Diet and scooped up Alice's morning portion. "So, what are you going to teach me today?"

He found this question ironic. He'd not taught her much of anything yet, but he did have a plan for their last day together. "I thought you could spend the day reading. I have an entire library of books upstairs in the first spare bedroom off the hallway. After you feed Alice, go up there and choose a book. Then, come back and read while I work on the porch." The girl definitely needed more to do. Lafayette Elementary didn't challenge her nearly enough, assigning books way below her reading level and math homework she could do in her sleep.

"Hmmm...I was hoping to help you replace the boards on the porch. As your construction assistant, it's probably in my job description to see the project through. But..." she paused, her face contorting as she puzzled something out in that highly inquisitive mind of hers, "...the idea of visiting a library *upstairs* trumps anything else. It's like you have a whole other world up there that I know nothing about."

"I'm afraid you—"

"What sort of books do you have? Mysteries and thrillers? Do you have *Fifty Shades of Gray* by any chance?" She raised her dark eyebrows and grinned.

Astounded, he stared at her. "What on earth would an eight-year-old know about *Fifty Shades of Gray*?" Theo had never read the book, but as someone who kept attuned to literary news, he knew without a doubt that Penelope should know *nothing* about it.

"Eight-and-a-half. Remember? I just had my half birthday. You came—"

"Yes, yes, I remember."

"Anyway, an eighth grader I know brought *Fifty Shades* to school a while back. It got confiscated by the lunch duty teacher almost as soon as she pulled it from her backpack. All I really know is it has a bunch of wild stuff in it. I'm thinking it's one of those banned books I should probably read before the radical conservatives burn it."

"Oh, is that right?" Theo swallowed hard. The taste of his peaceful morning coffee lingered on his tongue. It was too early in the day for a discussion on banned books or radical conservatives, although he certainly had specific opinions on both. "Here's the thing, Penelope Pie. You won't be reading fifty shades of anything while you are my responsibility." Only a few more hours, he thought. But a twinge of guilt crisscrossed his mind as he wondered about Ivy's plan for spring break. If Penelope didn't mention it before the end of the day, he might ask.

Penelope shrugged. "No sweat. I'm not surprised by your narrow view, but it was worth a shot. My mother says you'll never get what you want without first opening your mouth and asking the universe for it." Penelope dropped the scoop she'd used to feed Alice back into the bag of kibble, wiped her hands on her flamingo-pink pants, and raced upstairs.

Theo's views of the world were *not* narrow! On another day, he might have provided Penelope with proof of his ability to give open-minded commentary on a variety of social issues, but his time with the precocious little girl was winding down, and he could practically hear the ancient plants calling to him from the box on the dining room table. He poured another steaming cup of coffee, relaxed into his recliner, and savored the momentary silence.

Penelope wasn't upstairs long enough for Theo to take more than a few swallows of coffee. He heard her clattering down, and when she sprang into the family room, she was balancing a cardboard hat box in her hands. "Look what I found, Mr. Theo!"

The box wasn't all that large, but in her small hands it was bulky and cumbersome. Theo's breath snagged and his fists clenched. "That is most certainly not a book."

"No, it's a round box!" She looked surprised; likely she had never seen a hat box before.

He placed his coffee cup on the side table and stared at her. "Yes, hat boxes are always round. But I asked you to choose a book."

"I know, but I got sidetracked when I saw this on the bottom of your bookcase. It was calling out to me, practically saying, *Hey there, Pea, why don't you see what treasures I hold?* So? Can I look inside?"

Time seemed to slow for the briefest of moments. Theo stood, inhaled deeply, and consciously relaxed his hands. He took the hat box from Penelope, disturbing the fine layer of dust coating the lid. "No, Penelope. This box is personal. That means keep your grubby little hands off."

Penelope took a step backward as though he had physically shoved her. "Jeez. I'm sorry, but it says 'toys' on the side. See?"

He didn't reply. He knew exactly how the box was labeled. He'd labeled it himself, years ago. A lifetime ago.

"I'm only human, Mr. Theo. Surely you know a toy box is irresistible to a kid, especially someone like me who is blessed with excess curiosity. And by the way, my hands are *not* grubby. I always remember to wash them every time I use the restroom. It's the best way to remove pathogens from the skin."

Theo took a breath and focused on preserving his fast-diminishing patience. If he didn't know better, he might think this child had been sent to test him. "Penelope, would you like me to choose a book for you?"

"No sir, thank you, sir, I'll go get one now, sir!" Penelope saluted, with a stiff hand to the side of her owl-like eyeglasses, and then sprinted from the room as though he had set an egg timer for her return.

The box felt light in his hands, as though filled with crepe paper flowers or old Valentine cards, or even a straw hat like the one his mother had worn when she toiled in their West Texas garden, but as Theo carried it to the laundry room and placed it on the dryer, he was acutely aware of its weight. The heaviness of another lifetime lay inside. Later, he would find a better spot to store it, somewhere Penelope wouldn't stumble upon it. Of course, by the end of the day, she would return to her life, and he to his. This realization brought him a measure of relief. He was suddenly looking forward to returning to his solitary ways more than ever.

Penelope was upstairs fifteen minutes…twenty minutes…much longer than was necessary to choose a book. Theo finished his coffee. He began wondering if she was pouting, or hiding, or rifling through his personal things just to be spiteful. But he'd never known her to pout or hide or act spitefully. What did he really know of her, though? He rinsed his coffee cup and decided to accept the quiet for the splendor it was.

When she finally returned, she was carrying three books. "You sure have a bunch of old books up there."

"Well, I'm an old man. Let's see what you found."

She dropped the books with a thud on the kitchen table and arranged them side by side.

A Confederacy of Dunces. To Kill a Mockingbird. Crime and Punishment.
"Dostoevsky. Really?"

She nodded.

Was she simply trying to get a reaction from him? Theo considered all three novels to be literary masterpieces, but even with her aptitude, he didn't believe she could grasp the nuances of each. "Why did you select these particular books? There are plenty of more age-appropriate choices up there." Theo was not one to ever get rid of a book. Even as a science teacher in Mount Pleasant, he had encouraged his students to read, filling his classroom with classics, popular mystery series, and Newbery award-winners, and letting students borrow from his personal collection. One of the best things about buying a house had been finally unpacking his boxes of books.

Penelope studied the covers of the three novels before launching into her reasoning. "*Crime and Punishment* sounds dark and intriguing to me, and since it's huge, I imagine it must be filled with words I don't know yet. I like the idea of expanding my vocabulary. Plus, I've never read any Russian literature, and that seems like an important thing to do." Next, she lay a palm against *A Confederacy of Dunces*. "I like the title and even though I don't fully understand the meaning of it, the cover makes the story look funny. And last, I've never read the *Mockingbird* book, but I've seen the movie, the one with Gregory Peck. It was very compelling, and since my mother says books are always better than movies, why wouldn't I want to read it?"

He couldn't argue with her reasoning regarding any of the books, but still, he thought there had to be something upstairs more fitting for a kid her age. What had he been reading at age eight or nine? He vaguely recalled borrowing books from the county bookmobile whenever it came to their area.

"You know, Mr. Theo, now that I think about it, you favor Gregory Peck. Has anyone ever told you that?"

A belly laugh escaped him. Did she come up with things to say just to hear herself talk? "No, I can honestly say those words have never been uttered to me." As soon as the girl went home for the day, *forever*, he would throw some steaks on the grill, call Winn and Julie, and invite them for dinner. Maybe next week, he would air out his tent and go camping for a few days, take Alice and find a secluded spot on the Buffalo River, or even rent a cabin at Devil's Den, where he and Annie had spent so much time together. After all, the herbarium work had been labeled 'No rush'.

She studied him, eyes squinted, a finger on her chin. "You're tall like he was, and your hair is mostly dark."

Theo sighed. He would have a scotch as soon as she went home. Maybe two. He would sit on the porch until dusk tinted the sky, and then he would go to bed early. Maybe he'd start a new book and read until he fell asleep, the book splayed on his bare chest. Maybe he would re-read *Crime and Punishment*. It had been years.

"Do you dye your hair, Mr. Theo?"

He rubbed his eyes. "No, of course not. Do you?"

She laughed. "I'm just a kid."

All evidence to the contrary.

SOON, AS THOUGH her battery had finally run dry of juice, Penelope curled into his recliner, intent on reading *To Kill a Mockingbird*. He didn't know if the book was age-appropriate, but he reasoned that if Ivy let her watch the movie, it was probably the best choice of the three. Besides, what did age-appropriate mean for someone like Penelope Pie? Theo tried to imagine what might lie ahead for her, with her unique intelligence, but found it hard to push his imagination past what he knew of her complicated family situation. Life was hard enough without the challenge of poverty. Even during his loneliest, bottom-of-the-pit days, he'd held on to the cushion of inheritance money, bequeathed from family who had come before him.

Theo abandoned his plan to work on the porch. Replacing boards was a project best started during the early morning hours, when he was fresh. He ignored the plant specimens as well. The meticulousness needed for that project required an alert mind and a steady hand. While Penelope read, Theo studied a hiking trail map of Kessler Mountain, the topo lines a comfortable language for him. Tomorrow, he would pack a sandwich for himself, and a few treats for

Alice, and they would set out on a day-long hike in the woods. Lulled by the house's silence, his eyes grew heavy. He felt himself almost nodding off.

Penelope shifted positions, and *To Kill a Mockingbird* tumbled to the floor, startling them both. "Oh, I'm so sorry for dropping your book, Mr. Theo." She scrambled to the floor and picked it up.

"It's okay Penelope. No harm done. It's just a book." He began refolding the trail map.

She dusted the cover with her hand, even though it wasn't soiled, and crawled back into the recliner, cradling the book. Theo thought she looked like she might cry.

"Sometimes I think books have feelings, like people. Don't you?"

Had he ever met such a fanciful girl? "No, not at all. Books are inanimate objects."

"But how do you know?"

"It's the simple truth. Books are made from paper and ink and glue."

"I know, but still. Unless you spent part of your life as an actual book, how can you be absolutely positively sure?"

Theo rubbed his forehead. "Penelope, you're mixing up science and fairy tales. Facts are backed by proof. Some things aren't debatable."

"Oh no, Mr. Theo, every—"

Just as she began to debate the undebatable, the telephone rang, silencing her and surprising him. Theo's landline rarely rang anymore. It was probably a wrong number.

"You mean to tell me that thing actually works?" Penelope jumped from the recliner and rushed to the sofa side table, picking up the receiver before he could get it. "Mr. Theo's ancient phone," she said in a sing-song voice, the cord curling around her arm.

Oh, boy.

"Yes, I'm his assistant. Who may I say is calling?"

"Give me that!" Theo held out his hand toward the phone, but clutched only air.

"And your last name, sir?" She pushed her eyeglasses up her impossibly small nose. "Mr. Theo, are you available for a Mr. Winn Berton?"

He snatched the receiver from Penelope. "Sorry, Winn. Hold on a minute." Theo put his hand over the receiver, and sent Penelope off to wash her hands (again).

The child was always underfoot.

"That was a super short conversation," Penelope said when she returned from the bathroom.

"Not everything has to be a dissertation. Winn and I have lunch together every Friday, but he called to say he can't come today, which is a good thing, because I had completely forgotten about it. Restaurants aren't open right now anyway." During the early years, they had rushed to squeeze lunch in between lectures and office hours. Once they had retired, the practice had continued, only at that point it also included a cold mug of beer and sometimes a game of darts at Maxine's. Now, with restaurants closed, or open for take-out only, their tradition would have to continue at home, at least for a while. Theo was unnerved to have completely forgotten about a standing lunch date, something that was as routine as putting the recycling out each Sunday, or buying groceries on Monday morning. It was further evidence of his disrupted schedule.

Penelope released a gigantic exhalation that very nearly deflated her tiny body. "That is so sad."

"Not really. Sometimes life happens, and people have conflicts. There's no reason to be sad about it."

She squinted her eyes at him. "It's really not up to you to decide what makes another person sad. Have you ever thought of that?"

He hadn't. And it was a profound comment, when he thought about it. "By the way, Winn did say he was sorry to miss meeting my assistant."

She grinned. "Maybe he can come next Friday."

Next Friday he would be basking in quiet.

"By the way, Mr. Theo, what sort of crazy name is Winn? Is it short for Winnie the Pooh?" She shook her head rapidly back and forth as though trying to rid the confusion of it from her brain.

Theo frowned. "You know, Penelope *Pie*, it's really not up to you to decide which names are crazy and which are conventional, now, is it?"

A playfulness came into her eyes. "Oh, I see what you did there, Mr. Theo. Bravo. You get a point for that."

He hadn't realized a game was afoot.

THEO FORMED GROUND BEEF into patties while Penelope busied herself at the kitchen island, sketching her interpretation of Alice on a section of spread-out butcher paper. "Mr. Theo, don't forget, I'm a vegetarian, so I'll take my cheeseburger without meat, please."

He was glad Penelope had agreed to forgo her regular lunch and join him for a burger, but a *meatless* burger? He recalled their spaghetti dinner, and how Penelope's dish had been only noodles and butter. "I don't think that will qualify as a cheese*burger,* but sure. Basically, you want the same plain sandwich you have every day?"

She shook her head, continuing with her drawing. "That's not only rude, it's false. I want a cheeseburger, not a cheese sandwich. There's a world of difference."

"How?"

"Bread and accouterments, of course," she said, stumbling through the pronunciation of accoutrements, which he found charming. She began sharpening her pencil with a small square sharpener, letting the curl of shavings fall onto a tissue. "A cheeseburger is made with a bun that is either warmed in a skillet or toasted in the oven. It includes pickles and mustard and sometimes a very thin slice of onion if I'm in the mood for it. And because the bun is hot, the cheese melts, all delicious-like and gooey. A cheese sandwich is super basic in structure— a slice of American cheese between two pieces of soft white bread. I like mine with mayonnaise and nothing else, although sometimes I arrange two plain potato chips underneath the bread. But they have to be plain chips and not the ruffled kind, otherwise they don't crunch right when I bite into the sandwich." She looked up at him, and he could read her expression, plain as day. *See how obvious the differences are?*

"Okay—"

"Oh, and there's also the classic grilled cheese sandwich, which is a whole other thing."

She returned to her sketch. It looked nothing like a dog to Theo.

"What about the fact that the mere word 'burger' means meat?"

"Again, not true. What about veggie burgers? My mother makes a delicious chickpea burger."

That sounded horrible to Theo. "I don't think America's cattle farmers would agree with you."

"I don't know any cattle farmers."

"So?"

"So what?"

Theo had sunk to the level of an eight-year-old (albeit a brilliant one), but he found it entertaining and couldn't stop himself. "So you think it's okay to culturally hijack the word 'burger' and use it for your vegetarian purposes?"

"Words belong to the masses."

He sighed. This could go on infinitum. "You win. One meatless cheeseburger coming right up," he said.

Penelope's eyes lit with excitement. "We're tied one to one."

While she concentrated on her drawing, he placed the two patties in the skillet. He would have one for lunch and save one for supper. Penelope would be gone by then. He would at least be able to enjoy *that* meal in blessed silence.

As the meat began sizzling in the skillet, she planted herself beside him and asked, "Mr. Theo, what happened to your wife? Did she leave you?"

"What makes you think I ever had a wife?"

"For one thing, that wedding picture in the dining room. Isn't that you in the picture with the bride?"

"Well, yes." He had forgotten about the picture. "If it's all the same, I don't want to discuss my private life."

"Why?"

"Because by the word's very definition, private means not for public consumption."

Penelope giggled. "I know what private means. During the past five days as your official student, lots of questions have been building up in my mind, and they have nowhere to go but through my lips. Also, since we have a special teacher-student relationship now, I don't think you can lump me in with the general public. I'll probably have even more questions next week."

Penelope obviously had no idea she wouldn't be spending spring break with him. He wasn't going to mention it. He thought that was a conversation best left to Ivy.

"So, why did she divorce you?"

He inhaled. Exhaled. Thought of Annie, the only woman he'd ever loved. God, how he hated cancer. Again, he pressed the spatula firmly against a hamburger patty. The release of hot oil into the skillet and the aroma of cooking beef made him suddenly ravenous. *Only three more hours.* Soon, his time would be entirely his own again. At least until Monday week, when spring break would be over, and Ivy might ask for his help again.

Penelope frowned and looked him up and down as though trying to work something out. "Oh, duh. I get it," she said, opening her palms toward him as though offering a gift. "Your wife left because you're gay, and Winn is your partner. I can't believe it took me so long to figure it out. By the way, that's perfectly fine by me. I'm fully supportive of the LGBTQ community. In fact, I've always wished for a gay friend because, in my opinion, gay people are way cooler and much more interesting."

"For Pete's sake, I'm not gay. Winn and I are just friends. Old friends from way back. And before you ask, no, I'm not homophobic either."

"Oh." She deflated a bit, her smile falling, her expression disheartened. "So, just to be clear, you identify as a heterosexual man?"

Theo sighed. "Just to be clear, I am an old, boring, heterosexual white man who prefers a life of solitude. And you, Miss Penelope Pie, are making that very difficult. You know that?"

Her dark eyes narrowed behind her eyeglasses, and he could almost hear the ticking of her overactive mind. "*Soooo* if your wife didn't leave you or divorce you...." She pressed her fingers against her cheek, pondering Theo's past life; a life which he would prefer to keep private. Then, she gasped. "Does your house have a basement?"

"A basement?"

"I saw this movie a while back, I forget the name of it, but this crazy old *white* man was keeping his sick wife down in his basement. It was so creepy! He was trying to take care of her but at the same time he held her hostage. Look, Mr. Theo." Penelope shoved the sleeve of her shirt up to her elbow and held her arm in front of him. "I get goosebumps just remembering that movie. Not that I truly think you are like that psycho man or anything."

"Penelope. Listen to me. I'm not hiding my wife in the basement."

"So you *do* have a basement!"

He sighed and considered pouring himself a bourbon with lunch. "I do. It is a dark, damp place filled with rusted garden tools and old canning jars." A vision of Annie flitted through his mind, her hair tied in a messy knot, the kitchen counters covered with jars and lids and tongs and piles of vegetables from his backyard garden—pole beans and cucumbers and tomatoes. They had made a good team—he the gardener, she the food preservationist. But that had been another life.

"So your wife died then. That's the only other option, and I was hoping for a happy ending to your story. I despise sad endings. I bet you were really lost when that happened."

Theo swallowed the lump in the back of his throat. He had been lost and broken *before* Annie. With her, the cracks in his spirit had finally begun to mend.

"I was married for sixteen wonderful years, but my wife died of cancer. It was terribly sad, and yes, I felt lost, but she's been gone almost twenty years now. There's no need for you to be upset. And, by the way, my story hasn't ended yet. Last I checked, I'm still breathing." He would never admit it to her, but he often believed the end of his story *had* come. He would coast along for the rest of his days, gluing plants to archival paper, eating hamburgers on Fridays, and feeling a bit unmoored.

She nodded slowly, although her face expressed skepticism.

"What was her name?"

"Annie."

"Oh! Those are her initials carved on the bench under your tree. A plus T."

"Yes, I—"

"That's so romantic and heartbreaking."

"Well—"

"Mr. Theo, I don't think anyone can truly be lost, because we leave little bits and pieces of us everywhere we go, like a trail. If I ever became physically lost, like in the woods, I would leave a trail, like Hansel and Gretel did, so my mother could find me, only I wouldn't use breadcrumbs because of the hungry birds." She cocked her head in contemplation. "I suppose a person with amnesia might truly be lost, because being unable to remember yourself is the very definition. Right?"

Exhausted, Theo exhaled slowly and nodded his head. "I suppose so."

"So, Mr. Theo, where's your kid? From what I know about you, I'm guessing you have a son, but he's all grown up and living someplace exciting. Maybe Los Angeles?"

Theo moved the hamburger patties onto a paper towel. "First of all, Nosy Rosy, you don't know me. A few days provides very little insight into the lifetime of a person. Second, I've never had any children, nor do I understand why you would assume such a thing. Third, why are you compelled to ask so many personal questions?"

"That you know of."

"That I know of *what?*"

"You've never had any children that you know of. It's really up to the female to let the male know."

"Oh, good grief." He stopped himself from saying anything more and instead focused on browning the buns in the hot skillet.

"I thought you must have at least one kid because you have that secret box of toys. That's all." She explained her reasoning in such a forlorn tone that Theo suddenly began to feel sorry for both of them.

"Things aren't always as they seem, Penelope. You're maybe a little young to know this, but before long, you will."

She didn't say anything more on the topic—a minor miracle in his estimation. Theo began assembling his burger and her cheese sandwich, adding pickles, lettuce, and a thin slice of purple onion. He wished he'd thought to buy potatoes for fries at the grocery store, but decided they would make do with a bag of Doritos. While they ate, Theo explained about the toys. He decided not to worry about whether such profoundly personal information would be too much for her to handle; he just allowed his words to flow calmly.

"Inside the hat box are the toys my little brother and I played with as kids. My parents and brother died a very long time ago, in a car accident. I try not to think about it, and I don't like talking about it. Sometimes people really are in the wrong place at the wrong time."

Penelope blinked so slowly he thought she might close her eyes altogether. Then, she teared up.

"There's no reason to get upset, Penelope. Like I said, it was a long time ago. I'm okay."

She gripped his wrist. "But you can't be okay, Mr. Theo, not after something that unspeakable happened to you. I've never met anyone cursed with such awful luck! Based on what I've just learned about your wife and your parents and your brother, it's obvious that horrible luck follows you around like a black storm cloud. Thank goodness you have me now."

He took a drink of his iced tea. He wasn't sure what to say to that. Theo didn't believe in luck, good or bad. He couldn't afford to put his trust in such a thing.

"Mr. Theo, what was your brother's name? Or is that too much of a nosy rosy thing to ask?"

He smiled. "His name was Michael."

"Thanks for telling me. I believe it's healthy for the soul to share secrets. My mom doesn't, though."

Eight

A misty rain moved into the area and hovered over Theo's rooftop, thwarting his weekend hiking plans. He spent much of Saturday at the dining room table mounting a series of fragile specimens. Initially, Theo found the silence delicious. Without Penelope underfoot asking questions and chiming in about one thing or another, the house was as quiet as fog. By Sunday morning, however, an unexpected sense of desolation set in. It was a strange feeling for someone who typically craved silence. By mid-morning, Theo had lost all interest in working. He felt no physical symptoms of illness, yet wondered if he was coming down with something.

"Alice, come, girl!" He opened the sliding glass door and called to her when the gloominess truly began to gnaw at him. What harm could really come from it? He knew Alice was well-behaved, and he had moved the university specimens safely out of reach.

The dog's reaction to being allowed in the house provided a curious distraction for Theo. She was polite and shy, not straying far from the kitchen door. She probably assumed this unusual turn of events was a trick and she would soon need to dart back outside. Trust took time to build—Theo knew this—so he patiently urged Alice further inside, offering her one of the bacon treats he'd purchased at the pet store. It didn't take long before she was on his heels, following him around the kitchen as he made a pitcher of iced tea and then again as he looked for his iPhone, which he'd misplaced by simply laying it on the sports page spread across his coffee table.

Theo picked up his phone, turned, and nearly tripped over the dog. "Maybe I'll call you Alice the Shadow?"

Alice stared up at him with bottomless eyes, and he imagined her response—*Are you sure I'm supposed to be in the house?*

"You're okay, girl. I invited you inside. Remember?"

Alice's slight tail-wag was an exploratory movement, more provisional than passionate. Theo imagined how surprised Penelope would be to learn he had invited Alice inside. He considered calling her, but quickly dismissed the idea. He was supposed to be busy, doing all the things he'd not been able to do with her around. *What were those things?*

On a typical Sunday afternoon in March, Theo would be at Baum-Walker Stadium with Winn, watching the Razorbacks play baseball. Or, if the game was being played on the road, they would catch it at a sports bar on Dickson. But coronavirus had quickly changed everything. The College World Series had been canceled and, subsequently, the university canceled the remainder of its season too. It was shocking to Theo, yet he acknowledged that it shouldn't be. With soaring infection numbers and climbing death statistics, the virus had obviously dug in its heels; it wasn't going anywhere for a while. Without baseball to fill his spring and summer, he would focus on his handyman list, maybe clean the gutters and even grow vegetables in the side garden again.

Penelope's questions last week about Annie, and their nonexistent children, had unsettled him, had him falling back into memories that made him sad over all he had lost. Meeting Annie in the most clichéd of ways, stumbling on the steps outside Mullins Library, dropping a stack of notebooks at his feet. Being drawn in instantly by her kind spirit. Worrying over their eight-year age difference until they both decided age didn't matter. Their intimate wedding ceremony, the air scented by dogwood blossoms. Her unabashed tears and promise of everlasting devotion. Because of Annie, Theo had discovered joy truly *could* follow loss and pain.

As he climbed the stairs to the bathroom, his mind spun him deeper into his memories.

"You know what we need, Mr. Gruene?" Annie had said one Sunday morning, over eggs and coffee.

"What's that, Mrs. Gruene?"

She was smearing pear preserves onto a triangle of toast. They had canned them the previous summer. "A baby. My clock is ticking faster and faster every year."

Later, Theo would remember that breakfast conversation with pain, wishing he could take back his teasing response, so flippant in hindsight. *A clock doesn't tick faster, it winds down.* The notion of having a child had terrified him at first. He had never been around babies, and the responsibility of raising another human seemed an impossible challenge to him. But eventually, after nudging and even pleading from Annie, he agreed. He had unwavering faith in her nurturing abilities. But then, over the course of six years, she suffered three debilitating miscarriages. The last one, an ectopic pregnancy, had almost been more than either of them could bear.

Three years later, during a weekend away at Devil's Den, Annie brought up the subject of adoption. "But I'm old," Theo said, somewhat surprised she was bringing it up. He had turned forty-five in February, and while that wasn't old in the span of a typical lifetime, it seemed to him too late for such a conversation.

Annie squeezed his hand and flashed a smile that creased his heart. "Silly man. You aren't old. We're steady and solid and in a good place. Don't you think?" After more late-night conversations, they'd begun to research the steps required for adoption, deciding it wouldn't hurt to become educated about the process. Then, on her thirty-seventh birthday, something shifted inside Theo, and he said, "Let's do it. Let's adopt. A baby or a toddler. Hell, a teenager, I don't care. I just want us to be happy and grow as a family." He had never been so sure of anything.

But it never happened. After signing with an adoption agency and matching with a birth mother, a phone call after a routine mammogram changed everything. Despite trying to forget, the vivid memory stayed with him. The color draining from Annie's cheeks. Her trembling voice. *Okay, sure, yes, I can be there first thing tomorrow.*

Theo shook off the memories and returned to his chores. Alice continued following him as he gathered up the bathroom towels and stripped the sheets from his bed, then padded downstairs with laundry in his arms. When he entered the laundry room, Theo saw the hat box, still on the dryer, exactly where he'd left it. He forgot all about doing laundry and carried the box to the dining room table. He suddenly felt an unshakeable urge to revisit his earliest memories.

A chilly wind blew from the northwest as an unpredictable spring was making itself known beyond the dining room window. The viburnum hedge bordering Theo's yard had exploded overnight into a froth of pink blossoms, but he barely noticed nature's offerings. He was focused on loosening the lid of the hatbox, sealed tight by nothing but time. Finally, like a genie being released from a bottle, the musty scent of a stored-away childhood found him.

The hatbox was a time capsule, the items inside an archeological dig of Theo's childhood: the orange and navy ball caps he and his brother wore the summers they played Babe Ruth baseball; his stack of comic books, still in relatively good shape—*Dick Tracy, Tom and Jerry, Popeye, The Avengers, Archie*; a Folgers can containing small die-cast cars and tractors; a like-new harmonica inside its worn cardboard box (one of his mother's many failed attempts to make her sons musical); a paper sack filled to the brim with small trinkets; marbles, stored away in their original canvas pouch. *Wouldn't Penelope get a kick out of these old toys?* Lastly, his collection of faded green army men. There must have been thirty soldiers posed in various stages of combat.

Theo lined up the army men along the edge of the table. He and Michael had spent countless hours defending the Alamo beneath their mother's clothesline, but those toy soldiers had done little to prepare him for the real-life battles he'd have to fight. Growing up during the volatile era of the Vietnam War, the possibility of being drafted into military service after high school had hung over him for as long as he could remember. Everyone had the same worry, watching older brothers and uncles being called up, families torn apart daily. Theo picked up an army soldier and studied it more closely. He remembered the boy who had worked for his dad. He had enlisted, trained at Fort Wolters to fly helicopters, and had been shot down during his first week of combat. It seemed all of West Texas did nothing but talk about that boy. *He was only nineteen*. No one knew if he was a prisoner of war, or if his remains had been lost to the Gulf of Tonkin. Theo tried to recall his name—*Henry, Harold*—but he couldn't remember.

Theo had tried to avoid Vietnam, but part-time community college and a job at the local newspaper hadn't saved him from the draft. He'd tried to steel himself to the idea of killing and war, and dying; had thought it would be best for everyone to just say goodbye at the bus station, and not subject his family to a long drive to Fort Wolters and a protracted goodbye at an army base. A wave of familiar melancholy rushed over him. If only they'd let him go by himself, the accident would never have happened. The pain of his broken femur, cracked ribs and punctured lung had been nothing compared to the devastation of losing his entire family. Even after decades of trying to come to terms with it, the irony would sit with Theo forever. Vietnam had not taken Theo's life; at least not directly. His life had been destroyed on an innocent-seeming stretch of Interstate 20, just south of Midland, Texas.

Mr. Gruene, you're at Houston Memorial Hospital. You were in an accident. Can you tell me your birthday? Can you tell me who the president is?

Sixteen days had passed before Theo's awareness began returning in slow drips of excruciating memory. Remembering nothing of the accident couldn't spare him from learning the horrific details. The tire of an 18-wheeler had exploded, and hurtled onto their Buick. The car windows had shattered and the hood was crushed upon impact. The accident was an ambush, immediate and savage, with no time for bargaining or prayers. If a bright spot existed during that dark time, it was that Theo no longer had to serve in Vietnam. After two femur surgeries, months of physical therapy, and with persistent nerve pain, the military considered him unfit for service.

Theo wiped the tears from his face, angry that he had fallen back into such a painful memory. Why had he hung onto all these old toys for so long? It made no sense to him. Maybe he would re-pack the box and drop it off at Potter's House.

A flash of green on the chair at the head of the table caught his eye. It was Penelope's paint swatch. *Good Luck*. He read the other names on the swatch. *Folk Tale. End of the Rainbow. Mischievous.* The names couldn't have fit Penelope Pie better if he had chosen them himself. That quirky, pesky, smart-as-a-whip little girl had certainly taken up residence inside his head. He would save the swatch and return it to her when she visited again. Of course, after claiming to be too busy to watch Penelope in the coming days, he'd ruined any chance of that happening.

What was wrong with him?

Ivy had asked for his help, *needed* his help, and he had been unsympathetic and selfish. There was no reason for it! His mother's words echoed in his head—*kindness is always the right choice*. The truth was that he really *enjoyed* being around Penelope. Her unique energy revitalized him somehow. Theo stared at the paint swatch, recalling her exuberance over such a nothing thing, and he burned with shame. *Good Luck?* He didn't deserve good luck. Something good had come his way—*new friends for God's sake!*—and he had sabotaged any opportunity for change or happiness. And in the process, he had likely hurt Ivy and Penelope.

Theo would fix things straightaway. He would call Ivy, apologize, and offer his time. It was a step in the right direction.

A CHORUS OF SPRING PEEPERS filled the night air, full and frenzied and thrilled to welcome spring. Alice, equally frenzied, was investigating each corner of the backyard, her highly sensitive nose attentive to scents magnified after a weekend of drizzle. Theo inhaled and smelled nothing but the earthiness of wet mulch. He urged Alice to do her business so they could go back inside. A shadow passed in front of the garage apartment window. So Ivy and Penelope *were* there. Theo had not connected with Ivy all afternoon; her phone had gone unanswered, and when he'd knocked on the apartment door, he'd heard only silence. Was she avoiding him? He wouldn't blame her if she was; it's what he had wanted. Even so, being ignored by Ivy and Penelope panged him squarely in the gut.

Before Theo went to bed, he spread a pallet of blankets and quilts on the floor beneath the bedroom window. Alice had been good company for him all day, and now that night had come, he found her presence comforting. She took to it immediately, stretching out and nosing around until she found the perfect position for her body. The weekend had mentally taxed Theo, and slumber came quickly, but each time Alice whimpered in her sleep or readjusted her body, he jolted awake. He'd been sleeping alone for so many years. Eventually, Theo gave up trying to get back to sleep. He stared at the patch of dark ceiling above his head and ruminated on the changes in his life. He was a seventy-year-old man with his first dog. Alice was snoring soundly, three feet away. At one a.m., the truth of it seemed tragic, a glaring symbol of everything he'd missed out on.

He saw his grandparents' homestead in his mind's eye; the old, unpainted farmhouse with wide planks leading from the wooden front porch steps to the gravel driveway. A yard full of chickens chasing him and his brother around. The red barn out back. His grandparents died in the mid-sixties, one after the other in quick succession, and his father had sold the farm—around two hundred acres—depositing the proceeds in an account at Midland National Bank and saving most of the money. A few years later, when the money passed to him, the balance had grown to almost forty thousand dollars.

He thought of his mother, then, conjuring the details of her face, her aquamarine eyes and dark wavy hair, her softly arching eyebrows, the slight gap between her top front teeth. She'd been gone so long, though, that he couldn't see her face in focus; her features were blurred, like a muddled dream. Theo's parents' story had been one for the ages. Lying there in the dark, he conjured up the little boy he had once been, remembering how entranced he had been, every time he heard his all-time favorite adventure story—the one that featured his parents. His father, George, leaving the farm at sixteen, trading in fieldwork for a better opportunity. Working on a Mississippi River steamer, earning passage to New Orleans, and later, hopping a train west to Fort Worth. Hearing there was money in oil rigs, George had hitched a ride to Brownwood, ducking inside a gas station to ask the wide-eyed girl behind the counter about the next bus to Odessa. *It leaves at eight tonight. I'll be on it too. I'm going to see my aunt.* Halfway there, George had learned there was no aunt in Odessa. *Love at first sight, boys, that's what it was.*

Eventually, Theo drifted off again. He slept in fitful snatches, dreaming of his mother's homemade Johnny cakes, West Texas dust storms, and tumbleweeds as large as wringer washing machines. At five o'clock, Alice woke him, and he was up for good. He went downstairs and penned a short note to Ivy.

Ivy—If you still need someone to watch Penelope this week, I would be honored to help out. Please give me a call. Theo

Lavender dawn was still breaking when he secured the note to the door of the garage apartment, where Ivy would be sure to find it. Walking home he noticed clusters of golden daffodils circling the trees in front of the old Catholic church, waving in the breeze as though cheering him on.

Nine

There was very little traffic on College Avenue at 7 a.m., and the grocery store parking lot was mostly vacant. Were people actually following the CDC's advice to stay home? Walking toward the building, he noticed access had been changed; certain doors were designated for entrances and others for exits. A massive blue banner flapped in the wind above the door—*Masks Required*. As a young man, Theo had been fascinated by the great influenza of 1918, reading everything he could about the virus that had claimed the lives of fifty million people. As a botanist, he knew about the blight that had eliminated the entire species of American Chestnuts in eastern hardwood forests, and how susceptible American Elms were to Dutch Elm disease. Still, he couldn't quite believe how quickly the pandemic was changing even Fayetteville, Arkansas.

Theo didn't have a mask, but a lady, busily wiping down shopping cart handles with Clorox wipes, directed him to a box of complimentary ones. She offered him a shopping cart, as well, its handle still damp. Had Harp's always wiped down their grocery carts? He didn't think so. After securing the mask over his nose and mouth, Theo pushed his cart into the store feeling he had entered a strange new world.

Buying the weekly groceries had always been his job, even when Annie was alive. It was a task he enjoyed, but now, the experience was disorienting. When he went to get a jar of peanut butter, a young woman squeezed past and shot him a look of alarm. It was then he noticed that there were arrows on the floor. The store had become a maze of one-way aisles.

Theo's favorite wheat bread was sold out, so he bought a sourdough loaf instead. Toilet paper was limited to two rolls! He took his allotment despite having plenty at home. The local news had been right. Supply chain disruptions were even affecting his city.

Theo abandoned his grocery list and started filling his cart with staples to last at least a month. He would stock up, go home, and not venture out again until the craziness subsided. Hamburger meat. Dried beans. Brown rice. Flour. Sugar. Two gallons of two percent milk and a box of powdered milk in case things got really bad. Canned soup. Frozen chicken. Hot dogs and buns. A double package of sliced cheese. Two giant bags of coffee beans. Coffee would be the one thing he would most hate to do without. And, even though he had not heard from Ivy, he tossed in a box of green tea bags for Penelope Pie.

The employee who checked him out was standing behind a newly installed Plexiglas wall.

Theo had little confidence in society's ability to endure a cataclysmic disaster, but he was impressed at how efficiently Harp's had instituted its pandemic policy.

On the way home, he stopped at the gas station and topped off his gas, just in case. He recalled the oil embargo of the early seventies, gas shortages rocking the country, the speed limit on the interstate being lowered to a tortuous fifty-five miles per hour. Everything was cyclical, especially the economy.

It wasn't until Theo turned into his driveway that he realized his hands were clenched against the steering wheel. The straightforward task of buying milk and bread had become completely convoluted with mask-wearing, one-way aisles, and the requirement to stand six feet apart in the check-out line. For the first time since hearing of the virus, its implications became real to him.

After three trips to the truck and back, Theo's sacks of groceries covered the kitchen counter. He was still contemplating the sweeping changes at his grocery store when movement in the backyard caught his eye. Penelope was sitting on the bench beneath the white oak, her mouth pressed almost to Alice's ear. They seemed to be sharing deep secrets. Seeing her instantly eased his lingering grocery store tension.

He tapped on the door before walking outside. Both girl and dog looked up, but Alice was the only one who came racing over.

"You're back," he said, patting Alice but looking at Penelope. After leaving the note for Ivy, he had been disappointed not to hear back from her. But now she was here, and he was relieved.

"I'm back," she echoed, but her voice was flat.

"Are you okay?" He didn't think she was all that happy to be there.

She shrugged her thin shoulders. "I'm always okay."

Not wanting to press her, Theo invited her inside. "I bought you something today."

Her eyes brightened slightly. "What is it?" She hopped to her feet and followed him inside.

"Help me put away the groceries, and I'll show you." He began unpacking the sacks, spreading everything out on the kitchen table.

"This is unbelievable, Mr. Theo. I've never seen this much food except at the grocery store. You must be a millionaire." Her voice was filled with awe.

"Hardly. I just thought we should stock up. And since you'll be here all week—at least I *hope* you will be—I'll start making your lunch, if that's okay with you. I bought lots of cheese." *Would* she be there all week? He still wasn't sure, and didn't want to assume anything.

"You know, Mr. Theo, I thought we were going to be besties, and it really hurt my feelings when I found out you didn't want me to come over anymore. But then you wrote that note and invited me back. I think you might be a little passive-aggressive. Have you ever thought of that?"

Her words sliced right through his weary heart. "I apologize, Penelope. Sincerely." He pressed his palms together as though in prayer and dipped his head remorsefully. "I realized my misstep almost immediately. I hope you can forgive me."

Alice, who had apparently taken Penelope's side (if sides were being taken), stood with her nose in the folds of the girl's rainbow-colored skirt while Penelope rubbed her neck. Now, neither made eye contact with him.

"You *do* realize Alice is in the house, don't you?" Penelope said eventually, smoothing Alice's coat, the nametag jingling.

"Yes, I invited her inside yesterday. I even made her a bed upstairs, and she slept in my room last night. I think she's been missing you."

"Really? You do?"

He nodded and was relieved to see Penelope's brow soften, and her eyes widen. The last thing he wanted to do was hurt her feelings.

"Okay, Mr. Theo, in light of this positive change in circumstance, I am willing to be your friend again. I believe in second chances, and I think you must too. My mother said she wants to have a talk with you when she gets off work this afternoon. Would that be okay?"

"Of course." Theo suspected Ivy and Penelope had been through enough drama in their lives; he would make a concerted effort not to add to their problems.

"Oh, guess what?" she said, scratching Alice's ears. "I saw a Boo Radley hole when I was walking over here."

He frowned.

"*Hello?* Boo Radley. From *To Kill a Mockingbird*."

"I know who Boo Radley is." Then he realized what she meant. "So you saw a hollow in an old tree?"

"Yes, a Boo Radley hole. I can show it to you later. It was shaped exactly like a heart. Well, not the actual organ, because that's more like a fist, but the shape used for Valentine's Day. Anyway, I finished the book. It's in my backpack, by your thinking tree." Penelope scampered outside to retrieve her backpack, pulled the book from inside, and offered it to him. "Can we discuss it? Like in a real book club?"

Penelope's energy had begun to spread through his house again, like shimmery bubbles blown through a plastic wand. She was almost back.

"We'll talk about the book later. First, let's put away the groceries and have some breakfast. Here's what I got you." He held out the box of green tea for her perusal.

For the first time that morning, her eyes truly sparkled. "Oh, thank you! I've never tasted green tea before."

"I thought you preferred green tea."

"No, I never said that. It just intrigues me. And, because it's such a good source of antioxidants, I'm giving you another point! I think you're actually ahead now, two to one."

Theo was glad to know their game was back on, but he had to wonder if Penelope was really as brilliant as she seemed. Did she *understand* all the information she spouted, or did she repeat words and facts she heard, like a parrot? "So tell me, what are antioxidants?" he asked, testing her.

"Mr. Theo, surely you know about the incredible benefits of antioxidants. Antioxidants fight free radicals, and free radicals are what hurt cells and contribute to disease. How old are you, Mr. Theo?"

"Seventy."

Penelope's stare reflected her disbelief. "I don't know if you realize this yet, but you sure are lucky to have me around. At your age, you need to become besties with green tea."

He laughed out loud, happier than he could have imagined to have her back.

IVY'S FACE EXPRESSED no emotion. She unfolded a single sheet of lined notebook paper and began enumerating the reasons she had needed his help and expressing her desperation when he had let her down. Sitting directly across from her, Theo pressed his lips closed and listened without interrupting, feelings of sympathy and indignation warring within him. When she said, "We've had enough people ghosting us lately," he decided it was time for him to speak.

"I'm not sure what you mean."

"Disappearing. Vanishing. Wimping out on commitments. That's been the theme of my entire life so far, and I couldn't be more over it."

Theo was annoyed by Ivy's portrayal of the situation and, in fact, thought it was incredibly unfair. He had *not* wimped out on a commitment, nor had he vanished or disappeared. They had conversed face-to-face about his inability to watch Penelope during the week of spring break. Really, it was more an unwillingness than an inability, but that was beside the point. He had never ghosted anyone. He couldn't manage to ghost his own ghosts!

"I won't disappear on you and Penelope," he said, shoving aside the irritation growing within him. He wanted to defend his behavior, explain how exhausted and overwhelmed he had been after a week with Penelope. He wanted to reiterate his assumption that Ivy must have had some kind of plan in place already for spring break. But he saw that there was no point in discussing any of that with this young lady, whose life was so fraught. Theo glanced out back and saw Penelope tossing a tennis ball to Alice. "I promise to help you get through this hump. You have my word. And if something should change, I'll give you at least one week's notice. No, two weeks. How's that?"

Ivy's demeanor softened slightly. The defensive hunch of her shoulders relaxed, and she began presenting her other talking points with greater ease. When she asked Theo to avoid taking Penelope to public places like Lowe's, he agreed without hesitation. He had learned his lesson at the grocery store and didn't plan to go anywhere anytime soon.

Ivy rooted around in her bag. "I brought these N95 masks from the hospital. If you have to go somewhere, wear these."

The national news had reported that there was a shortage of N95 masks. He realized this was not a small thing she was giving him.

"Mr. Theo? Mostly, during this weird time, I want my daughter to be safe, and enjoy being a kid. I don't want her watching the news and worrying about coronavirus." Ivy glanced at the paper in her hand and continued reciting her 'don'ts' as though each broke her heart a little.

"Don't let Pea watch *Dr. Phil* or *The View* or—"

"Let me interrupt you right there, Ivy." *The View*?! "We won't be watching any television, especially talk shows or that reality nonsense, so don't worry yourself over that." Theo would probably not possess a television if not for Razorback sports.

She smiled, and her shoulders further relaxed.

"What else?" he asked.

"You already know about her peanut allergy, but don't let her eat too many sweets or junk food, especially after lunch. And don't let her play games on her iPad. Her iPad was provided by the school, and it's for schoolwork only. Same with her phone. We have a very basic plan, with limited minutes."

Theo resisted sharing his opinion on society's dependency on electronics. So far, he agreed wholeheartedly with everything Ivy had said. He might have written the same list for anyone, including himself.

"Mr. Theo, I'm gonna be honest. Penelope is super smart, but she can be a lot to handle. And you better believe she will test whatever limitations she's given. Her schoolwork is the least of my worries. I'd rather she spends time learning something real. Something that will help her down the road. Maybe you could teach her about plants, since that's your specialty?"

Now that, he could certainly do. Nothing gave him greater joy than introducing a willing student to the wonders of nature. When he had been the Mount Pleasant Junior High science fair facilitator, there were always a handful of students who embraced every aspect of their projects, whether they were demonstrating the process of photosynthesis or testing the importance of nitrogen in plant growth. He imagined at least a few of them must have followed their love of science into adulthood. Maybe he could make that kind of a difference in Penelope's life, too.

For the next while, their meeting turned into a rather pleasant discussion as Ivy continued sharing her ideas and expectations, while Theo added his input. As he took in the calmer expression in her placid blue eyes, he noticed a tiny curved scar above her left eyebrow and wondered how it had come to be.

"Mr. Theo, things will get a lot worse before they get better. And at the end of the day, I don't think it will matter if Penelope completes a bunch of math assignments. Do you get what I mean?" Ivy was both serene and commanding as she spoke.

Despite her relative youth and stretched-thin circumstances, Theo was beginning to realize Ivy was a force to be reckoned with. This young woman might single-handedly set the world on fire. His eyes narrowed as he thought about her latest point. Not turning in assignments went against his core beliefs. "How about we get assignments done *and* learn about plants?"

"Deal." Ivy extended her hand to shake. "I hear you have your own library upstairs. Giving her challenging books to read is a great idea too. A whole lot of people want to ban books these days. You know?"

The apple certainly didn't fall far from the tree.

Later, after his conversation with Ivy had marinated, Theo scribbled a few ideas on a legal pad. If he was to be Penelope's substitute teacher, he would give it his all. And to give it his all, he needed supplies. Theo placed an online express delivery order with Walmart for the first time in his life, and then settled in to re-read *To Kill a Mockingbird*. It had been decades since he'd read it.

Ten

Penelope rapped on the front door just as the clock chimed for the eighth time. She was nothing if not prompt. Theo had been waiting and watching for her. He welcomed her inside with such zeal he barely recognized himself.

"You seem different, Mr. Theo." Penelope stood flat-footed in the entryway and gave him a good looking over. "If I didn't know better, I would think your secret twin brother had taken over your body—the cheerful one I never knew existed. What gives?" She slipped off her worn sneakers in the foyer.

Theo laughed. "Nothing. I'm glad to have another chance to be your teacher."

Penelope's licorice-dark eyes pierced into him. "For real? This isn't a trick? I saw this movie about a kid who was kidnapped and—"

"Seriously, kiddo, when do you watch all this trash television? Come inside." He was eager to tell Penelope about the schedule he had planned for them.

Penelope looked around the family room like she'd never been inside his home. When she glimpsed the dining room, she skipped over and swung her backpack into a chair. "Wow, Mr. Theo, you've made us a classroom. This is clutch!"

Clutch? Theo primarily associated the word with a vehicle transmission, but estimated by her exuberance that she was using the expression positively. He watched, with a small smile, as Penelope circled the dining room table, commenting on all the supplies he had purchased—a large box of Crayola crayons, markers, poster board, pencils and pens, glue sticks, a ruler, construction paper, packages of stickers, three blank journals, and two packages of colored index cards. He had even affixed a small whiteboard to the wall beside the buffet.

Theo stood before the whiteboard, opened the notebook he'd chosen for his new teaching career, and uncapped a blue marker. The pungent smell of the ink reminded him of long-ago school days. "I've come up with a schedule that I believe will benefit both of us. Before you say anything, let me lay it all out." He began transferring the schedule from his notebook to the whiteboard. While he wrote, there was no sound in the room other than the squeak of marker.

8 – 10: Botany for Beginners
10 – 11: Nature Walk
11 – Noon: Lunch
Noon – 1: Free Reading Time
1 – 2: Science Experiments & Whatnot
2 – 3: Book Discussion
3 – 4: Wrap Up / Walk Alice

"Okay, let me elaborate," he said as he gazed at his writing, pleased with his plan. "From eight until ten we will have a basic botany lesson. This will be a hands-on, learn-while-we-go endeavor. Since spring is here, the flower beds need lots of attention. We can fertilize the roses, weed, plant fall-blooming bulbs, test the soil, and so on." His blood rushed just thinking about it.

Penelope raised her hand.

"Yes?"

"Is it okay if I take notes?"

"Of course. That's a great idea." He handed her a fresh new spiral notebook, and she selected a pen from the cup where he had placed them.

Penelope began writing furiously.

Theo frowned, wondering what she could already have to say about his botany lesson idea, but he returned to the whiteboard and continued explaining. "At ten o'clock, we will go for a nature walk through the neighborhood. Again, my plan is to teach you interactively. I'll point out trees and flowers, explain the scientific names, and we might even start a collection like the one the university herbarium maintains. I've always thought creating a personal specimen collection would be interesting."

Penelope scribbled something else in her notebook, her pen rapidly moving across the page.

"Next is lunch. We probably won't need an hour to eat, so extending our afternoon nature walk on the front end or reading time on the back end will be doable. You can help with both meal planning and meal prep. This will give us a chance to talk about vegetables and fruits and the chemistry behind cooking."

Penelope stared at him silently, then made some more notes in her notebook. He had no idea what she was thinking, but he wasn't going to ask before he finished his presentation. "Also, once a week, depending on the weather, I thought we could forgo our regular schedule and spend the day hiking the area trails. We could go to Mount Kessler, Mount Sequoyah, or even Lake Leatherwood in Eureka Springs." He took a deep breath. "Okay. What do you think?" It had been years since Theo had developed a lesson plan, but it was an ingrained skill. He still had it.

Penelope placed a hand on her face, tapped a finger against her cheek. "Is it okay if I approach the whiteboard?"

"Well, sure. This isn't a courtroom." Theo pulled out a chair and took a seat while she walked over to the buffet.

"Professor Theo, do you have a pointer, by chance?"

"A pointer? No."

She glanced at the school supplies arranged across the center of the table and reached for a ruler. "I can make do with this," she said. Then she began reading her notes verbatim, in one long discourse without pausing between thoughts and without giving him a chance to address each individual remark.

"One—am I to become your house elf? Is my whole purpose for being here to pull weeds and make your lunch? Two—I will not stray from my commitment to vegetarianism no matter what you make me cook. Three—I like the idea of reading and having a book discussion, but when will I have time to do the schoolwork assigned by Miss Markum? Four—when is art time? Art is an important element of creative development and something I very much need in my life. Five—what exactly falls into the whatnot category?"

When she finished reading her notes, she took a deep breath and placed the ruler on the edge of the table. It had served no purpose.

"Okay. I take it you don't like my schedule." Theo chuckled, but felt a tad injured.

"It feels confining."

"Do you have an alternative recommendation? You can't just sit around jibber jabbering and wasting time not learning—"

"Mr. Theo. It is my belief this time is a unique gift. Instead of being forced to sit in a boring classroom all day at Lafayette Elementary, I can use this time to do something *stupendous*." She flung her arms above her head as though she had just successfully landed a gymnastics vault routine.

"Okay. I can work with stupendous. What do you have in mind?"

"I'd like to write a book. Maybe a memoir."

Theo could not control his laughter any more than Penelope could control her wild imagination. "I'm sorry," he said through his snickering, "you make writing a book sound as easy as stopping by Harp's for a carton of milk. He paused, remembering the one-way aisles at the grocery store. "Not that going to the store is all that easy anymore. Penelope, I know many published authors, English professors who have published novels that took a lifetime to write, and scientists who publish volumes of research as part of their profession. It's not so simple as deciding to do something and doing it. And you're a kid. What personal chronicle could you possibly have to write already?" Theo simply could not stop laughing, despite the wounded expression clouding her eyes.

"I wouldn't expect someone with zero imagination to understand. Mr. Theo, maybe you should excuse yourself until you can rein in your emotions."

"I think you're right." Theo pressed his lips together as he exited the room. He went to the bathroom and dabbed the tears from his eyes. It felt good to laugh, but he felt guilty about doing it at Penelope's expense. *Write a memoir.* The kid was something else.

After a few minutes, Theo returned to the dining room, ready to discuss further what he believed was a solid school schedule. Penelope, it seemed, had other ideas. She was sitting on the opposite side of the table, flipping through the blank pages of one of the journals he had purchased to record their nature walk observations.

"Mr. Theo, I've heard that ideas flow better when an author uses paper and pen instead of typing on a keyboard, so would it be okay if I use this journal for my writing?" Her eager eyes reflected none of her annoyance from minutes ago. It was as though he had never dissuaded her, and he was glad.

"Sure. By all means. Who am I to get in the way of the next S. E. Hinton?" And for the rest of the day, he followed his student's lead, letting her sit for hours writing and drawing, simply enjoying her presence. He would try again with a modified schedule tomorrow.

Eleven

Theo turned off the television and put his coffee on to brew. The noise of the news was replaced with the sound of Alice whining at the back door. He let her out and quickly closed the door against the early morning chill. A rosy sunrise illuminated the sky between the branches of his oak tree. He missed Annie most during the early morning. *Come look at the sunrise*, he had always called to her, while their coffee brewed, and she would join him, watching at the kitchen window, or outside on the deck during the warm months, her arm around his waist.

The world had certainly changed.

Theo had become fixated on news of the virus, but he limited his intake to the early morning, or late afternoon hours once Penelope's school day had ended. Watching the drip of the coffee, he tried to concentrate on the rich aroma, but he couldn't get the news images from his mind. Refrigerated trucks were now serving as makeshift morgues for the overflow of dead bodies in Brooklyn. The reporter broadcasting that morning might as well have been a war correspondent—this pandemic ravaging New York City was not really that dissimilar to explosives annihilating a series of underground shelters in Saigon *or* a car crash on I-20 just south of Midland, Texas. No matter the cause—an infectious microbe, a C-4 malleable explosive, a hundred-pound semi-truck tire—the end result brought loss of life.

The grim images of New York City were particularly unsettling to him. Theo had fled there in '73, four years after the death of his family. What a strange time that had been! With his inheritance to provide financial breathing room, Theo had leased a room at the West Side YMCA and worked odd jobs as a cook in a financial district deli and as a doorman in a Midtown walkup, primarily to keep himself busy. Anonymously disappearing into the noise of the big city helped ease the maelstrom of pain that extended far beyond his bodily injuries. As the sky continued to brighten beyond his kitchen window, he tried to reconcile the morning's bleak shots of New York to the vibrant images of the city that lived in his memory. It was nearly impossible.

Theo had met Winn at a group therapy session in the city, and they connected from the beginning. Winn had been a broken human too, suffering significant trauma in Vietnam. Theo learned then that shock came in different forms. The Vietcong had been exceptionally skilled at creating entire worlds underground; not only bunkers, but meeting rooms and communities of living quarters. Winn had been a tunnel rat, part of a troop tasked with finding and destroying tunnels, whether or not they were occupied. As he talked of near-paralyzing claustrophobia, nights spent hunkered down in a rice paddy, the air reeking of scorched earth and sweltering excrement, Theo began opening to someone else's pain. He understood the crash that claimed his family had saved him from a type of hell. What an awful, heavy notion for a bereaved young man to carry.

Gradually, therapy helped Theo face the loss of his family, and he stopped shoving his memories of them away. He missed them with an ache he knew would never dissipate, but began allowing himself to feel again. He started noticing the beauty around him, the crabapples blooming in Central Park and Manhattan's glittery skyline after sunset. His mother had always dreamed of seeing the Empire State Building and visiting the Statue of Liberty, yet never had. Three years after his arrival in New York, Theo began visiting tourist locations for her, trying to see the city through her eyes, inhaling the aroma of roasting chestnuts at Christmas time, longing to catch a Yankee game with his dad and brother. The next fall, he packed his meager belongings and headed back to Texas. Even though he no longer had family there, home tugged at him. He enrolled at Texas Tech as a twenty-six-year-old freshman, and started out his major in agricultural science. The land was one of the few things that still felt permanent to him.

Sometimes, his past didn't seem real.

Theo poured a cup of coffee. It was going to be one of those perfect spring days, cool in the morning but warm and pleasant later, ideal for an afternoon walk with Penelope and Alice. Two weeks had passed since his meeting with Ivy, and to Theo's surprise, the time had passed quickly. There had been no need for a strict classroom routine. Penelope spent hours writing each morning, sitting at the dining room table or on the bench beneath the white oak. Exactly what she was writing, he couldn't fathom. She cut her eyes at him the first time he asked and said, "Please don't interrupt me when I'm in the zone." The child deserved an A+ for extreme dedication, that was for sure.

Theo had been productive too. During Penelope's writing time, he applied a final coat of stain to the porch, weeded the flowerbeds of chickweed and bittercress, and raked leaves from the front yard. Afternoons had been devoted to nature walks, with Alice in tow, followed by reading and book discussion. So far, *To Kill a Mockingbird* had spurred talks on a wide range of topics, including the court system, Jim Crow, racial bias, and mockingbirds. Penelope had been most fascinated by the gifts Boo Radley left for Scout and Jem in the hollow of the tree. With each passing day, Theo was becoming more and more attached to her. She was an incredible child, capable of grasping meaning and nuance, yet often as green as a tender sprout.

Outside, Alice began whining. Theo hoped she had not cornered a critter of some sort on the deck. Instead, he found Penelope there, sleeping, curled in a chair, buried beneath the green raincoat and a quilt he had never seen. He approached her as though she were an injured animal, softly touching her shoulder.

"Penelope? What on earth are you doing out here?"

She moaned and rubbed her still-closed eyes. Then, alarm jerked her fully awake, and she booted the quilt to the deck, vaulted from the chair, and began kicking at Theo's shins. "Why wouldn't you answer the door! Why!?"

"Whoa, whoa! Hold up." Theo kneeled, firmly held her shoulders, and stared directly into her wild eyes. "What's going on, kiddo? Talk to me."

"It's…my…mommy…I think she's dying." Penelope buried her face inside her cupped palms, her small body racked by hysterical sobs. She was a fledgling, fragile and helpless. He felt desperate to stop the flow of her tears.

"Tell me what's happened. Should I call an ambulance?" His anxiety bloomed as he remembered the grim news coming out of New York; ill patients lining the halls of hospitals, morgues overrun with the deceased.

"She's already at the hospital. She's been there all n-n-n-ight." Penelope was crying so hard her words released in a jagged stutter. Swallowing hard and sniffling, she ran the back of her hand across her nose.

Tears made Theo both uneasy and ready to spring into action. It was as though a water pipe had sprung a leak and the whole world would flood if he didn't fix things right away. He guided Penelope inside, lifted her into a kitchen chair, and wrapped the quilt around her shivering body.

"Take a deep breath, and here, blow your nose." He yanked a tissue from the box on the table and held it to her face. She weakly blew a puff of air into the tissue. "It'll be okay, but you have to calm down." He said the words as firmly as he could, despite having no idea if it *would* be okay.

"I can't calm down. I've had an awful night." Her sobs began again.

"Why didn't you call me? I gave you my phone number—did you lose it?"

She shook her head again, and her bottom lip trembled. "Don't yell at me pl-pl-pleeeaase. I've been extremely traumatized." She covered her face with her hands again.

Had he been yelling? He'd not intended to. Theo pulled a chair over and sat beside her, offering a weak smile. "I'm sorry for yelling. How about we start from the beginning? Tell me what you know, Penelope Pie. We'll figure this out together."

She gazed at him with puffy eyes, her cheeks raw and pink. "Okay, I'll try. But the thoughts in my mind are as shattered as a broken windo-o-o-o-w-pane."

"I understand." He patted her knee, hoping that was an encouraging thing to do.

"All I know is my mom never came home from work last night, even though she said she would be home by six, and she asked me to set the table and promised to bring home a cheese pizza because they are two dollars off on Thursday night at Eureka Pizza. By eight, when she still hadn't come home, I called her cell phone, which I'm not supposed to do while she's at work, except during an emergency—and I figured this was one—but she didn't answer."

"Okay." He thought of the breathing exercises he had learned years ago as a way to work through panic attacks. "Take five deep, slow breaths, all the way in and then all the way out."

She closed her eyes and began breathing while Theo got her a glass of water. After taking a gulp, she continued. "Anyway, finally, Mom called to say she had gotten sick at work and couldn't come home until later. She said, 'Pea, keep the door locked, fix yourself some supper but don't use the stove, and don't stay up all night worrying. I'll be okay. Call Mr. Theo if you get scared.'"

Theo stared at Penelope, worry building inside him. As soon as possible, he would try to call Ivy for clarification.

"My mother was being very calm about the whole thing, so I asked her if she was playing a joke on me, like a late April Fool's joke. She said, 'No, Pea, I wouldn't do that, and besides, it doesn't work that way.'" Heavy tears rimmed Penelope's swollen eyes.

"What doesn't work that way?" Theo was trying his best to keep up, but Penelope's explanation had become difficult to follow.

"April Fool's jokes. They don't work except on April first, and today's April third."

Theo wondered if the kid had an attention deficit disorder.

"And for the record, Mr. Theo, I *did* call you. You didn't answer your pho-o-o-ne." She moaned, yanked another tissue from the box, and swiped at her nose.

His phone was right there on the kitchen table. The truth flashed on the screen with one touch of his finger—*5 missed calls*. He picked it up and looked at it, as though staring more closely might change the situation. "I don't know how I missed…" He dropped the phone on the table, aggravated with himself. When had he set his phone on silent?

"When you didn't answer for the fifth time, I climbed the fence and knocked on the back door. You didn't answer the door either, and Alice didn't even bark. I worried you both might be dead, that the horrible virus had slipped right underneath your back door and suffocated both of you while you worked on those old plants you love so much."

Penelope must have come to his door around dusk, when he'd been out walking Alice around the neighborhood. But had she *slept* on his back porch?

"I'm a survivor, Mr. Theo." Penelope straightened in the chair, wiped her cheeks, and then tapped the back of his hand with her damp fingertips. "I went back to the apartment, locked the door, and sat on the couch thinking about my new circumstance. I decided to pray as hard as I could that my mother would get well very soon, and I decided not to eat anything whatsoever for supper because I can't eat when I'm distressed; plus, I thought God might help me better if I fasted the way Jesus sometimes did. Finally, I fell asleep on the couch, and the next thing I knew, daylight was coming in the window. I figured I would come back over here because I knew you would let Alice out to pee soon. I'm getting pretty good at climbing the fence. I've been thinking putting a ladder back there might be a good idea. On both sides of the fence."

Whew. "Let me make sure I understand. Your mom has Covid-19? And she's in the hospital?"

"I can't swear she has Covid-19, but she's got something alright. They think it's contagious, so they took her to the regular hospital."

The regular hospital? Theo began pacing and ranting. "I can't believe no one from her place of employment would think to check on you. Ivy is a single mother, for goodness sake!"

At this, a rogue snuffle escaped from Penelope. "My mother never told her boss about me. People don't like to hire single mothers."

"Now, why would you think something like that?"

Penelope glared at him. "Because it's the truth. No offense, Mr. Theo, but what would a seventy-year-old straight white man know about discrimination in the workplace? Especially discrimination against young women?"

"Excuse me, but I—"

"Remember what Scout's father said? 'You don't know what someone else is going through until you walk in his shoes.' I think that applies here."

"Okay...well..." While he despised being lumped in with *any* group of people, he *certainly* didn't like being thought of as someone who would discriminate against anyone. "You're right. I don't know what it's like to be a young female in the workplace," he said. "And I'm sorry your mother has to deal with that sort of unacceptable behavior."

She croaked out a tired, "thank you," and began crying again.

BEING IN SOMEONE ELSE'S SPACE made Theo uneasy, so he planted his feet by the door and watched Penelope as she scampered around, gathering items and piling them on the table. She added a stack of mail to the growing pile of pajamas, socks, and toiletries. "Mr. Theo, I should probably take some of my clothes too. If that's okay?" Penelope's voice was so earnest, so desperate for something good to cling to, he could barely stand it.

"Good idea. If you bring me a suitcase, I'll pack up your mom's things while you get your stuff."

"We don't have a suitcase. But there are some grocery sacks in the kitchen."

A suitcase was such an ordinary thing. Not having one spoke volumes to Theo. He went to fetch a few sacks and began filling one with Ivy's belongings, grateful for something to do. The morning had rattled him, and he still didn't feel completely himself. Discovering Penelope sleeping in the deck chair. Witnessing her fragility. Seeing so many phone notifications—five missed calls! The realization had hit him squarely in the gut—it was solely up to him to calm the child. Thankfully, she did calm down, and he had walked her upstairs to the guest bedroom, turned down the covers, and stayed with her until she fell asleep. Finally, he slipped downstairs to call Ivy. Hearing her voice and learning first-hand what had happened brought him some relief. She had had a sudden fever and excruciating headache, had passed out at the nurse's station. Because these were all symptoms of COVID-19, the on-call doctor sent her to Washington Regional right away.

"Can you believe every coronavirus test in Arkansas has to be processed at one facility in Little Rock?"

Ivy's voice was edged with frustration, but Theo took her complaining as a hopeful sign. He promised to watch Penelope and made a quick list of the things she needed from home.

Penelope had slept long and hard. When he finally heard her stirring and went to check on her, he was relieved to see her propped against the pillow whispering to Alice, who was curled beside her. He hated delivering bad news, though. Having to explain to her that her mom would be in the hospital a little longer, and seeing her small body deflate, deflated him too. But he was cheered beyond measure when he saw her face brighten after he invited her to stay with him a few days.

"Did you hear, Alice, I get to stay! Can this beautiful yellow room be my official bedroom while I'm here?"

Penelope's wide-eyed question had shaken loose other memories: Annie's joyful expression—*close your eyes, don't peek*!—upon first seeing the freshly painted room; assembling a Jenny Lind cradle they found at a yard sale; and later, after Annie died, emptying the room of all baby-related things, and worrying he would never survive the pain.

"What's the name of the paint color?"

Penelope's question had brought him back to the present, and made him chuckle. "Whatever you want it to be," he'd told her, glad he'd never re-painted the room.

Now, Theo watched as Penelope placed some of her things inside a sack—the notebooks and papers stacked on the kitchen table, a pair of bright pink flip-flops, and clothing she emptied from a small cabinet beside the couch. She put on her lime green raincoat even though it was a clear globe of a day.

"Okay, I'm ready to go." With only three sacks packed, the apartment seemed stripped bare.

DURING THE SHORT DRIVE to Washington Regional, Penelope chatted away about keys. The child never ran out of things to talk about.

"Don't you think keys are interesting, Mr. Theo?" She held the key to their apartment in her palm and flipped it over. "We use keys to lock up rooms and safeguard our lives." She looked over at him.

"Safeguard our lives? That's pretty deep."

She shrugged. "I know. I'm as deep as the ocean sometimes."

He smiled. "Yes. I think you are."

"Have you seen the ocean, Mr. Theo?"

"Sure."

"Will you describe it to me?" Penelope's curiosity seemed to sit with them like a third passenger in Theo's old Chevrolet.

"Let's see...." He thought for a moment, driving along Gregg Avenue on autopilot until a memory came to him in full color. "The first time I saw the Atlantic was during my time in New York. Winn had bought a sixty-six sky blue Cobra for next to nothing, and we decided to drive along the coast all the way to Florida. We actually saw KISS in concert at The Daisy on Long Island, and let me tell you, that was really something else. They were up-and-coming musicians back then, and we just lucked into tickets." He paused. "You probably have no idea who KISS is."

"Actually, I do. They were in a Scooby-Doo movie, well, not the *actual* group, but their cartoon version. After I saw it, I looked them up. Did you know Gene Simmons has the longest tongue ever? In fact, he has a cow tongue sewn into his mouth. How gross is that?" Her voice had become more animated than usual.

"You can't believe everything you read or hear. Do you know how large a cow tongue is?"

She shook her head.

"It's the size of a pot roast. Under no scenario could a human head be surgically implanted with a cow tongue. Gene Simmons' tongue may be long, but it's all his."

"Well, it's interesting to think about. I've never been to a real live concert, but I'd like to see Taylor Swift. Are you a Swiftie, Mr. Theo?"

He knew who Taylor Swift was, but wouldn't have been able to identify any of her song titles from a list of multiple-choice selections. "I don't think so."

"That's a shame. So, what about the ocean?"

"We never made it any further than New Jersey on that road trip. The car turned out to be a real lemon, and when the motor burned up, we left it on the side of the road near Atlantic City and took a Greyhound back to Manhattan. But I saw a lot of the Atlantic Ocean during that trip."

"You've been friends with that Winn man a long time, haven't you?"

"Sure have. We met in New York, lost touch for a while, and reconnected some years later. I recommended him for a position at the university. That's how he ended up here."

Penelope nodded and began spinning the round keychain on her finger. "You know what, Mr. Theo? I'm going to start thinking about keys in a more positive light. Instead of seeing keys as a way to lock things up, I'll think about how they can make the world more accessible."

"Right now you need to put that key away before you lose it." Theo pulled into the parking lot at Washington Regional just as a vehicle was leaving a prime parking spot near the doors.

"Will you put it on your key ring? That way I know it won't get lost." Penelope beamed at him and handed him the key.

He took it automatically, feeling a little strange. "Okay, I'll run your mom's things to the front desk and be back in one minute. Don't unlock the truck, and don't leave. In fact," he teased, "don't move a muscle!" Theo affixed one of the N-95 masks to his face.

"What if there's a fire?" There was a mischievous glint in her eye.

"A fire?"

"Or, what if an extremist starts shooting up the parking lot? Can I move then? At least duck and hide on the floorboard?"

"You know what I mean."

EVEN THE EXPANSIVE HOSPITAL entryway was buzzing with a frantic kind of energy. Theo suspected local healthcare workers must already be overwhelmed. The lady behind the information desk was dressed as though Ebola was rampant; along with a mask, she wore plastic gloves and a clear protective covering over her scrubs. Theo placed the sack on the counter and asked her to give it to Ivy Palmer.

"I'll make sure she gets it right away," she said.

Theo had no idea of the extent of Ivy's sickness. If she had coronavirus, it was possible that he and Penelope had been exposed. If they had, how long would it be before their symptoms appeared? He took one of the COVID-19 information sheets on the table and pumped disinfectant into his palms from a dispenser by the hospital door. He returned to the truck feeling slightly paranoid about everything.

Penelope was sitting exactly as he had left her. This surprised him.

Twelve

Life certainly had a bizarre sense of humor. Twenty years ago, he couldn't imagine being seventy and being a widower. He'd certainly never imagined home-schooling a kid he'd not known six weeks ago, or dealing with irksome specks of silver glitter embedded in the crevices of his dining room table. Theo straightened a stack of red construction paper (another unimaginable thing) and then erased yesterday's whiteboard notations, careful not to disturb the six small hash marks Penelope had added at the bottom. She had been tracking Ivy's days in the hospital since her admittance. According to last night's phone conversation, she would be released in a day or two. *Thank goodness.*

Theo was consulting the list of botanical vocabulary words he had saved in a note on his iPhone when it began vibrating. *Wash Reg* flashed on the screen. In the split second before he answered, Theo mentally rearranged Penelope's school day. They would not study vocabulary words or take Alice for a morning walk to Wilson Park. Instead, he and Penelope would drive to the hospital and get Ivy.

That's what he expected, anyway.

A nurse identified herself and asked him to verify his name. Then she began explaining that Ivy's blood oxygen level had dropped to a concerning level, describing her condition with phrases unfamiliar to Theo, like *pressure in her chest* and *blue lips*. "Dr. O' Ryan transferred Ms. Palmer to ICU for more extensive monitoring," she said. Her voice was calm, but Theo could hear the concern in it.

His anxiety rocketed. He found it impossible to concentrate on what the nurse was saying. Everything was impossible. "I'm sorry, but this can't be right. She was doing so much better yesterday. Can you please repeat everything you just said?"

Why did terrible news always come so quickly, with no time to prepare? Yesterday Ivy's fever had been low-grade, almost normal. She had lost her sense of taste and smell, but her appetite had returned. She had expected to be home by the weekend! With that reassurance, Penelope had turned her attention to crafting a welcome home sign, using poster board, red and blue construction paper, and, yes, a vial of silver glitter she had pulled from the bottom of her backpack.

The nurse advised him to wait a few hours before calling ICU for an update. "Let her get settled, Mr. Gruene, and just know she is in good hands. I take it you are her father?"

"No. No relation. I'm just a friend." *I barely know her.*

"She listed you as her emergency contact person."

"Me? Are you sure?" He blurted the words out without thinking. Ivy had made it clear she had no family to help care for Penelope, but listing him as her emergency contact seemed extraordinarily tragic. They had met only because of sheer happenstance, because Penelope had appeared on his porch, sopping wet, chattering on about missing the bus and needing to use the toilet. What if he'd been at the grocery store? What if he had ignored the incessant rapping and continued working on his plant specimens? Penelope might have knocked and knocked until she eventually ran to someone else's front stoop, Nita Johnson's, for instance. If that had happened, Nita would be having this conversation with the nurse, and he would still be contentedly working on his plant specimens, his home forever glitter-free. But that wasn't what had happened. And now here he was. In a few minutes, Penelope would come inside with Alice after their morning game of fetch, and it would be up to him to explain Ivy's worsening condition. What a mess he was in!

PENELOPE PEERED inside the hat box as though she was looking down into a deep well. "Oh, sick, Mr. Theo. They're so old-timey. Can I touch them?" Her dark eyes remained on the toys, but she resisted reaching inside until he gave her the go-ahead. If she wondered why he was finally letting her see his childhood toy collection, she didn't let on. He wasn't sure he understood it himself. Something in the nurse's voice, the raw tenor of her words, had sent Theo looking for any distraction from their regular routine. He didn't consider himself a procrastinator, but he was prudent. No good would come from upsetting Penelope with limited information. He would explain things *after* he spoke with an ICU nurse and obtained an update.

Penelope began removing the first few items from the box, handling them as though they were made of fine bone china. She pursed her lips, blew into the harmonica, and winced at its grating noise. "Oh, sorry, Mr. Theo, but is it supposed to sound like a barking seal?"

He laughed at her description. "No, but I can't say I've ever heard a pleasing noise come from it."

Penelope untied the canvas pouch and poured a few marbles into her small palm. She picked one out and held it toward the dining room light fixture, turning it this way and that. "It's like a teeny planet. If I arrange them just right, we could have an entire solar system. This one looks like the sun."

Theo brightened. "That was my brother's favorite marble. Michael called it his good luck charm and carried it to school whenever he had a test. Once he thought he lost it, and my mother turned the house upside down searching for it. She found it in the bottom of the laundry hamper; it had fallen from his pocket." Sometimes Theo thought of his childhood like a dated newspaper clipping; factual, but yellowed and unclear. Other times, something as small as a marble brought with it a flood of crystal-clear memories.

"It might bring you good luck too, if you didn't hide it in a dusty box. It has probably been suffocating for a hundred years."

He chuckled. "I'm not quite that old, but maybe you're right. Where should we put it?"

Penelope strolled around the dining room, examining every surface, corner, and window ledge. "How about here?" She nestled it in the soil of a potted rhododendron. The golden center of the marble glowed in a slant of afternoon light.

Theo agreed to the new home for the marble, thinking that Michael would have approved.

Penelope continued looking through the box. "You have a whole army battalion in here?" She began lining the army men up on the table.

"Good word, battalion. Your vocabulary is impressive."

"I know. I'm highly gifted." She said this as though reporting on the day's weather. "My IQ is one sixty, in case you are wondering. What's yours?"

Theo had never taken an IQ test. "I'm average, if I had to guess. Gifted at nothing, really. Maybe growing things." Theo had grown Oncidium orchids a lifetime ago, as part of his master's thesis. His apartment kitchen had become a makeshift greenhouse as he propagated and studied orchid genomics.

"So you like plants and army men?"

"Michael and I played with these army men for hours." All these years later, the loss of his brother still rippled just beneath the surface of his life.

"Well, I'm a pacifist, so I won't be spending much time with these little soldiers." She pushed them toward the center of the table. "I don't believe in killing people. No one won the last war, and no one will win the next war. Eleanor Roosevelt said that, by the way."

"They're just toys." He reached for an army man. The base of the particular one he picked up had teeth marks on it. From their dog, he wondered? For a moment, he was back in their Midland backyard, the creosote-saturated air smelling like rain, his mother's insistent voice calling to them through the screen door, "Boys, come inside! Lunch is ready."

She never had to ask twice, because they were always hungry, "growing like weeds," his dad always said. Every race to the house was a friendly competition. First to reach the porch steps. First to finish their lunch. First back outside to the soldiers waiting for the next battle. Theo was older and taller, but Michael had short, fast legs. The winner wasn't a given.

"Mr. Theo, don't you think giving a kid a toy promotes whatever that toy stands for? In this case, extreme violence?" Penelope plucked two of the army men from the pile. "Look at these guys. One's throwing a bomb, and the other is about to shoot someone with an AR-15."

"Technically, that one's a hand grenade and the other is an M16. Those rifles were popular during Vietnam."

"Guns should never be popular."

"Have you considered joining the debate team at school? Or maybe you could go ahead and enroll in law school. I'll write you a glowing letter of recommendation."

"I would if I could, but debate team is for high schoolers. And no way do I ever plan to be a lawyer. I want to do something that matters."

He snorted. She was clever but still too young to comprehend the way the world worked. "Don't you think lawyers do work that matters? Especially to their clients?"

She shrugged her thin shoulders, and he sensed she was growing weary of their conversation. "You know, Penelope, sometimes war is necessary. Take World War Two, for example. Some Americans believed we should never have gotten involved. But being neutral is sometimes the worst possible response, especially when freedom is at stake. Hitler rose to power relatively quickly, and Germany became a dictatorship within only a few years. It's impossible to know exactly what our lives would be like today if the United States had not joined forces with the Allies, but I believe fascism would have continued to spread unchecked." Theo felt himself getting worked up, and was conflicted over how much or how little to say. "I know this may sound like a copout, Penelope, but this is a very complicated subject. To your point, though, Eleanor Roosevelt was right. A wartime winner is never clear cut."

Penelope's eyes widened. "Were *you* in a war?"

"Almost. I wasn't able to serve because of the car accident I told you about. The accident with my family."

"Is that why you sometimes limp a little bit?"

"Well, that, and because I'm just getting old."

She pushed her glasses up on her nose and stared solemnly into his eyes. "Well, I'm glad you didn't go, but to tell you the truth, I wish I didn't know your position on war."

"Then maybe you shouldn't ask so many questions."

She sighed, and for a moment seemed defeated. "I wish I didn't ask so many questions too, but I can't help it. I'm inquisitive. Even someone with an average IQ should be able to see how war doesn't protect life. It ends life." Her demeanor was serious as she scooped up the army men, dropped them in the box, and took out the paper sack filled with trinkets.

"Even with my average IQ, I know we should move on to another topic." Theo wasn't up for further explaining or defining when and under what circumstances war was justified or necessary.

Penelope peered inside the paper sack. "Oooh, these are interesting." She poured the objects onto the table. "Look, a tiny green frog, and a compass, and there's even an old penny in here. These little toys remind me of the gifts Boo Radley left for Jem and Scout."

Theo seized on this opportunity to discuss the book again, the reason behind the gifts in the tree, and the symbolism of the tree itself.

Later, after lunch, they set out for their daily nature walk. Theo led Alice, and Penelope skipped along beside him, stopping frequently to inspect any interesting leaf, acorn, or insect in their path. She carried her notepad and a pencil to record the location of any additional tree hollows they discovered. Routine was important, Theo thought, and searching for Boo Radley holes had become a favorite afternoon activity. The best ones were low on the trunks, at eye level, or lower even, because Penelope could better see into them.

"I'm glad you aren't mad at me," Penelope said.

"Why would I be mad at you?"

"Because I ask too many questions about war and stuff. Derrick always got mad when I asked too many questions."

Derrick? "Who is Derrick?"

"He was my mom's despicable boyfriend. He's gone, and I'm glad. He broke Mom's heart and stole all her money."

This was the first Theo had heard of Derrick. He wondered how long he and Ivy had been together. "Well then, I'm glad he's gone too. And, no, of course, I'm not mad. Asking questions is always good, even when we may not like the answers."

Penelope considered this before replying. "I agree. One hundred percent."

Three blocks over, they noticed a large cavity in the trunk of a sugar maple tree. Penelope plopped onto the grass and began sketching out the shape of the hole on her notepad. "I can't believe we've walked by this tree so many times but never noticed this hole until right this very second. Do you think Boo Radley holes magically appear when we really need to see one? Sort of like the Room of Requirement at Hogwarts? My mom loves the idea of a Room of Requirement." She giggled.

Theo knew nothing about a Room of Requirement, but he was familiar enough with Harry Potter to know Hogwarts was the wizarding school created by author J. K. Rowling.

"Do you, Mr. Theo? Think they are magic?"

"You know, this tree hole all began with an injury." Theo pressed his fingers to the smooth lip of the cavity like he was taking the tree's pulse. "Years ago, a broken limb or lightning strike wounded the tree. And because a wounded tree attracts more insects than a healthy one, it also attracts hungry woodpeckers looking for a meal. A woodpecker probably pecked away at the injured area, feasting on bark beetles and borers, and eventually excavated a hole. Over time, the heartwood of the weakened tree rotted away. It's still alive, the tree, I mean. All this time, it has been growing around the hollow part." Theo touched his palm to the firm tree trunk. *All of us—trees, woodpeckers, and humans—are just fighting to survive.* He thought of Ivy trying to fight off a novel virus. When their walk was over, he would call the hospital for an update and tell Penelope of her mother's deteriorating condition.

"But what's your answer? About tree hole magic?"

Magic?

His childhood, spent playing with marbles and toy soldiers, seemed vastly different to the childhood experienced today, with virtual games played on cell phones, but there were points of commonality. Much like Penelope, good books had captivated Theo, and his brother too. When visiting Grandpa Gruene's house, they liked to pretend the back of the bedroom closet opened to the world of Narnia. He'd not thought of that in years, but suddenly recalled woolen clothing hanging on wooden hangers and the stuffy smell of mothballs.

Penelope was waiting patiently for his answer.

For reasons he did not truly understand, the well-being of this dazzling child temporarily rested with him. Keeping her grounded and level-headed, helping her decipher fact from fiction, real from make-believe—these undertakings were now part of his job description. But he expressed none of this to her. Instead, as though a different part of his brain commandeered his tongue, he said, "Yes, Penelope. Magic is real if you believe it to be."

THEO AND PENELOPE sat on the bench beneath the thinking tree and took turns bouncing tennis balls off the back fence for Alice to chase. "What if she doesn't get better? What if she dies?" Penelope's tentatively-spoken words came like breath on a cold night, raw and honest, chilling Theo despite the warm evening. He had delayed as long as possible, but after speaking to an ICU nurse, and eating Cheerios for supper (Penelope's choice), it had been time to break the news that Ivy's condition had worsened and that she was in the ICU.

"Your mom will be okay. They've moved her to a part of the hospital where she will be more closely monitored. She will get the best possible care there." A magnificent sunset made the low-hanging clouds in the east appear crimson. Theo found it hard to look directly at Penelope. He watched the changing colors of the sky, hoping what he was saying was true.

"You don't know that."

"Yes, I do. That's what happens in the ICU. And we have top-notch hospitals here."

Penelope lay her head against his arm. "Do you miss your wife?" She traced her finger on the initials he had carved on the bench years ago.

"Of course. Every day."

Penelope nodded and then leaned heavier into him.

He pulled her closer, feeling protective, wishing he could erase all her worry.

"As long as I can stay here with you, I'll be okay," she said.

Theo squeezed her shoulder. Such a young child should never be faced with such heavy concerns. "Of course, you'll stay here, and your mom will get better, and everything will be fine." There was no way to know what would happen, but expressing this certainty was all he could offer.

"Mr. Theo, I have a very important question. I've been thinking about this, and I know you'll know the answer." She tilted her face toward him, anticipation written in her eyes.

Without hearing her question, he could guess it. Theo rubbed his palms back and forth against his thighs, a nervous habit that helped him focus. What would he say to her? How much truth could an eight-year-old handle? *If your mother dies, you will become a foster child. Our time together will end.*

"What's your question?" In the pause that followed, Theo wanted to promise Penelope the moon, but it wasn't his to give. The spring peepers screamed their twilight song. An owl hooted nearby.

"I've been wondering why Boo Radley's father put cement in the tree."

"Oh…well, um…." Relieved, Theo exhaled. "You want to know why he filled the hole in with cement?"

She nodded, the last of the fading light flickering on her glasses.

Sometimes being wrong brought the greatest relief. "Well, years ago, people thought filling a hollow area with cement would save the tree, or at least keep it from further decay. Today, we know that's not true; a tree will grow around a hollow spot. But, to answer your question about the story, I believe Mr. Radley wanted to stop the gift exchanges between Boo, Jem, and Scout."

"But why?"

"Well, isolation is one of the themes of the story, right?"

"Uh-huh."

"When Boo began to interact with Jem and Scout, Mr. Radley put an end to it by cementing the hole in the tree, since that was the way they communicated. He wanted to keep Boo isolated from everyone in Maycomb."

Penelope huffed. "That's just sad and unfair and extremely rude. Boo was only trying to make friends with Jem and Scout. Being lonely isn't a crime. At least not yet, it isn't."

Theo agreed with Penelope's assessment, then suggested they go inside while they could still make out the pathway to the back door.

Thirteen

Nita Johnson stood at Theo's front door, a platter of raspberry shortbread cookies in her outstretched arms. "I came to thank you for last night," she said, her voice muffled by the mask worn tight over her nose and mouth.

Theo suspected her real purpose for being there was to meet Penelope, who had been staying with him for a few days already. "Oh, no thanks necessary," Theo said with a wave of his hand, trying his level best to ignore the shortbread cookies arranged beneath the plastic wrap. Nita was a spectacular baker; her cookies were among the best he had ever tasted. "The poor creature was terrified and glad to be free."

"No doubt about that, but I'm grateful for your help." Nita dipped into a clumsy curtsy on his doorstep, almost spilling the cookies before righting the platter. "Oops. Grateful but not very graceful."

He smiled despite himself.

The afternoon before, just after walking Alice, the phone had rung. It had been Nita, frantic, asking for help. A squirrel had gotten into her house, and she was beside herself, with no idea what to do. At first, Theo had told her he couldn't come over because of possible coronavirus exposure, but Nita had been adamant.

"I don't care, Theo! The thing is clinging to the wall above my kitchen stove, and he's shrieking!"

Theo, feeling sorry for the squirrel, had put on a mask and walked over, while Penelope stayed with Alice. He'd managed to shoo the squirrel out through an open window without much effort and then accepted Nita's offer of a beer. Agreeing to one beer with Nita Johnson seemed easier than declining, although his willingness *did* make him wonder if he was coming down with the virus. Sitting six feet apart on Nita's side porch, Theo commented on the lushness of the maple trees behind her house. Talk of the maples led to a brief conversation on how lucky they were to live in a place with wide-open spaces.

"Those poor people in New York City—how are they keeping sane?" she said, and then began chattering on about how she was spending her time now that the furniture store where she worked part-time had temporarily closed. Writing haikus. Joining an online Tai chi class. Having her groceries delivered and sanitizing cans of soup before allowing them into her house. *Sanitizing cans of soup?* He thought her behavior toward canned food was extreme, but he sipped his beer and kept quiet.

Still she went on.

Weary of talking about the all-pervasive subject of coronavirus—the very topic had become a virus!—Theo redirected the conversation to himself. And, even though he immediately recognized what a blunder it was, he couldn't stop himself from explaining his new role as Penelope's temporary teacher since Lafayette Elementary had gone virtual. Thankfully, he had the forethought not to divulge Ivy's current status as a Covid patient at Washington Regional, or that Penelope was temporarily living with him. But Nita had been positively enthralled and peppered him with questions. *What's she like? What are you teaching her? It must be so fun to have a child around all day!*

And now here she was, standing on his front porch, offering up a platter of his favorite cookies in the world.

"Who is it, Mr. Theo?" Penelope called out.

"Just a neighbor. Please keep on with your reading."

She sighed with all the might such a tiny girl could muster.

"Wait a minute. Is that Penelope? I want to meet her."

Seconds later, Penelope slipped beneath Theo's arm and stood next to him like a baby bird beneath its parent's wing. "Yes, ma'am. I'm Penelope Palmer. Mr. Theo is my grandfather."

Theo jerked away as though she had scalded him. "No, I'm not! Good lord, why would you say that?" He hadn't meant to shout, but this was too much.

Penelope's face drooped, and she shrugged. "Well, we've basically adopted each other, so it's kinda the same thing."

"No, it absolutely—" Theo stopped talking when Nita stepped closer and shoved the edge of the cookie platter into his stomach, forcing him to take it.

"Aren't you the cutest thing?" Nita said.

Penelope sidestepped around Theo and bowed to Nita. "Thank you so very, very much for the compliment."

"I'm pleased to make your acquaintance, Penelope. I'm Nita Johnson, and I live down the street."

"Oh, I know," Penelope said in a knowing tone, as though she held a big secret tucked inside.

"Really?" Nita raised her eyebrows.

"Yes, ma'am. We walk around the neighborhood every day as part of Mr. Theo's nature school. He talks about plants and shrubs, while I mostly search for Boo Radley holes. Mr. Theo has pointed out your house several times, because he is always trying to—"

"Okay, I don't think Ms. Johnson wants a play-by-play of our nature walks." *Good grief.* With Penelope itching to divulge everything she knew and Nita drawing out information like a human magnet, Theo was outmaneuvered.

"Sure I do." Nita's eyes brightened and Theo knew she was grinning beneath her mask.

"See, she does." Penelope giggled.

"Ms. Johnson makes the best cookies, Penelope." Theo extended the platter toward Penelope, hoping to refocus the conversation.

"My almond raspberry shortbread cookies are your grandpa's favorite." Nita winked at him, which made him uncomfortable.

Penelope let out a little cheer. "Raspberries are the merriest of all the berries!"

"We can enjoy them out here on the porch. That way, we can practice our social distancing." Nita said this as though social distancing required lessons, like learning to play the saxophone.

Any control of his day had been completely yanked away. Feeling powerless, Theo followed Nita across the newly stained porch. He watched her unpack the tote bag she'd brought, depositing everything on the porch swing—three paper plates, three cloth napkins that looked to have been made from red bandanas, and a small plaid tablecloth which she draped over the wooden table where he and Winn played the occasional game of chess or Scrabble.

"It's a party!" Penelope cheered. "Can we make tea, Mr. Theo?"

Theo knew when he was outnumbered. "Black or green?"

"Ooh, green! Do you know about antioxidants, Ms. Nita?"

He placed the cookies in the center of the table and went to put on the kettle, leaving Penelope to chatter on about free radicals. When he returned with three steaming cups of green tea, Nita was wearing clear plastic gloves, the type a restaurant worker might wear. She placed two cookies on each paper plate and passed them around. Alice was perched beside them as though waiting for her share.

The afternoon was perfect for a tea party; Theo would give Nita that.

"Your front porch sure looks nice since you redid it, Theo."

"It was long overdue." Theo bit into a cookie, and an automatic "Ummm" escaped his lips. She truly did bake the most fabulous cookie.

"I helped," Penelope said. "Didn't I, Mr. Theo?"

For a moment, delicate sweetness melting on his tongue, Theo had no idea what Penelope meant. Helped with what?

"Ooh, these cookies are amazing. They're like clouds of heaven," Penelope said.

Nita beamed. "Thank you, Penelope. Now tell me, how did you help with the porch?"

Oh, the porch. He devoured the remainder of his first cookie.

"As Mr. Theo's assistant, I counted and measured the new boards needed using a measuring tape, and I went with him to Lowe's when he bought sandpaper and rollers and stain. He wouldn't let me touch his electric saw, but he let me sand the top of the railing with his hand sander. Didn't you?"

Theo nodded as he stuffed his second cookie into his mouth.

"When it came to actually staining the deck, I mostly stayed out of the way and worked on my homework. That was okay by me because I disagreed with the color anyway. I guess it's grown on me, though, and now I can sorta understand why he chose it."

Nita's forehead rumpled with confusion. "You didn't agree with the stain color he chose?"

"Yeah," Theo interjected. "She wanted me to paint the porch neon green."

"False. Totally false." Penelope shook her head as she nibbled a cookie. "I just wondered if there wasn't a better color than driftwood, that's all. Honestly, I think Mr. Theo could use a little color in his life. He lives in a gray house and dresses like he is trying to blend into the background of the world. His spirit animal must be a leaf-litter toad."

Nita nearly blew green tea through her nose. "Well, she certainly has your number, doesn't she, Theo?"

Theo took a gulp of his tea. It tasted like wet socks.

"Ms. Nita, can you teach me to make these cookies? I'm an outstanding student, and I've been known to act as my mother's sous chef."

"Oh, is your mother a chef?"

"No. She's an almost-nurse who makes the most delicious cherry hand pies. Doesn't she, Mr. Theo?"

Theo nodded his agreement and took another bite of cookie, letting it sit on his tongue and tasting the sweetness as it melted like a sugar mint.

"I'd be happy to give you a cookie-baking lesson. I taught my granddaughter to make these last Christmas."

"No. Covid!" Theo, simultaneously enraptured by Nita's cookies and annoyed by said rapture, heard himself spit out the words. He had intended to say more: *No, because of Covid, you can't come into the house; no, because you get on my nerves, you can't come into the house. No! No! No!*

Nita and Penelope completely ignored him.

"Really? You will!? Maybe next week?"

"I would love it. And don't worry about catching the virus from me. I've been extremely cautious, and I've not been around *anyone* except Theo in at least two weeks. Maybe we could start our own safe group, the three of us."

"Like a club?" Penelope asked, her eyes glistening like melted chocolate drops.

"Yes. A safe Covid club."

Theo's head spun from sugar and annoyance. He piled more cookies onto his plate as the situation moved from bad to worse. Just as he had been unable to stop Nita from meeting Penelope, he could not keep the child quiet about her mother's health situation. Theo chewed stolidly through several more cookies while Penelope spilled everything she knew to Nita, starting with the night her mother didn't come home from work and ending with last night's update from the ICU nurse.

"Even though she's been in the hospital for almost two hundred hours, I know she will make a complete recovery. I've been praying super hard about it. I believe in the power of prayer, do you?"

Nita nodded enthusiastically. "Absolutely, yes I do. I'm sorry about your mom, and I'll put her on my prayer list."

Penelope beamed. "How many people are on your prayer list?" She began nibbling her second cookie. Theo had lost track of the number he'd eaten and thought there was a good chance he might be sick.

"Well, I'm not completely sure—"

"Is that too nosy rosy to ask? Mr. Theo sometimes gets frustrated because I ask too many questions. I can't help it though; I just like to know things."

Nita smiled. "It's fine, I just—"

"How old is your granddaughter? And what's her name?"

"Sophia just turned twelve. She lives in Minneapolis, and I don't see her nearly as often as I would like. Especially now with Covid."

"That's sad. But if you'd like, I could be your pretend-granddaughter. Just so you don't miss her too much."

"That's sweet. Thank you."

Theo knew Nita had an adult son living up north, but he didn't recall ever hearing about a grandchild. Strangely, he found this new knowledge about Nita comforting.

"So, I'm curious, do you and Mr. Theo ever go out on dates?" Penelope's eyebrows lifted so high they arched over the top of her eyeglasses.

Theo choked and sputtered. "No, we aren't dating!"

"Well, we did go out a couple of times, once to a new restaurant in Bentonville, and then later to a movie, I forget the name of it, but it was violent and I didn't care for it. Lots of blood." Nita shook her head as though shaking off the unpleasant memory.

Penelope leaned toward Nita and lowered her voice to a near whisper. "Did you know he believes in war?"

"What's that, hon?" Nita asked.

Theo sprang to his feet and began gathering the empty paper plates. "Okay, thank you for the always excellent cookies, Nita, but we need to get back to our lessons. Maybe a session on manners," he added under his breath.

Penelope and Nita continued talking as though Theo was invisible.

"Men really are from Mars, Penelope. You'll understand it someday. The bottom line is Theo and I really aren't romantically compatible. We're just friendly neighbors."

Theo rolled his eyes. Getting less friendly and less neighborly by the half-second, he thought.

AFTER DINNER, Theo called the hospital for an update and was surprised to actually speak to Ivy. She sounded fully alert and had a thing or two to say about still being in the hospital. Again, Theo interpreted her grumbling as a good thing. When Annie had been at her sickest, she could barely summon the energy to breathe, much less complain. Passing the phone to Penelope, he heard the re-telling of their impromptu tea party. It was true—every story had two sides; the kid's version of their afternoon sounded positively enchanting.

"Oh, Mom, Ms. Nita brought the most delectable raspberry-filled cookies, and Mr. Theo served green tea in real teacups with saucers, and we had red bandana napkins and a tablecloth and everything." Penelope detailed how they sat on the front porch for safety reasons, with chairs spaced out and masks worn between the eating and drinking. "No one sneezed or coughed, and Alice was a guest too, even though she was just an observer. Being outside only added to the garden party atmosphere. I wish you could have been here!"

Despite his earlier frustration, Theo couldn't help but be amused as he watched Penelope talk on the phone. She was such an expressive child, with enthusiasm so intense he could almost see it floating around the den. He wondered if he had been transported into a bizarre fairytale—if so, clearly he was the ogre.

"Oh, yes," she continued, replying to something Ivy said that wasn't audible to Theo. "Now that's pretty interesting! They used to date but broke up because he's from Mars, and they are mostly incompatible." Fully animated now, she nodded and grinned at Theo. He rubbed his forehead and wondered if he was fevered. A curtain of fatigue fell over him.

Later, after Penelope got into bed, she called out to him. "Mr. Theeeeeoooooo—can you please come in here? I need to tell you something exceptionally important."

Theo shook his head and whispered, "No," to his weary reflection in the bathroom mirror. His exhaustion was tremendous, like a heavy person riding on his shoulders. Was there no end to the child's talking? Last night, he had heard her talking in her sleep!

"Mr. Theeeoooo? I know you can hear me."

He returned his toothbrush to the cup holder and trudged down the hall, his fatigue riding piggyback.

"What is it, Penelope?"

She lay in the center of the bed with the quilt pulled to her chin, her small body barely displacing the covers. Without her glasses, her dark eyes looked as small as coffee beans.

"I'm curious about something."

"Well, go on then before I pass out in the doorway."

"Do you know the thread count of these sheets?"

She had summoned him to ask about thread count? "I'm sure I don't have a clue."

"Well, I really like this bed." She freed her arms from beneath the covers and moved them in slow arcs, up and down, reminding him of the way he and Michael had made snow angels during the Texas panhandle winters. "It's extremely comfortable, probably because of the amazing sheets, although it could be the mattress. I've never had my own bed, much less my own bedroom, so I will never forget this one. I just wanted you to know."

Theo's heart twisted, and his voice caught in his throat. "I'm glad you like it."

"Is it one of those expensive sleep number beds?"

"No. It's just a regular bed. Now let's get some sleep."

"Okay."

Fourteen

The forecast was perfect for a spring hike, so for the second time in two weeks, Theo and Penelope set out to have school in the forest. Last week, Theo had taken her hiking along the nearby trails of Mount Sequoyah. It had been a test of sorts, which she had passed with flying colors. He had wondered about Penelope's stamina, and how willing she would be to trek through the woods without access to her art supplies and books, and with no convenient way to wash her hands. He needn't have worried. Her curiosity made her a natural student of nature, and with so much to see, she had been quite willing to explore every marked trail, wade across shallow creek beds, and search for morel mushrooms in the leafy understory. It helped that Theo had bought her a proper pair of hiking boots. Since the hilly Ozark terrain was no match for Penelope's flip flops and flimsy worn sneakers, they'd donned their N95 masks and braved Potter's House, looking for thrift-store options. When a pair of like-new, all-terrain Keens turned out to be just her size, he gladly paid the ten-dollar ask price. She was absolutely thrilled, and declared them the perfect shoes for scientific discovery, mainly because they were brown and tan, which were serious colors.

This week, Theo had chosen Yellow Rock Trail for them to explore. As the sky began to lighten, Theo exited the highway and pulled onto the shoulder of the road. To the right, almost close enough to touch, water trickled down a sheer limestone wall.

"Are we there?" Penelope's words were thick with sleep.

"Not yet, but soon." He couldn't make out her expression in the meager light, but he heard her rifling through her gear. After last week's hike, Theo had created an explorer kit for her, from items left over from his years as a seventh-grade science teacher. A magnifying mirror, a set of plastic vials with tweezers and nippers for collecting specimens, a refillable water bottle bearing a faded 'Get Outside' sticker—it didn't take much to make Penelope happy, and when he saw her delight over the kit, he was glad he'd stored away his classroom equipment in the attic.

"Then where are we, and why are we stopping? I'm excited to get there, but I don't get why we had to leave under the cover of darkness."

He laughed at her choice of words. "Stop messing with the things in your backpack, and you'll see why we left under the so-called cover of darkness."

Penelope lifted her head and looked at him. He nodded toward the front window of the truck, and her eyes followed his gaze.

"Oh!! It's super glorious. How did you do that?"

"Do what?"

"Make the sun come up right when we happen to be in this exact spot! I mean, look outside, Mr. Theo. This is the most magical place I've been in my whole entire life! Oh, you get a very gigantic point for this!" She pointed to the valley below them, where the first rays of morning light were brushing the forested landscape.

"Penelope, you realize the sun rises daily, right? I'll gladly accept a point, even though my only involvement with today's magic was checking the forecast for clear weather and setting my alarm to drive us here on time. It's not rocket science."

"No, but it's earth science. Mr. Theo, I've never seen the sunrise, not like this, and whether you want to believe it or not, you had everything to do with it simply because you brought me here. Timing really is everything sometimes."

How true that was. Both good timing and bad timing. He wondered what the score was, of the game he'd forgotten they were playing.

The sun was fully up by the time they stepped onto Yellow Rock Trail, with Theo leading and Penelope following. The week before, after walking into a spider web, Penelope had declared the lead position was not for her. "I can appreciate spiders, but no way will I ever be friends with them," she'd said, shuddering from head to toe while wiping her arms with her fingertips. Now, as Penelope followed behind him, Theo found himself growing frustrated. She kept aiming to step directly on his footprints, but more often trod on the back of his shoe. When she wasn't doing that, she was making frequent stops to look through the plant identification book he had given her.

"I'm going to find all of these plants. Every single one," she said, now lagging several yards behind him. "Wait up! How will I find all these plants if you are in such a hurry?"

Theo stopped, inhaled slowly and deliberately, and reminded himself that the whole purpose of the hike was to teach Penelope about nature. He trudged back to her. "I'm not in a hurry; I'm just hiking. The point of the book is not to find *every* plant, but to look up the ones you have questions about. It's better to let nature present itself to you."

"Listen, Mr. Theo. Do you hear that?" She froze in place.

"I hear you talking."

"No," she whispered. "I hear someone."

Once they both stopped talking, Theo could hear rustling leaves. That sound usually meant a squirrel was near, but seconds later, a beautiful doe appeared among the trees, only feet from the trail. Time paused as they stared at each another, all three of them. The doe's white tail was flicking, her liquid eyes unblinking, trained on them. Penelope was actually struck speechless, for a change. Theo could feel his pulse thumping. Deer typically travelled in pairs. He scanned the area carefully, only moving his eyes, but no second deer materialized. As quickly as she had appeared, the magnificent creature left them, leaping effortlessly over a moss-covered log and vanishing back into the woods.

"I think that was my Patronus," Penelope whispered, gazing after the deer.

Theo had no idea what she meant, and wasn't convinced he had heard her correctly, but to avoid a nonsensical discussion of something unrelated to nature, he just nodded.

The sighting stifled much of Penelope's chatter for the remainder of the morning. She followed Theo quietly along the trail, no longer leaping to fill his footprints, utterly absorbed in her thoughts. He couldn't help wondering what she was thinking about, even while he enjoyed the peace.

Later, they came across a stone outcropping that offered magnificent views of the valley. It was a good place to stop for a while.

Theo took a long swig from his water bottle while Penelope examined patches of blue-green moss growing at the base of a boulder. "Look at this, and look at this," she said repeatedly, moving her magnifying glass into different positions around the boulder. "There's a whole world growing out of the moss, like teeny tiny trees or something. Can you come see, Mr. Theo?"

Theo squatted despite his complaining joints. "Yes, there's lichen growing on it. Moss is a plant, but lichen isn't actually a plant at all. Lichen is algae and fungus growing in a symbiotic relationship."

"I don't get what you mean." She moved the magnifying glass closer.

"Imagine an algae-fungus sandwich. That's lichen."

"That's weird. Since there's a lot here, can I take a tiny sample?"

"Of course." Theo was pleased she had remembered last week's trail rule of never over-harvesting any species. Samples could be taken only when growth was abundant. Single flowers should be left to multiply.

Penelope snipped off a piece of the moss, dropped it into one of her vials, and raised it to the sunlight. "A whole little world right here in my hands." She carefully tucked the vial back into her pack.

After eating the lunch Theo had packed—a cheese sandwich for her and turkey for himself, along with bananas, green grapes, and carrot sticks—they continued hiking the circuitous trail which would eventually take them back to the trailhead starting point. Penelope stopped occasionally to study various plants that caught her attention. She asked questions when she couldn't identify a particular variety in her guidebook, and snipped specimens here and there, filling the remaining vials. When she spotted small pale-blue flowers blooming beneath the shade of a dogwood, she said, "Well, hi there, Mr. Jacob's Ladder." Then she grinned at Theo, proud to have recognized the native plant without any help.

He gave her a point for that.

THEO DUMPED NOODLES into boiling water while Penelope, working at the kitchen table, carefully transferred her collected specimens to the wooden flower press Theo had built decades ago. Sitting at the kitchen table, deep inside her own world, she whispered to each stem and blossom while arranging them for drying. "Now, you will fit right here, and, let's see, you will go here…no, you guys can't touch…there, that's better." A particular sort of tranquility often followed a full day spent in nature, and Theo felt it then, treasured it much like a night of solid sleep. Sunshine and exercise followed by a hot shower—what more could he ask of a day?

Penelope added her last specimen to the press. "I had a really fun time hiking that trail at Devil's Den today, Mr. Theo," she said. "But to tell you the truth, I was a little disappointed we didn't find evidence of Bigfoot out there in the woods. I thought for sure the rustling sound we heard was going to be Bigfoot."

Theo laughed at this newest wild notion of Penelope's.

"Don't you think Bigfoot might live in the Ozarks?"

"I think Bigfoot lives in the imagination of pranksters."

"Oh, no, there have been sightings. I read an article about Bigfoot in one of those *National Geographic* magazines at our apartment. For real."

He chuckled again and gave the noodles a stir. He had developed a strong affinity for the kid, and was glad at how well they were getting on, but nevertheless, each day felt surreal; his routine unrecognizable, her future cloaked in uncertainty. Ivy had been in the hospital eleven days now, with five days in the ICU. Each time Theo called the hospital for an update, he was told her condition was stable but she still required intensive care monitoring.

"That deer we saw, what did you call it?" he asked Penelope. She had come to stand beside him, was peering into the pot of noodles.

"A Patronus. It provides protection from dementors."

Patronus? Dementors? He couldn't remember the last time he'd been so confused.

"Harry Potter's Patronus was a deer too, only his was a stag and mine is a doe."

Finally, he understood. Another Harry Potter reference.

She looked up at him, frowned, and cocked her head. "I really doubt you could produce one."

"What do you mean? Why can't I have one?" He found the idea that Penelope doubted his ability to do something oddly perturbing.

"Well, it's based on the spell-caster's concentration on very happy memories. And you have lots of sad ones."

Suddenly Theo desperately wanted a Patronus; wanted Penelope to *believe* he could "produce" one. Maybe he should check out a Harry Potter book from the library when it reopened. He might be missing out on a mysterious way to connect with her, much the way he'd connected with his science students over Kung Fu.

"I guess you don't believe in aliens either."

"Aliens? Nope."

"What about mermaids or unicorns?"

"Again, no and no."

"Ghosts?"

This recitation of imaginary creatures might go on all night. Theo didn't answer, but began looking through the utensil drawer for the cheese grater.

"You *must* believe in ghosts! You sure do live with a bunch of them."

"How about you grate this parmesan for us?"

"I'm talking about your brother, Michael, who practically lives inside that box of toys. And Annie still lives inside your head, you know?"

"Give me a little credit. I know the ghosts you're talking about."

She shrugged. "I'm not a mind reader. Oh, I know! What about the Abominable Snowmonster? Do you believe he's real?"

"Good grief."

Penelope's laughter caught him, and hilarity ensued—as he rinsed cherry tomatoes and began preparing a basic green salad to accompany the pasta, she leaped around the kitchen, acting out her vision of all the fantastic creatures that populated her imagination. Eventually, after she imitated the basilisk from Harry Potter (a beast

127

Theo was unfamiliar with, yet guessed because her flickering tongue was serpent-like), he decided it was time to try and rein in her flights of fancy.

"Tell me something you learned today. Something true and tangible."

She scrunched up her sunburned nose and thought briefly. "Well, I learned about nature's sandwiches. It's pretty cool how nature takes care of itself, one thing thriving only because of another thing."

"Kiddo, I think my job here is done. One point for you." He found himself quite pleased by her comment.

"Well, *my* job is just getting started," she retorted, rather seriously, which concerned him a little.

Theo poured the cooked noodles into the colander and inhaled the warm steam rising from the sink. It had grown dark outside, and when he glimpsed his reflection in the window, the smiling face reminded him of his younger self. That pleased him, too.

Fifteen

Theo almost didn't answer the phone; usually the only people who called his land line were spam callers. But he did answer, and when a lady identified herself as a housing relocation specialist from Sequoyah Trail Village, the local retirement community where Winn and Julie lived, his curiosity kept him on the line. "It's your lucky day, Mr. Gruene," she said, sounding genuinely excited for him.

"Oh, yeah? What did I win?" He was willing to bite because he was in an extraordinarily good mood. Yesterday, he and Penelope had received excellent news; Ivy's health had improved and she was being moved from ICU into a regular room. He had woken that morning feeling energized and optimistic, and his positive feelings had lasted throughout the day. Another week as Penelope's teacher had almost passed, and they had accomplished everything detailed in his lesson plan.

"A two-bedroom cottage is becoming available on August first. I bet you never thought we'd get to your name." Her laugh sounded effervescent. She had the perfect voice for radio, or maybe even television commercials. "Are you still interested in joining our community?"

Joining your community? "I'm sorry, but I think you have the wrong number." Sequoyah Trail Village was the type of place a person could age into, living first in a cottage or duplex unit and later moving into a high-rise apartment when additional care was needed. The waitlist was notoriously long, but he had never added his name.

She repeated his name and verified his current address, which were both correct, then said, "Your application was submitted on May fifth, nineteen ninety-seven."

She was so cheerful and upbeat that Theo almost wished her information was accurate. "No, I never...I'm pretty sure I would remember filling out an application. My memory isn't that bad." He chuckled but a sinking feeling came over him. Years ago, someone in Florida had accessed his Mastercard, charging thousands of dollars in electronics and hotel rooms. What a mess that had been to straighten out. Had he been victimized again?

"That's odd...." He heard the shuffling of paperwork. "Oh, I see. Your wife, Annie R. Gruene, submitted and signed the paperwork. Should I discuss this with her?"

Annie? "No, I'm afraid that's impossible. Annie passed away some time ago." No matter how many times he said them, those words always held an edge of disbelief.

"Oh, I'm so sorry, Mr. Gruene. Please accept my condolences."

He swallowed hard and muttered, "Thank you," vowing to cancel his landline by day's end. His good mood had been snuffed out by sadness.

"Mr. Gruene, I'm sure you know openings here are a commodity. Would *you* like to consider the cottage? After all, the application is in your name."

"No, no, you can remove me from your list. I plan to die right here in my house." Theo glanced around the room. His plant specimens were spread across one corner of the dining room table, and Penelope's art supplies across the other.

This time, the lady didn't laugh. "Well, take some time and think about it. We don't need an answer until the end of May. I believe you would be very happy here."

What could she possibly know about his happiness?

She provided a return phone number, which he didn't bother to write down. He would *never* move. He had painted every wall, re-caulked around every bathroom tile, buried crocus bulbs on cold autumn days; his roots in this place had grown as deep as those of his beloved oak tree. The mere thought of moving brought a cold prickle to his skin.

After the call ended, Theo wandered into the kitchen, feeling numbed by the bewildering conversation. Getting a call about something Annie had done so long ago was almost like hearing from her. But the idea of it was jarring; the application, the waitlist, all of it. Never once had they discussed moving to Sequoyah Trail and certainly not in '97, when battling her cancer had been their only focus.

He heard Penelope laughing in the backyard, and Alice barking. Were dogs even allowed at Sequoyah Trail? He didn't subscribe to a belief in predestined occurrences, yet recognized that the timing would have been ideal if he *had* wanted to sell his home. Fayetteville repeatedly made the national list of best places to live, and houses in the historic district, like his, often sold within hours, usually above the asking price. If he didn't know better, he might have thought the unexpected call was a nudge from Annie.

He opened the refrigerator and stared inside.

Annie had been insightful and forward-thinking, someone who could visualize things into being. Any social activities they enjoyed or trips they had taken had been because of her planning. To imagine Annie adding his name to the Village waitlist, knowing he would be a seventy-year-old widower with no family by the time his name reached the top, was mindboggling. But, it was exactly like something she might have done; her way to gift him an option when he might need one, or maybe simply a way to make him contemplate change, to shake him out of a rut.

He closed the refrigerator without getting anything to eat.

Theo preferred living inside the comfortable rut of routine.

His cell phone vibrated in his shirt pocket, and when he saw *Wash Reg* on the screen, his eyes sought out Penelope in the backyard. His first thought was that finally, after two long weeks, Ivy was being released from the hospital. He would hang the glittery welcome home banner Penelope had made days earlier, and by nightfall, Ivy would be home. *Home?* Ivy could stay in his other spare bedroom until she fully recovered. It was a quiet room, at the end of the hallway, one that had become a convenient place to store items he planned to donate yet never had—old textbooks, Annie's sewing machine, and Christmas decorations used once upon a time. There was a queen-sized bed in there. He would clear out the space and ask Penelope to help him put fresh sheets on the bed.

He answered the phone. While Penelope giggled and chased Alice in the backyard, he reeled, toppled by a flood of words he couldn't quite grasp. O*xygen saturation. Air sacs. S*i*lent hypoxia.* Such an unexpected update may as well have been delivered in a foreign language. Theo had been wrong about numerous things in his life, but to be so exceptionally wrong in this instance...he felt like he was grappling with a cruel joke.

"...*inflammatory cells* and *excess fluid*...and so there's the concern of—"

"Whoa, whoa, WHOA! Slow down, please." He felt bad for shouting but he had to interrupt the flow of information and reset his muddled mind.

The line went quiet. Theo hoped the doctor had hung up on him. He hoped the call had been meant for someone else.

"Mr. Gruene? Did I lose you?" The doctor was still on the line.

"Yes. No. I'm here. Sorry, it's a lot to take in."

"Understandable," he said kindly, his voice sounding altogether different. The doctor started from the beginning, speaking slowly and more clearly, giving Theo time to scribble a few words on the back of his electric bill. Still, it was all too much.

"Ms. Palmer began suffering from severe breathing difficulties early this morning. With a rise in arterial carbon dioxide and a fall in her blood pH, mechanical ventilation is helping to normalize the flow of oxygen."

"In other words, she's on life support?"

"Ventilation is a type of support, yes. Think of it as the best way to help her breathe while her body fights the virus."

Theo was struggling to believe this news. He and Penelope had just spoken to Ivy the night before. Her voice had been clear, and when Penelope had described their hike at Devil's Den two days earlier, she'd asked questions and sounded fully engaged.

"She's back in the ICU and has likely suffered mild lung damage," he continued. "And while the ventilator won't heal her lungs, it will help push oxygen further into them. It's the best treatment protocol for her." Theo thought the doctor sounded hopeful. But perhaps that was just his wishful thinking. When the call ended, Theo dropped his iPhone on the counter, looking at it in horror, as though it was responsible for the news it had relayed.

Penelope spotted him standing at the kitchen window and waved. Theo waved back numbly and thought he might be sick. It was almost four o'clock. At four o'clock they usually took Alice for a long afternoon walk, and while they walked, they began planning what they might make for supper. He couldn't continue on with their schedule and pretend everything was normal. But, how on earth would he explain a ventilator to Penelope?

Theo was still trying to process the news of Ivy's deteriorated health when his phone rang again. He had never given much credence to the idea that good or bad news came in threes, but the third call of the day sent him to his knees.

Winn had *died* of coronavirus.

"MR. THEO? ARE YOU OKAY? Your face is as pale as a slice of white bread."

Theo heard the buzz of Penelope's voice but couldn't form any words in response. Alice was lapping water from her bowl, the sloshing noise magnified strangely. He had no idea how much time had passed since Winn's wife had called. *Ten minutes? Two hours?*

How could such a thing be true?

Theo's mind told him it couldn't be true, but he knew in his bones it was. Julie's sobbing had been deep and boundless, and when she finally choked out the two ragged words, "Winn's gone," it had taken Theo a moment to equate *gone* to *dead*. His mind had snagged on images of Winn gone to Whole Foods for his favorite dark chocolate sea salt caramels, which he purchased in bulk. Or gone fly fishing on the White River, a relatively new hobby for him. Or he could have gone off the deep end, falling into a Vietnam flashback only to become trapped there.

But no.

Julie was typically unruffled and even-keeled, and when she had choked out those two words, Theo couldn't immediately process what she was really saying. When his mind had finally started working again, he knew his only real friend in the world had died.

"Mr. Theo? *Hel-loooo?* You're scaring me."

Penelope's voice drifted to him from a dark, distant place. Her palms were against his face, and although he sensed the touch of her warm fingertips, still he saw nothing. Said nothing. Heard the truth repeating like gunfire... *GONE—GONE—GONE!* An invisible line connected life and death. A faint pencil mark. The sun vanishing below the horizon. Here and then no more. His mother and father. Michael. Annie. And now, Winn? How many times must he suffer the death of others before his own?

"Winn's dead," he said plainly, as there was no other way to say it. A throaty sob churned from deep inside and hot tears brimmed his eyes. "I need to be alone." Stone-faced and blurry-eyed, he staggered to the pantry, grabbed a bottle of scotch from the liquor shelf, and taking it outside, sank onto the ground beneath the white oak. He barely noticed Penelope watching him from the back deck as he leaned against the bench and began swigging the amber liquid straight from the bottle. Caring had brought nothing but devastation, so what was the point of it?

THE SHADOW OF THEO'S hunched body grew longer beneath the oak tree as the sun sank lower in the sky. Any relief to be found in a bottle of scotch would come only as his body numbed and his world blurred. Just before dusk, a smudge of bare toes appeared inside his murky shadow. A slight sound entered his ear canal and vibrated his eardrum.

He took another drink from the bottle but no longer tasted it.

Again, the voice. Like the incessant buzz of a mosquito. His mushy mind registered a few words.

"I know...went upstairs to my room...two weeks now...think I should go—"

On some level, Theo remembered his responsibility to Penelope—he was a teacher. *Her* teacher. But his cognitive state was compromised, his thinking illogical. Her presence barely registered. "Just talked to him last Monday." The whiskey had flooded his bloodstream. Theo was collapsing back into the broken person he had worked so hard not to be. Through barely open eyes he imagined the solar system spinning lazily above his classroom—Jupiter with its rings, red-tinged

Mars, and lovely Venus, her pale face obscured by a wisp of clouds. Inhaling, the air seemed thick with chalk dust. He heard the loud punch of a staple gun, stars exploding in the sky.

"I can stay in my—"

"Leavemealone." *Not her parent.* Never *a parent.*

Penelope backed away from him, taking small steps at first and then turning and running.

Grief smothered Theo. Liquor anesthetized pain but magnified every recollection. At one point, he thought he heard his mother crying out to him. *Theo!*

Soon after, he heard nothing at all.

Sixteen

Time passed in the deadened way it does for the unconscious, and when Theo eventually stirred, bright morning light pricked his barely-opened eyes. For a fraction of a second, Theo had no idea why he was lying prone in his backyard, damp and cold thoroughly permeating his limbs, while a male cardinal scrutinized him from its perch on the lowermost branch of the oak tree.

But the truth was a persistent, heavy thing. Winn was dead. Ivy might be.

Theo gulped air into his lungs and tasted stale whiskey. An empty bottle of scotch lay toppled beside the bench; what he hadn't poured down his throat had spilled onto the grass. The afghan from his couch lay over his stiff body, stretched to his shoulders. Alice lay curled nearby. Theo shoved the afghan aside with a thrust of his leaden arm and realized Penelope's green raincoat was tucked around his chest and stomach. As if his heart wasn't already shattered, knowing that Penelope had covered him with her cherished raincoat threatened to push him completely over the edge. Or had he already gone over?

How could he have done what he'd done? Theo tried to blame his abhorrent behavior on extenuating circumstances, circumstances that would have driven anyone to behave recklessly—learning that his best friend just died, only moments after hearing Ivy was on a ventilator; it had all been too much! But the path of blame led right back to him. There was *no* excuse for leaving Penelope to fend for herself. An eight-year-old girl! Where was she? And how had Ivy fared since the doctor's call? The self-loathing he felt was as intense as the bright morning sun dazzling his eyes. A black hole had swallowed Theo's night, and now, in the light of morning, panic and guilt smothered him.

"Penelope!" Theo's voice was a dry croak. The effort required to even roll over almost brought the contents of his roiling stomach up. He focused on a single dandelion to ease the spinning. Theo had not tied one on so completely since Annie's death, and during that horrendous time, Winn had helped him. Now, he had no one.

Using the bench for support, Theo slowly raised his stiff body. Alice bounded to her feet and began whining and turning in a tight circle, celebrating his survival. Typically, the lush green of Theo's backyard would remind him of new life, but not that morning; *that morning,* his foolishness was on full display to every blade of grass, every plucky flower. As Alice herded him to the back deck, playfully tugging at the afghan and raincoat he carried in his shaky arms, death and devastation walked with him.

The kitchen lights glared. Had they been on all night? Just as he flipped the switch off, familiar voices drifted from the dining room. Penelope's lilting voice. Nita's firm and steady response to her. Hearing them brought immediate relief, but embarrassment rooted him to the floor. What would he say to them? He dropped the afghan and raincoat on a kitchen chair, wishing he could disappear through the floorboards.

"He's awake!" Penelope rushed into the kitchen but abruptly stopped when she saw him. "Oh, you don't look so good." She turned back toward the dining room and dramatically repeated her announcement. "He doesn't look so good."

Nita appeared, wearing yoga pants and a flowy black top, her feet bare on his pine floor. She was holding a coffee mug he'd never seen before.

Theo cleared the gravel from his voice. "Good morning." His voice echoed in his head, mockingly. *Good morning?* Mourning was the more fitting word. Mourning the loss of his friend. Mourning the loss of his good sense. "What time is it? I don't know where I left my phone."

Penelope and Nita stared at him, seemingly blinking in unison. Theo's head throbbed and his throat felt raw. He took in the kitchen as though he'd never been there before. Wet blueberries draining in a colander. A glass mixing bowl and a bag of flour. An open carton of eggs, the top of each stamped with the red Eggland's Best logo. He thought he was going to be sick, and for a long, quiet moment, concentrated on not vomiting.

Penelope was the first to speak. "It's almost breakfast time. Ms. Nita is about to make blueberry pancakes for me and bacon for you. Scrambled eggs, too, if you can stomach them." Penelope's eyes dropped to his midsection, and she grimaced like she could see straight through to his churning gut.

Heat flushed his face. There was so much he should be saying, but his tongue was fat and thick and incapable of delivering more than a few stunted words.

Nita reached into the utensil drawer, pulled out a wire whisk, and pointed it at him. "Can you eat something?" Her words were plain, but laced with concern. And in that split second, he saw Nita caring for her dying husband. Or making breakfast for her granddaughter when she came to visit.

"Not yet, I don't think." Sour acid rushed to his throat. He swallowed hard, wincing at the taste in his mouth.

"You know, Mr. Theo, you should take better care of yourself. If your body is a temple, like the apostle Paul said, then your temple is filled with poison this morning."

Theo nodded. The entire room swayed. He pressed his fingertips to his aching brow and leaned against the kitchen countertop for balance. "I know. I'm sorry." *Sorry. Mortified. Humiliated.* He would give anything for a do-over.

Nita opened a cabinet, separated a skillet from the other pots it was nestled with, and made a clanging sound that rattled his teeth. "I'll make some coffee, if that sounds good. Or maybe a cola to settle your stomach? Or toast? Toast is always good."

So many words.

"I'm very sorry about Mr. Winn," Penelope said.

"It's a horrible thing, Theo. Just unbelievable." Nita shook her head but her voice sounded detached. Angry, probably. He didn't blame her.

"I still can't believe it," he said and rubbed a hand over his achy forehead.

Nita cracked an egg against the rim of the mixing bowl and its slippery contents dumped in. Theo's stomach turned. He couldn't quite connect the dots of the past twenty-four hours and wondered if the scene playing out in his kitchen was a psychotic episode. "Nita…um…" He cleared his voice. "Have you been here all night?"

"Of course she has!" Penelope interjected loudly.

Theo winced, feeling the full weight of his negligent behavior. He had been a fool last night, allowing himself to fall back into the old habits that had consumed him after the death of his family. That had been prescription drugs, and this had been alcohol, but did it really matter what substance he used? Abdicating his responsibilities and leaving Penelope to fend for herself was inexcusable! Thank goodness she was a resourceful kid.

"I went to her house last night and knocked on the door and told her you were acting extremely recklessly, drinking whiskey straight from the bottle, and I thought you were going to die right outside underneath your thinking tree. Ms. Nita rushed over to see about you, and sure enough, she said you were drunker than Cooter Brown. We both tried to get you to come inside, but you were jabbering nonsense. We almost called 9-1-1, but after you puked in the grass, which was completely disgusting by the way, Ms. Nita said you probably just needed to sleep it off. We covered you up, and Alice kept watch. I don't know who Cooter Brown is, but I sure hope I never meet him."

"Here, drink this." Nita offered him a glass of water.

One long gulp eased his nausea. He thought he might actually live if he took a shower.

It was then Theo noticed all his childhood toys spread out on his dining room table. He stepped closer and saw the pouch of marbles, the army men lined up in formation, the harmonica.

"I've been showing Ms. Nita your toys. I hope that's okay." Penelope exchanged glances with Nita. They seemed to be sharing some kind of secret, and he strongly suspected he was the subject of it.

Theo caught a glimpse of himself in the mirror over the buffet. A smear of dirt marked his face, his grass-matted hair stood in all directions, and puffy purple circles rimmed his eyes. He wasn't in any condition to argue, or question anything, and he sure didn't deserve compassion from Nita or Penelope. "I think those army men attacked me in the night," he said, before climbing the impossibly steep staircase and surrendering to a long, steamy shower.

THEO WIPED AT THE FOGGY bathroom mirror until his reflection came into focus. His eyes were bloodshot, and his face a bit puffy, but overall, he looked the same as he had yesterday morning. He found this oddly disappointing. Somehow he expected his outward appearance to reflect his internal agony. He wished he could crawl back into bed and sleep off his hangover. But he couldn't. He would go downstairs and get on with the conversation he had put off for too long. Apologizing for his behavior last night would not be the half of it. Explaining Ivy's worsened condition to Penelope was what he most dreaded doing.

He found Penelope and Nita sitting at the kitchen table with a pad of paper between them. "Yay! You're still alive." Penelope dropped the pen onto the paper. He realized they were playing a game of Hangman.

Even his face hurt when he smiled. "Barely." He pulled out a chair and slowly lowered himself into it, his leg pain flaring. Breakfast was over, but the kitchen still smelled cloyingly of warm maple syrup.

"There's fresh coffee if you can stomach it. Shall I make you some toast?"

Nita's benevolence only underscored his remorse. "Toast sounds good, but I can make it," he said, although, really, he wasn't sure he could. Standing again seemed impossible.

"Not sure I believe that," Nita said reproachfully, as she quickly sprang into action, pouring him a cup of coffee and popping bread into the toaster.

"You look lots better. Do you feel better? When you came inside, we thought you looked like one of those zombies from *The Walking Dead*, didn't we, Ms. Nita?"

"I felt like the walking dead. Still do, if I'm being honest." He took a tentative sip of coffee. It tasted good, so he took another sip. In his peripheral vision he could see Nita scurrying around, loading dirty dishes into the dishwasher, opening and closing the refrigerator, returning the syrup to the pantry. His head spun. He looked down at the table, focusing on the pad of paper. Half of the word had been solved, and half of the man had been drawn. "Who's winning?"

Penelope shrugged. "It's hard to say. Until the last stroke of the pen is made, it could go either way. I feel sorry for the guy, though. I don't want him to hang."

Theo wondered if they were still talking about the game.

"Can I ask you a question about Mr. Winn?"

The earnestness in her eyes was almost more than he could bear. Theo didn't want to talk about Winn—he still couldn't believe he was really gone—but after being so irresponsible the night before, the least he could do was be there for Penelope. "Of course."

"How did he die, exactly? I mean, I know he died from the virus, but how does the virus actually kill someone?"

Theo suspected she was paralleling Winn's illness and her mother's. This would make what he had to say even more difficult. "I don't know any of the details, but I'm sure each case is different. I think the age and overall health of the patient come into play."

She slowly nodded. "I guess that makes sense. Mr. Winn probably didn't have enough antioxidants in his diet."

"Probably not."

Nita set a plate of toast in front of him and scooted the butter dish within his reach. "My husband could never stomach any dairy when he was nauseous, but you might want some." She handed him a napkin. "I think I'll head home now, unless you need something else."

He still couldn't tell if Nita was angry, but it made no difference in what he needed to say. He swallowed a bite of dry toast. "Please, stop being so nice to me, Nita. You, too, Penelope. After the stunt I pulled last night...well, I don't deserve any compassion from either of you. But I need to say some things, and if you could stay a little longer, Nita, I would appreciate it."

Nita returned to the chair across from him, clasped her hands together, and rested them on the table. Exhaustion was etched on her face.

"I owe you both a huge apology. And I hope you can forgive me." He looked directly at Penelope. "I told your mother I would take care of you, but then last night, I did just the opposite. I was very reckless, inexcusably so."

Penelope's eyes began to tear, and he felt even worse.

"Nita, thank you for stepping in. For staying all night with Penelope." His own eyes began to sting.

Penelope lightly patted him on the arm. Her touch was reassuring.

Nita dropped her hands into her lap. "Theo, you've been traumatized. Not only did you lose your closest friend, but it happened quickly, without any warning or time to prepare. I'm sure it will take a very long time to process. I can't speak for Penelope, but I appreciate and accept your apology. But drinking like that…well, maybe we should talk about that later." She glanced at Penelope, and he realized she wanted to speak privately.

"Sure. Of course."

"No way! We're all in this together." Penelope jumped to her feet. "I'm not a baby."

Nita didn't react to Penelope's outburst; she sat quietly, her face expressionless. Theo realized it was his move. He thought of Ivy, now on a ventilator at Washington Regional, and desperately hoped her condition had improved during the night. "The thing is, I suspect Ms. Nita wants to lay into me about my behavior last night, which I absolutely deserve. She wanted to talk privately about it, not because she thinks you're a baby—neither of us has ever thought that—but because she doesn't want you to worry any more than you already are. I was out of control last night, and even though I feel terrible about it today, I still need to take responsibility for my actions. I'm sorry to you, Ms. Nita, and myself."

Penelope nodded and sat back down. "It's okay. Everyone makes mistakes. I forgave you earlier, when you came inside looking like a zombie."

He pressed his palms flat against the table to keep them from trembling. "Thank you for that, Penelope. But I have something else to tell you too. Something about your mom."

Penelope looked directly at him, blinked slowly, and chewed on her bottom lip. "What? What's happened?"

"A doctor from the hospital called yesterday. Your mom was needing a little extra help with her breathing, and so, she's okay, she's just getting—"

"She's on a ventilator?" The color in Penelope's face drained away and tears welled up in her eyes. "Everyone on ventilators dies!"

Nita's eyes had widened.

Theo remembered this was news to her too. "No, no, that's not true. It's helping your mom get better." Theo knew he was in over his head and tried to remember exactly what the doctor had told him. "Think of it as a tool that helps her breathe so her body can heal faster."

Penelope covered her ears with her hands. "Please don't say another word, Mr. Theo. I don't want all this negativity in my brain. My mother has to be okay. She just has to."

Theo understood the need to shut out bad news. But after trying to do that very thing for years, he had learned a valuable lesson: without facing the truth, there could be no real solace. He reached for her hand, gently pulled it away from her face, and lightly squeezed it. "Kiddo, I really believe your mom will be okay. We'll call the hospital and get an update any time you want. Right now, even."

She nodded.

"What you said before is true, you know."

"What did I say?"

"That we're all in this together."

"Oh. I guess I did say that. But coming from you, it sounds a little cheesy." She grinned through her tears, laced her fingers through his, and gripped tightly.

"Maybe so, but that's okay." Theo had been expecting Penelope to pepper him with questions and completely break down, like she had when her mother was first admitted to the hospital. Now, her composure worried him as much as his initial concern over telling her the news. Maybe even more. "Will you promise to come to me if you have questions? Or if you're afraid?"

Nita had become very quiet, but she quickly added, "Or, me too. You can call me anytime, honey."

Penelope nodded slowly and let go of his hand. "I'll try."

Seventeen

Theo dressed in dark gray slacks and a maroon and navy plaid shirt. After fumbling for a while with a tie he found hanging in the back of his closet, he gave up. His fingers couldn't seem to tie a proper knot. The service was to be casual anyway.

"Just come as you are. That's what Winn would want," Julie had said, her voice as hollow as a reed. No, Winn wouldn't want that, he'd thought. Winn would rather go to Hugo's for a cheeseburger. He'd rather be watching the Razorbacks play baseball or playing checkers on the front porch. He most certainly wouldn't want to be the guest of honor at his own funeral.

Theo moved through the motions of his morning in a fog. Nothing much mattered, certainly not his sartorial choices. Since learning of Winn's death ten days ago, he had tried to go about his days pretending all was well, that the news of his death had been nothing more than misinformation, but debilitating swaths of darkness would hit him unannounced, as though the pause button in his mind had been pressed, and he could do nothing but succumb for a while.

It was the end of April now, and coronavirus had spread across the globe, disrupting lives and altering routines. Even time-honored traditions like burying the dead had to be changed. Winn deserved a proper funeral, but his service would be limited to a few words spoken at Veterans Memorial Park at Lake Fayetteville to just a handful of mask-wearing friends. Theo knew that Julie planned to sprinkle Winn's ashes someplace special. "I haven't decided where yet," she'd said. Theo understood her uncertainty, recalling his indecisiveness after Annie's death. For the longest time, even the most straightforward decisions had stacked up before him like insurmountable obstacles.

"Mr. Theo, can I go with you?" Penelope appeared in his bedroom doorway wearing a white and pink polka dot skirt he'd never seen, with her lime green raincoat draped over one arm. A red plastic headband held back her curls, framing her face and accentuating her wide, pleading eyes.

From the moment he'd met her, Penelope had been like a fledgling, doing her level best to understand and fit into the world, often trying too hard to be part of something that wasn't hers. The past ten days had been especially hard for Theo to navigate. Ivy's condition was the same; she was still on a ventilator. Staying positive was becoming more and more difficult. And now, his resolve nearly cracked. Penelope had done her best to clean up and dress up, that was obvious to him.

"Penelope, I'd like you to stay here." He needed quiet on the drive to the service. Listening to her chatter on about this or that would be more than he could bear.

"Why?"

"Because this is a private funeral and attendees are limited. You never even met Winn."

"Can I at least ride with you? I never get to go anywhere because of stupid Covid." It was a miserable statement of truth.

"Wouldn't you rather stay with Alice? I've already asked Ms. Nita to come over and be with you while I'm gone."

Penelope's expression rearranged itself from piteous to incredulous. "Mr. Theo, how many times do I have to remind you that I'm not an infant. I am plenty capable of taking care of myself. It's just that I would like to support you in your time of great need. We're family now, and that's what family does."

But we aren't family.

The girl was getting too attached.

"Please, Mr. Theo, can I? I'll take my book and read the whole time. You won't know I'm there."

Theo sighed and ultimately gave in. Since Winn's death, his energy level seemed to drain quickly, and with it, his willingness to continue explaining himself to Penelope. He messaged Nita and let her know she wouldn't be needed that afternoon after all.

True to her word, Penelope was mostly quiet on the first part of their drive across town. Theo's mind was a blank. Think nothing, and there's no way to remember anything.

"Mr. Theo, when I said I would be quiet, I had my fingers crossed. There's something serious I need to discuss with you. I understand this might not be the best time, but I've been distracted the past few days, and you've not been very approachable. Not that I blame you. But would now be an okay time to talk about my future?"

It took a moment for Penelope's voice to register with Theo, and when it did, a flash of frustration hit him. *She had promised to be quiet!* He inhaled, squeezed the steering wheel, and waited a few seconds to speak. "That's quite the topic for a short drive across town."

She shrugged.

"Go ahead."

"What I need to know is...what's going to happen to me if my mom dies?"

Theo swallowed hard. For a moment he couldn't think what to say. This was not a conversation he could have while driving to his best friend's funeral. Finally, trying to sound unruffled, he said, "Penelope, that's not something we need to worry about."

"But I *am* worried." Her voice was small.

"Well, don't be."

"You can't tell me how to feel. *I* can't even tell me how to feel. Emotion is a naturally occurring thing." Side-eyeing him she added, "For me, anyway."

As they neared the park where Winn's service was to be held, Theo tried to think of something helpful to say. There was no way around it; despite the happenstance of their initial meeting, it was now his responsibility to put Penelope at ease. He tossed out everything he knew to be true, and started explaining that worry never helped any situation. He encouraged her to concentrate on the positives.

"Like what?" she asked. "I can't see any positives."

"Like...well, your mom is young and healthy (was she healthy?), and she's in a well-regarded hospital receiving excellent care. Odds of a full recovery are definitely in her favor." Were the odds good? Every day, the news reported an increased mortality rate for those on ventilators.

For a moment, Penelope stared straight ahead, saying nothing, twisting the hem of her skirt in her hands. Finally, she said, "It's quite reasonable to plan for the worst-case scenario. In case you've forgotten, I'm a kid totally dependent on my mother. And if something should happen to her, like *permanently* happen to her, I will have to live in an orphanage or worse. I bet you never imagined Mr. Winn Berton would die, but he did."

Her last comment cut him to the bone. How could he respond to such a thing? Winn's death had upended life as he knew it. "Penelope, I can't predict the future. No one can. But I have every reason to believe you will have a good life filled with good things."

"Why?"

"Because you are gifted and observant and sensitive to the world around you. And you have a kind heart. A kind heart is more valuable than gold." Oh, good lord, he was spewing out platitudes like an insane Pollyanna.

Penelope gazed out the window at the passing scenery. "Okay, well, I am glad you think so, but if I had a pile of real gold, I'd give it to the doctors and beg them to make my mother well. If you could spend a little time thinking over my situation, I'd be grateful. I don't want to be homeless again."

"Kiddo, we won't let that happen." Theo spoke with complete sincerity, but inside his guts lurched. He wondered if he'd just made a promise he wouldn't be able to keep.

THEO SAW JULIE, and recognized her sister, but knew none of the other handful of attendees gathered at the park. He approached, stopping to collect himself a few feet away beneath the shade of an enormous sycamore tree. He pulled at the scratchy collar of his shirt, squinting against the harsh sunlight reflecting off the distant lake. There was no denying reality anymore. Sorrow hung heavy in the late April afternoon.

Julie approached him but stopped a few feet away. "Sorry, there's a no hug rule," she said, twisting a handkerchief, her hazel eyes grief-stricken above her mask.

"I'm so sorry, Julie," he said. His voice cracked. Someone was playing "Dust in the Wind" on acoustic guitar. Theo had never much liked that song.

"I know. Me too. He loved you so much."

All Theo could do was nod and swallow the anguish swelling in his throat.

It felt odd to be there, standing in a large circle of mourners, and for a moment, it seemed absurd, like they might all start holding hands and sing "Kumbaya." He wanted to laugh, and sob, and curse. He bit his lip and stared at the enormous photo of Winn, propped on an easel like an oil painting. It looked nothing like him and captured none of his spirit. Theo wondered when it had been taken, why on earth Winn had been wearing a suit and tie.

There was a guest book splayed open on a folding table, its pages secured by small rocks from the nearby garden bed, and beside the book, a plain terra-cotta urn which he knew held Winn's remains. Theo looked at it, a whole life reduced to that, and the words kept running through his mind. *No more tomorrows. No more tomorrows.*

One by one, people took turns paying tribute in some way, speaking a few words or sharing a humorous story. Theo kept staring at the guest book, the corners of its pages fluttering in the wind. Someone read "Funeral Blues" by W. H. Auden, a poem that never failed to move Theo.

When his turn came, he worried his knees might buckle. He had prepared nothing, and could think of no fitting words for such an unbelievable situation.

Standing across the circle from him, Julie nodded, urging him to go ahead.

A cardinal called out from a nearby elm tree, and for a moment, he searched for it, his eyes needing something beautiful to focus on while his mind attempted to gather up words. "I'll start with an apology," he said. "I didn't prepare anything because I can't quite bring myself to believe he's gone. Winn deserves so much more than me standing up here rambling." With a tight-lipped smile, he scanned the faces around him without really seeing anyone. "He should be here. He would enjoy hearing all your stories and seeing everyone at this lake he loved."

Theo paused, wondering how much he should say about his very private friend. "We met in the Bronx in the early seventies, in a group therapy session, sitting in a circle, much like how we are standing here today. I wasn't someone who let many people into my orbit; I'm still not, if the truth be told. But we became buddies right off, the best of friends. Maybe because we were both screwed up and suffering from loss." He shrugged. "He was from Wisconsin, and I was from Texas, and although our backgrounds were very different, we were like brothers joined together by a force stronger than genetics. Winn's friendship is the main reason I'm still standing today. When I think of the trauma he suffered in Vietnam, well, I'll just say he was the strongest person I ever met, a real hero, who deserved so much more."

The cardinal began trilling again, and despite everything, Theo smiled. "Some people believe loved ones appear as cardinals. Of course, Winn would say that's baloney."

At this, chuckles and nods circled the group, lifting the mood a smidgen.

"I'll finish by saying thanks for everything, buddy. Rest easy." He took a deep breath, glancing upward to search for the cardinal. He didn't find him.

He felt a small poke in the small of his back. "That was really nice, Mr. Theo," Penelope whispered.

He spun around. "What are you—"

"I thought you might need my support. Sue me." She wormed her way into the circle and took his hand, swinging his arm like they were skipping along a sidewalk.

He stopped the swinging with a squeeze of his fingers and concentrated on Julie, who had begun wrapping up the service. She thanked everyone for coming and apologized there would be no repast because of Covid restrictions. People began to scatter, appearing dazed and slightly relieved, but Theo just stood there. His feet refused to move.

"Should we go, Mr. Theo?" Penelope tugged on his hand, returning him to the present, where irritation temporarily overwhelmed his sadness.

Theo spoke quietly, through gritted teeth. He was anxious to get home and didn't want to draw attention to himself by lecturing the kid in public. "Excuse me, but please explain why you couldn't wait for me like you promised? Was the truck on fire?"

"No, your truck's fine," she chirped, looping her arm inside his elbow and leading him toward the parking lot. "It was getting a little hot, though. There wasn't much breeze coming through the open windows."

"Theo, wait up. I have something for you." Julie was rushing toward him, carrying a paper sack. "I found this in Winn's closet. There's a note inside; he wanted you to have it."

The sack contained a black, rectangular box like the one his dad used for storing important documents. He thought of airplane black boxes that recorded all the flight details, conversations, and decisions. "What's in it?"

"Lots of old pictures of people I don't know; his family, I suppose, grandparents and great-grandparents, old letters he saved, and paperwork dating back to his time in Vietnam. Did you know he was awarded a Bronze Star? It's in there too, quietly hidden away." Her eyes were wet with tears.

"I had no idea." He took the sack from her, wondering if Julie regretted their decision to remain childless. Of course, someday there would be no one to take his family mementos either. He pushed away the depressing thought.

"It means so much that you came today. Thank you for saying what you said." She squeezed his forearm lightly and then jerked back. "Sorry. I forget these are non-contact days."

BACK HOME, Theo considered pouring himself a beer but opted for a glass of iced tea instead. His recent bender still weighed heavily on him. He had apologized several times to Nita and Penelope, and they had graciously accepted his apology, but still, he had promised them—and himself—to lay off the alcohol for a while.

Theo took the box to the dining room table, where the light was good. He saw the note as soon as he opened the lid. Seeing Winn's handwriting jolted him, but reading his words somehow brought peace.

If something happens to me, give this box to my brother, Theo Gruene. He saved my life over and over again. W.

"Ooh, are you looking in the mysterious box?" Penelope peered over his shoulder, her words prickling his ear. "Can I see, or would you rather be alone?"

If she hadn't asked so nicely, he would have sent her off to read, or play with Alice, but she had been quiet and respectful on the drive home, and genuinely concerned over his welfare; he let her join him.

The Bronze Star was encased in plastic. They must have logged thousands of hours talking through the years, but Winn had never mentioned being awarded such a high honor. It represented all he had witnessed, sacrificed, and suffered. Theo removed the medal from its plastic sleeve and held it in his palm. Winn had survived one of the worst assignments in Vietnam, only to be taken by a virus. It was so unfair.

"Can I look at that medal?"

It was a vital history lesson, after all. They inspected it together, studying the small bronze star and its attached ribbon, red with a single vertical blue stripe down the middle, edged in white. On the back, were the words, HEROIC OR MERITORIOUS ACHIEVEMENT.

Penelope read them aloud. "What did Mr. Winn do to get this?"

"I don't know, but every soldier who fought in Vietnam probably deserved one."

"Is it valuable? Like a gold bar?"

"It's valuable in its rarity."

She nodded. "You should keep it someplace safe."

Theo began sifting through some of the old photographs in the box. Even though the people and their stories had long been forgotten, each photo provided a compelling glimpse into the past. He studied a picture of a couple with a child, and thought the man resembled Winn.

"Look at this picture, Mr. Theo." She showed him a photograph of a large family standing in front of a barn. "Not a single person is smiling. I'm glad I didn't live back then. People today are way happier."

But were they? He didn't believe so. "Today we expect people to smile in photographs, even if they don't feel like it. I think the custom was just different back then."

"Well, it was a weird custom."

They put the stack of photos aside and continued looking through the box. There was a yellowed bookmark with the Lord's Prayer, and a smashed coin imprinted with the faint outline of a fish and the words *New York Aquarium*. He handed the coin to Penelope, remembering getting a similar one from Six Flags Over Texas. His family had gone there one summer not long after it opened. It had been a rare family weekend outing, he and his brother almost unable to sit still in the back of his dad's Plymouth, his mother trying to find good music on the radio, his dad smoking Pall Malls and smashing the butts in the dashboard ashtray.

Penelope returned the coin to the box and plucked a marble from a corner. "Gosh, does every old man keep a box of old marbles and things?" She held it toward the kitchen window, and the afternoon light made the center swirl glow.

"I guess so," Theo said, chuckling. He had no idea what significance the marble might have had to Winn.

Penelope placed the marble beside the one in the potted plant. "Now they can be marble friends. Just like you and Winn were friends."

"I like the thought of that." He removed the only things left in the box: a mailer stuffed with yellowed newspaper clippings; several tightly-folded squares of lined notebook paper, the type a student might pass to a friend in the school hallway; and a few letters that had been mailed to Winn when he lived in New York.

"Can we cook a pizza, Mr. Theo? I'm starving and this is sort of boring now."

Theo was hungry too. The funeral, as well as the time they had spent looking through Winn's things, had left him drained. "Sure thing, kiddo." He returned the mailer to the box without looking through it, along with the with the family photographs, bookmark, and souvenir coin from the aquarium.

LATER THAT EVENING, Julie called to thank him for attending.

"I was really dreading it, Julie, but it was a nice gathering. So much better than a serious church funeral or a graveside service."

"He wouldn't have wanted one of those, Covid or not," she said.

They briefly discussed Winn's Bronze Star. It turned out that Julie hadn't known about it either.

"He never said much to me about his tour in Vietnam, only that he was a sapper; that's the term he used. Until the day he died, he had frequent nightmares about tunneling underground and not being able to breathe. You think you know someone, especially after twenty-five years of marriage, but I guess you never really do," she said. "By the way, the little friend you brought today, was she the neighbor girl Winn mentioned to me?"

"Oh yeah, Penelope. Now, there's a story for you." He lowered his voice, even though Penelope was upstairs and he was relatively confident she couldn't hear him, and explained all that had happened. "After almost two months, it actually has begun to feel like the kid has always been around. I've become her caretaker."

"She doesn't have other family?"

"Nope. From what I've pieced together, her father died several years ago. Ivy is a single mom with no one to depend on."

"Wow. What's going to happen if, you know..."

"No idea."

"Okay...."

Julie was a retired attorney, and although her specialty had been property law, Theo suspected she was putting on her legal hat. He was right.

"I know you didn't ask me for advice, but I can't not ask—do you have a power of attorney or medical consent form? The child is a minor."

"No, I have nothing like that. I was just helping Ivy during the day, like a babysitter. Then, she became sick at work one night and was sent to Washington Regional. Now, here we are. What was I supposed to do?"

"Honestly, Theo, you need to be careful. You've opened yourself up to liability. What if something happens to Penelope on your watch? Like an injury or sickness?"

"I can't just send her back to her apartment to live alone."

"You know as well as I do—it's really a situation for Child Protective Services."

"She's only eight years old."

"That's exactly my point, Theo."

Eighteen

Theo started in the side garden as soon as the sun provided enough light. Turning the compacted dirt took little concentration, but required more physical effort than he'd expected. It had been some time since he'd manned a hoe. Muscles in his shoulders ached from the repetitive movement, and he knew that lifting his arms would be a challenge by sundown. *Use it or lose it.* He hated how those clichéd sayings often proved true.

Summer had been his favorite season as a kid. With the school year behind them, he and his brother would zip through their chores and then spend the day playing baseball, riding their bikes, or swimming at Lake Colorado City whenever they could hitch a ride there on a passing farmer's truck. Now, spring was his favorite time of year. He appreciated the morning's fresh air cooling his bare ears, and then, later in the day, the afternoon sunshine was balmy—not oppressive, like it could become in July and August.

It had been two weeks since Julie's fateful phone call, and the truth of it was that Theo had spent very little time with Penelope. He fed her, answered her questions, but mostly he had just left her to write in her journal and read whatever she fancied from his personal library. Most nights after dinner, he fell asleep on the couch, the newspaper spread over his belly. He was buried alive in loss, moving through the days and nights as though the ground beneath his feet might give way at any moment. For the third time in Theo's life, a tornado of grief had touched down on a perfectly calm day, upending everything. Theo thrust the hoe into the soil again, feeling his shoulder scream. He asked life for very little, but perhaps that was his problem. Maybe he needed to demand more; clarify his expectations to the universe. Turning over another clump of compacted soil, Theo began talking to the clouds drifting overhead. "You win. I give up. Either bother someone else, or strike me dead in this garden plot. I'm done playing the 'woe is me' game." As soon as the words passed through his lips, a sense of calm determination came to him, an understanding as clear as the chirping of the chickadee watching from the fencepost. To grieve over the loss of his loved ones was one thing; to believe he was a victim of their deaths was ludicrous. He had no control, influence, or even one speck of power over such things.

Theo continued moving the sharp blade of the hoe through the rectangular patch of ground and thought of Annie. They had grown a vegetable garden every year in this very spot, canning so many jars of salsa, tomato juice, and spicy pickles that their pantry shelves would overflow by fall. He paused, propped his arm against the handle, and listened. It was the first day of May. *May Day, and the chirping birds are celebrating.* He heard the distinctive chirruping of a sparrow and the hammering of a nearby woodpecker. A city garbage truck emptied a trash bin on a street nearby, it's racket an unwelcomed disruption to the morning. Theo had forgotten to wheel his container to the curb. Forgetting trash day would have typically dismayed him, but he dismissed the oversight as a sign of his recent distraction. Another trash day would come soon enough. Theo got back to work, still listening to the birds and thinking about Annie. She had been gone almost twenty years, but being there in the side garden, turning over the soil they had both worked together, made her seem near. And that put him in better spirits. He would lose no more time to personal anguish.

"There you are. I couldn't find you." Penelope's voice nudged him back to the present. She'd begun sleeping late, until at least ten, so he'd expected to have an hour or two alone to prepare the bed for planting. She squatted to pick up a discarded clump of hairy bittercress. "Whatcha doing?"

Reclaiming my life. Burying my pain. Starting over. "Hoeing this bed," he said. He'd finally found a good rhythm with the hoe, which he didn't want to lose, so he continued his weed chopping and dirt turning.

"Are you planning to bury something back here? I saw this movie once where—"

"Yes, that's exactly what I'm going to do. And you're going to help me."

"Oh, no, Mr. Theo. I like you a whole lot, but I can't be a party to—"

"We're going to bury seeds. It's called gardening. How's that sound?" Theo loosened another clump of dry soil and tried to remember when northwest Arkansas had experienced its last good rainfall.

"*Ohhh*...I get it." A grin brightened her face. "You had me worried there for a minute." Penelope continued chattering, once again spinning a story worthy of shelf space at the public library. "So, we're going to grow our own food in case this pandemic turns out to be biblical? You know, Mr. Theo, you might be right in your assumption because all signs point to the end of time. Have you thought about storing water too? Because when the power grid goes down and—"

"Penelope, this isn't about zombies or sentient robots or Russians who poison our food supply. There's nothing apocalyptic happening here." He straightened his body and looked at the sky overhead. In the distance, he heard the comforting lullaby of a train. He inhaled a lungful of early spring air, smelling crumbled earth and wild carrots, leaf litter slowly decaying to give nutrients to new life. "Here's the deal. I promised your mother I would teach you something while you're my responsibility, and I'm afraid I've not done a very good job of that in the last two weeks. The thing I know best is plants. Combine that with our current situation of quarantining in place, and growing a few vegetables seems like a practical lesson plan. Besides, it's high time I weeded this area behind the garage."

All the while he had been explaining his plan, Penelope had been walking along the railroad ties that marked the edge of the garden bed. Slowly, she moved one foot in front of the other, her arms floating to the side, carrying herself as though she were balancing a dictionary on her head. "Are you watching me? I'm a gymnast warming up for the balance beam. Maybe I'll be in the Olympics when I'm older. I wonder if there has ever been an Olympic athlete who is also a mezzo-soprano? What do you think?"

"I think you have a high opinion of your ability to walk a plank and sing opera. Did you hear anything I said?" Theo propped the hoe against the back fence. He would take a coffee break and send Penelope off to read a very long book. *Crime and Punishment*, maybe.

"Every word." She stopped her balance beam walk, stood at attention, and recited verbatim in a deep voice that he supposed mimicked his own, "Here's the deal, Penelope. I promised your mother I would teach you something while you're my responsibility, and I'm afraid I've not done a very good job of that in the last two weeks. The thing I know best is plants. Combine that with our current situation of quarantining in place, and growing a few vegetables seems like a practical lesson plan. Besides, it's high time I weeded this area behind the garage."

Theo stared at her. "Okay then. I guess you get several points for that." It had been some time since either of them had mentioned their game of wits—in fact, he wasn't sure they were still playing— but her ability to repeat exactly what he had said was worthy of resuscitating it.

"How many?"

"Umm…three?" He pulled a number from the air.

"Thanks! I forgot the score of our game, but I'm pretty sure I'm winning," she said, resuming her balance beam stroll around the perimeter of the bed. "You know, Mr. Theo, I can do more than one thing at a time. It's called multi-tasking. And I think growing our own food is a positively brilliant idea, so count me in. I am fully committed to the project; just tell me what to do. I'm at your service." She gave him a little salute and added, "you know, Mr. Theo, you're actually quite intelligent."

"Survive life this long, and a person tends to learn a few things." As soon as he uttered the words, he wished he could take them back. Ivy had been on a ventilator for two weeks, with no real improvement. Theo couldn't remember the exact percentage, but just yesterday, PBS news had reported the mortality rate for patients on ventilators was much higher than predicted.

"I'll be right back, Mr. Theo. I need to get something."

She disappeared around the garage. He continued regretting his prior comment, a sinking feeling growing in his stomach. When she returned, she was wearing her lime green raincoat.

"I don't think—"

"I know what you're going to say, and no offense, but feel free to save your energy for something else, Mr. Theo. I know it isn't raining, and based on the lack of cloud coverage, I realize rain is not imminent."

"Then why—"

She cut him off with a sharp glance. "Not everything is meant to make sense. I'm pretty sure those are your words, by the way. But since my raincoat is obviously driving you crazy, I'll take this opportunity to explain." She resumed her walk around the railroad ties, this time stepping counterclockwise. "Last year, my mother gave me ten dollars for my birthday and said I could spend it however I wanted. Ten dollars probably means nothing to you, but we never have money to spare on frivolous things, so it was a huge deal to me. We went to Potter's House, and I walked up and down the children's clothing aisles, trying to find a raincoat and rain boots or maybe a bright-colored umbrella. I don't know if you remember last fall very well, but it rained a lot, and I was always getting soaked waiting for the school bus. Anyway, at first, I found nothing worthy of my money. Then, just as I had decided to wait and shop another day, I began looking through the adult clothing. You never know when things have been put in the wrong place. And wouldn't you know it, I discovered this raincoat in the women's section, and it still had its original tag on it! So even though it came from a place that deals in used clothes and things, I found something brand new and only paid five dollars for something that originally cost thirty dollars at the Gap." Penelope stopped walking, held her arms out, and presented Theo with the full view of the raincoat.

"Nice find," he said.

"It's big on me, but I'll grow into it and be able to wear it for a long time. So it's even more valuable than it seems at face value. Plus, it's the first new piece of clothing I remember having." She grinned.

Theo appreciated the story of the raincoat but still didn't understand why she wore it when the weather was warm and sunny. "And why exactly are you wearing it today?" He walked over to the hose, turned it on, and took a long drink.

She sighed. "You know how Harry Potter had an invisibility cloak?"

"Not really, no," he said. Everything he knew about Harry Potter had come from Penelope. Theo turned off the spigot, and the water trickled until it stopped.

Again, she sighed. "Okay, so Harry Potter got a cloak one year for Christmas. It was an anonymous present that turned out to be a significant magical artifact because it gave him the power of invisibility. When he wore it, he could sneak into hallways and rooms at Hogwarts without detection. Later, we find out the cloak had originally belonged to James, Harry's father, who was murdered by Voldemort. We also learn Albus Dumbledore was the anonymous gift-giver. You really should read the books."

"I know. I keep forgetting." He truly would check out the books soon. "But I still don't understand the reference, because I can see you. You aren't invisible."

"I know! This isn't an invisibility cloak." She spun it like a bullfighter cape. "It's my *protectability* cloak. It gives me strength and keeps me safe during battle."

Theo didn't think protectability was a word, but he kept that thought to himself. "Who are you battling?"

"The world, of course. It's crazy out there, Mr. Theo. Especially for a kid like me."

Like me? What exactly did that mean? Smart? Quirky? Small for her age? Several questions popped into Theo's mind, but when he asked her what she meant, she only said, "Oh, I'm referring to general meanness at school, you know, kids being rude about my clothes or shoes. That sort of thing."

His face began to burn at the thought of Penelope being bullied. Bullies were the lowest form of humanity.

"The truth is, Mr. Theo, I don't mix very well with other kids, but there's nothing super serious going on, like sex trafficking or anything."

"Well, I'm relieved about the lack of sex trafficking, but you shouldn't have to deal with playground bullies. Tell me who's bothering you, and I'll tie a knot in their heads right now."

They both laughed, but his dander truly was raised.

"Mr. Theo, since I told you something, maybe you could tell me something."

"That seems fair."

Once again, she began walking around the railroad ties. "Let me think…oh, I know…I'm curious if you like the name Crystal? For a lady, I mean?"

"Crystal? I don't know, why?"

"No reason other than I like to think about names. Don't you?" As she walked, her arms balanced at her side, the raincoat was almost dragging on the ground.

"No, not really."

"Well, I think it's a pretty name, and I was wondering if you know anyone with that name?"

He stared at her, bemused. "You are an interesting kid."

"We've already established that, but can you please just answer the question."

He searched his memory, but the only Crystal he could recall was from the *Dynasty* television series that had been popular when he was in graduate school. "No. I don't think so."

"Okay. I was just wondering."

"Do *you* know someone named Crystal?"

"Nope."

Interesting kid, indeed.

For the next hour, Theo put Penelope in charge of removing dandelions from the bed. She became quite proficient at the task, pushing the hand weeder beneath the tap root of each dandelion before pulling it free. While Theo dug compost from his mostly-ignored compost bin nearby, he told Penelope about the pros and cons of the weed. The roots aerated the soil, and the greens were edible and healthy, but if left in the bed, whatever vegetables they planted would have to compete with them for nutrients. This led to some compelling commentary from Penelope on mother nature and human interference. She was adamant that survival of the fittest was the natural way. "Nothing good seems to come when you fight nature."

Even with all the time he had spent with Penelope, hearing such advanced thoughts come from an eight-year-old still amazed him.

"Sometimes human interference is a good thing, though." Ivy was the perfect example. Without medical care, the mortality rate of coronavirus would no doubt be even higher than it was. But since Theo didn't want to remind Penelope of her mother's condition, he decided not to say anything more.

"Look at what happened in *Jurassic Park*. Those scientists took a bunch of dinosaur DNA and made T-Rexes and those shrewd velociraptors and terrible things happened."

"*Jurassic Park* was a fictional movie."

"But it could happen, don't you think?"

He shook his head. "No. I don't. Dinosaurs went extinct sixty-five million years ago. DNA can't survive that long."

She shrugged. "Well, you don't know everything."

"I never said I did."

After weeding, turning the soil, and enriching it with several buckets of compost, they sowed radish and carrot seeds purchased at the neighborhood garden center. When they finally finished and went inside, Penelope spent the afternoon in her bedroom, reading and writing in her journal, while he watched an ESPN rebroadcast of Nolan Ryan's seventh no-hitter. A day spent gardening and watching baseball, even a game played thirty years ago, felt good to Theo. Normal, almost.

Later, Theo made vegetable soup and cornbread for supper, along with a salad that included a few dandelion greens. They ate in the type of weary silence that came after a long day that included hard physical work.

"What do you say to an early bedtime tonight? I'm bushed, and I bet you are too." Theo spooned the last of his soup into his mouth.

"You probably need extra rest, but I plan to stay up writing. I'm really getting to a good part in my story."

"Yeah? Care to give me a hint?"

"No, you'll have to wait and read the book when it's finished. Is it okay if I don't eat all of my salad? I know there are millions of food insecure kids in Sudan and Syria, and I've been hungry many times too, but I liked these dandelion leaves better when they were attached to flowers."

Her tendency to flit between topics still caught him off guard. "Sure." While Theo didn't like to waste food, he didn't subscribe to his grandmother's clean plate rule either.

"I am glad to know dandelions are edible, though." An edge of sadness crept into her tone. "If I ever live in the woods, I can eat dandelions rather than starve to death."

Her words shook Theo. He wasn't sure what to say, so he simply laughed it off. "Always glad to help."

When Theo collapsed into bed, he was more tired than he'd been in some time. His face was warm with sunburn, and his eyelids were so heavy he couldn't manage even a few minutes of bedtime reading. He slept a sound, heavy sleep, until sobs woke him in the dead of night.

"Penelope?" He jerked upright and hobbled down the hallway to her bedroom, the blood moving slowly to his tired legs. She was sitting against the headboard, her covers all twisted. Had she been thrashing about? "What's wrong? What is it?"

"I need my mommy. I need to *see* her."

Still half asleep, Theo couldn't think clearly and wasn't sure what to do. Awkwardly, he patted the top of her head. "We'll call tomorrow and check on her. I bet she's sleeping now."

"She's been sleeping for two weeks! She's on a ventilator, Mr. Theo. That's one step from being dead!" Penelope gulped out another sob. "I had a terrible dream that we planted seeds as big as marbles and then the next day a giant weed had grown all the way into the sky. And I climbed up it, sort of like "Jack and the Beanstalk," but up at the top, in the clouds, I found my mother sitting in a swing, and she was wearing this white dress, and she had butterfly wings, and she said, in this exhausted voice, 'You can't be here because *I* shouldn't be here.' What do you think that means, Mr. Theo?"

"I think it means you are extremely tired from all that gardening we did today. When you're rested tomorrow, we'll call the hospital and check on your mom, and everything will seem much better. You'll see."

"But what if we are dreaming right now, and "Jack in the Beanstalk" *is* my reality? What then?" She dissolved into sobs again.

Penelope's pain wrenched Theo's heart. Powerless to truly help, he sat on the edge of the bed and gathered Penelope into his arms, ignoring his discomfort at such physical closeness. He was accustomed to distance, space. Theo recalled her words earlier that day—*you don't know everything*. How true that was, especially concerning the care of a young child. He held her tight and rubbed circles on her back, like his mother had always done for him when he was upset, so many decades ago. "You're okay, Penelope. I'm here now, and we're going to get through this."

She nodded against his chest and muttered, "I hope so."

He knew they would.

Nineteen

Penelope disappeared onto the front porch, having left a trail of water droplets behind her, from the kitchen floor to the entryway of his house. The watering can was heavy for her, but she insisted on carrying it anyway. "The flowers are my responsibility, so I *need* to do it, Mr. Theo!" They had planted purple petunias in pots along the front porch steps after Penelope selected them at the nursery. "These smell like grape Laffy Taffy, and that's my favorite candy!" she'd said after dropping her face into a large swath of purple blooms and breathing them in. Theo had thought Laffy Taffy was banana-flavored, but she quickly set him straight, reciting the candy's long list of available flavors off the top of her head.

Penelope continually amazed him. Even such a small task as watering flowers mattered greatly to her. Her passion seemed to bubble up from an endless source, deep within. As he watched the door close behind her, his cell phone rang. He stared at the caller's name on his screen—*Wash Reg*—but could not bring himself to press the answer button. After four weeks in the hospital, including seventeen days on a ventilator, this call would bring bad news. The worst news. Theo sensed it like he sensed storms brewing on gusty spring afternoons.

Theo's cell phone rang a second time. He couldn't avoid whoever was on the line, he knew that. He also knew Penelope would be returning to the kitchen for more water soon. Theo rushed upstairs to the privacy of his bedroom and steeled himself for the news to come. Once more, Penelope would need him to be rock solid.

He answered on the fourth ring. "Theo Gruene." He kept his voice unemotional and businesslike even while his stomach churned.

The nurse on the line released a rapid string of information into Theo's ear. Her voice was upbeat, the news so unlike what he had expected that he thought his mind was playing a trick on him.

"Can you say that again?"

Theo could hear how happy she was to be repeating good news. Ivy had received a positive evaluation. She would be removed from the ventilator later that afternoon.

"Ms. Palmer will likely remain in the ICU for a while, but after twenty-four hours of self-breathing, the doctor will assess her next steps," the nurse said. "You still won't be able to visit, because of current hospital restrictions, but she will be able to take phone calls as soon as she is moved to a room."

Relief flooded Theo. He thought he might actually weep. An exquisite sunrise had appeared after a grueling, month-long nightmare. He hurried downstairs, bursting to share the news with Penelope. They nearly collided as the kid bounded through the front door, swinging the water can, empty but for a few remaining drops that landed on the tile floor.

"Mr. Theo, look who I found!"

Behind her stood Nita in her N-95 mask, an over-filled tote bag hanging from her shoulder. "I'm here to finally give Penelope that cookie-baking lesson I promised. Can I come inside? I've not been around a single soul since I last saw you."

How odd that someone who had thoroughly irritated him not long ago had become one of the only adults he saw. Theo waved her inside. Considering the fantastic news he had just received, perhaps this timing was serendipitous. A cookie-making lesson might be the perfect way to celebrate Ivy's improved health.

Nita began unpacking supplies from her canvas bag: baking ingredients that looked to be pre-measured and stored in various-sized containers; a large plastic mixing bowl; wooden spoons; and a small hand mixer. "I brought everything with me. When I cooked breakfast for you that morning, you know...*after*...well, I did an inventory and realized you didn't have many baking ingredients or a mixer," she explained.

"Smart thinking." Theo wished he could forget the condition he'd been in when she'd last been around, and felt somewhat exposed knowing she had snooped through his pantry. If he did still have a mixer, he had no idea where it might be stored. Annie would have been the last person to use it.

Nita began to hum as she arranged everything she had brought on the kitchen countertop. He didn't know how she'd been able to fit it all into one tote bag. "I didn't bring a cookie sheet, though. I thought you might have one."

"Now that, I do have." Theo opened the bottom drawer beneath the stove and removed it with a clatter. "Penelope, before you get busy baking cookies, I have some excellent news about your mom."

Penelope had been assessing all of Nita's items, but at this, her head popped up. Her eyes pierced his. "You do?"

"A nurse from the hospital called to say your mom is doing much better. She is being taken off the ventilator."

Joy spread across her face. "For real?"

"For real."

Penelope burst into tears and covered her face with her hands.

"Honey, this is such wonderful news!" Nita gave her a side hug. "Everything's going to be fine now, you'll see."

"I'm crying tears of happiness," she sputtered as the sobs came with more intensity.

Nita drew Penelope into a proper hug. "Go right ahead and cry it all out. Releasing all those trapped up feelings is good for your soul." She patted Penelope softly on the back, as though urging every last tear out. "Then, when you're ready, I'll teach you my secret cookie recipe, and soon, you'll make them for your mother's homecoming party. How about that?"

Penelope pulled away from Nita, nodded, and swiped her tears away with her fingertips. Theo wiped a tear from his eye too. The intensity of the moment surprised him, especially the overwhelming gratitude he felt toward Nita. She seemed to always know what to say and do. Finally, after being drowned by a constant rush of bad news, they could all breathe again.

SOLITARY WALKS had become a thing of Theo's past, but that afternoon, while Nita commandeered his kitchen, he snapped on Alice's leash and slipped out the door. He was still exhilarated by the news of Ivy's imminent release from the hospital. Thoughts of what he would do if she didn't survive had filled his head for days. The fatality rate for COVID-19 was up to fifty percent higher than that of the seasonal flu, according to reports from John Hopkins University. Even so, Americans had become wildly divided on the subject of the seriousness of the virus, which he attributed to the country's polarized political climate. But Theo was a scientist. He had little patience for those who dismissed scientific research in favor of rumor and hysteria. The year wasn't quite halfway over, yet there were over a million cases in the States alone. And close to two thousand deaths! He wondered how many people would die before a vaccine could be developed.

Theo pushed these dark thoughts from his mind and focused on the sunshine warming his face, and the rhythm of his steps. Alice had become a first-rate walker, heeling at corners and waiting for him to move forward before she took another step. When a couple walked by on the opposite side of the street, their two Schnauzers barked wildly and pulled against their leashes, but Alice continued padding calmly along, unfazed.

"Good girl!" Theo wished he had brought a few dog treats. Alice really did deserve them.

Along Gloria Rice's front fence, bearded iris grew in a dense row, filling the air with one of Theo's favorite fragrances. He stopped to inhale the familiar scent and admire the midnight purple blossoms. Closing his eyes, he was immediately transported to his childhood backyard. His mother had grown a variety of iris species and colors, planting them in straight rows like most folks grew sweet corn, amassing an impressive collection of blue ribbons from the South Plains Fair. One year, a local women's group had come to see her iris garden in full bloom. He and Michael had climbed on top of the old smokehouse, lain flat on their bellies, and watched as the finely dressed ladies walked around looking and whispering and making cooing sounds. After the ladies had gone, Theo's mother had returned to the backyard, looked right up at where they were hidden, with her hands on her hips, and told them to come down. Theo remembered with a smile how surprised they'd been that she had spotted them there in the first place. She'd threatened to take a switch to them—*I know I'm not raising spies!* Feeling suitably guilty, they promised to never spy on her again.

As Theo considered the possibility of olfactory preferences being passed from mother to son, a black Porsche Cayenne slowed on the street beside him. He watched as it turned onto Gloria Rice's long driveway and disappeared around the back of the house. Gloria had evidently returned from Aspen. How nice that she'd returned in time to see her irises in full bloom.

Theo and Alice continued walking. The afternoon burst with goodness as they circled the downtown square and eventually passed the stairs leading down to Hugo's. On the sidewalk out front, a sign announced *Take-out Orders Only*. Not being able to enjoy a burger at one of the tables inside felt like a personal loss. The fact that he would *never* return with Winn, even once the virus was eradicated, returned a lump to his throat that he couldn't swallow.

Nothing would ever be the same.

THE AROMA of toasted almonds and brown sugar teased him and roused his empty stomach. "It sure smells good in here," he called out, detaching the leash from Alice's collar and walking into the kitchen.

"That's because you've entered our baking laboratory. We aim to wake your sense of smell with aromatic molecules. Right, Ms. Nita?"

Nita and Theo exchanged glances. The child was a regular Albert Einstein.

"And, lucky you! You're just in time to help. We're about to add the filling!" Penelope was surveying the cookies, which were spread out across a wire rack. Each of them had a round indentation in the center.

Nita spooned a dollop of seedless raspberry jam into the thumbprint center of the first cookie.

"That's beautiful," Penelope said, her nose only inches from it.

Nita grinned and filled several more before handing the task off to Penelope. She took to it easily, and soon all the cookies were filled.

"That was so fun! They look like happy little flowers, don't they, Mr. Theo? Daisies with scarlet centers."

"Yes, I guess they do. Speaking of flowers, the irises in front of the Rice house are in full bloom. I don't like playing favorites when it comes to flowers, but irises really do take me back to my childhood." Again, he thought of his mother. He lifted the jar of leftover raspberry jam to his nose and inhaled the sweet aroma. "Mmmm. Smells just like a raspberry iris."

Penelope giggled. "You're silly."

Theo dipped a finger into the sticky jar and made a great show of savoring the taste. "By the way, Gloria Rice must be home. I saw a black Porsche pull into her drive."

Penelope abruptly turned and dropped the spoon from her hand. It clattered against the side of the countertop, and a smidgen of jam splattered onto the floor. She bent to clean it up but said nothing at all.

Theo had only made the comment in passing, but he saw that it had altered the atmosphere in the kitchen. He wondered if he'd revealed some big secret, or ruined a surprise.

"Oh, yes! I can't believe I forgot." Nita said. "Kat Montgomery told me something you aren't going to believe."

Nita was fairly unremarkable, physically, but when she was about to deliver gossip, her shoulders stretched, and her green eyes sparkled. Her voice lowered, becoming thick and rich, as though each syllable was coated with dark chocolate.

"I'm not sure I care to know," Theo said. He was watching Penelope wipe the jam from the lower cabinet. Gossip made him uncomfortable.

"Trust me, you'll want to know this."

"Who is Kat Montgomery?" Penelope asked, placing the spoon on the counter.

"Only the biggest busybody around," Theo said. Was it his imagination or did Penelope's face look flushed?

"She's not a busybody. She's a very reliable source of neighborhood information." Nita plunged the mixing bowl into the soapy sink water and began washing it.

"Alice needs to go outside," Penelope blurted.

Theo watched her quickly slip out the kitchen door, with Alice following on her heels. Something was going on here, but he had no idea what. Penelope Pie would never voluntarily miss out on Nita's gossip.

"The idea that something like this would happen in our neighborhood is unbelievable, to say the least." Nita waved her hands in the air, slinging around droplets of soapy water.

"Oh good gravy, tell me already," Theo said. The gratitude he'd felt earlier toward Nita was quickly diminishing with each moment she spent drawing out her story.

Nita inhaled deeply, as though the information she was about to deliver would take an incredible amount of energy to relay. "Okay, so Gloria's daughter, Elizabeth—she lives in Tulsa or Oklahoma City, I forget which, not that it matters…." She paused and frowned, as though it did, indeed, matter a great deal.

Theo motioned impatiently, his hand executing the internationally recognized sign of *Get on with the story for Pete's sake.*

"Anyway, Elizabeth went by Gloria's house a few days ago, to let some guys in to service the air conditioner. When they went out back to check the unit in the guest quarters, she discovered someone had been living there!" She pointed out his kitchen window, in the direction of Gloria's house.

He blinked. "Wha—"

"Squatters have been living in Gloria Rice's back house. Can you believe it?"

Squatters? "But that's—" Theo clamped his lips shut. Ivy and Penelope had been living in Gloria Rice's guest apartment since Valentine's Day, and before that, they had lived in several other places, an apartment off Leverett, a motel, and even in Ivy's car for a few days—wasn't that what Ivy had told him? Had someone begun squatting in their apartment since Ivy had been admitted to the hospital, or were she and Penelope the squatters? Nita's continued yammering made it impossible for him to think clearly, but he was certain Nita had no idea Ivy and Penelope lived there. The topic of their address had never come up.

"Did someone break in? Did they catch the person?" He refused to give credence to the suspicion knocking around in his mind.

"Kat didn't say anything about how they got inside, whether they smashed a window or broke the front door lock, or whatever. She did say whoever's been living there really wrecked the place; clothes were everywhere and there was food in the refrigerator. Isn't that the craziest thing you've ever heard?" She dried her hands with a dish towel and draped it neatly over the edge of Theo's sink.

Ivy said they were renting, hadn't she?

"Can you imagine? Homeless people breaking in and taking over such a lovely place, like a wild pack of raccoons. Besides the bout with porch pirates last Christmas, this has always been a safe neighborhood. I've never felt the need for a security system. During the day, I don't even lock my back door! You better believe that's going to change."

Theo found himself incredibly aggravated by this. Nita was acting so horrified, but he could see how entertaining she was finding this gossip. "I don't think you should be spreading rumors around the neighborhood," he snapped. He had first-hand experience with rumors. Bored people latching on to anything they heard and spreading falsehoods like a panhandle dust storm, desperate to distract themselves from the emptiness of their days.

"I'm not spreading anything around the neighborhood; I'm just telling you." Nita seemed affronted. She began packing her kitchen gear into her tote bag. "This affects everyone living here. I thought you would want to know what's going on right under your nose, but evidently, I was wrong."

He thought back to the few times he had been inside the apartment. The space had been clean and tidy when he ate supper there. Later, when he returned with Penelope to gather up clothes and things for Ivy's hospital stay, the place had looked lived in, sure, but it wasn't any more wrecked than his own house. And they had a key to the place. *He* had the key. He glanced at the small bowl on the kitchen counter where he kept his keys. Squatters didn't have keys, did they?

"Do you know if Gloria called the police?"

She slung her bag over her shoulder and stared at him. "I may know a little something about that, but I wouldn't dare further spread my information around the neighborhood."

"Touché, Nita." If he conceded, maybe she'd tell him what he needed to know. "But you've already spread it to me, so you can't just leave me hanging."

"Well, I *could*. But it wouldn't be very nice. According to Kat, Elizabeth filed a police report because Gloria was still in Aspen."

It must have been Elizabeth's Porsche that Theo had seen earlier.

"I assume Gloria has a security system, but Kat didn't know."

A slew of emotions moved through him. Confusion. Guilt. Worry. Embarrassment. Anger. Theo was not one to jump to conclusions, nor did he like to judge others. "Well, I won't lose any sleep worrying about this. The whole story sounds like regular neighborhood chin-wag to me."

Nita huffed. "You just go right ahead and stick your head in the sand. I plan to be on high alert." With her tote bag swaying, she opened the back door and stepped onto the deck.

Theo followed her. "I don't have my head stuck in the sand."

Nita ignored him and called out to Penelope. "Hon, I'm leaving now. You sure were a good student, and I'm so glad your mother is coming home soon."

Penelope, barely making eye contact, said, "I would come over and give you a proper goodbye, but as you can see, I'm quite busy." She had filled a bucket from the shed with water from the hose and was rubbing Alice down with a cloth Theo didn't recognize. Alice, a natural water lover, was alternately drinking from the bucket and plopping a paw in to create a splash.

"That's okay. I'll see you again real soon. Remember, you invited me to look for Boo Radley holes."

"Oh, yeah." Penelope glanced at Theo for a flash, then looked away again.

If ever someone appeared guilty, it was that little girl. Once Nita was out of the way, Theo went over to her, determined to address the situation head-on, but before he could say anything, she shook her head. "Please don't say anything, Mr. Theo. Not now. My mind is extremely occupied." She didn't look up at him, keeping her eyes on Alice.

"Well, my mind is occupied too, and I don't like the thoughts filling it."

"Try thinking about something else, why don't you? That works pretty good when I'm upset."

Theo sighed. "Penelope, you can't run away from your problems. I need to know what's going on."

She continued stroking Alice's back. The dog was a wonder, sitting so still while Penelope continued with her nonsense.

"What exactly are you doing, anyway? It's not like you're bathing her; you've got no soap."

"At first I wanted to baptize Alice, you know, to wash away any sins she might have, not that she could possibly have any. Then we just kept playing. She really likes water. I think she might be part duck."

Alice's sins? Theo snorted, marched over to the white oak, and plopped down on the bench. Whatever was going on here was now at least partly *his* problem, and Penelope's refusal to say anything was trying his patience. Still, he knew he had to step lightly. She was just a kid, dragged by her mother into whatever this drama was. If he kept calm, she would likely volunteer the truth in short order. After all, the girl *did* love hearing herself talk.

Theo studied his backyard. He noted bare spots in the grass, and decided he would sow white clover seed for the summer pollinators. The climbing rose, given to him by department colleagues at his retirement luncheon, had grown wild and unruly. He would reattach it to the fence trellis and coax it to grow upright, rather than sprawl along the ground. Then a strong power washing to the house walls, to remove pollen and grime. That would freshen up the exterior. Theo had always thought that once he retired he would stay on top of his house chores, and spend hours enhancing his garden, maybe even adding a new peony bed along the side fence. Instead, retirement had given him permission to procrastinate. He shuffled chores down his to-do list while focusing on his herbarium work or spending idyllic spring afternoons at Baum-Walker cheering on the Razorbacks. Now, he only addressed issues when they ballooned into massive problems, like the front porch floorboards crumbling. It was ridiculous, the things he had ignored.

Sunlight drained from the afternoon. Penelope continued dousing Alice in water and cooing to her. Eventually, after a period of quiet during which the only sound was the distinctive hoot of an owl, Theo tried again.

"Penelope—"

"Mr. Theo—"

She had spoken at the same moment he did. They made real eye contact for the first time since he had come outside. "You go first," Theo said, waving a hand as though inviting her to open an invisible door for her words to pass through.

"I was wondering if I could make an appointment with you. I'm famished, and I thought maybe we could meet and discuss things after we eat."

An appointment? A vein throbbed in his temple.

The owl hooted again, loudly. It must be nearby. Theo scanned the canopy overhead, trying to locate the bird. He suspected it was a barred owl; he had spotted one a few weeks ago through his binoculars.

"Is that an owl?" Penelope stood and started looking for it too.

He nodded. For a moment, they searched together, but the creature stayed hidden.

"Are you hungry?" she whispered.

"No. I'm upset and want to know what's going on."

"See? Really, I suspect you *are* hungry. Being hungry can often translate to anger. Your blood sugar is probably out of balance. You ate a whole lot of cookies."

He lurched from the bench, nearly sending it toppling. "Okay. *Fine!* I'll go make us something to eat."

"What time, do you think?" Her voice was tiny.

"What time do I think what?"

She hesitated. "What time do you think you might pencil me in for an appointment?"

He shook his head and didn't answer. *Why wouldn't she tell him what was going on?!* Frustration bubbled inside him, so he chose his next words carefully. "I'm going inside to heat up some of the broccoli cheese soup I thawed out this morning. We can talk about this later."

Once inside, Theo dumped the soup into a small pot and put it on the stove on a low flame. While the soup warmed, he searched online through recent conversations on the Fayetteville section of the Nextdoor website. People were quick to post about feral cats and trash pickup issues, but he found no mention of squatters in Gloria Rice's home. If it was true, the lack of such information on a public forum didn't surprise him. He imagined Gloria had a staff of folks to handle every task, from monitoring her investments to quashing gossipy neighborhood information.

Theo put some slices of bread in the toaster, then held his breath to a count of five, released, then held his breath again. He repeated the process several times, until the toast popped out, and then again while he buttered it. Despite his attempts at the calming trick he had learned years ago, the sick feeling remained lodged in his belly. *What was he going to do!?* He ran through various scenarios in his mind. If Ivy and Penelope were squatters, what would happen to them? Charges had already been filed, according to Nita. What would the consequences be? A hearing and a hefty fine? Jail time for Ivy? And what would happen to Penelope? He recalled Julie's advice. *It's really a situation for Protective Services.*

He peered outside. Penelope Pie was pacing around the white oak and whispering to herself. Had he been a party to misconduct by merely eating spaghetti and cherry pie at the kitchen table with them? Ms. Rice would have security cameras around her house—of course she would! The thought of his picture appearing on a security tape intensified his anxiety. What on earth would she think of him? What would he say in his defense?

He gave himself a mental shake. *Pull yourself togethe*r! "Penelope, dinner is ready, please come inside."

She nodded but continued pacing. Alice raced past him and began rolling her still-damp body around on the rug in the den.

"Penelope," he called louder, "you said you were hungry, so come inside and eat. It's almost dark."

"Would it be possible for me to eat outside? I thought I would have a nighttime picnic with the owl. I heard him again."

"No. It is *not* possible." Theo's jaw clenched. The child was really testing him.

"The truth is I'm a little afraid to come inside, knowing what you know. You know?"

"Well, I don't know anything, but by now, you should know I can be trusted."

"I don't know anything for sure, Mr. Theo. And neither do you."

He wanted to bang his head on the door. The day had started out to be such a good one, with excellent news followed by a long, leisurely walk. But now *this?* Theo gripped the handle of the sliding glass door and thought of several retorts, all ridiculous and childish. *I know plenty of things. I know that my life was peaceful before you knocked on my door. I know what it's like to be scared and alone, but what was your mother thinking, committing the crime of breaking and entering? Trespassing?* But he said none of these things, knowing that truly, none of this was the fault of this eight-year-old in his care. No matter how precocious she was.

Penelope continued circling the white oak, dragging her feet through the meager grass. He really should sow clover seed before the days grew too hot.

When Theo finally spoke again, his mother's words spewed from his mouth. "Penelope, if you don't come inside by the time I count to five, I'm giving your soup to Alice. She's hungry, and you will have to go to bed without supper."

Penelope dropped to the bench and looked at him, the day's waning sunlight reflecting in her eyeglasses. "You don't have to threaten me, Mr. Theo. I'm coming. I needed some time to think over a few things and prepare for our meeting." She stood, dusted the grass from her legs, and strode toward him.

"Okay. Good." Theo slid the door wider for her. Once more, he was struck by how tiny she was. She was just a kid, and whatever was going on wasn't her fault. He had to rein in his temper; it was unfair of him to be taking out his anger at the situation on her. Penelope couldn't be held accountable for her mother's transgressions.

She tiptoed past him, saying, "Well, you went to all that trouble to cook for me, so it's the polite thing to do. And, by the way, I don't think dogs should eat broccoli cheese soup. Dogs are mostly lactose intolerant."

Penelope usually chitchatted throughout mealtime, asking questions and pontificating about one thing or another, but that night, she was silent. As their spoons clinked against the bowls, Theo watched her expressionless face and wondered what she was thinking. Sooner or later, she would spill every detail. Keeping quiet went against every fiber of her being.

"Thank you for the soup," she said, dabbing at her lips. She folded her napkin, placing it beside her bowl. "I'll put the bowls in the dishwasher if you'd like."

"That would be fine," Theo said, making an effort to keep his voice measured and pleasant. He didn't want to intimidate her into talking, but he didn't want her to think he was a pushover either.

"Exactly what time is our meeting, Mr. Theo? I was thinking a morning meeting might be more productive than a nighttime one, since you're a morning person and all." Penelope's smile was hesitant, and her eyes wouldn't meet his.

She looked so tiny and vulnerable. "Our meeting starts in exactly five minutes. Meet me in the dining room after you put away the dishes, please." He added the *please* because he didn't want to sound angry. And really, he wasn't angry. Any anger had faded to worry, laced with exhaustion. Soon, he would get the truth from her, and that meant he would have a decision to make.

Penelope carefully gathered the bowls and spoons. She carried them to the sink as though they were filled to the brim with boiling water.

He left her to deal with the kitchen and went to the dining room, where he cleared away the evidence of his herbarium project and her school work, moving art supplies aside and placing her journal on top of her mathematics book. From where he stood, he could see her stacking the bread plates on the bottom shelf of the dishwasher. Something about the meticulous way she arranged the dishes and then arranged them again, moving them to a different position, broke his heart a little. He looked away, trying to focus on what he would say and how he would say it, but a magnificent sunset drew his eyes to the window. The sky had melted into a sweep of fuchsia and tangerine, so glorious it seemed the sun was reaching out to touch him, to remind him of the important things in life.

A lump formed in his throat as he pulled out a chair and sat. *What was wrong with him?*

"Okay, I'm here." Penelope came into the room looking a little pale and weary eyed. And she was wearing her lime green raincoat. "I see you have a yellow pad of paper," she said. "Will I need to take notes? I could go get my iPad."

Suddenly, Theo felt silly, sitting at the head of the dining room table with a legal pad in front of him. Good grief. This wasn't an inquisition. He remembered the series of depositions taken after the death of his family, all the starch-collared attorneys and bland-faced insurance professionals gathered around a polished mahogany table. No one involved had wanted to be blamed; no one wanted to assume responsibility. It had simply been an accident. Everyone in the wrong place at the wrong time.

"No, you don't need to take notes. I just need to know what's going on." He pushed the legal pad away.

She nodded. "That's reasonable, but I don't think I should talk to you without representation. I know my rights."

"Penelope, I'm not a police officer, and you are not being charged with a crime."

"Mr. Theo, I don't respond well to passive-aggressive behavior."

Theo sighed. He had no idea what to do.

"Maybe you could submit your questions to me in writing," she continued. "I could answer them tomorrow, when my brain has rejuvenated. I'm just a kid, and I'm tired all the way to my hair follicles."

"You're being manipulative. I don't respond well to that sort of behavior," he said.

She offered a tired smile. "Most of the time I really like you, Mr. Theo, and I hope this situation doesn't mar our friendship."

"What exactly *is* the situation? I wish you would enlighten me. And for heaven's sake, could you please take off your raincoat?"

"I've already explained, it's not a raincoat; it's a protectability cloak, and I don't know why it bothers you so much when I wear it. Maybe you shouldn't concern yourself with the superficial and instead concentrate on the important. Like relationships and kindness and human beings struggling to survive day to day without basic necessities." She slipped from her chair, grabbed her journal from the buffet, and then fingered through the cup of pens and pencils until she found her favorite, a retractable ballpoint with four different ink colors. "Goodnight, Mr. Theo. I need to journal out my feelings and then go to sleep. If you want to write down your questions on that legal pad and slip it under my bedroom door, I'll answer them in the morning."

He stared at her, his mouth agape. Did he only worry about the superficial?

Twenty

Theo's sleep had been restless, his dreams a mixture of technicolor snippets: his brother running down a dirt road, the air thick with dust; a stark white hospital room crowded with nurses in starched uniforms, each carrying a clipboard; Annie, cooing and rocking a fussy baby in her arms, her long hair pulled into a side ponytail. He woke exhausted, yet with a plan. In the hopeful light of this fresh morning, Theo would feed Penelope a hearty breakfast as soon as she came downstairs, and then he would skillfully unearth the truth, not through harsh demands, or threats, but by offering his assistance.

Relief would come in the knowing.

Theo dressed and made the bed the way Annie always had, with hospital-cornered sheets and the quilt folded neatly at the foot. It was a task he rarely skipped, because making it represented an accomplishment. On those days when a neatly-made bed represented his *only* accomplishment, he wouldn't consider the day a total waste of time.

He went downstairs, put oatmeal on to simmer, and fried six strips of thick-cut bacon in his iron skillet. Penelope may not eat meat, but he did. He devoured the first two crispy pieces while stirring the oatmeal. When breakfast was ready, he set the table and began picking up the den, straightening cushions and refolding the afghan.

It was almost nine-thirty by the time Penelope padded barefoot downstairs. She climbed onto a kitchen chair and sat like a pretzel, with her legs crisscrossed and her knobby knees flared to the side. Theo was glad to see that she was not wearing her raincoat.

"Good morning, kiddo," he said, careful to maintain a friendly tone despite his eagerness to get on with things.

"Mornin', Mr. Theo. How did you sleep?" She yawned.

"Okay." No need to share how he had *actually* slept. "I hope you like oatmeal." He placed a bowl in front of her, along with a small ramekin of golden raisins and dried cranberries. "You can add some dried fruit if you'd like."

"Thanks. I like oatmeal okay. On my list of favorite breakfast foods, oatmeal is number twenty-one, right behind cheese grits. That's a decent ranking, considering all the foods a person might eat for breakfast." She sprinkled a few raisins and berries into the bowl and stirred them into the oatmeal before taking a tiny bite.

"You've ranked breakfast foods." He wasn't all that surprised.

"Of course," she chirped.

"What's number one on your list?" Theo thought it essential to keep the conversation flowing, but he was curious too.

"Bear claws."

"Like a donut?"

"Hmm." Her forehead wrinkled as she compared the two. "I would describe a bear claw as more of a pastry or a Danish than a donut, but the sugar content is probably similar. I only had a bear claw once, in kindergarten, when Louie England's mother brought them for a treat. Once was all it took, though. It was quite exceptional—like something that would be served to the angels in heaven for breakfast."

"Interesting. I never envisioned St. Peter serving bear claws at the Pearly Gates, but why not?" Clearly, he had lost his mind. Theo's version of heaven was a hardwood forest undisturbed by humans, or perhaps a deep, restful sleep on a cool night. As for a heavenly menu, obviously bacon would be served. He smiled as he crumbled two pieces on top of his oatmeal.

"I've never seen anyone put bacon in oatmeal."

"Bacon makes everything better."

"Even ice cream?"

"Maple bacon ice cream is delicious," he assured her, although he had only read about it in the recipe section of the newspaper.

"You're kidding me."

"I would never kid a kid about bacon."

They ate quietly, the atmosphere thick with unspoken words. Theo studied Penelope's T-shirt choice for the day. It was suitable for the conversation to come—an oversized purple shirt with a taco in the center, and underneath it, the phrase: *Let's taco 'bout it.*

"Mr. Theo, can I tell you something?"

Finally, she was ready to talk. "Please, go ahead."

"Last night, when I went to bed, I told myself I would never consume another bite of food cooked by your hands. I was worried you were so upset that you might poison me or something. But this oatmeal doesn't taste altered in the least, not that I would necessarily be able to detect toxins." She scooped another spoonful of oatmeal and held it close to her face to inspect. "Even knowing your position on war and all, I still doubt murder is in your wheelhouse of tendencies." She took another big bite and smiled. "I may decide to move oatmeal up the list."

He stared at her, speechless. He refused to be sucked into a crazy conversation about the ranking of breakfast foods *or* how to poison a houseguest.

Penelope drained her small glass of milk and wiped the milk mustache from her upper lip. Then she pulled out a tightly folded square of notebook paper from the waistband of her jeans. She unfolded it, put it on the table, and smoothed it out, using her hand as an iron. Then, she passed the paper across the table to him, so that whatever was written there was face down.

"Here's my statement about recent allegations. If you'd like to use it as evidence, feel free. Also, before we start, would it be okay to have another glass of milk? I'm thirsty and expect to need lots of nourishment today."

This should be interesting. Theo went to get the milk carton and refilled her glass, placing the carton within reach in case she wanted more.

"Okay. Are you ready to taco 'bout it?" He reached for the paper, trying to keep things light. No matter what Penelope had chosen to reveal to him, no matter what the situation turned out to be, he would calmly review the facts before considering the next steps. Perhaps there was an obvious explanation for the rumor.

"I guess so." She picked at her cuticles.

Theo had never actually seen Penelope biting her nails, but they were ragged and chewed. He flipped over the paper and stared, silently, at the sheet of paper. It was blank.

"Did you write your statement in invisible ink?"

Once upon a time, he and Michael had eaten Chex cereal every morning for an entire year, trying to win invisible ink pens and secret agent decoder rings. He felt just as gullible, now, as he had back then. He would do his best not to express it, but he was fuming. This was too much.

"No, sir. My statement *is* invisible because I am choosing to exercise my rights under the Fifth Amendment to the United States Constitution."

The wooden kitchen chair groaned as he leaned back.

"It's a legitimate legal response, you know. I've seen it on *Law & Order,* and politicians do it as a common practice on C-Span."

Theo's anger simmered.

"I'm sure my mother will explain everything when she gets home from the hospital. I don't want her to be upset with me if I say the wrong thing. Besides, and this is really important, I don't want to give away any key plot points of the story I'm writing. I'm almost finished with it."

Theo stood, pushed his chair away, and began pacing. "Penelope, I'm trying to be patient, but you are really testing me here. I need to know what's going on, and I need to know this very minute."

She blinked her impossibly long eyelashes, and for a moment, he thought she might divulge everything. But she stayed silent, picking at her ragged cuticles.

"Listen to me. If you don't tell me what's what, I will call Gloria Rice and find out everything for myself." He didn't have Gloria Rice's phone number but suspected he could easily get it.

"I'll consider that, Mr. Theo, but right now, I'm going back upstairs to work on my book. Thank you for breakfast and for not poisoning me this morning." Penelope turned and left the kitchen as though exiting a stage.

THE SIDE GARDEN was a place of isolation and privacy, so filled with memories of Annie that he thought he caught a whiff of her favorite body lotion on the breeze. Theo dragged a folding chair to the corner and sat down with a heavy thud. He was glad to have reclaimed the area, but for a moment, he regretted having shared such a special spot with Penelope.

Theo closed his eyes. "What should I do?" He took slow breaths and tried to summon Annie's face, her touch, her hand squeezing his. Even though he couldn't feel her, he knew what she would say—*Give the situation a little space. Don't let someone else's drama become yours.* After mulling things over for a while, he settled on the simplest, most obvious solution: He would do nothing—at least, not immediately.

Theo gave the water spigot a swift turn, and the hose came alive in his hand. Careful not to deluge the garden, he lightly sprinkled the raised bed. A squiggly row of tiny, bright green radish shoots caught his eye. Theo kneeled to look closer. The seeds he and Penelope had planted had germinated in only five days! He snapped a photo with his phone. He wanted to tell Penelope, but thought it best they avoid one another for a while longer, so he continued working outside, mowing the backyard, cutting deadwood from the climbing rose, and then reattaching it to the trellis with twine. Working the soil, in all its varieties, was always good for him. By the time he had finished, he was feeling calm again, and his mood had lifted.

Inside, Theo washed his hands, splashed water on his face, and opened the pantry, looking for lunch inspiration. A burger and fries sounded better than anything staring at him from the pantry shelves; he should ask Winn if he wanted to meet downtown.

Reality punched him like a rock-hard baseball to the gut. Winn was gone. He was the same gone as Theo's parents and brother. And Annie.

Gone was the most permanent thing he knew.

He shook off the melancholy that threatened to destroy his calm, and decided to make grilled cheese sandwiches for lunch. Surprised when the aroma of crisping buttered bread and melting cheese didn't lure Penelope down to the kitchen, he went to the bottom of the stairs and called for her.

She didn't respond. He assumed she was ignoring him.

"Penelope, you don't have to talk to me. Just come down and eat lunch."

Again, no response came. Theo's shoulders and thighs were already stiff from the morning's excessive yard work. If the girl knew how badly his body ached, she wouldn't make him go up there. Or, maybe that's precisely what she would do. He shook his head and trudged upstairs.

Theo was surprised to see Alice sitting outside Penelope's bedroom, staring at the closed door as though on guard duty. Penelope *never* closed her door. "What's she doing in there?" he whispered to Alice, giving her a pat on the head. Putting his ear to the door, Theo expected to hear a petulant *I can hear you talking about me*, but there was nothing, only silence. The kid had to be either reading, or writing in her journal, or perhaps she had fallen asleep.

He knocked, but there was still no answer. *This is getting ridiculous.* Theo cracked opened the door and looked inside. Penelope wasn't reading or napping, and she wasn't sitting at the writing table. The emptiness of the bedroom felt vast. Alice padded into the room, her toenails tapping against the hardwood floor providing the only sound in the house. She jumped onto the bed, stretched herself out quite comfortably, and stared at him, as though to say *Look what you've gone and done now.*

"Well, help me find her then!" A pinprick of anxiety grew in Theo's belly. He searched each room of his house, upstairs and downstairs. He checked his phone, but there were no missed calls and no text messages. When he called for her from the back deck, the only response came from a crow perched high in the oak tree, its characteristic caw sounding like manic laughter.

Theo began looking to see if anything was missing. Not because he thought Penelope might have stolen anything, but because identifying something missing might lead him to her. There was nothing missing from the pantry or refrigerator. Truth is, the girl barely ate anything anyway; food probably wouldn't be the first thing she would take. He opened the junk drawer and unzipped the leather bank bag, where he kept two hundred dollars for emergencies. The money was still there.

As panic began to course through him, Theo thought about Penelope's journal. He wasn't one to snoop through a private diary, but maybe she had left clues in it.

He rushed to the dining room, to the corner of the table where she usually left it. Her art supplies were there, but the journal was missing.

Then he noticed the empty space on the coat rack where her raincoat usually hung. Penelope had run away. She must have left while he was working in the garden!

Panic almost overpowered him, and for a few seconds he questioned everything that had brought him to this point. Good lord, as Penelope's temporary caretaker, and the *only* adult in the immediate picture, he had been trying to do his job. But he had made a mess out of everything—putting too much pressure on her, probing too forcefully for answers, and making her so uncomfortable that she ran away!

The wretchedness that gripped him soon gave way to pure fear. Where was she? Was she safe?

He rang Penelope's cell phone, heard her perky voice say, "*Hi. You've reached Penelope's very own voicemail. Say something fascinating and I'll call you back.*"

He stuttered. "Hey, Penelope, um, I have a fascinating idea. Call me. I promise I'm not mad at you…so please, Penelope Pie—"

The phone beeped, and he was cut off. Theo hoped his odd message sounded friendly, and not as alarmed as he felt. He redialed and left a shorter, more direct message. "Call me, please." Then he snapped on Alice's leash and snatched his keys from the bowl on the countertop. He would drive through the neighborhood looking for her, and if that didn't prove successful, he would move on to step two. Only he had not worked out what step two was, yet.

His cellphone rang shrilly in the quiet kitchen. "Hello!" He answered quickly, relieved that Penelope had got his messages and called him back.

"Mr. Gruene. It's me, Ivy."

Theo didn't know what to think or feel. Ivy's voice was as coarse as sandpaper, almost unrecognizable. She coughed, and then apologized for coughing.

"Oh, Ivy! My goodness, how are you?" His heart was thumping. He opened the back door and allowed Alice to race outside, dragging her leash across the freshly mown grass. "We've been so worried about you," he said, hoping she'd think the tremor in his voice was for her, not because he had no idea where the other half of the 'we' had disappeared to!

"I'm a little weak, and I think I've lost a lot of weight, but I'm okay. I will be, anyway."

"Good. That's great news." Worries about Penelope's whereabouts cluttered his mind, making concentration difficult and the right words impossible to summon. He glanced at the roof of Gloria Rice's garage apartment. Had Penelope gone over there to try and hide evidence that would identify her or her mother?

"I'm being released in a day or two. At least that's the story this morning," Ivy said, each word a flicker, a flame trying not to wink out. "Can I talk to Pea? I want to tell her the news myself."

Theo could hear the joy in her halting words. "Sure. Of course. But…um…." He glanced around the kitchen as though she might suddenly reappear. "She's not here. She's out. Gone for a walk." Good grief. He couldn't string together a coherent sentence. He didn't dare admit Penelope was missing, nor could he question Ivy about the situation that had led to the disappearance, not over the phone, not when her health was still compromised.

There was a long silence on the other end of the line. Theo held his breath, waiting for Ivy to call out his lie. Despite illness and absence, he expected her mothering instincts were still sharp; that she would pick up on the uneasiness in his voice and see right through his weak attempt at normalcy. Ivy had trusted him with the person most important to her, and he had failed miserably.

Finally, she spoke. "Oh, okay. It's probably good she isn't there."

"It is?"

"Yes. I think so." Ivy's voice began trembling, and then a sob sputtered into Theo's ear. That sob led to full-on weeping and wheezing, followed by a coughing spell.

"Ivy, what's wrong?" Helpless to do anything, Theo's overwound brain ticked off the possibilities. Was Ivy's sickness more than coronavirus? Did she know Penelope was missing?

"Nothing at all." She half-sobbed, half-laughed. "I'm sorry. It's just that I've been so emotional today, like super weepy. And I really need to pull myself together before I talk to Pea, so it's probably good she's gone out to walk Alice. The truth is I'm grateful to be alive. And I can't get over everything you've done for us. Taking care of my child all this time…well, you're my guardian angel. I could never make it up to you, even if I spent the rest of my life trying."

Theo leaned against the kitchen island and inhaled a quivering breath. He was the opposite of a guardian angel. Penelope had run away, and he had no idea where to find her.

WITH ALICE RIDING shotgun, Theo drove up and down every street in the neighborhood, his eyes peeled for flashes of neon green. He looked between houses and down alleyways. Theo had figured Penelope's protectability cloak would be easier to spot than the girl herself, but it turned out that the whole world was clothed in shades of bright spring green. Wherever Penelope was hiding remained a secret.

Theo parked in front of Gloria Rice's home, studying the house and surrounding yard. The blinds in the main house were still closed, and he couldn't see the garage apartment from his curbside vantage point. He felt like a common stalker. Being parked there was a waste of precious time.

As much as Theo hated to involve Nita Johnson, he was out of ideas. He drove to her house and knocked on her front door, fighting the urge to rush back to his truck and speed away. She opened the door before he could change his mind and flee.

"Theo. What a nice surprise." She was wearing a cloth mask. He wondered if she always wore it, even inside her home. "I was just thinking it's such a gorgeous afternoon I should weed my flower beds, but now here you are to save me from such a terrible chore."

Nita did not enjoy getting her hands dirty, unless it involved sprinkling flour over dough and forming it into cookies.

"Is Penelope here?" he blurted.

"Here? No. Why? Have you lost her?" She chuckled, but then her eyes narrowed. "You *have* lost her, haven't you?"

Theo nodded. It was a relief to tell someone about Penelope's disappearance, but in explaining the situation, he was forced to tell Nita the reason behind it too.

"Don't worry, we'll find her, Theo, and when we do, this will all get straightened out. I refuse to believe Penelope and her mother were the squatters." Nita looked full of resolve as she climbed into Theo's truck. Alice, sitting between them, thumped her tail against the seat, excited over this new experience. "I'm to blame, at least partially. Me and my big mouth! I should have never spread Kat Montgomery's gossip." Nita latched the seatbelt with a forceful shove.

Theo couldn't blame Nita for Penelope's disappearance, and he told her so. "Penelope is so stinking smart, it's easy to forget she's only eight. In fact, if anyone should be blamed, it's me. I've been trying to get clarity surrounding the squatting rumor and obviously put too much pressure on her. She's just a kid. I feel like a real jerk. I should have waited to talk with Ivy."

Nita reached around Alice and squeezed Theo's wrist.

He was so tightly wound up, he almost jumped at the touch. But somehow, the unexpected touch settled him.

"A jerk and a gossip—boy, we make a good team, don't we?" She rolled her eyes and shook her head, clearly bothered by her role in the situation.

Theo started the truck and pulled away from the curb. Nita's willingness to help him search for Penelope felt like a gift he didn't deserve. He reckoned it was true; misery loves company. He certainly felt better with Nita sharing the load.

"Let's think about this systematically. Where would she go?" Nita gazed out the window. She seemed to be searching her own mind for the answer. Turning back toward him, she asked, "Did you ever run away from home?"

"No. I had great parents and a happy childhood. It was idyllic, really. But my brother Michael ran away once when he was a first grader." The memory reappeared to him, fresh and undisturbed despite the decades since. "I was riding my bike over to the baseball field, taking the long way around by the school playground so I could jump the hill by the creek. In West Texas, hills were a real commodity. Anyway, there he was, dragging a lumpy pillowcase across the playground, looking like he'd lost his last friend. When I asked him what he was doing, he said, 'I've run away from home, but now that it's happened, I'm not sure what to do next.'"

"So what happened?"

"I convinced him to come play baseball, and that was that. I remember thinking that since I was older, it was my responsibility to protect him, and convince him not to run away. I also thought he was really clever, because he'd thought to pack his pillowcase with such important things—clean underwear and socks, a jam sandwich, and his plastic piggy bank."

"That's so cute." Porches and lawns slowly passed them as Theo drove without a destination in mind. "So your brother ran away to the school playground, a familiar place. Do you think Penelope might have run away to her school?"

"She doesn't seem too enamored with school, but it's worth a shot." Having no better idea, he drove to Lafayette Elementary and slowly circled the campus. On a typical early afternoon in May, the schoolyard would have been buzzing with activity, the students on the energy high that always increased just before school let out for summer. But now the entire place—the main building, parking lot, and playground with its brightly-colored equipment—sat jarringly empty.

"Okay, well that was a bust," Nita said, after they'd driven all around the campus and not seen any sign of Penelope. "What about walks you've taken together, with Alice? Or hikes?"

Theo thought back to their hikes to Kessler Mountain and Devil's Den, and their numerous strolls around the neighborhood, with

Alice on the leash and Penelope always stopping to sketch Boo Radley holes. And then it came to him. "Nita, you're brilliant!"

"Well, yeah." She winked at him. "Took you long enough to notice. But why?"

Theo turned the truck around sharply and headed in the direction of Wilson Park. During the short drive over, he explained. "We were walking around Wilson Park, not long ago, and Alice ran to the creek—if there's water around, you'll find it, won't you girl?" Upon hearing her name—or perhaps it was the word 'water' that excited her—Alice's tail beat wildly against the seat, and she tried to climb into Theo's lap. Nita had to restrain her with the leash. "Anyway, Penelope raced after her and noticed a giant hollowed-out tree near Scull Creek. She called it the door to a magical kingdom and said if she was ever homeless again, she would live inside that cozy tree. I bet that's where she's gone."

Unlike the school playground, the park was busy with joggers, dog walkers, and Frisbee golf players. Nita pointed out an empty parking spot, and Theo pulled into it, anxious to find Penelope and make things right.

"You go ahead," Nita offered. "I'll walk Alice around the loop and meet you back here."

"You're sure? I might need your help persuading her to come back with me."

"I doubt that. You'll do fine."

Theo appreciated Nita's vote of confidence, but as he walked toward the creek, he wasn't sure what to say if he found her. He corrected himself. *When* he found her.

The tree-covered park encompassed twenty-two acres, but he quickly found the pathway leading down to the creek and located the tree with no trouble—it was the only hollowed-out tree in the area. But Theo's hunch had been wrong. Penelope wasn't in the hollow of the tree. Small footprints marked the soil and mulch all around it, evidence the spot was frequented by lots of kids. He wondered if any of the footprints belonged to Penelope? Maybe she had been there earlier.

Theo bent down and stuck his head inside anyway, looked up, and called out. "Hellll-oooo?" He and Michael would have certainly claimed a tree like this as a secret hideaway or home base during games of tag.

"What are you doing, Mr. Theo?"

Theo startled, half-stood, and whacked his head on the edge of the hollow. An explosion of stars filled his eyes, momentarily claiming his balance and voice.

"Are you okay? Let me help you." Penelope took his hand and guided him away from the tree.

"Jeez, Penelope. I've been looking everywhere for you. Where have you been?" The relief that ran through him was far stronger than the pounding in his head.

"I've been right here. Um, Mr. Theo, I don't want to freak you out, but there's blood dripping down the side of your face."

Theo reached up and felt the stickiness of the blood. Pulling a mask from his back pocket—these days, he was never without one—he held the fabric against the wound.

"If you need stitches, I can probably do it—I saw my mother stitch up a patient once. It's not hard to do."

He smiled. "I'll keep that in mind, but I'm pretty sure it's just a scratch. Head wounds always bleed a lot."

They moved from the trail into the expanse of the park. The smell of barbecue saturated the air; someone was grilling nearby. Theo was about to suggest they go home, but decided to do his talking immediately, right there in the park, before the moment's urgency passed. "Let's go sit down for a minute. I need to say some things."

"Sure thing, Mr. Theo. We can go over there, if you'd like. That's where I've been working all day." She pointed to a wooden picnic table a few yards away, where he saw her green raincoat spread over the bench like a cushion. Theo draped an arm over her thin shoulders, the urge to protect her strong. Approaching the table, he saw her journal, several colored pens, and the refillable water bottle he'd given her to take on hiking trips. She slipped onto the bench and swiftly moved her materials aside.

"So, what do you want to talk about?"

"You know…well…I realize I've been putting too much stress on you. I still don't know what's going on with the apartment, you know, but…well—"

Theo had become a sputtering, stuttering mess. He closed his eyes to calm himself.

"What's wrong with you? Do you have a concussion?"

Penelope reached an arm across the table and pressed her fingertips into the back of his hand. The pressure was consoling. He wondered if he might be the one about to lift off and disappear.

"No. This is nothing." Theo removed the mask from the side of his head and peered at the splotch of dried blood. The wound had already stopped bleeding. "I don't know what's wrong with me. Actually, yes, I do. I've been worried sick since you ran away. I'm sorry for making you feel like you couldn't stay. Your mother will be home soon, and I promise to save my questions for her. But, Penelope, if you need to talk to me about something, anything, I hope you know you can."

His words, as ragged and stammering as they were, transformed Penelope. She sat taller on the bench and her whole face lit up with her smile. "Mr. Theo, sometimes you can be a little bit hard to take, that's the truth, but cross my heart, I didn't run away. I would *never* run away from you and Alice and your magnificent house. I want to stay there forever and ever." She looked up at the sky, a dreamy expression on her face, then at the dense tree canopy running the length of the creek.

He stared at her. "But I thought…then, what were you doing? Why did you disappear? You've been gone so long."

"Time is nothing to a writer. I'm learning it takes a long time to write a book, and there's power in a change of scenery. This morning, when you were in a mood and I couldn't concentrate, I remembered you said you think best out in nature. So I thought this would be a good place to come."

Theo heard Penelope's words, but couldn't really believe she had not left out of anger or fear.

"I know what you're thinking; it's stamped in that skeptical expression between your eyes. Yes, I should have told you where I was going, but I couldn't find you. You weren't in the house, or sitting out back under your thinking tree. I thought you were probably on the front porch, so I packed my things and planned to tell you as I walked out. Mr. Theo, you may not be able to relate since you aren't a writer, but when the muse speaks, time is of the essence. I had this idea swimming around in my brain and really, *really* needed to get it on paper." She blinked and swallowed, looking at him intensely, but he was still speechless. "So…anyway, I rushed down the porch steps and practically raced to the park, super eager to write. I planned to text you when I got settled—I brought my phone with me—but when I got here, I discovered it was totally out of minutes. It's like the universe probably knew we needed space from each other. Don't you think?" She was nodding at him, wide-eyed, urging him to accept her explanation.

He *thought* it was more than a little ridiculous. All of it. But he maintained a neutral expression. "Penelope, you're a kid. You can't vanish without a word. No matter how optimistic or enthusiastic or inspired you might be, the world is not always a safe place." It might be a cliché, but he knew it was true. "Believe it or not, there are some really bad people out there." Theo waved his arm through the air as though the bad people encompassed the Frisbee throwers at Wilson Park.

"Mr. Theo, even though I'm just a kid, my brain contains lots of mature information. I know about drugs, and creepy stuff like child porno. Poor people like me and my mom are acutely aware of the world's dark side. It's sort of necessary for survival." She shrugged her bird-like shoulders. "And really, I'm pretty used to doing my own thing, you know, when my mom's at work, so I didn't think much about it, even with a dead phone. I sure didn't think you would *miss* me." She flashed him a beaming smile.

He shook his throbbing head, and took a deep breath, inhaling barbecue smells that made his stomach clench with hunger. He thought of the grilled cheese sandwiches he'd made for lunch, only to abandon them in the skillet. They would be cold by now.

"How did you find me, anyway?"

"I remembered the tree by the creek, and how you said you could live inside it."

"Well, that turned out to be a miscalculation on my part. I did go sit inside the hollow for a bit, but it was too dark to write, and the air smelled like mushrooms. The picnic table turned out to be much better. What time is it anyway?"

Theo looked at his watch. "Four o'clock."

"Oh, awesome. It's true what the experts say. When a writer gets into the zone, time flies. I didn't mean to be gone so long. Really, I didn't."

Penelope gathered her things, and they walked back to the truck, where Nita and Alice were waiting. During the short drive home, Nita gently scolded Penelope for disappearing without a word. "You scared us to death, young lady. You can't just up and disappear like that. Mr. Theo was beside himself with worry, and now look, he's somehow injured himself while rescuing you."

Theo had been running on adrenaline all afternoon, and now that Penelope had been found, exhaustion coursed through him. He willingly let Nita be the mouthpiece for both of them.

"I know, I'm so, so sorry. I didn't mean to worry anyone. Honestly, I didn't. It was all just a humongous misunderstanding." As she spoke, Penelope was trying to control a very excited Alice.

Theo heard the remorse in her voice and knew her words were sincere. She continued, explaining to Nita what had happened, and how she had planned to call, but her phone had run out of minutes. "Really, if anyone is to blame for the confusion, it's my muse. She was working overtime."

"That's nonsense, Penelope. You are responsible for your muse, not the other way around."

Nita's snappy rebuke made Theo smile. Penelope apologized again.

Back home, Nita commandeered his kitchen for the second time in as many days, announcing, "We'll have breakfast for supper."

Theo was hungry and tired, and the notion that she would prepare him a meal felt like a real treat. He was even more appreciative when she declined his offer of help.

Theo plopped down in a kitchen chair and watched the activity unfold. Eggs cracking. Onion being diced. Toast slices springing from the toaster. Penelope was underfoot, wanting to help, so Nita put her in charge of buttering the toast. Theo just sat there, reflecting on the past few weeks. He knew that life didn't happen in a straight line; everyone faced multiple forks in the road, some that meandered pleasantly and others that took them wildly off their predicted course. Destinations were not predetermined. Some sixty-odd days ago now, Penelope's knock on his door had obviously been a fork for him. And now, after being so confused and upset, and then experiencing the sheer panic of thinking she had run away, Theo felt...well, *different*. He felt like he had...expanded, somehow.

"This feels like a real celebration," Penelope said, once they had started eating. "Even though I wasn't lost, I sure feel found now. Does that make sense?"

"It makes perfect sense," Theo said. "Today feels like Thanksgiving without turkey. When I was a kid, my family always went around the table and said what we were thankful for. I'm thankful you are safe, kiddo. And I'm thankful for Ms. Nita too." He felt exceedingly vulnerable, but resisted the urge to clam up—his typical reaction. He turned to Nita. "Without your help, I would still be out searching. And I would be starving too." He chuckled. "These eggs are delicious."

Nita smiled and accepted the compliment graciously.

"And there's something extremely important I forgot to tell you, Penelope. And it's the best thing that's happened in weeks." It wasn't true that he had forgotten to mention it. He had purposefully saved the good news until they were settled back home.

Penelope stopped eating and stared at him, her eyes wide and inquisitive. "What?"

"Your mom called today. I actually talked to her. She sounded good, and she's definitely coming home!"

This news propelled Penelope to her feet. She began cheering and dancing, capering around the room, then stopped abruptly. "Are you really sure? Like a hundred percent sure?"

"No hesitation." He rarely gave such high odds to anything, but after talking to Ivy, he thought it was a sure bet.

Twenty-One

Ivy was going to be released from the hospital in two days, and her return became Theo and Penelope's sole focus. They threw their efforts into planning and preparing an elaborate welcome home meal and making the house festive. They scrubbed every surface to eliminate any possibility of germs that might harm her fragile recovery. After spending an entire afternoon clearing out the bedroom that was to be Ivy's while she recuperated, Theo dropped off an entire truckload of things at Potter's House. Annie's sewing machine had been the hardest thing to let go of, but imagining someone making good use of it had eased the sting.

Now, with excitement and tension riding along with them in the truck, the five-mile journey to the hospital seemed to Theo like it might last forever. Unable to sit still, anticipation coursing through her like sugar, Penelope was tapping her fingers against her knees and wiggling her naked toes, the heels of her feet pressed into the dashboard.

He did a double-take. "I see you've lost your shoes." She *had* been wearing pale pink plastic sandals.

"No, they aren't lost. They're back there." She thumbed her hand toward the back truck window.

"At home?"

She shook her head quickly, as though dispelling a foul smell from the air. "No, no. In the truck bed. I've always wanted to ride in the back of a truck, like ride all the way to the Rio Grande River, or Hollywood, or someplace equally exciting, with the air blowing my hair into tangles and the aroma of pine trees filling up my nostrils. I imagine it would be like the covered wagon days, but tons better, because of McDonald's fries and gas stations with free-to-use bathrooms, you know? But I didn't bother asking if I could ride back there to the hospital, because I knew you would say no and give me that look of yours. So instead of getting into a whole big thing about it, resulting in your annoyance and my disappointment, I tossed my shoes back there. At least my shoes will enjoy the experience."

For a fraction of a second, Theo wondered if he was dreaming. What a long year the past nine-and-a-half weeks had been, since the kid first knocked on his door. "Penelope, shoes don't have feelings. Please tell me you understand that."

"That's your opinion."

He shook his head. "Is there anything you want to talk about? You seem more…overwrought than usual."

"I guess I *am* a little overwrought. My insides are swirling with excitement because my mother is finally coming home! I mean, I always thought she would completely survive the virus and eventually leave the hospital—she's very strong and all seven of her chakras are open and freely flowing—but when living inside a tough situation, sometimes it's hard to believe in good things. Bad thoughts tend to slip right in and hang out. You know?"

Theo knew very well how negative thoughts could overwhelm positive ones, and because Annie had practiced yoga, he actually knew enough about chakras to be able to respond intelligently. "Why don't you take some slow, cleansing breaths? That always helps me when my energy is blocked up." He was partially teasing, but was quite pleased that Annie's yoga terminology had returned to him.

"That's a good idea, Mr. Theo. One point for you!" Penelope pressed her hands against her thighs as though bracing for impact, then closed her eyes and began inhaling and exhaling slowly and steadily through her mouth.

As Theo waited for the light to turn green at College Avenue and North Street, he wondered if Penelope had actually kept track of the score of their game, because he certainly couldn't recall. But he was enjoying the silence too much to ask her. He watched Penelope, saw her chin moving with each breath and her lips puckering like a goldfish. Just as traffic began to move again, her eyes popped open and she turned toward him, her shoulders swaying back and forth as though she was performing a seated dance. "It's working! I feel calmer inside and joyful outside."

He took a deep breath. "Penelope, I have a favor to ask."

"You do? No one ever asks me for favors."

"The whole issue over the apartment, you know, what Ms. Nita said about squatters and the day I thought you ran away, but you said you didn't?"

"Yeah, how could I forget." She pressed a hand to her heart.

"I was hoping you wouldn't mention any of that to your mom."

"So you want me to lie?"

"No, no. I just don't want you to bring it up. Let me talk to her about it after she's had time to recuperate. We don't want to bombard her with upsetting things right away."

She side-eyed him and pursed her lips. "I can't make any promises, but I'll try. Sometimes my words just come gushing out. Mr. Theo, do you think keeping quiet about something is different than lying?"

"Well, I think it depends on the circumstance."

She nodded slowly. "So, aren't you going to say anything about my fashion statement and my hairdo?"

Once again she dizzied him with her abrupt change of subject. She was wearing the same white and pink polka dot skirt she had worn for Winn's funeral, but this time, she had fashioned her hair into two lopsided Princess Leia braids spiraled above her ears. "You look cute as a bug."

"Bugs aren't cute."

"That's a matter of perspective. How about ladybugs?"

She considered this and nodded. "Okay. I agree ladybugs are cute. And roly poly bugs are cute in an intriguing way."

He laughed. "My mom used to say they were 'so ugly they're cute.' By the way, those little pill bugs belong to the family *Armadillidiidae*. See if you can't store that bit of scientific trivia away in that dazzling brain of yours."

She nodded and repeated the word several times, committing it to memory. "Mr. Theo, will we be home by four o'clock? Since four is my second favorite number, I think that would be a lucky time to get back. I have our whole night mapped out in my mind and right here on this paper. Wanna see?" She pulled a folded slip of paper from her pocket and fluttered it in his direction.

"I'm driving."

"Oh, yeah." Penelope referred to the paper and gave him the highlights. According to her, dinner would be at six—Theo had already assembled a vegetarian pasta dish and she had made a batch of raspberry shortbread cookies for dessert, with Nita's help. "After we eat, I think we should all watch a fun movie, something light-hearted, and then go to sleep early. We'll need our rest, because tomorrow I have a full day planned." Again, she began wiggling her toes and tapping her fingers against her legs.

"Hold up there, Penelope. Don't get ahead of yourself. Just because your mom is being released from the hospital doesn't mean she will be ready to turn back flips."

She nodded. "I know, and I hear you, and I have no gymnastics planned for us. But can I please tell you about the surprise I'm dying to release from my brain?"

"By all means."

"Okay, you're going to love this. During the past two days, in between all the cleaning and planning, I've been working on my book. I stayed up late last night—I was super quiet, because I didn't want to wake you up—and I finally finished it!"

"Oh, you did, did you?"

"I did!" She was positively brimming with enthusiasm. "It doesn't fit clearly into one particular genre. Really, I don't think the best books do. But if I was forced to choose, I would say it is a memoir told in fairy tale."

"Is that a real thing, memoir told in fairy tale?"

"Of course. Anything imaginable is a real thing."

"*Well...*"

"Also, I've written it as a graphic story, but I've decided that for my debut, I will simply do a read through. Maybe I'll invite Ms. Nita to come hear it. What do you think?"

"I think a graphic story sounds inappropriate."

Penelope pressed her hands to her forehead in exasperation. "Your old man brain is not thinking about the various uses of the word graphic. A graphic story is like a comic book with illustrations. Not graphic like X-rated!"

"Then why don't you call it a comic book?" Theo couldn't help but enjoy Penelope's enthusiasm, but the conversation was beginning to tire him out.

"Because it's not cartoonish. Not to brag, but the whole thing is incredibly inspired. And the ending is the coolest part." She beamed with such joy it seemed to Theo that the sunlight brightened.

"Well then, I'm looking forward to it."

Theo followed the hospital signs for patient discharge and slowly pulled into the area identified for short-term loading and unloading. That morning, a hospital representative had called to review detailed discharge instructions with him, the process being different because of the virus. Visitors still weren't allowed into the hospital proper; Theo was grateful he wouldn't have to navigate the confusing corridors to secure Ivy's discharge.

"There's where we go!" Penelope pointed at someone in sky blue scrubs waiting out front beneath the awning, holding a clipboard.

Theo pulled up behind two other vehicles, secured a face mask over his mouth and nose, and rolled down the window, waiting his turn. Once the instruction came, he pulled into parking spot number four as directed and waited for the nurse who would bring Ivy down. The pandemic had certainly become a lesson in efficiency.

Soon, Ivy was there, an orderly wheeling her through the doors of the main hospital and over to the passenger door of his truck. An overstuffed plastic bag hung from the back of her wheelchair, and she carried a glass cylinder of pink gerbera daisies in her hands.

Penelope vaulted from the truck and collapsed onto her mother, crushing the daisies. "I thought you would surely die, and I would never see you again!"

Theo had sensed their reunion would be highly charged, that Penelope's excitement would be impossible to contain, but her reaction turned out to be even more dramatic than he'd expected. "Why don't we let your mom get into the truck, Penelope? Let's get her home. Okay?"

Penelope quickly jumped off her mother, and with the help of the orderly, Ivy stood, shuffled closer to the truck, and managed to hoist herself inside.

"Thank you, Mr. Theo."

He smiled at her. Ivy was thin and pale—almost unrecognizable—her mass of wild curly auburn hair tamed into two long braids, her sweatshirt hanging limp on her shoulders. But then she smiled back at him, and her silvery-blue eyes came alive. Shakespeare may have said that the eyes are the windows to the soul, but in that moment, Theo glimpsed Ivy's heart. Hers was so grateful, his breath snagged.

Penelope was relatively subdued on the short drive home until Ivy asked about her schoolwork and what she had been learning. That brought her back to her usual voluble self. "I've learned so much, thanks to my new botany teacher! I know some flowers are weeds, and some weeds are edible. We've been hiking at Mt. Kessler and Devil's Den, and Mr. Theo gave me my very own trail backpack, and we've been creating a personal herbarium catalog from the plant specimens we find. Radishes are easy to grow—ours germinated in five days!—and purple petunias smell like grape Laffy Taffy. Also, those cute roly poly bugs belong to the family…" she cut her eyes to Theo and squinted. "Don't tell me. Oh, I remember. Arm-a-dillo-day."

Ivy chuckled and then began coughing. "Don't make me laugh, Pea. It hurts."

"I didn't tell a joke. It's the truth, right Mr. Theo?"

"It's the truth." Her pronunciation was a bit off, but he didn't correct her. "I'm afraid my teaching is rusty, but lucky for me, Penelope is a sponge. She learns despite my poor efforts." He turned onto College Avenue, trying to drive smoothly, without jerks or sudden movement.

"Everything looks so green and lush," Ivy commented, her gaze trained on the landscape outside the truck window. "Seems I've been gone an entire season."

Theo understood what she meant. Mother Nature was steadfast, never failing to go about her daily business, shaping and changing the landscape again and again in miniscule, incredible ways. The changes weren't necessarily noticeable when constantly exposed to them, but being away always brought them into sharp relief. And poor Ivy had been away for quite a while.

Penelope was continuing to describe their routine to Ivy. "The dining room is our classroom, but really the whole world of nature is our classroom; the dining room table is just our home base. I do my school assignments and art projects there, and Mr. Theo works on his plant specimens. He's doing highly important things—basically he's saving the world by preserving plants."

"Well, that's a bit of a stretch." Theo chuckled, but at the same time he felt a sense of pride. She understood that the world was worth saving.

"Not really. Hey, Mom, did you know Mr. Theo's best friend, Mr. Winn, died of coronavirus? It's been a really sad thing, and Mr. Theo got super smashed on whiskey, and I went to the funeral to help him."

"Wait, what? Your best friend died? That's horrible." There were tears in Ivy's eyes. "I'm so sorry. What a terrible thing."

Theo nodded. "It was a complete shock. Still is. Penelope, I don't think your mom needs to know all the details."

"It's okay. My mom understands grief." Penelope talked about Ivy as though she wasn't sitting right there beside her. "And mom, you better prepare yourself. We have a huge surprise waiting for you at home…um, at Mr. Theo's home."

Home.

Theo had shoved the issue of Gloria Rice's apartment to the back of his mind, but he had not forgotten. According to Nita, nothing more was being discussed about it on the neighborhood grapevine. Most people had fleeting attention spans, after all; one outrage would soon be followed by the next. Theo hoped the whole thing was nothing more than a misunderstanding; gossipy neighbors jumping to conclusions. Still, his gut urged him to broach the subject with Ivy as soon as possible.

They turned onto his street and Theo pulled up to the front curb, in full view of the huge banner Penelope had crafted. It was an impressive art project, made with alternating sheets of red and blue construction paper, the edges hole-punched and tied together with twine.

WELCOME HOME!!!

"Wow! It's amazing, Pea!" Ivy rolled down the window to get a better look. The banner spanned the railing like patriotic bunting, colorful and celebratory, worthy of a soldier's homecoming.

"I've been working on it for days. Mr. Theo tied it to the porch railing, but I did all the letters and designed the glittery parts and everything." Penelope's smile bloomed wide across her face, as resplendent as the petunias lining the front porch steps. Theo felt his smile match hers.

Twenty-Two

Theo put away the last of the supper dishes, poured himself a glass of tea, and went to find Ivy. She was on the front porch, sitting on the swing. It swayed gently as she gazed toward the setting sun.

"Mind if I join you?" Theo hated interrupting her quiet moment, but Penelope was playing with Alice in the backyard, and he wanted to take advantage of her being out of earshot to discuss the rumors surrounding Gloria Rice's guest apartment. Ivy had been with them already for four days; it was time.

"Please do. Your front porch is so nice and peaceful, I could live out here forever." Ivy waved a hand through the air dramatically, reminding Theo of her daughter. The resemblance between them went deeper than their curly auburn hair and heart-shaped faces. Their mannerisms were almost identical.

"I know what you mean. The porch is one of my favorite things about this house." Sinking into the rocker across from Ivy, Theo felt the weight of the past few weeks settle in his bones. According to the hospital discharge information, the rule-of-thumb recovery time was one week for every day on a ventilator. Ivy's frailty was obvious to him. After seventeen days on a ventilator, her road to recovery would be long. The slightest expenditure of energy made her breathing difficult.

"I really like the way the porch turned out. I meant to tell you before," Ivy said.

"Thank you. Penelope was a big help. Although if she'd gotten her way, the whole house would now be painted bright green, like her raincoat."

She laughed, looking wistful.

Theo wondered what she was thinking. So much had happened since the windy March morning when she had asked him to fill in as Penelope's teacher. Penelope had become an important part of his life in the past two months, but he still knew very little of Ivy.

"Nita's vegetarian lasagna was amazing. And that zucchini bread! I would love to have her recipe. I ate too much, though." She patted her flat belly, contentedly, and grinned. "You're lucky to have her as a neighbor."

He nodded. "I guess I am." He'd never considered himself lucky to live so close to Nita, but he knew he was fortunate for all her recent help. Earlier, when Nita had dropped off the food and they had invited her to stay for dinner, she'd declined. "I made some zucchini bread for Gloria Rice, too. She got back into town yesterday, and I want to drop it off before it gets too late." Theo had no idea if Nita had really made a loaf for Ms. Rice, but he certainly appreciated the information she was passing along to him.

"I get the impression you have a history with her?" Ivy said.

"Not really. We're just neighbors." He kept his voice light, hoping to dismiss the topic with a wave of his hand. He had more urgent things to discuss with Ivy.

"Oh, yeah?" She raised an eyebrow, and he could tell she thought there was more to the story.

"That's it. We're just friends. My dating years are way in the rearview window." He felt ridiculous even mentioning his dating years. A few years after Annie's death, he'd gone out a couple times with friends of Julie's, and yes, with Nita twice, but he had always felt uncomfortable, and ended things before relationships could progress. The thought of having a romantic relationship with anyone other than Annie just felt like betrayal to him.

"Well, I think you should ask her out again. She's amazing!"

Theo shook his head. He didn't like the direction their conversation had gone. He needed to ask her about the apartment and the rumor, and this chatter was getting in the way. *Just spit it out. Rip off the Band-Aid. Spill it, for Pete's sake!* "Look, Ivy, I need to talk to you about something, and I've been waiting for a time when Penelope wasn't around."

"Oh, okay. You sound serious."

"The thing is...it's just that...I'm curious about your lease with Gloria Rice. What's the term? When does it renew?" Until he had reason to believe otherwise, he would give her the benefit of the doubt.

"My lease?" She was looking him straight in the eye, and certainly showed no outward sign of guilt. "If this is your subtle way of asking me to return to the apartment, you can just say so."

"No, not at all."

Blinking slowly, she said, "Well, I guess you could say the term is month-to-month."

"So you *do* have a rental agreement. Really, I don't want to pry into your business, but if you've been—"

"It's complicated."

His stomach sank, but he was determined to remain unruffled even if Ivy's ambiguous reply meant there was truth to the rumor. If there was one thing he had learned last week, it was that pressuring Penelope had not gotten him any closer to the truth. In fact, it had almost been disastrous. The panic he had felt when he thought she had run away was still fresh to him. "Yeah? How so?" He took a drink of tea and wished it was scotch. But after drinking so excessively after Winn's death, he was determined to lay off the hard stuff for a while longer.

"Well..." Now she was looking at the neighbor's oak tree across the street. "Is that an owl I hear?"

Theo nodded. "He lives around here. I hear him occasionally, but rarely see him." Either Ivy's mind danced from topic to topic the way her daughter's did, or she was stalling. No matter which turned out to be true (and perhaps they both were), his impatience began growing.

"Wow. That's cool."

For a moment, neither spoke as the owl continued hooting.

"Ivy, I heard you were a squatter." Finally, he spoke the words he had been holding in for days. "Rumor is you broke into Gloria Rice's apartment and have been living there without permission. I need to know if it's true."

"A squatter?" Again, she looked toward the oak tree. He searched her face for clues but found nothing decipherable. Was she confused? Exhausted? Afraid? He imagined all these things might be simultaneously true, but her blank expression provided no real hints.

"Either you are, or you aren't. If there's a gray area, I'm too dense to see it." Calm had settled over Theo now that he was finally close to learning the truth. Just putting his question out there had already brought some relief.

Ivy ran her hands through her hair and fashioned it into a knot on top of her head. It was something he'd come to recognize about her—she fidgeted with her hair when she was uncomfortable, or in deep thought.

"You have no idea what it's like to be me. No idea...." She dropped her hands to her lap.

"You're right about that. I don't. But I've been in my share of sad situations. I know what it's like to be lost and alone, to hit rock bottom."

She glanced around the porch and then out to the yard. Theo noticed a slight tremor in her hands as she began twisting the thin silver ring on her pointer finger.

"Ivy, I understand you have no family to help you, and I can't imagine what it must be like to be a single parent. But—"

"That's right. No offense, Mr. Theo, but you can't imagine surviving on food pantry handouts and payday loans that exist only to keep poor people in debt. Or trying to make living in a hatchback seem like a grand camping adventure. So don't even—"

"Please, Ivy, just be *honest* with me. What trouble are you in?"

She straightened in the swing, crossed her arms defiantly, and stared at him with shiny eyes. "I'm not in trouble, unless being destitute is a crime."

Theo sighed. He was getting nowhere.

"You have this nice big air-conditioned house with food in your refrigerator. You retired from a career you love, and from what I've observed, you have enough money to sleep at night. What do you know about real trouble?" She held his gaze, blinked slowly, and then blew a stream of breath through her teeth. "Oh god, I'm so sorry. I shouldn't have said that. You've been so kind to us." Her voice cracked.

"It's okay, you can say whatever you want to me. I've got thick skin. See?" He tapped the fingers of his right hand against his left forearm, hoping to lighten the mood.

She smiled a little, but it wasn't a full smile.

"Listen, Ivy, everything you said about my house and career and being able to sleep at night, well, those things are true now, but that sure wasn't the case when I was your age. Far from it. Contentment and success aren't tied to money. There's—"

"They are if you don't have any," she retorted.

He shook his head. He had hoped for a logical explanation. Or, even if the truth was something terrible, he thought she would trust him with it. He had never seen this side of Ivy, and wondered what he could say to help her. "Ivy, misery isn't a contest. Life holds enough pain to go around. I've inflicted it, been consumed by it, and barely survived it. And trust me when I say, you *can* get through whatever this is. I'll help you if I can, but first you have to talk to me."

"Why? Why do you want to help me? You've already gone above and beyond. I don't want to involve you."

"Because helping one another is what makes us human. Look Ivy, I'm far from perfect, and I know I often come across as a curmudgeon. When you first asked me to teach Penelope, I was very reluctant; even after I agreed, I didn't handle things well, especially at first. Sometimes it's almost impossible for me to break outside of my comfort zone. But I did, and I have, and I want to help you now. "Believe me, I haven't survived seventy years without getting plenty of help myself. I may never have suffered financially, but I lost my entire family when I was only nineteen. And then my wife, when she was only forty. I needed a lot of help to get through that, and I was lucky to get it. I don't like to think of what would have become of me if I hadn't." Theo remembered some of the people who had helped him through the years: the surgeons and therapists who provided physical and mental healing; Annie, his soulmate; and of course, Winn. Without Winn, he would never have survived the loss of Annie.

Theo swallowed hard. Speaking so openly was arduous for him, and he had never intended to reveal so much. But sharing his story seemed to be having a positive effect on Ivy. Her demeanor had softened noticeably, so he continued. "Helping someone doesn't have to be a grand gesture, Ivy. Take Nita, for example. Since Penelope came to stay, she has helped both of us in so many small ways. The least I can do is pay kindness forward whenever I can."

"Mr. Theo, I knew your family died when you were a teenager, and I can't imagine how painful that must have been for you. But I've never really had much of a family."

"You have an incredible daughter," he said, gently.

At this, she began to cry softly. Theo wanted to walk over and give her a hug, but he held back. He didn't want to overstep or make her feel even more uncomfortable.

She twisted her ring again and then clasped her hands in her lap. "I'm tired, and I really don't want to talk about any of this."

Theo saw the weariness in her eyes and heard the strain in her voice. She was fragile and far from being fully recovered, and he certainly didn't want to add to her problems. So he decided to change his approach. If he shared more of his own story, maybe she would be willing to share some of hers. "Ivy, can I tell you a story?"

She sniffled and uncrossed her arms. "Okay, I guess so."

Suddenly, he needed to tell his story as much as he needed to hear hers.

"Ivy, when I was nineteen years old, I developed a drug problem, and I overdosed."

She shuddered, avoiding his gaze.

"When my parents and brother died…it's hard to convey just how lost I was without my family. The car accident happened a few months after I received my draft notice; we were on our way to Fort Bliss so I could report for basic training. Three weeks later, I woke up in a Houston hospital with a broken body, an incredible amount of rehabilitation ahead of me, and no family other than an aunt, who had her own issues."

"Mr. Theo, you don't have to tell—"

"To this day, I can't really describe what happened to me other than I completely spiraled—mind, body, and spirit. I was in unbearable pain from a series of surgeries, and mentally, I was a complete wreck. It was the early seventies, and back then there was a much greater stigma surrounding mental health. And, I was so young..." Theo's voice faltered, and he had to pause for a few seconds to regain control. "You know, one of the biggest mistakes I made was thinking pain pills were the answer to my problems. I thought addicts got hooked on heroin or cocaine, not medication prescribed by a doctor and dispensed from the drugstore. For a long time, I didn't realize I had a drug problem, or if I did, I excused it. But the day came when my physical injuries were fully healed and my prescription expired. That's when I knew I had a real problem."

"What happened?"

"My sole focus became getting my hands on pain medication. I went to a new doctor who wrote me a prescription for Valium. I abused that too." Theo had not told anyone his addiction story since he'd told Annie, and that had been so long ago. They had only been together a few weeks when he shared all of it, the car accident, the pain, his drug problem. Spilling out his soul to her had cracked open the possibility of a new life. Now, as he relayed his family tragedy to Ivy, he was surprised to view it with such objectivity. For the first time, he didn't feel defined by that awful period of his life!

She began rocking the swing, her hair lifting and floating around her shoulders. "Did you overdose on purpose?" Ivy was hugging herself. She looked so small.

He shrugged. "I don't really know. When it happened, I was still living in Midland, working at a small paper company. I didn't show up for work one morning, and my boss, Mr. Giasano, came looking for me. He had known my father and sensed how troubled I was. He was the person who called for an ambulance." Theo paused as the memory of that reckless time consumed him. He would always regret the trauma he must have caused that kind man. "Midland was the only home I'd ever known, but nothing was the same without my parents and my brother there. I was hurting, and I believe on some level I didn't want to live without my family. When pain is that raw, it's impossible to separate yourself from it. At least that's how it was for me."

"I'm sorry you had to go through all that. It's not fair."

"I completely agree with you, Ivy. Life is often unfair. The thing is, everyone experiences these low moments at some point, but thank goodness, we don't all get bulldozed at the same time. There's always someone out there to lean on, someone who wants to help; a therapist, doctor, or even a friend, like *me*." Again, he paused and wondered if he was saying too much. Expecting too much.

Ivy nodded as though she could relate to what he was saying. "Who helped you?"

"Oh, so many people...." His voice trailed. "I knew the only way to survive and move forward was to leave Midland. So I sold the family home, and took a Greyhound to New York City, hoping a huge metropolitan area would allow me a fresh perspective and a chance to start over. I thought about the hordes of immigrants who came to America with nothing, at the turn of the last century, leaving behind friends and family to escape famine or persecution. I imagined myself the same way, on the hunt for a new life in a new place, determined to reinvent myself."

"And it worked?"

"Eventually, it did. In New York, I could separate myself from my past. And, even though I had money, I got a job, just as I had done when I was still in Midland—actually, I worked multiple jobs; it was essential that I stayed busy while attempting to find direction for my life. I went to group therapy sessions several times a week too. That's where I met Winn, in a support group in Manhattan. He had just returned from Vietnam, and was struggling in ways I couldn't fathom. Asking for help is a huge part of recovery, and meeting other people trying to live with loss taught me to think outside myself. I learned that everyone is trying to get over something."

Ivy was leaning forward, her bare feet pressed into the porch floor, the swing no longer moving. "Wow, I never would have imagined...." She seemed to be studying his face, and he sensed he was finally connecting with her. "It really is true what they say, that we can never know what someone else is going through...."

Twilight was closing in. Theo reveled in the vivid colors, fuchsia and blood orange streaking the horizon, Venus already twinkling above the tree line. The setting sun cast long shadows across Ivy's face. Dusk typically gave Theo a feeling of emptiness, a sensation of not having accomplished enough, of time passing too swiftly. But that night, he felt strangely content.

"Mr. Theo, did you ever think...." Ivy had a strange expression on her face. "The accident that killed your family probably saved your life? It kept you from going to Vietnam."

"Oh...*constantly*. Especially in the beginning. For a long time, I couldn't get past it. Just the idea of it...." He rubbed his forehead and struggled with how to explain something that had long been central to his thinking. "The idea that a freak accident could take the lives of the people most important to me, yet somehow be a catalyst for *my* safer future...well, that went beyond the pale. It was impossible to understand. It's why I numbed myself with pills; I didn't want to think about it. But Ivy, the point I'm trying to make is there's always a solution, even to the worst problems. It may not be the solution you want, and it probably won't be the easiest one. Sometimes we have to get out of our own way, ask for help from unlikely people and places, and accept it when offered." Theo drained the last few drops of tea and returned the glass to the side table. An unfamiliar sense of serenity came over him.

"Thank you for telling me your story," Ivy whispered.

Theo couldn't turn off the spigot of words. "Oh, there's more." He reached for his glass before remembering he'd already emptied it. "To this day, I can't remember anything about the car accident itself, but weeks later, I learned that *I* had been driving. That knowledge...even though the accident happened in a flash, and rationally, I know that there was nothing I could have done to lessen the damage inflicted by a truck tire smashing through our windshield, the fact remains; if my dad had been driving, *he* would have survived. Not me."

She didn't say anything, and he had said all he could say. Early evening provided the only sound for a while—the creak of the swing, the lonesome whistle of a train passing through downtown, roosting birds calling to one another.

Eventually, Ivy spoke. "I'm ready to tell my story now." She clasped her hands and looked toward the last of the day's sun.

Theo waited silently. He knew how difficult sharing could be—whatever he was about to discover of her truth would come in Ivy's own way.

"Okay...so, I was with this guy, Derrick, for almost a year." Ivy sounded detached and emotionless, like she was relaying someone else's story. "We met on campus just before I finished my first nursing classes. He worked for a company that did maintenance work for the community college. He had a talent for fixing things and could solve any problem, whether plumbing, mechanical, or electrical. I rarely let anyone into my life because I've not had much reason to trust people, but right from the beginning, he seemed different. He had this way of listening to me, like he was *really* hearing me, like he cared about everything I had to say."

She paused and inhaled deeply before continuing. "After a few months, he moved into the apartment I was renting over on Leverett. Splitting the rent gave both of us a little breathing room, and he really seemed to enjoy being around Pea. She liked him too; he made both of us laugh. But then things outside our control started falling apart. The company Derrick worked for began laying off people, and he was suddenly let go. He was a hard worker, though, so he placed an ad on the neighborhood website and started picking up handyman jobs right away. We didn't worry at first. But then our landlord decided to sell the apartment building, and we were given thirty days to vacate. Right at Christmas, too! It was something I should have suspected might happen, I guess, because tearing down older apartments to make room for fancy student housing, and those really expensive townhomes, has become the norm here."

Theo nodded. He was no real estate expert, but knew exactly what she meant. Income in the area wasn't keeping pace with inflation, and the lack of affordable housing had become a hot topic in northwest Arkansas.

"So, I began looking for a new place in the area—I didn't want to change Pea's school because she was doing well at Lafayette Elementary, and the teachers really nurtured her. But finding something in the neighborhood that we could afford was almost impossible, and before long, our eviction date came. I loaded up our stuff, and we all crashed with Derrick's friend for a couple of weeks."

Again she paused to gather herself. "Anyway, one afternoon, when Pea was at school and I had just gotten off an early shift, I went on a job with Derrick at Gloria Rice's home. It was supposed to be a quick repair, and then we planned to check out a nearby efficiency apartment. Well, the job took much longer than Derrick expected—a complete electrical box upgrade—and it was so cold that day, drizzling freezing rain, really miserable. At one point, Ms. Rice came out to check on the progress, and when she saw how cold I was, she told me I could wait for Derrick in the apartment. I took her up on the offer right away. I went upstairs and used the restroom, and I admit I looked the place over. It was cute and clean, and I couldn't believe no one lived there. It seemed so unjust. Derrick and I were desperate to find a place to live, and Ms. Rice had an entire unused apartment."

"So you thought you'd just move right in?" He spoke more brusquely that he'd intended.

"No! Please let me finish."

Theo promised to keep quiet.

"Derrick's first job for Ms. Rice led to another, and I rode along with him when I could. Occasionally, I saw her, and she would always strike up a conversation with me. She seemed very nice. Maybe a little lonely. One day, I mentioned to her that I sometimes cleaned houses for extra money, and she asked if I would clean the apartment. Ms. Rice is a big theater donor, and she had offered the place to an actor who was coming into town for a show."

Ivy's long story was making Theo antsy. He was becoming impatient to understand how all of this would tie into the squatting rumor, but he controlled his impatience, and nodded without speaking.

"You know, Mr. Theo, it's amazing what people will reveal to someone they've just met. Ms. Rice told me all about her travel schedule, how she planned to spend several months in Aspen beginning in February, and how lucky she was to live in such a safe neighborhood. She even told me her house wasn't monitored by a security company."

"She doesn't have a security system?" Theo found this oddly reassuring.

"No. The signs around her yard are only meant to be a deterrent. Anyway, I did a few more jobs for her, running errands and taking her poodle to the groomer. When the actor left after a few weeks, Ms. Rice asked me to clean the apartment again. She paid very well, and I thought meeting her was going to be a real turning point in my life. Derrick had rented us a room at the Chief Motel by then. It's cheap and clean and on the city bus route, and Derrick was friends with the manager, Jerry. Things seemed solid again. I kept checking apartments, and there were a few that looked promising. But then I came home one night and Derrick wasn't there, and all his things were gone. He didn't answer his phone when I called. Jerry told me he'd gone back to his wife."

Even in the twilight, Theo could see her shaking her head.

"We were together for almost a year and I had no idea he even *had* a wife!"

Before Ivy could continue, Penelope appeared on the porch. "I can see you are in deep conversation, so it's a-okay if you don't want to come with us, but Alice needs to go for a walk before it gets too dark. We'll just go from that intersection to that one." She pointed to the north and south intersections bordering Theo's block with a dramatic sweep of her hand. "If someone tries to kidnap us, I'll scream real loud and run right back. We are both fast runners, aren't we, Alice?"

Alice stared at the leash rattling in Penelope's hand and gently wagged her tail.

Theo appreciated Penelope's interruption. It saved him from having to think of a response to Ivy's tale of woe. "Good idea," he said, with a chuckle.

"Don't you want to put on some shoes?" Ivy asked.

Theo winced. Had he overstepped by granting his permission before Penelope's mother could say anything? Now that she was back, she was the decision-maker when it came to her daughter. He was, well, nothing more than a friend.

218

Penelope looked at her feet. "No. While I walk, I'll be forest bathing. I read about it in one of Mr. Theo's nature books upstairs, the one with the green cover."

"Forest bathing? Okay...."

"Yes, by walking barefoot, I can better connect to the earth. Of course, we'll mostly be on the sidewalk." With a bright smile, she and Alice were off to forest bathe as the night's first stars began to show themselves above the treetops.

Theo watched as the pair passed in front of Nita Johnson's house.

Ivy laughed. "She's a lot, isn't she?"

"She's wonderful," Theo said. "You're fortunate to have such a remarkable daughter."

Ivy nodded, inhaled deeply, and said, "Now, where was I?"

Theo remembered precisely where she was in the story—Derrick was married! Had there been signs? Clues that later left her reeling over their obviousness? What a lowlife. *Poor Ivy.*

"Yeah. So, Derrick...well, he went back to the wife I didn't know he had, and worse, he took all the cash I had been saving for a deposit at a new place. Most of my housekeeping jobs were paid in cash, and I knew it was foolish to have so much money on hand, but I'd not had a chance to make a deposit. Honestly, I think I went a little crazy after that. I couldn't think what to do..."

"So you moved into the apartment?"

"We stayed in the room at the motel a little while longer, but I started getting a strange vibe from Jerry. Maybe I was being paranoid, I don't know, but I no longer felt safe there. I tried to stay at a nicer hotel, but when the clerk ran my credit card, the charge wouldn't go through." She sighed heavily.

He waited for her to continue, but as the seconds ticked by, she said nothing. *What was she not telling him?* Finally, he spoke. "So where'd you go?"

"We lived in our car for two weeks."

Ivy said this almost proudly, a bit defiantly, he thought. Had he made her feel judged? He'd hoped not.

"The thing is I'm just an aide at the VA. Until I finish my nursing degree, I'll never have any money. Sixteen dollars an hour doesn't go very far."

"Oh," he said, then immediately regretted his lacking response.

Penelope and Alice had been walking back and forth in front of the house, over and over, and Theo had become so engrossed in Ivy's story that he had been only slightly aware of them. But now, Penelope raced up the porch steps with Alice, declared, "Our forest bath was a huge success. But we're both thirsty."

"I wish I had some of your energy, kiddo," Theo said, laughing.

Once they went inside for a drink of water, Ivy continued explaining. "Do you remember the snow we got in February? How cold it was? I told myself Ms. Rice wouldn't mind if we stayed in the apartment, but really, I didn't think anyone would know. I only planned to stay a few nights, until I could work out a better solution. And we were very careful."

Theo's stomach was tied into knots over all he had just been told. It was true—*they had been squatters*. The relief he'd expected to feel after he learned Ivy's story didn't materialize. Instead, he felt overwhelmed and sympathetic, and he only wanted to make things right for her. *But how?* He thought of Penelope. She was resilient, but also impressionable, and her wellbeing was foremost on his mind. "Did Penelope know what was going on?" he asked, keeping his voice neutral.

"Not at first, no, but eventually I had to tell her. Penelope needed to understand our new rules. It was important that no one noticed us, so we tried not to use much electricity, and mostly lit candles at night. I know you must think I'm a terrible mother, but I was desperate, and it was just a temporary situation. That's what I told myself."

Ivy rocked quietly in the swing. The setting sun cast long shadows across her face, making her look even younger than she was.

She was a survivor. That much was clear to him. "Ivy, you have no reason to beat yourself up. You are a great mother. Your daughter impresses me every day, and that starts with you."

She smiled sadly. "Thanks for saying that, but I've made a lot of mistakes."

"Don't we all?"

She nodded and sniffled, and he hoped there would be no more tears that night. Question after question came to him, but even though he needed more answers, he didn't want to bombard her.

"Where's your car now? And what about your mail?" Theo couldn't believe he'd not thought to ask about these things before.

"I sold my car to Jerry. Parking that clunker in front of Ms. Rice's house would have drawn attention, and I needed the five hundred bucks he offered me. Since the VA is so close, I can walk there, or ride the bus if the weather is bad. And my mail was already going to a post office box on Dickson—I need to pick it up soon," she added, as though just remembering.

"So, anyway, we stayed in the apartment a few nights, which turned into a few weeks. It all seemed to be okay, and I felt myself relaxing. I had found a way to keep us off the streets while I saved up to replace the money Derrick stole, so I could put down a deposit on an apartment. But then everything got really crazy. Penelope's school closed, I got sick, and here we are."

Here we are, indeed.

Theo felt an overpowering need to take charge and fix everything. He had felt much the same way when Annie had been diagnosed with cancer. But he told himself to slow down, and think a moment about what he really wanted to say. He couldn't erase what had happened; he could only offer support. "Ivy, I just want to say…well, I want to thank you for sharing your story with me. I know that must have been difficult." He could barely see her face now, but the growing darkness made it easier for him to speak freely. "You've had some real challenges, but for what it's worth, I think you are doing a phenomenal job. I hope you don't think I'm patronizing you, because that's not my intention. Also, I would like to throw this out there—if you want me to, I would be happy to call Gloria Rice and explain everything to her. But only if you are okay with that."

"I appreciate everything you've said and all the things you have done for Penelope and me, but please don't call Ms. Rice. This is my problem, and I have to make everything right. I promise, I will. I have a plan."

Penelope came back outside, still full of energy and animated with news of Alice. "She can shake hands now. Watch." Penelope squatted beside Alice and offered her palm. Alice put her paw onto her hand. "See?"

Theo and Ivy began cheering for this new trick Alice had learned. It was a good way to end a tough evening, he thought.

When he crawled into bed later, bone-tired but unable to sleep, he couldn't stop thinking about the heartbreaking things Ivy had revealed to him and wondering about her plan to fix everything. He *wanted* to explain the situation to Gloria, to show his support of Ivy, but he wouldn't. He couldn't. It was her problem to work through. Theo closed his eyes and waited for sleep. He thought of the garden he and Penelope had prepped and planted, the radishes and carrots already growing so well. Outside, he heard the faint hoot of an owl again.

Twenty-Three

Theo poured a dollop of glue onto the Plexiglas work surface, spread it thin, and carefully pressed the crane-fly orchid into it, then lifted it from the glue and transferred it onto the mounting paper. Collected from Petit Jean Mountain in 1955, its array of tiny dried flowers was remarkably whole, and its basal leaves, though faded, were still marked with distinctive purple spots. Theo pictured the orchid as it may once have been, growing in a mountain holler beneath a fifty-foot tall Ozark Chinquapin. The tree was endangered now, but had been plentiful sixty years ago. He tended to feel a personal connection with every plant he preserved, but to this specimen, in particular, he felt a special kinship. It had been collected the year his little brother was born. All these years later, it felt to Theo like an indirect link to his family.

It had been over a week since Theo had worked on specimens. He had put the project aside in preparation for Ivy's hospital release, and then, once she was back with them, cooking had taken up more of his time. Theo was making sure Ivy ate three nutritious meals a day. But he had woken early, before Ivy and Penelope began stirring, feeling relieved to finally know the truth behind the squatting claim and eager to get back to work.

In a stillness reminiscent of his life before Penelope, he affixed another orchid to mounting paper, deciding he would incorporate his morning work into Penelope's botany lesson for the day. Years from now, when Penelope was busy living her adult life as a writer, or actress, or scientist, he hoped she would think back on their time together and remember how much he had taught her of the interconnectivity of all living things.

"Mr. Theo, where's my mom?" Penelope appeared beside him as though he had summoned her with his thoughts, her unexpected voice startling him. Alice, who had taken to sleeping in Penelope's room, had followed her.

"I thought she was upstairs."

"I can't find her anywhere. What if she's still in the hospital?"

"Wha—"

"Like, what if I've been dreaming this whole time, and none of this is real? What if she never left the hospital, and she's never coming home?" She covered her face with her hands and stood beside him trembling.

Theo understood trauma. He pulled Penelope into a hug, astonished at how natural it felt. "If that's all true," he whispered gently to her, "we've been living the same dream. And that would be something else, don't you think?"

She nodded, sniffling, and looked up at him. "I overreact sometimes."

"You have a vivid imagination. That's a good thing."

As quickly as she'd entered the room, she wriggled out of his arms and plopped down on the floor beside Alice. "Well, what should we do about her disappearance?" Penelope sounded alarmed, as though she believed her mother had been snatched off the street by someone in an unmarked van.

Theo moved the orchid to the box where he kept other completed specimens. "She'll be back. She probably walked down to the Co-op. We're out of milk." Theo didn't know where Ivy had got to so early in the morning, but he suspected it involved the apartment and her plan to make things right with Gloria Rice.

Almost on cue, Ivy came through the front door. "I brought breakfast," she announced, presenting a white pastry box and a mischievous smile. Theo noticed a flush of color in her cheeks. Her breathing seemed to have improved overnight.

The worry on Penelope's face disappeared as she ran to her mother, took the box, and peeked inside. "You got bear claws? I sure hope I'm not dreaming!"

Number one breakfast item, Theo thought.

"Bear claws and blueberry muffins. And I invited someone for breakfast. She'll be here soon, so go get dressed."

"Like fancy dressed, or regular dressed?"

"Regular." Ivy glanced at Theo, who had begun to clear his herbarium supplies from the dining room table. "I hope that's okay," she said.

"If it's who I think it is, by all means."

IT HAD BEEN YEARS since Theo had seen Gloria Rice. She had to be in her mid-eighties. He watched as she exited the gleaming black Mercedes, then tottered down the sidewalk with the aid of a cane. She looked downright diminutive, but she was still classic Gloria, dressed like she'd just come from a board meeting, her cotton-white hair slicked into a chignon, a mask covering her nose and mouth.

Theo greeted her midway down the sidewalk.

"Theo. It's been ages." She reached out, took his hand, and squeezed.

"That it has," he said. "It's good to see you."

Gloria clutched his arm, and he helped her up the steps to the corner of the porch, where Ivy was arranging a plate of muffins and bear claws on the game table, along with steaming cups of freshly brewed coffee.

"We thought it would be best to sit on the porch so we can socially distance," Ivy said. She offered a chair to their guest.

"Oh, pish posh. Let's sit on this delightful porch because it's a splendid spring day, not because of some nasty virus." Gloria eased onto one of the straight-backed wooden chairs and hooked her cane around the railing. She took one of the coffees offered but declined cream and sugar. "And this must be the famous Penelope I've heard so much about."

"Yes, ma'am. My full name is Penelope Pie Palmer. I will be nine years old on September fourteenth. Although I'm not famous yet, I will be. Right, Mr. Theo?"

"Absolutely. Our Penelope is going to be a writer or a scientist. Maybe both."

Penelope had her hair in pigtails, a red bandana tied over her mask, and was wearing bright pink shorts. Apparently, a revered social media influencer had declared red and pink to be hot summer colors. He couldn't imagine two colors less well suited, but thought she looked like an adorable outlaw.

"I'm almost finished with my first book. It's a mixed-genre graphic fairy tale. Maybe you'd like to read it someday?"

If Gloria was confused by the book description, she didn't let on. "I'd be honored. You just let me know when it's available."

Penelope's bright eyes widened. "Oh yes, ma'am, I will." She jumped from the swing, grabbed a bear claw from the plate, and wrapped it in a paper napkin. "It was stupendous to meet you, but now I need to 'make myself scarce' so the adults can speak in private." She encircled *make myself scarce* with air quotes.

Once Penelope disappeared back into the house, Gloria wasted no time getting straight to the point. "Ivy came to chat with me this morning about the squatting hullabaloo. When I heard what she had to say, I thought it best for all three of us to meet, since this concerns you too, Theo."

"It does?" Gloria's take-charge attitude made Theo feel like a guilty accomplice.

"It surely does." With a slight tremor in her hand, she removed a corner of her mask, lifted her cup, and took a sip of coffee. "You see, I'm afraid my daughter, Elizabeth, can be melodramatic sometimes. I was in Aspen when she discovered someone was living in the garage apartment. She took it upon herself to file a police report without my knowledge. When I'm away, she helps me with things at the house, considers herself my keeper, I suppose. Sometimes I probably need one!" Gloria's gentle laugh pleated the soft wrinkles around her eyes. "Really, I'm sure the Fayetteville police officers have more urgent issues to deal with, particularly since nothing was taken and there was no property damage. But the law is the law. Once a report is filed, it takes on a life of its own. The thing is, Theo, the police got their hands on a bit of security footage with you in it. That's why I say you are involved."

He felt blood rush to his cheeks. "I see."

"Oh, I didn't send any tape over; I don't have a security system. But my daughter asked the new neighbors across the street if they had noticed anything odd, and they volunteered video recorded from their doorbell, if you can imagine. It seems a doorbell has been spying on my house! But that's a conversation for another time. They had a considerable amount of footage involving Ivy and Penelope, and a film of you walking around the house several times. It's lucky that I returned home when I did. They were about to question the lot of you."

She laughed, but beneath his facemask, beads of sweat prickled Theo's upper lip.

"I contacted the sergeant at headquarters—I know him rather well—and explained the whole thing was nothing more than a misunderstanding. I clarified that Ivy was staying in the apartment *at my invitation*—that she had been doing some work for me, and since she needed a place to stay and my apartment was vacant, I'd offered it to her. I reminded the sergeant that affordable housing in this city is of grave concern and something, in my opinion, the city leaders should take more seriously. As of this afternoon, the case will be marked expunged, or resolved, or whatever they choose to call it."

Ivy and Theo exchanged glances. He was so relieved!

"Thank you so much, Ms. Rice," Ivy said. "Really, I am so, so grateful."

The long-ago words of Theo's mother came to him—*Son, the things you worry about the most will likely work themselves out.*

"What matters is that everyone is okay. Now, unfortunately, I need to skedaddle. I have a doctor's appointment up in Bentonville. When you get to be eighty-six, you spend the remaining time you have left seeing one doctor or another. It's really rather ridiculous." Gloria took a final sip of her coffee, returned the cup to the table, and readjusted her mask. She glanced at her Mercedes, still idling at the curb. "Would it be okay if I take a muffin for my driver, Albert? He has quite the sweet tooth."

Ivy vaulted from her chair, fetched a large Ziploc from the kitchen, and placed a muffin and a bear claw inside.

Theo walked Gloria to her car.

"Let's do this again, Theo. On my back veranda next time."

Watching the Mercedes pull away from the curb and disappear around the corner, it felt to Theo as though a pleasant breeze had just moved through the neighborhood.

Back inside, Theo found Ivy washing the plates and cups they had used. "Can you believe it?" she said.

"What exactly did you say to her this morning?" Theo took a bear claw out of the pastry box that still sat on the table. Full of nervous energy, he ripped off a large bite, sugar blooming against his teeth. Wow. Penelope was right—bear claws deserved a spot high on the list of breakfast treats.

"I heard Nita say she was home from Aspen, and I went to beg her forgiveness. When I opened my mouth, my entire story spilled out. She really is such a classy lady." Ivy placed the plates and cups on the drying rack beside the sink. "Did you know she grew up in the foster care system? She's a self-made woman."

Theo had forgotten that, but it was something he had heard before. He nodded, but Ivy didn't notice, she just kept talking, news gushing from her mouth like water from the faucet.

"At first she seemed uber-upset. I worried she might have me arrested on the spot! But then I realized she wasn't actually upset with me, she was mostly annoyed that her daughter had made such a big deal out of it. Although, honestly, I don't blame her daughter at all. I told Ms. Rice I would pay back rent as soon as I save some money, but she said that was ludicrous."

"I know that must be a huge relief, Ivy." He had gone to bed last night relieved to finally know the truth, but this latest news felt like true liberation. Ivy wouldn't be charged with a crime, and he wouldn't be implicated in any way. Best of all, Penelope would truly have her mother back. So much worry had probably been slowing Ivy's recovery.

"Yes, huge! And that's not all; she offered me a full-time job! Twenty-five dollars an hour to be her nurse, companion, and general errand runner, and—you aren't going to believe this—she said I could stay in the apartment. It *comes* with the job. How about that?!"

Ivy's happiness was infectious; Theo felt himself being swept up in it. "That's amazing. What about your job at the VA?"

"Oh, I would much rather work for Ms. Rice. The pay is much better, and I wouldn't be around so many sick people all the time. I'd be crazy not to take her up on the offer, don't you agree? I mean, we get to stay in the apartment, rent free! Just think—we'll be out of your hair in no time. I can't believe it." Ivy's eyes were shining as they locked with his. Her smile was so bright it brought a lump to his throat.

"There is a sad part to all this, though," Ivy continued, her excitement almost visibly fading. "Ms. Rice has been diagnosed with stage four Hodgkin lymphoma, so she really does need my help during the week, when her daughter can't be there. Isn't that awful?"

"That *is* terrible." All this news was coming at him quickly, too quickly, like a sudden hail storm thrumming his brain. He thought about the short visit they had just enjoyed with Gloria. She had walked with the aid of the cane, and sure, she seemed even more frail than he remembered, but for eighty-six, she seemed to be sprightly, still as sharp-witted as ever. It was all very hard to absorb.

"Ivy, I understand why this would be a wonderful opportunity for you. But I'm a little worried."

She was staring out the kitchen window now, not looking at him. "Why?" she asked, tentatively.

He hated to spoil her excitement and weighed his words carefully. "Well, the timing doesn't seem very good to me. You are still getting over a very serious case of coronavirus—it's only been five days since you left the hospital, and you've not been approved to return to work. Being around Ms. Rice, taking her to doctor appointments, running errands for her, all those things will put you into contact with more people. What if you have a relapse?" Ivy worked in healthcare; surely she knew all this!

She wiped her damp hands on a dishcloth and turned toward him. He saw determination in her eyes. "I appreciate your concern, seriously, I do, and I understand the risk of relapse. But my job is taking care of sick patients." She folded the dishcloth and placed it beside the sink. "I told Ms. Rice I couldn't start immediately; she knows I'm still recovering. But I'm already feeling stronger."

"Well, I can—"

"I can't afford to pass on her offer. I really need the money."

"What about your insurance? I assume your job with the VA comes with insurance."

"Ms. Rice said I will be an official employee of her company, which comes with both medical and dental. You're being a worry-wart, and that's very sweet, but I really can't see a downside." Ivy paused and stared at the ceiling. She seemed to be weighing her words too. "You know, last night you told me about all those people who helped you during tough times. Ms. Rice is one of those people for me. She's doing pretty well, I think, considering her diagnosis, but I really think I can help her too. This will be a good thing for Ms. Rice and me."

Theo nodded, wanting to show Ivy he was still with her, still listening, but inside, he was reeling. He understood what an attractive opportunity this was for Ivy. And he certainly understood the desire to repay a kindness. But still, everything was happening so quickly that he was having trouble processing it.

"Pea's school will be out for summer in a few days, and even though I probably won't start my new job until the end of the month, at the earliest, maybe we can move back to the apartment in a week or two." Ivy spoke quickly, as though she was working through the timeline on the fly. "You'll have your life back. Finally, right?" She was so completely rejuvenated by her astonishing change of fortune.

And with that, everything became clear to him. There *was* more to his worry, he realized. He had known they were only staying with him temporarily. At times, he'd worried they might never leave! But Ivy's declaration—*we'll be out of your hair in no time*—had hit him with abrupt finality. Soon, he would be alone. Again.

Twenty-Four

"I bet you're looking forward to having your house back, Mr. Theo." Ivy sipped her morning coffee and peered out the dining room window as heavy rain continued falling. "I can't believe how fast everything is happening. For the first time, I feel like I'm on the right path."

Theo placed a delicate Buffalo clover on mounting paper and pressed it down lightly with his tweezers. A courier from the herbarium had recently delivered another package of specimens, and he had been devoting much of his time to preserving a native clover collection from Newton County. "I'm glad you feel good about things. I'm happy for you." He *was* happy for Ivy. He'd watched her health improve slowly but steadily in the two weeks since Ms. Rice had changed her fortunes. Rest and the passage of time delivered a powerful remedy, especially when combined with the magic of being a young adult. But as for himself, a leaden feeling of stagnation was weighing him down. Later that afternoon, Ivy and Penelope would be moving back into the apartment. Already, the upstairs was emptied of their things; sacks of clothing and shoes, books, and toiletries lined the entryway, waiting for Theo to load them into the truck. His life would be returning to normal, and normal suddenly seemed...lackluster.

"I've already stripped the sheets from our beds," she added. "I put them in the washer."

Theo nodded. The growing lump in his throat prevented him from speaking, so he kept focusing on the specimen before him. It had been raining all night; he wondered if the gloomy weather was adding to his blue mood.

"I know you're probably tired of hearing me say it, but I am truly so grateful for all your help. And I'm grateful you are still willing to help me when I start working for Ms. Rice. There shouldn't be as much for you to do, though, now that Pea's school is on summer break."

"Penelope has been no trouble." He tapped the trifoliate leaves into the glue, then looked across the table at Penelope, enjoying the sound of her pen scribbling across paper. For the past few days, she had been spending hours at the dining room table illustrating essential plot points of her story. "And like I said before, she is welcome to come here anytime you are busy, even if you just need a break."

"Hello...you're both talking about me like I can't hear you, but I'm sitting right here in plain sight!" Penelope dropped her pen and frowned at them, looking a little cross.

"Ivy, do you hear someone talking?" Theo looked around the room, pretending not to see Penelope. He bent down and looked under the table.

"Yes, it sounded a little like Penelope...oh, there you are, Pea! You've had your nose stuck in that journal so much we thought you'd disappeared into whatever world you're creating."

Penelope shook her head. "You're both acting weird. Mr. Theo, I was about to make a suggestion. Now that school's out for summer and we won't have to waste any more time on math and stuff, I thought we could hike more. And take Alice with us. Especially after I finish my story."

"I would love that, kiddo." He wanted nothing more than to get back to a regular hiking routine. The few times he and Penelope hiked together had been both enjoyable and educational. School might be out for summer, but he hoped to continue teaching her about nature.

"So when can we read this masterpiece?" Ivy took another sip from her cup.

Penelope closed the journal, lay the pen across the cover, and counted on her fingers. "In five days."

Ivy seemed taken aback. "Really? That's very specific."

"Yes. I have it all planned out. I'll be hosting a backyard salon on Sunday afternoon, the way Gertrude Stein did in Paris for all those up-and-coming creatives like Picasso and Ernest Hemingway. It will be a very nice affair, and Ms. Nita and Ms. Rice will come. I hope the timing works for everyone, and I sure hope it won't be raining that day." She glanced toward the window. "I've already discussed my salon idea with Ms. Nita, and she's excited to attend. She doesn't know anything about the story—I provided no spoilers—but she said she would be in charge of costumes if I needed a designer. Which I probably do."

Costumes? Whatever next? "So... I presume the backyard you mention will be mine?"

"Oh, yes, for sure. I should have probably asked you first, but you don't mind, do you? Your yard is perfect!" Penelope clapped her hands and wiggled in her chair.

Theo's melancholy mood was beginning to lift with Penelope's excitement over the play and her mention of hiking. Having something to anticipate was always a good remedy for the doldrums. "What can I do to help with the *salon*?" He pronounced the word in his best French accent, which wasn't any good, and resulted in a funny look from Penelope.

"Let's see...the most important thing is to bring curiosity and an open mind. Some refreshments would be good too. And I will graciously accept monetary donations. Being a writer is a solitary endeavor that, so far, doesn't pay anything."

Theo smiled. It had been nearly three months since Penelope first knocked on his front door, but she continued to astound him. "Noted."

"Mr. Theo, I realize we're moving back to the apartment today, but I thought I would leave my art supplies here. It's not like I won't be back. After all, we belong to each other now. Don't forget."

"I won't." Her words touched him deeply, but he still couldn't shake the feeling that something essential was vanishing from his life.

Suddenly, Ivy looked at her phone. "Oh gosh, I didn't realize how late it was getting to be. My appointment is in twenty minutes!"

Theo watched as she hurried to the kitchen and poured the last of her coffee down the sink drain. "Are you sure it's okay if I take your truck?" she called out. He heard the jingle of his key being taken from the bowl.

"I'm sure. We aren't going anywhere, are we kiddo? Especially not in this rain."

"No, I am super engrossed in my work."

"Okay, be good, Pea. And thanks again, Mr. Theo. When I get back, hopefully the rain will have stopped and I can load our stuff into the truck." She slipped on her raincoat and rushed to the front door, stepping gingerly around their things. "I can't believe how much stuff we have accumulated!" Ivy giggled. She sounded so young.

Once she was out the door, Penelope rolled her eyes and muttered, "I'm always good. My mom tends to forget that."

"Nah. She doesn't forget. That's just a thing moms say, I think." It had always been the last thing his mother said, too, as he and Michael raced to the school bus, or walked to the baseball field on Saturday morning. Really, anytime they were leaving her, for any period of time. *Be good, boys.* Suddenly a thought struck him. "You know, maybe the phrase 'be good' holds more than a literal meaning. Maybe it's a blessing of sorts, protection tendered from mother to child. What do you think?"

"*Oooh*, I like that. Do you think saying 'Take care' or 'Be safe' is also a blessing?" Still scribbling away, Penelope remained focused on the journal. Theo marveled at the ease with which she could hold two thoughts.

Again, he thought of his mother. "Yes, I think maybe so."

"Mr. Theo, that's a pretty deep observation. You've earned another point."

This surprised him. There had been no mention of their game since Ivy's release from the hospital. "So what's the score of our game?"

She shrugged. "Who knows? That doesn't matter—our game is not about the score. It's just a fun way to cheer each other on."

Penelope's perceptive explanation stunned him. "That's a pretty insightful way of thinking, young lady. You've earned yourself another point too."

"Thank you!" Her face seemed to light from within. "I really don't get why the whole world hasn't learned to play our game."

Indeed.

TWO HOURS LATER, Ivy returned from her doctor's appointment, flitting into the kitchen and dropping his truck key into the bowl. "Gosh, something sure smells good! What is it?"

"Quesadillas." He lifted the skillet lid so Ivy could see, and the aroma intensified. It was almost noon, and his stomach was complaining. He wanted to ask about her appointment, to know what the doctor had said, but he knew she would tell him when she was ready.

"*Bean* quesadillas! Mr. Theo is eating more vegetarian dishes, thanks to me. Right?" Penelope was meticulously folding paper towels into squares and placing them beside the water glasses on the kitchen table.

"Right. But, my recent vegetarianism has happened only due to convenience. It's easier for me to make the same thing for everyone." He sliced the quesadilla into large wedges using a pizza cutter and put a wedge on each plate. He handed the first serving to Ivy.

"And you are way healthier for it! Again, thanks to *moi*."

Theo laughed. She was probably right about his healthier lifestyle. Sure, his legs still became stiff when he worked too long at the dining room table, and a day of yard work still made his back ache, but he was sleeping better, and he seemed to have more energy at the end of a long hike. He dished slices onto two more plates and placed them on the table.

"My appointment took so much longer than I thought it would," Ivy told them once they were seated. "Twelve patients were ahead of me, and we were all told to wait in our cars. It was relaxing, sitting in the cab of your truck, listening to the rain. I'm grateful to feel so good, you know?"

Grateful to be alive, Theo thought. "And? Did you get a good report from the doctor?" Since she had finally brought up her appointment, he decided it would be okay to ask about it.

"Yes! My oxygen level and heartbeat were both normal. My blood pressure was still a bit elevated, but my doctor said that was to be expected. He said I should keep doing what I'm doing, and that my recovery is going better than most patients who have been on a vent."

"Yay!!" Penelope cheered. "I knew you were cured! I've been praying about it every night." She took a big bite of quesadilla and began laughing as a string of gooey cheese stretched from the tortilla.

Theo felt tremendous relief over Ivy's news. He had presumed her recovery was going well—her energy level had increased significantly, and the color had returned to her cheeks—but now, with confirmation from her doctor, Theo felt he could let go of his worry over her health.

"It's amazing, really. I survived Covid, a much better job practically fell into my lap, and as soon as the rain lets up, Pea and I will move back into the apartment. This time with permission," she added sheepishly.

For the first time, Theo realized how different the apartment would be for them. Ivy and Penelope would be able to actually enjoy the place. They would no longer be hiding out and living a lie. How stressful that must have been for both of them.

Once they finished eating lunch, Ivy took the dishes to the sink and Theo turned on the midday news to check the weather forecast. But the weather wasn't on. The local news had been delayed by breaking news out of St. Paul. Crowds of protesters. Burning buildings. Vandalism and looting. Theo had not watched the news since the morning before. It quickly became apparent that something ugly was unfolding.

"Ivy, have you seen the news today? Something terrible has happened."

Penelope came rushing over, sliding on her socked feet to stand beside him. "What is it?"

He knew she shouldn't see what was happening, but he was frozen in place, unable to stop watching.

Ivy's reaction time was instantaneous. Dashing in from the kitchen, she snatched the remote and turned off the television.

"I didn't mean for her...I'm sorry, Ivy." The flash of news Theo saw had been horrendous. A Black man dying at the hands of a white police officer. A crowd of horrified witnesses. A bystander recording it with her phone! Theo stared at the dark television screen and swallowed the swirl of emotion rising to his throat.

"What happened to that man?" Penelope asked. "Turn it back on. We need to know."

"Not right now. We have things to do." Ivy gave Theo a woeful look. "I think the rain is letting up."

The rain wasn't letting up. It continued pouring for two more hours. During that time, they played gin rummy and spades at the kitchen table. Theo's heart wasn't in it though. He would have much rather parked himself in front of the television. He needed to know what was happening in Minnesota. Penelope, however, was a natural card player, her focus intent on each discard. In fact, Theo thought she was instinctively counting cards. At a blackjack table, she would probably bring down the house.

THE RAIN FINALLY STOPPED in the late afternoon. Theo packed the truck with Ivy and Penelope's things, insisting on doing it alone. He *needed* to do this one last thing for them. Ivy must have understood because she and Penelope began busying themselves in the laundry room, folding the freshly washed towels and bedding, and returning everything to the linen closet.

Packing their things took no time. Driving to Gloria Rice's house and carrying their sacks into the apartment took no time either.

"It's so clean!" Penelope took in the apartment. The place smelled strong of Pine Sol, and every surface gleamed. Theo remembered how Nita had first described the rumored squatters as a wild pack of raccoons. Thank goodness that was all behind them.

"I came over yesterday and cleaned it up. We deserve a fresh start," Ivy said, her eyes bright with gratification.

"You do," Theo said, feeling honored to have played a small role in their new beginning. He left them joyfully unpacking their things. Their next chapter was just starting, and now he needed to focus on his.

Once he got home though, Theo felt the emptiness. But still, Alice was there, enthusiastically wagging her tail, greeting him as though he'd been away two days. "It's just you and me again, girl," he told her, giving her ears a quick rub before getting her supper.

Since inadvertently hearing the news report earlier, Theo had been anxious to learn more about what had happened. Now he could turn on the news and watch all night without fear of Penelope overhearing. He grabbed a bag of potato chips and settled onto the couch, turning the channel to CNN. And there it was. George Floyd's very public murder. He could hardly believe it. Theo dropped the chip he was holding back into the bag. His stomach turned. *Twenty dollars in exchange for someone's life?*

The world had gone mad.

His mind began racing. Why hadn't someone done something? Bystanders just watched it happen; someone even videoed it! If only the man had cooperated and followed the cop's instructions, he would still be alive. But almost as soon as the thought formed, Theo chided himself. No one should be murdered, *period. End of story.* Theo wanted to believe, no, *had* to believe, that if he had been among the crowd of bystanders he would have said something, done something.

He began scrolling news channels, flipping from one to another every few minutes, the atrocious scene burned into his mind. *I can't breathe! I can't breathe!* When he found a channel on which George Floyd's murder wasn't being replayed, the news was reporting live footage of a growing protest in Minneapolis-St. Paul. He would never understand how people felt justified to loot and burn down businesses.

Theo had seen bleak times before, but this merciless act replaying on every news channel filled him with a sort of heavy-laden despair. He couldn't quite wrap his head around his feelings, but something made him feel culpable. The entire country was to blame! Mr. Floyd's death had been a purposefully cruel act; a white man purporting to serve their shared country, a man in uniform, for God's sake, kneeling on his neck until he died of asphyxiation. What profound pain that man's mother must be feeling. Her son had cried out for her with his dying breath.

Theo turned off the television and went to bed. He lay awake for some time, trying to comprehend the level of intolerance necessary to murder an unarmed man over a counterfeit bill. The only solace he found was in his inability to understand such hatred.

Twenty-Five

Theo spaced folding chairs beneath the oak tree, then started ripping open a package that held a sparkly red garland. Nita was carefully arranging a charcuterie tray and a platter of almond cookies on the nearby card table. "Thanks for helping with this, Nita," Theo said.

"Are you kidding? I'm honored to be included! It isn't every day I get invited to a debut story reading. Penelope said the reading would be an astonishing reveal. I'm not sure what she meant by that, and when I tried to pry it from her, she wouldn't elaborate. Goodness, she was bubbling with excitement though." Nita unwrapped a package of red and white polka dot napkins, pressed and twisted the stack between her palms, and presto, the napkins fanned into a design worthy of Martha Stewart's table. "That should do nicely," she said, surveying the table and scanning the backyard. "Do you want me to hang that garland for you?"

Theo had forgotten he was holding it. "Um, yes, thanks. I thought this would be a good idea when I saw it at Lowe's, but now I'm unsure what to do with it." He handed over the jumble, glad to be liberated from it. "I think it's a Fourth of July decoration."

Nita untangled the garland and skillfully draped it along the backyard gate. "It's perfect. This will be the first festive thing everyone will see."

"I thought Penelope would like it."

"That little girl has sure rubbed off on you."

A rush of blood flushed his cheeks. "Oh…well…she likes sparkly things…and I just want to make—"

"Theo, I'm not criticizing you. I think it's adorable how you've bonded with Penelope. I've grown quite attached to her too."

Theo had become accustomed to wearing a mask over the past few months. The anonymity it gave him felt protective, as if the thin cloth might hide everything about him. That afternoon, he wasn't wearing one, not in his backyard where the air was fresh and the world his own, but he found himself wishing he could hide his reddened cheeks behind one. He couldn't think of a word to say.

Nita took the plastic wrapper from Theo, her fingers incidentally brushing his. "How has it been since they left? Really quiet, I bet?"

"Yes, my house is as quiet as a coffin," he admitted. "I've really been looking forward to seeing everyone today. I sure do need the distraction. Other than walking Alice, all I do is watch the news. As my dad would say, the world's gone to hell in a handbasket, and I can't stop watching it burn."

Ivy and Penelope had moved back to the apartment five days ago, and since then, Theo's world had been moving at a different pace. He had become obsessed with the news, his entire afternoons consumed with live feeds of nationwide protests. "I can't breathe" had become a rallying cry across the world, and a specific call for Theo to take a long hard look at his own prejudices. He had lost interest in almost everything—growing carrots and preserving dried columbine seemed pointless when the country was boiling with hate.

"I actually participated in a protest downtown; I carried a sign and everything," Nita said. "I've never done anything like that, and even though it probably won't make a lick of difference, it felt good to do something. You may not know this, but my son lives in Minneapolis with his family, not too far from where it happened. I've been so worried." Nita shook her head quickly, as though expelling terrible thoughts. "I just can't stick my head in the sand, you know?"

Theo nodded. He had never taken Nita for an activist, and he admired her strength in taking a public stand and marching in front of the courthouse. He preferred donating money to local organizations he believed in, like the 7hills Homeless Center and the Northwest Arkansas Food Bank. Two days ago, he had even mailed his first ever political donation to the Black Lives Matter cause. Theo had no illusions that two hundred dollars would help much, but it made him feel a smidgen better. Still, he wondered if he was sticking his head in the sand.

"Oh, I almost forgot." Nita reached into her tote bag and pulling out a bag of candy. "I bought some Laffy Taffy. Penelope mentioned you like the banana ones, and she likes grape-flavored." She tossed him a single yellow piece, and he caught it in midair.

"I've not had one of these since I was a boy. Probably Halloween, in sixty-two or thereabouts." Theo unwrapped the candy and popped it into his mouth. The familiar taste brought back memories of school carnivals, and the lady at the supermarket who offered a piece of candy to every kid who passed through her checkout lane. What an innocent time that had been! After a few chews, he spit the sticky taffy into a paper napkin.

"Is it that bad?" Nita laughed.

"I'm not sure my old fillings can take it!"

Alice, sitting at the back door, heard the car before anyone else. A whine led to a single woof, then full-fledged barking. By the time Penelope rushed through the gate, Alice was in a frenzy.

"Alice!!" Penelope hugged her ecstatically. Standing on her hind legs, Alice seemed to be hugging her right back.

Next, Ivy and Gloria ambled up the driveway, arm in arm. Extremely happy to see everyone, Theo was struck by a strange feeling—that something interesting would soon unfold.

"Wow! It's a real fancy garden party." Penelope danced around the backyard, taking in every detail, her mouth agape. "Ms. Nita, did *you* do all this?"

"I was in charge of the food, but Mr. Theo hung the balloons, arranged the chairs, and made a stage from wooden pallets. And he bought the sparkly red garland decorating the gate." Nita glanced at him and winked, her eyes bright.

Penelope threw her arms around Theo's waist. "It's even more dreamy than I imagined."

Theo was caught off guard. He couldn't remember the last time he'd been hugged like this and was surprised, unnerved even, to realize how warm and...whole, it made him feel. He stroked Penelope's hair a bit clumsily. "Ms. Nita even brought your favorite candy."

"Laffy Taffy?" She released her grip on Theo's waist and stared up at him.

He nodded.

"Boy, you and Ms. Nita thought of every single incredible thing. This is unbelievable!" She twirled around the table before plucking a piece of candy from the bowl and holding it tightly in her hand. "I'm gonna save this for later. I need to go inside real quick and mentally prepare." She vanished into the house. The adults exchanged glances, shrugging.

"Ivy, do you know what Penelope's story is about?" Nita asked.

"Not really. She's been very secretive. I've not been allowed to even peek at it." Ivy turned to Theo, offering him the paper sack she was carrying. "Thanks for doing this, Mr. Theo. Maybe you should save these for later. It seems desserts are well covered."

He opened the bag and inhaled the fresh-from-the-oven aroma of cherry hand pies with great pleasure. "Oooh—thank you! I'll be having one of these for breakfast tomorrow."

Penelope was only inside a few minutes, and when she returned she strode to the stage Theo had built, opened her journal, and sent a darting glance his way. "Thank you for coming. Today I will be reading my debut story, *The Almost Princess*. There will be one intermission, but don't worry—the story isn't very long, not compared to *Crime and Punishment* or even *To Kill a Mockingbird*."

Clapping and cheering, they made quite a spirited fuss for such a small audience.

Penelope paused and grinned. Watching her own the moment, Theo felt a surge of pride in the kid. He could see her on an actual stage someday.

"Once upon a time, in a faraway land of sand and copper, a raven-haired child was born to undeserving parents who had chipped ice hearts," she began in a dreamy, faraway voice. "The baby was heaven-sent, as all newborns are, blessed with starlit eyes, sweet milk skin, and cheeks tinted by the first rose petals of May. But despite her fair attributes, the child's father, who some say was part wolf, and distantly related to the Robber Bridegroom, declared a newborn as useless to him as a crystal vase. And so the mother, who rarely spoke and only ate black licorice, called the baby Crystal from that day forward.

"Pauper poor, without much affection or any real guidance from her unfit parents, the years passed, as Crystal went about her days and nights with only the moon and sun to protect her from the world's lurking evils." Penelope paused and looked up, making eye contact first with her mother and then with Gloria, before moving to Nita and Theo.

Already, Theo thought the story was bizarre.

"And evils were aplenty."

As Penelope continued, turning page after page with a soft flutter, Theo's attention began wandering. The balloons tied to the lowermost branches of the oak tree were barely moving in the warm afternoon air. Midway up the tree canopy, there was a massive nest built in a fork near the trunk. He had never noticed it before.

"It was years ago, and life was still mostly new to Crystal...."

Theo was mesmerized by the clump of leaves, twigs, and moss, marveling over the construction talent of gray squirrels. He was pleased that his favorite tree was providing a home to such a skilled animal family. Perhaps the squirrel living in his tree was the same one he had chased from Nita's kitchen. He chuckled, then fake-coughed into his hand as Penelope said, "unknown future, dark and foreboding." Evidently, whatever section of the story Penelope was now reading was not a laughing matter.

Ivy glanced back at him, grimacing. Had she realized he'd lost track of the story? Theo shifted in his chair, pressed his feet firmly into the grass, and tried to concentrate.

"...and then Crystal understood. She was doomed to follow the path of her ancestors unless she forged a new one for herself and her soon-to-arrive baby."

Her baby? So now Crystal was grown up herself and having a baby? Theo felt incredibly guilty for his distraction. Maybe it was the warmth of the afternoon sun or the faraway tone of Penelope's voice that had lulled him. He wished he could ask her to start over, but that would make things worse. She'd know he hadn't been paying attention.

"Everyone had troubles to navigate and secrets to bury along the way...."

Theo saw Ivy lower her head. He looked at Gloria, sitting next to her. She certainly didn't look sick. Exuding style, as ever, she wore a midnight blue pantsuit, and her hair was in its signature chignon. Thank goodness she was the forgiving type. Things had certainly worked out well for Ivy.

"As fall turned to winter and attentions turned to holiday feasts and celebrations, Crystal contemplated her future, searching for a remedy to the curse that had befallen her. She had no parental support, and no money beyond the coins she scrounged working odd jobs, but she wished on stars and watched for answers in the nocturnal sky. And all the while, she hid the life growing inside her."

Hadn't Penelope asked him if he knew anyone named Crystal? *What do you think about the name Crystal? Do you know anyone named Crystal?* Yes, she definitely had, but when? Theo tried to remember the details of their conversation, but it remained distant. He straightened in his chair and forced himself to focus on Penelope's words.

"Three days before Christmas, her miracle occurred. It was a literal sign from above, written in newsprint and wrapped around a two-day-old broken pretzel given to her by a kind sidewalk vendor. The ad said: *Pregnant, frightened, and alone? Dear Baby provides love and solutions. Call for support today!* Before finishing her pretzel, Crystal dialed the number from a downtown pay phone, made an appointment, and breathed again for the first time in months."

This sent Theo back to his memories. He and Annie had traveled a considerable distance down the path to adoption before she fell ill. For a moment, Theo allowed himself to remember Annie poring over birthing books, and corresponding with the prospective mother. They had even planned to meet her before the birth.

"It was the perfect solution to an imperfect situation. A real family would give her princess the life she deserved."

They had even started making lists of baby names.

". . . grew and grew and for a while contentment spread over the land. . ."

Annie had been gone twenty years, but sometimes, when he least expected it, her presence felt as tangible as the sunshine warming his brow. Theo pressed his fingertips against his face, trying to hold on to the sensation.

Penelope turned another page, paused, and said, "This concludes act one. There will now be a short intermission while I prepare for act two. Please reserve conversation for the conclusion of the story." Penelope stepped off the pallet stage and went inside the house. Ivy followed her without a word or glance at anyone.

Theo stood and stretched his back into a shallow backbend. Alice appeared at his side and nudged his leg. "Hey girl, you missed the first part of the play." He'd missed most of it too. He drained a plastic cup of iced tea and refilled it, grateful Nita had thought to make a pitcher. Nita and Gloria were complying with Penelope's request for a quiet intermission, but even in silence, the ladies looked happy, smiling as they nibbled on crackers and cubes of cheddar cheese.

Theo sat down again just as Ivy came back outside, her eyes downcast, arms crossed as though shielding herself. A pang went through him. What was wrong?

Penelope then emerged from the house. Two bright blue tears, the size of English ivy leaves, now decorated one side of her face. Theo hoped she hadn't used the blue slick board marker; if she had, she would be wearing those tears for some time. He rubbed his forehead. Alice, now sprawled beside him, probably needed a walk. *He* needed a walk, he thought. His leg had started throbbing.

"News traveled slowly in the land of sand and copper, and when Crystal learned of the curse, it was too late for salvation. No matter how serendipitous, wished for, or perfect something seemed, some things were simply not meant to be."

His tea glass already empty again, Theo began crunching on a piece of ice. When the reading was over, what would he tell Penelope? She would ask his opinion of her story, and what would he say? The truth was, he had never liked plays. It was Annie who had loved attending live performances on campus. Being supportive, Theo always went along, even though he would have rather spent the time working in the garden or hiking a trail.

"Only weeks before the birth of Crystal's baby, the entire adoption unraveled. Not because the adoptive couple didn't want her baby, but because the wife was stricken with a terminal illness." Penelope's voice had risen, and her cheeks were flushed. "Her diagnosis was hopeless."

Theo shifted in his seat. Suddenly he didn't want to hear anymore. The style of the story was grating on him, and the scenario was uncomfortably familiar, a reminder of all he had lost.

"Life isn't always meant to be understood," Penelope continued. "That's what Crystal believed when her plan toppled. Dear Baby made assurances that she would be matched with another couple. But the princess arrived early, permanently changing her life, and the life of her descendants to come. Crystal held her baby for the first time, looked into her gray-blue eyes, nuzzled the top of her downy head, and vowed to keep her baby safe and healthy. Meanwhile, Annie died."

The name reverberated through Theo's skull. *What the hell?*

"The death of Annie became a turning point for Crystal and her almost princess."

Theo's head was whirling. Around him, everything had gone deathly quiet. Then a sudden barrage of incoherent shouting. "What in the world? Why would you—?"

He was the one shouting, he realized.

"Because it's true, Mr. Theo, Annie—"

"Stop it! Stop talking." He rocketed from his chair, sending it toppling backward into the grass.

"Wait, Theo. Don't go." Nita was instantly at his side.

He glared at Penelope. She teetered on the edge of the stage, the ridiculous blue tears radiant on her cheek, the late afternoon sun dazzling in her eyeglasses. Yes, she was a child, but after spending so much time with her, he knew emphatically how mature she actually was. Surely, she understood the callousness of her words. How could she have used his wife's name in her fairy tale?

Theo became acutely aware of Nita's hands gripping his arm. He watched, dumbfounded, as Ivy approached Penelope, murmured something in her ear, and then announced, with an apologetic smile, "I think we will take a short break."

Nita released her hold on Theo's arm, and for a moment he just stood there, his body heavy, his mind a muddled mess. Then he turned, walked to the back porch, and went inside. *Annie?* What was going on exactly? Theo filled a glass with tap water and swigged it down so fast he sputtered water back into the sink.

"Mr. Theo, can we talk? I only need a minute. Please, let me explain." Ivy had quietly followed him inside.

Theo couldn't look at her. He was confused and felt like the butt of some joke he didn't yet understand. "Why would Penelope use my wife's name in her story? It feels incredibly cruel to me."

"I'm so sorry, she would never ... she didn't mean to be cruel." Ivy sounded almost panicked. "If I'd known what Penelope's story was about, I would never have let her perform it for you like this. I...I need to tell you something."

Something in Ivy's voice pushed Theo from upset to unnerved. He tried to think more clearly but nothing was making any sense.

"I understand you're upset, but I think you need to know the whole story."

He turned around. She was blinking back tears and wringing her hands. He certainly had a right to be upset, but why was *she* so upset? "What is it, Ivy?"

"Penelope...Penelope's story was based on...on what she knows of her own life. You see...Crystal was my mother. And—" she swallowed hard. "—I was the baby you and Annie were planning to adopt."

The words were spoken softly, but they struck him like a sledgehammer. His mind began spinning. "What?"

Tears filled Ivy's eyes. She didn't blink them away or move her focus from Theo.

He was speechless; all he could do was stare at her.

"I know this must be incredibly confusing, but I swear it's true. I was trying to think of a way to tell you, but then I got Covid, and, well, you know the rest."

The rest? What on earth did she mean, he knew the rest? He knew nothing! "Not really, no. I'm beginning to think I don't know anything!"

"I mean, I was in the hospital, and Penelope was here. Of course, Penelope took matters into her own hands. I had no idea of the details of her story until she started reading. Oh, I know this sounds crazy, and I'm not explaining it right." Ivy covered her face with her palms.

Theo turned away from her, looking out the kitchen window at the trio of co-conspirators gathered around his beloved oak tree. He tried to think back to the weeks before Annie's cancer diagnosis, when they had been matched with an expectant mother. *Crystal?* He couldn't possibly remember her name after so much time had passed! Annie had corresponded with her a few times through the agency, but...

"During the intermission, when I realized what Pea's story was about, I tried to stop her from continuing, but she was so excited about sharing her story that I gave up and let her reveal it all. Not my best decision, I guess. Please, please don't be mad. We just wanted to know you. That's all."

Theo realized his hands were trembling. Cautiously, he put his glass down in the sink and turned back to her. He couldn't believe what he was hearing. *She was the baby?* He didn't know what to say. But it seemed Ivy had plenty more to tell him.

"I didn't know any of this until after my mother died. I only saw her sporadically; she had become an addict, with very little to her name, and being around her was too painful. But I kept up with her through her friend Marilee. Her *only* friend, really." Ivy's voice cracked. She paused for a few seconds and looked at him.

In the quietness of the moment, Theo saw a deep sadness gathered in her pale blue eyes. Her sincerity unsettled him.

"Penelope and I were living in Tulsa when I found out she'd died. I was barely treading water as it was, taking an online nursing aide class and working two part-time customer service jobs. Marilee mailed my mother's few belongings to me, and in her things, I found the letters your wife wrote to her. There was even a copy of Annie's obituary. It may sound crazy, Mr. Theo, but those letters became a real lifeline for me. I began to imagine how my life might have turned out; I became fixated on it, I suppose. At first, I just wanted to see you. To maybe catch a glimpse of what my life might have been like. And then—"

Tulsa? Annie's letters? Her obituary? Theo's heart pounded in his ears. His awareness heightened. He couldn't believe what he was hearing! "Wait a minute. Are you saying you moved into Gloria Rice's apartment so you could spy on me?"

A single tear silently slipped down her cheek. "I moved to Fayetteville to find you. But everything I told you before is true."

"When? When did you move here?"

"A little over a year ago," she said, in a voice that was barely a murmur.

Over a year ago? Anger flared inside, but he willed himself to keep calm. "Why are you just now telling me this? I can't understand how you could sit on this information for so long, especially after our conversation two weeks ago."

She flinched at what he'd said, just slightly, while his words continued spooling out in a measured voice he didn't quite recognize.

"Ivy, please help me understand. We sat together on the front porch, and you explained your problem in finding affordable housing. You told me all about Derrick, and how you and Penelope had to live in your car…but you didn't think to mention *this*?"

Her cheeks were slick with tears now, but she was staring directly at him. "At first, I couldn't figure out how to tell you. Then, I was too *afraid* to tell you. I *needed* to hold on to the idea that once I did tell you, everything would work out; that we might eventually have a relationship. But if you refused to hear me out, or didn't believe me, well, I was terrified by what that rejection would mean. I would have noth…nothing," she said, choking out her words. "But I swear, Mr. Theo, the rest of what I've said is true. I was taking classes at the community college when I met Derrick. He turned out to be a snake, but because of him, I met Ms. Rice. He really was doing some work for her. We were living in the motel, then Derrick left, and she had that empty apartment. The fact that it backed up to your property seemed like an incredible miracle. It was definitely a sign. I'm just so sorry that you found out this way. This wasn't at all how I wanted things to happen."

Theo thought his head might explode. She looked so vulnerable to him, like an injured animal or a frightened child.

"You have to believe me, Mr. Theo. I wanted to meet you since I first read the letters, but fear paralyzed me. Of course, Penelope took it upon herself to knock on your front door, and I knew I had no choice but to explain everything. I planned to tell you the night you came for dinner, but...." Her voice trailed off as she stared at her hands and twisted the ring on her finger. "I couldn't do it, not with Penelope there."

She swiped at a tear and sucked in a breath. Theo felt his stomach clench.

"Remember the next morning, when you were working on your porch, and I first asked you to teach Penelope?"

"Of course."

"That was the morning I had learned Penelope's school was moving to virtual classes, and I was completely panicked over what to do. I had no accrued vacation at work, and no one to help with my child. So, yes, I came over to ask for your help, but I also planned to tell you the whole story."

"But you didn't."

"I couldn't. Don't you see? Once you agreed to help with Penelope, I couldn't risk it."

He sighed. His confusion seemed to escalate with each of her attempts at an explanation. "What do you mean? Risk what?"

"That you might not believe me and that you would refuse to help me with Penelope." She had stopped crying now. Her voice was calmer, more determined. "I decided telling you would be much easier after you spent a week with Penelope. By then, we would no longer be strangers."

Theo rubbed his forehead. "But you ended up in the hospital before you could tell me."

"Yes. And when I finally got out of the hospital, the timing was still terrible. I was totally dependent on you. I wanted to get back on my feet, healthy and working again, before I told you. But...Penelope had her own timeline."

He was trying to process all this information, but Theo knew it would take him time. Turning to the window again, he was struck by the altered backyard scene, the merry celebration gone wrong. Penelope had been planning her big event for several days, but it was over. That much was obvious. He had ruined it in grand style, yelling at a little girl and storming into the house. Already he couldn't remember exactly what he had said, although that was probably a good thing. His eyes skittered to Gloria and Nita, sitting in chairs that had been moved into deeper shade. If they were talking, he couldn't tell. Even Penelope looked subdued, sitting cross-legged in a sunny patch of grass, her hand stroking Alice. For a moment he watched a blue balloon, still tied to a tree branch, idly spinning in the breeze. He wondered what Annie would have said to all this.

"Mr. Theo? What are you thinking?"

Ivy's voice was sweet and tentative. It almost made him cry. "I'm not really sure. But I wish Annie were here."

Twenty-Six

Theo had a fitful night, with little sleep. He couldn't see past his confusion, and knew that clarity would only come with a change of perspective. For once, his timing was perfect—making the call first thing in the morning, he snapped up the last available cabin at Devil's Den. He stuffed clothing in a duffle, and packed enough food for two weeks. He barely gave a thought to the plant specimens waiting in the box on the dining room table. They would still be there when he returned.

When Theo got to his cabin, he dropped his duffle onto the floor beside the fireplace and felt his soul sink beneath a flood of memories. A strong need to return home tugged at him. He took a deep breath, inhaling the ashen scent of the last fire that had burned in the room, and vowed to give himself time. If there was anywhere he could find a way to rebalance his world it would be here, deep in the forest at Devil's Den. It had been Annie's favorite place for quick weekend getaways, and they had celebrated several anniversaries there too. After her death, Theo had fled to Devil's Den to hibernate, and make some way towards healing. Remembering that, he stuck the first night out, telling himself he could always leave first thing the next morning.

The new day dawned bright and sweet, and his spirits rose. As the first morning passed at a slow, pleasant pace, thoughts of leaving disappeared. He thought he might stay forever. It was June now, the first day of June, and the warm day helped quiet his mind. When thoughts of Penelope and Ivy bubbled to the surface, he pushed them down again. Time for contemplation would come later.

He spent the first week hiking the trails, fished and skipped stones at the creek in the late afternoon, and watched for shooting stars late into the night. Theo was grateful to be there, tucked away in the Ozarks, far from horrible news of the pandemic and the constant noise surrounding the death of George Floyd. Without television, or even a Wi-Fi signal, he wasn't constantly being reminded that nothing much had really changed when it came to discrimination. Pleasant dreams filled his sleep, of family members lost long ago; his brother and father playing a game of catch in the front yard, his mother walking barefoot between rows of okra, harvesting pods and dropping them into the pocket of her homespun apron.

THEO WALKED TO THE SHORELINE near the spillway, then wandered, searching for stones to skip across the glassy water. He selected a pearly white one, held it first in the center of his palm before moving it into position. The perfect skipping rock was relatively flat and of a specific size, but it could not be chosen by sight alone. For Theo, it was a tactile thing. When he balanced a good stone between his thumb and forefinger, he sensed its suitability the way he knew Nita's raspberry shortbread would melt on his tongue simply because of how delicate it felt in his hand. This one was too thin and light to carry itself across the water, so he dropped it. He studied one rock after another, collected several in his pockets, and started tossing, knowing the instant they left his fingers whether he had chosen correctly.

Practice makes perfect. His mother's voice echoed in his memory. It was a trite saying, but he'd always found it to be true, whether for growing orchids, rebuilding a porch, or teaching Botany 101. When he'd arrived at Devil's Den, his rock-skipping skills had been mighty rusty. The first stone he tossed had hit the water and sunk instantly. But by the end of his second afternoon there, the childhood activity had returned to him as naturally as Alice had taken to splashing and swimming in the creek.

Theo arranged a dozen or so rocks along the trunk of a fallen tree near the water's edge. While Alice gnawed on a stick, he pitched the first stone and watched it skip five times before sinking into the water.

"I've still got it," he said to Alice, who said nothing in return.

Taking up the next stone, he adjusted his grip, cleared his mind, and flicked his wrist. The stone sailed toward the fuchsia sunset, skipping across the sparkling water—once, twice…six times! "Whoa! Did you see that?"

Theo didn't actually expect Alice to notice anything other than the stick she held expertly between her paws, but after a week of solitude he occasionally felt the need to stretch his vocal cords, and talking to

Alice was more enjoyable than talking to himself. He continued skipping stones, one after the next, never rushing the process. There was an art to it. His grip, the quick flick of his wrist and angle of release, the speed at which the stone touched the surface of the shimmering water—these were the essential components. "This one's for you, Michael." Theo flicked the stone, imagining his brother standing beside him, waiting his turn, their dad coaching and cheering them on. The stone skimmed the water and kissed the surface five times before gently disappearing.

"Yeah!" Theo cheered and pumped his fist, a tingle moving up his spine to the back of his neck. He felt he had witnessed something akin to magic. From the opposite shore, his shout echoed back to him. *Yeah...yeah...*for an infinitesimal flash, Theo almost believed his brother had witnessed the stone skip across the water, and that it was his cheering voice he heard.

"Okay, Dad, this next one is for you." He selected another stone from his pile, remembering the first time his dad had shown him how to skip stones, at the pond near Grandpa Gruene's house.

The sun dropped lower in the sky. Theo's mind was clear of everything except stone-skipping. A flat, arrowhead-shaped stone reminded him of his mother's fascination with Native American artifacts. The stone was too light to skip successfully, but he tossed it anyway, in her honor, and watched it spin over the water.

He saved the last of the day's collection for Annie. The rose-colored stone only skipped four times, and he vowed to try again the next day.

THEO LIFTED THE EDGE of the T-bone steak he was grilling for supper and checked for char lines. He leaned back into his chair and sipped from his cup of hot tea, the peaceful day settling into his bones. "It's smelling mighty good, Alice."

Alice, sitting in one of the two wooden chairs near the grill, watched without blinking, her nostrils twitching. She was now a chair-sitting dog. The first time he'd caught her curled in one of the club chairs inside the cabin, he'd been inclined to shoo her down, but he let her stay.

After all, they were practically camping, and camping rules were more relaxed. Later, when she'd jumped into one of the outside chairs, he just laughed and let her stay. What could it hurt? Not only was her loyalty beyond reproach, but she was the perfect buddy to accompany him on a peaceful retreat in the woods.

"I think it's done." Theo lifted the steak onto a plate and took it inside. Alice followed him around the small kitchen as he made some toast and fried two eggs. Adding a generous sprinkle of red pepper flakes to the eggs, he carried his plate back outside, to the picnic table by the cabin. Theo had taken to eating all of his meals outside, often timing breakfast and dinner to coincide with sunrise and sunset. "Now this is how you cook a steak," he told his canine companion, pulling a tender piece away from the bone. He offered her a bite, even though she'd already eaten her bowl of supper kibble. "We'll need our strength for tomorrow's hike to Holt Ridge," he told her as she gobbled the morsel from his palm.

The waxing moon rose higher in the dusky sky, but the early evening still held tight to the day's warmth. It was still almost two weeks until solstice, and Theo suspected it would be an extraordinarily hot summer. He pondered what it would be like to permanently live off the grid, to have no air-conditioning in August, to depend entirely on his wits for survival, hunting and foraging for food, hauling water from the creek. His savings would last longer, he reasoned. And probably his sanity. Fully disengaging with the frenzied world, even for a week, was the ultimate luxury. He already felt healthier for having replaced television news with the rustle of leaves and the cawing of crows. Other than the occasional hiker he came across on a trail, he'd heard no human noises besides his own. The other cabin dwellers kept to themselves.

Only two people knew where he was—the reservation clerk at Devil's Den and Nita Johnson. Theo had not particularly wanted to share his plan with Nita, but he believed it prudent for someone to know his whereabouts. With Winn gone, she had been the only person he could think of. Of course, he could have told Ivy, but he wasn't quite ready to talk to her. Theo hoped Nita was keeping her promise not to tell anyone where he had gone.

Theo sopped up the last of his egg with a wedge of toast just as the stars began showing themselves through the trees. Being in the woods centered him. With spongy leaf litter beneath his feet and the tree canopy above, he felt…bathed…in forest. Penelope's sidewalk foray into forest bathing flitted through his mind, but he stopped his memories, wouldn't let himself think about her. Not yet. Instead, he thought of his loved ones, long gone; they seemed to speak to him more here, piercing the veil to touch his world—sometimes almost imperceptibly, through starlight or warm rays of sunshine, sometimes through memories so vivid it felt like they were back with him in truth. Theo stayed outside until his eyelids grew heavy.

Twenty-Seven

Hiking Vista Point Trail to Holt Ridge took several hours. When Theo reached the overlook, the view was more breathtaking than he remembered. "Just look at that, would you, Alice?" Mile after mile of rolling hills and dense forest spread beneath a luminous sky. For a moment it filled him completely. He studied the landscape, the world resting at his feet. And again, he found himself wondering what it would be like to step off the trail, disappear into the woods, and never be heard from again. He could almost visualize it, the act of disappearing.

Uninterested in the view, Alice pawed at the plastic bowl attached to Theo's backpack, her signal for *I need a drink of water.*

"Oh, sorry. Right away, Alice." Theo turned his attention to her needs, filling the container with water from one of the several bottles he had brought along.

As Alice sloppily lapped water, Theo adjusted his binoculars and continued examining Lee Creek Valley below. In the foreground, not more than fifty yards away, a gnarly snag tree silhouetted against the bright sky captured his attention. Theo felt reverence as he looked at it, knowing its vital part in the native landscape. Dignified in its decay, the snag tree still provided a home to numerous creatures—squirrels and woodpeckers, lichen and moss. Eventually, it would decay further and collapse, but even then it would play its part, returning nutrients to the forest soil. Theo adjusted his binoculars to look further up the trunk just in time to see a bald eagle land on its uppermost tip. *Whoa!* He held his breath and stood stock still, hoping the raptor would stay perched there for a while longer, worrying even his slightest sound or movement would send it flying away. Feeling privileged and grateful, Theo watched the magnificent bird as it preened its wings and scanned the forest floor. Slowly, *s l o w l y*, he reached into the front pocket of his backpack for his cell phone. Lowering the binoculars, he snapped a picture with his phone, then zoomed closer and snapped another.

As he slipped it into his shirt pocket, his phone began to chime. "Shhhh," he whispered, as though the phone might heed his instruction and cease its noise. What a terrible time for his phone to ding! He'd not had a signal all week, and realized what must be happening—at this higher elevation, cell reception had momentarily been restored. He began receiving all the text messages that hadn't come through until now.

Last week the smallest interruption to the peacefulness Theo sought would have been met with resentment, but by this point in his retreat he was mostly just curious. The glaring afternoon sun made it impossible to see anything on the screen of his phone. He stepped off the trail into the shade of a large burr oak tree and, when his eyes finally adjusted to the change in light, he saw notifications for three missed calls and twenty-three new text messages. They were all from Penelope.

He leaned against the trunk of the tree and began reading.

Monday, June 1 at 10:30 AM
Mr. Theo, can you pls call me? P. (praying hands emoji)

Monday, June 1 at 1:05 PM
I really need to talk to you. Like really bad.

Monday, June 1 at 3:02 PM
Mr. T, I know you don't want to talk to me, but I would like to explain some things. My mom wants to talk to you too.

Tuesday, June 2 at 9:04 AM
Please, please, pretty please, call me.

Tuesday, June 2 at 8:15 PM
Do you hate me? Please don't hate me.

Wednesday, June 3 at 8:16 PM
I didn't text you for twenty-four solid hours hoping you would chill out and miss me. But I guess you haven't.

Wednesday, June 3 at 9:33 PM *I made cookies with Ms. Nita today. She assured me you aren't dead. I'm glad about that. P.S. She really likes you. Maybe you should think about this while you are off doing whatever you are doing.*

Thursday, June 4 at 4:12 PM
Mr. Theo, it's okay if u never want to see me but can u explain why exactly? Aren't we the type of friends who at least provide explanations?

Thursday, June 4 at 6:04 PM
How's Alice? I miss her with my whole entire broken heart.

Friday, June 5 at 4:10 PM
I begged Ms. Nita to tell me where you are hiding. She refused. I think the two of you are kindred stubborn souls. For real!

Friday, June 5 at 7:13 PM
I'm sorry you didn't like my story. Not every book is for every reader. (You didn't let me finish tho.)

Friday, June 5 at 10:06 PM
Please, can you call me just for like two seconds?

Saturday, June 6 at 8:47 AM
You are a very obstinate man. If the Guinness World Records has a category for being obstinate, you might win it.

Saturday, June 6 at 10:22 AM
I found a new Boo Radley hole yesterday. It was very tiny, like only big enough to hold one of your marbles. I think you would like it. Or at least, the old version of you would like it. The new version of Mr. Theo tho? I don't know him anymore. Btw, you said you would teach me to play marbles. I guess that's never gonna happen now.

Saturday, June 6 at 3:55 PM
Ms. Nita took me to the library today and I got five new books. I asked to get Fifty Shades of Grey but Ms. Nita said not on her watch. We had to do curbside pickup. Btw I got you the first Harry Potter book! If you won't come back to see me, maybe you'll come back for Harry.

Saturday, June 6 at 8:07 PM

Are you okay? I would be devastated if something happened to you. Obviously you don't feel the same way about me. It's okay. I'm used to that.

Saturday, June 6 at 8:10 PM
If you will send me your address, I will write you a snail mail letter. P.S. I heard our owl last night!

Saturday, June 6 at 10:11 PM
Mr. Theo, I'm sorry, and I am on my knees begging for forgiveness.

Sunday, June 7 at 10:15 AM
I skinned my knee this morning. It's a long story, but I will tell you about it if you will call me.

Sunday, June 7 at 1:01 PM
I really miss you Mr. Theo. There for a while, you were the best friend I've ever had. I know you despise me and don't ever want to talk to me again, but I want you to know I will never forget you. Thank you for teaching me about your world of nature. P.S. Our garden is looking pretty good and I pulled out a weird double carrot the other day. Yes, I climbed over the back fence and played in your backyard but it wasn't the same without you and Alice there. Even your tree looked weepy.

Sunday, June 7 at 1:05 PM
Please take very good care of Alice. (broken-heart emoji)

Sunday, June 7 at 8:09 PM
I really love you, Mr. Theo. I hope you know that. Also, I thought you were brave but now I understand you are just scared like everyone else.

Tears were running down Theo's cheeks by the time he read the last text. What a mess he was! He wiped his eyes, the sting of sweat and dust from the morning's hike feeling like a penance. *You are a very obstinate man.* It was true. He wore his pigheadedness like armor; it had protected him for years. But then Penelope had shown up at his door under the guise of having missed her bus. *Had she missed her bus?* He didn't really know. He did know she had wormed her way underneath his skin. He studied the dates of her messages. Nothing today. Had she given up on him? The possibility made him feel dejected.

Alice was whining.

"I'm okay, girl." He patted her head. "Penelope says she misses you. We miss her too, don't we?" He was surprised at his words even as he uttered them.

Alice swiftly licked him across his scratchy beard.

"Okay, okay." He laughed, pushing her away from his face. For a while, they stayed there, Theo leaning against the sturdy trunk of the burr oak, and Alice sitting beside him. He felt strange after crying; looser, somehow. He'd been carrying a knot in his chest for weeks without realizing. Now, it seemed the knot was easing.

He began re-reading each message, more slowly this time. When he reached the last one, he knew he had to do something. He didn't want to call or message Penelope, not yet, but he didn't want her to worry over him either.

What a strange, convoluted, intense relationship he had with Penelope and Ivy, two people he'd not known even ninety days ago. He had spent his adult life avoiding maddening what-ifs. What ifs had almost destroyed him after the accident. What if he'd taken the bus to Fort Bliss? What if his father had been the one driving? What if that damn tire hadn't exploded? He'd trained himself not to think that way. But now what-ifs loomed so large he couldn't avoid them. If Annie had not gotten sick, they would have adopted Crystal's baby as planned. *Ivy would be his daughter.* She would have grown up in his house, the yellow bedroom would have been hers after all, and he would have focused his energy on being a good parent, a devoted father. Theo felt it in his bones, knew it with certainty—life would have been more stable for Ivy. But what about Penelope? He found it impossible to believe she would ever have existed, let alone as her current brilliant self.

Theo's phone dinged again, and a message from Nita appeared on his screen.

Today 11:45 AM

Theo, sorry to bother, just checking to make sure you are okay. Any idea when you might come home? Everyone here misses you. (heart emoji)

Heart emoji?

Theo heard the familiar whir of a hummingbird as it whooshed by his head. He looked up and saw it hovering in a tangle of passionflower snaking up the massive trunk of a hackberry tree. Buzzing from one yellow blossom to the next, its ruby throat was brilliant in the slant of golden sunlight. Theo had noticed very few hummingbirds that spring. The season was getting on, and he still hadn't put out his feeders at home.

"Time to head back, Alice." He gave her an affectionate rub, then took a long drink from his water bottle before coaxing his tired legs to stand. Back on the trail, he remembered the eagle and focused his binoculars toward the valley, but it was long gone from the snag. Bright white contrails formed a perfect X in the sky above him. He thought of all the people traveling through the heavens above him, wondering where they were going and why they would travel during such an unsafe time. What weighty things did they carry with them? Sickness, hate, hopelessness, worry? Shattered, lonely hearts?

As the vapor trails faded, Nita's message dinged a second time, a reminder that he had not yet responded. Again he read her words and saw the red heart emoji.

He returned to the shade and typed a reply, not entirely convinced he would send it.

Will be here until Sunday. When I get home, I would love some of your cookies. And could you please let Penelope and Ivy know I'm doing okay?

He would never be the type to add an emoji to a text message (and certainly not a red heart), but he did end his message with *Thanks for checking on me.* And that was something. Theo re-read his words and pressed the send button quickly, while his phone still had one bar, before he could change his mind.

262

Twenty-Eight

The hit on the line was nothing more than a gentle touch, but it was enough to alert Theo. The second hit came with more pressure. When the line jerked and the bob dipped beneath the water's surface, Theo tugged and set the hook firmly—more from shock than skill. "Alice, I think I actually caught one!"

Alice, gnawing on the chew toy he had brought along, paid him no attention.

Theo's fishing experience at Devil's Den had been a great success, not because he reeled in supper every night—he'd not caught anything—but because sitting on the shore with his dad's pole in his hand had brought him peace. Theo was not a fisherman. Despite his father's fondness for the pastime, and the thrills Theo and his brother had experienced during their annual father-son fishing trip to Lake Balmorhea, catching a fish had never been his goal. Not then, or now.

Theo lifted his pole skyward, feeling the weight of the tired creature hooked on the line. It was a small fish that he would end up tossing back. With no other choice, Theo began reeling it in, wondering why a fish would take a bare hook. Perhaps even fish have desperate days.

He thought back to the day before. He'd been sitting in the same spot when a man had approached, carrying a curly-haired child on his shoulders, her bare feet dusty to her ankles. The little girl couldn't have been older than three. She had her hands smashed against the sides of her dad's face in a way that looked uncomfortable to Theo, but only resulted in smiles from the guy. During their brief conversation, Theo had learned that the man and his wife and daughter were traveling from Los Angeles to Boston, having decided to do something different and "epic" during their enforced time off work. When the guy had asked what type of fish were in the lake, Theo had guessed at bream, because he knew they were plentiful in Arkansas. He hadn't bothered explaining that he never fished with bait because catching fish wasn't his objective. He just wanted the solitude and stillness. When the man had continued his walk with his daughter, the little girl tugging at his hair and giggling, Theo had watched them go with an unaccustomed wrench to his heart. For the remainder of the afternoon and into the evening, the brief encounter had stayed with him.

Now, as the pole trembled and the fish struggled, he glanced along the trail leading into the woods, half-expecting the man and girl to reappear so that he could show them the fish he had caught. But the trail was empty, and yesterday's encounter felt like nothing more than a dream. When the tension on the line went slack, relief flooded Theo. The fish had gotten away.

Tomorrow, he would fish without a hook.

His time at Devil's Den was passing quickly, each day blurring into the next. He felt physically stronger, and when he went to bed at night, he slept until daybreak, barely disturbing the bedcovers. He felt, somehow, that each hour of deep sleep, each step along the trails, each time he dropped a fishing line into the lake, had helped him come to terms with his emotions. He hadn't found complete clarity—did such a thing even exist?—but he had reached a state of calmness that felt comforting. The hike to Holt Ridge had changed him, been an antidote of sorts to his confusion over all that had recently happened.

Since that hike, Theo had thought back to the afternoon of Penelope's play again and again, seeing in his mind's eye the cartoonish blue tears she had drawn on her face, the way she'd stood on the stage he had built, the way she'd read so proudly from the journal purchased at Walmart. With a bit of time and perspective, he couldn't help wondering, uneasily, if his reaction had been an overreaction. He was the product of his life experiences—but wasn't everyone? Life had a way of tormenting a person. Blessings came, but were snatched away. Occasionally, happiness might appear to dangle within reach again. After so much loss, had he learned to protect himself...too much? Theo felt as though Penelope's persistent text messages streaming in, one after another, had shaken him awake. He had re-read them at least a half dozen times, imagining how he might respond.

Certain words and phrases had felt like a gut punch. *Do you hate me? Please don't hate me.* Of course, he didn't hate Penelope. Thinking about all the people who had come in and out of his life, he couldn't name a single soul he had truly hated. He hated certain *things*, like horrible accidents and cancer that claimed good people far too soon. He hated how certain people were treated unfairly because of skin color or circumstance. Well, maybe there were a few souls he hated, like narcissistic leaders who behave without moral compasses and seem to believe they were above the law.

There had been times he hated himself too.

Mr. Theo, it's okay if u never want to see me but can u explain why exactly? Aren't we the type of friends who at least provide explanations? Yes, Penelope deserved an explanation for his reaction. Now, he saw that.

My mom wants to talk to you too. He hadn't known what to think about Ivy's revelation on the afternoon of Penelope's reading. Her news had hit the center of his deepest pain, and he'd needed time to process it. Over the past few days, he had come to realize that his inability to engage in a real discussion with Ivy had been because he *did* believe her story.

Theo pulled the fishing line from the water, creaked to his feet, and began searching the shore for stones. Once he had gathered a pocketful, he flicked the first one and counted five skips across the water. He couldn't deny it. If Penelope were there with him, he would be teaching her to skip stones.

"Grip it like this," he said out loud, taking the next stone from his small pile and demonstrating the proper way to hold it. He imagined Penelope taking the stone in her tiny palm, chattering the whole time. *Like this? It's too big. My fingers aren't long like yours*. He laughed. With a flick of his wrist, the stone skipped lightly across the water. "That was for you, Penelope Pie."

EVENTUALLY THE DAY'S WARMTH and humidity began to sap Theo's energy, and he began packing up his gear, eager to return to the cabin. By the time he'd trekked across the first hill, Alice padding silently next to him, his legs were aching with heaviness. Suddenly Alice darted off, disappearing beyond the curve in the gravel road. Calling out to her, he picked up his pace despite his tiredness.

In the distance, he heard a fit of wild barking. Theo worried that his laxness about using a leash when walking to and from the lake had got them into trouble. Had Alice treed a wild animal? Or worse, had a wild animal cornered her? Walking as fast as he could, Theo rounded the bend in the road and saw a flash of lime green. Instantly he understood the reason for Alice's behavior. Penelope was there, sitting cross-legged in the dusty gravel beside his truck, her arms encircling Alice's neck, her raincoat hanging from a nearby tree branch.

Theo was stunned. Had his daydream of teaching Penelope to skip stones somehow manifested itself? He felt like he couldn't trust his eyes, but after blinking several times, there she still was, lavishing attention on Alice. A surge of sheer joy broke through his tiredness, bewilderment, and surprise.

"Hello, Mr. Theo! It's me, Penelope!" She waved with one hand as Alice continued her exuberant greeting, all wagging and licking and whining. Penelope fell backward, giggling wildly.

Her glee was contagious, and he began laughing too. "How on earth did you get here?" He couldn't see any means of transportation.

"Well, I walked."

"You—"

"Just kidding! You know, Mr. Theo, Fayetteville is like twenty-five miles from Devil's Den, and I can't walk that far. Well, I probably could, but I didn't. Ms. Nita brought me. Her car is parked around front."

"Oh. You really had me for a second there, kiddo." After twelve days in the woods, he was rusty. He had to gear up again for Penelope's lightning-quick replies. This, too, surprised him. He propped his pole next to the back door of the cabin, trying to work out what he thought about this change of circumstance.

"To be quite honest, I did give some thought to hitchhiking. On a certain level, it sounds enthralling! But I decided it wouldn't be very safe, what with all the psychos in the world. Plus, a cop might pick me up and take me to foster care. I saw a movie where this girl—"

Theo needed some clarity. "Is your mom here too?"

"Uh-huh. We're all here. But they got too hot waiting outside and went inside the cabin. They didn't think you would mind, but really, you should be more careful and lock your door. You are just inviting trouble. By the way, we've come to save you."

"*Save* me?" There had been times when he'd needed saving, but was this one of those times? He didn't think so.

"Yep."

Despite Penelope's ubiquitous chattiness, Theo noticed that she had made no move to approach him, and she wasn't making eye contact, either. She was focusing all her attention on Alice. Was she scared of his reaction? "Save me from what?"

"From yourself, of course." Still not looking at him, she began listing the reasons he needed rescuing. "You left my backyard book reveal very agitated, without hearing the end of the story. Even though my mom tried to explain everything to you, you ran away from home. Just disappeared, without saying goodbye. You wouldn't take my phone calls or answer any of my text messages, so naturally, I spent all my time worrying about you, and—"

"I don't have cell reception here."

"So you say."

"It's true! I can show you." He began pulling his phone from his pocket, but stopped, realizing he was being childish.

"You pretend not to have any feelings whatsoever. But I know what's driving you, and you need to address it ASAP. Like very ASAP."

Penelope might be having trouble meeting his eyes, but she was fearless when it came to speaking her mind. He felt rather beleaguered by her scolding, but he *was* curious to hear her views on his motivations.

"It's fear, Mr. Theo. Fear drives your actions. The sooner you scale that mountain of fear you've been avoiding, the better you'll feel. Just my opinion, you know."

Theo could feel his cheeks burning. He couldn't think of a word to say.

"Would it be okay if I gave you a small hug, Mr. Theo? I've really missed you."

Finally, she was looking at him, and the look on her face smote his heart. He had to clear his throat to speak past the lump in it. "I think that would be okay."

Her face lit up and she practically leaped toward him. When she reached up and clasped her arms around his waist, he gladly hugged her back.

IVY AND NITA had made themselves quite at home, playing cards and drinking iced tea at his kitchen table. Not that he minded. *Did he mind?* The last time he saw them, he had been like a wounded animal, cornered and confused. Now, he didn't know what to feel, except surprise. And if he were truly honest with himself, a niggle that felt surprisingly like happiness.

"Theo. You're back. I hope you don't mind that we barged right on in." Nita placed her cards on the table.

"Yes, we waited outside for a while, but it was so hot!" Ivy also put down her cards. Unlike Penelope, she seemed happy to meet his eyes.

"No, you're fine," he said. "It's awfully hot today. Very humid." He was curious about how they were planning to "save" him, but willing to let their plan play out. He noticed a large manila envelope on the table beside Ivy. He resisted the urge to ask about it. For a while the four of them tiptoed around one another like polite acquaintances, exchanging pleasantries about the beautiful place Theo had temporarily been calling home.

Home. Nita updated Theo on their Fayetteville neighborhood. A young family from Chicago had moved into the rental house on the corner temporarily, to escape coronavirus in the city. Various people she knew had come down with the virus, including a friend of a friend of hers, who had passed away. "He was fine one day, sick the next, and gone by the following weekend."

Theo thought of Winn. Then, because he didn't want to think about Winn, he said, "You know, you didn't need to drive over and check on me. I'll be home Monday." Surely, whatever they were planning could have waited three more days.

Now wearing her raincoat like a cape, Penelope stepped forward and raised her hand. "It's totally my fault, Mr. Theo. I made them bring me."

"Made them?"

"Yes. I've been on a hunger strike. I've not consumed a single bite of solid food in two whole days, and I vowed not to eat until someone brought me to see you."

Theo was alarmed. Two days was a long time for a kid to go without eating! "Good lord, you're smarter than that, Penelope. Let's get some food in you right away!" He moved toward the kitchen.

"Oh, I ate a cheese sandwich already. My mom packed one and made me eat it once we were on the road. But really, Mr. Theo, my food strike had nothing to do with smarts. Sometimes we have to take a stand for the greater good. Take Alice Paul, for instance. She finally got President Wilson's attention by organizing a hunger strike while in prison. I mean, we women can finally vote, right?"

"And Alice the dog is named after Alice Paul the suffragist?" Theo said this in part to refresh his memory and in part to clarify for Nita, who was looking completely baffled.

"Yes, and she—"

"And how do you know these details about Alice Paul?" he asked, cutting her off before she could launch into an entire speech on the women behind the Nineteenth Amendment.

"I read, of course. Mr. Theo, I'm pretty sure there are more than a few cavemen in this country who would love nothing more than to take away my future right to vote. If we don't understand where we came from and how we got here, we won't recognize when it's snatched away from us."

Theo realized how much he had missed being ringside to this child's dazzling mind.

"You look skinnier than normal, Mr. Theo. Have you been on a hunger strike too?"

He chuckled. "No, I've been eating quite well. Alice and I have been hiking daily, so I've been getting more exercise than normal." He thought of all the trails they had traversed, and the daily walks to and from the lake to fish and skip rocks. He hadn't been on a strike. His was a pause from life. He had needed space and quiet. Since arriving at Devil's Den, Theo had allowed nature to reset him.

"I'm so glad you aren't mad at us anymore. You aren't, are you? Because that's the last thing in the whole wide world we wanted. Right, Mom?" Penelope patted Ivy on the shoulder.

Leave it to a kid to get to the heart of the matter.

Ivy nodded and said, "Right."

"No, I'm not mad anymore. So long as you've all been leveling with me." He took a deep breath and turned to face his three guests. If they were going to do this now, he would say what he needed to say. "Seriously, if there are any more secrets, I need to know them. Let's lay them all out on the table right now, just like those cards."

A stifling quiet blanketed the room. Nita stood abruptly. "I think I'll take Alice for a walk and give you all some privacy."

After the door shut behind her, Theo offered Ivy a weak smile. The proverbial elephant in the room was sitting on his chest. His pulse throbbed in the back of his throat. They were standing at a crossroads. One he'd not expected to reach until he returned home; one he couldn't imagine traversing if they were keeping more secrets.

Penelope gulped down some water, then set her glass down with a clatter. "I'll go first. I have something important to confess."

"Okay, let's have it." Sitting down directly across from Penelope, Theo stared into her dark eyes, wishing he'd had more time to prepare for her looming revelation.

"Remember the morning when I first knocked on your front door, how I was dying to pee, and you let me use your bathroom? And I told you how many sheets of toilet paper you had left? Remember that?"

"Of course."

"Well, I lied. And I would like to apologize."

"You lied about having to use the bathroom?"

"No."

Theo was baffled. "About the number of toilet paper sheets I had left?"

"No." She giggled nervously. "I lied about saying I didn't look in the cabinet under the sink. Even though my mother told me to never look in someone else's cabinet, I did. The things in someone's cabinet reveal a lot about a person, so it's a very difficult thing for a curious person like me to resist. I realize it's a weakness, and I really do want to change." Penelope offered this confession with great seriousness.

Theo felt an upswell of relief, fighting the smile tugging at his lips. "And what did you learn about me that morning?"

"Let's see...." She paused dramatically. "I learned that you probably have very clean ears, you don't live off government assistance, and you like to be organized and prepared, but not to a fault."

Now Theo had to fight off the chuckle that was threatening to erupt. "Interesting. And how did you come to those conclusions?"

She began counting with her fingers. "One—you had the most humongous container of Q-tips I've ever seen. Two—people without money never buy pillow-soft toilet paper or brand-name cleaning supplies like Windex. And three—everything under your cabinet was organized nice and neat. There were no stains under there either, not that I could see."

"Hmm."

"It works. I've looked inside Ms. Nita's bathroom cabinet too. It's a mess, but don't tell her I said that."

Theo laughed. He never would have thought Nita was messy; what he'd seen of her home was immaculate. He couldn't help but find this secret flaw endearing.

"Okay, I better go next." Ivy, who had been lightly tapping her fingers on the tabletop, stood, straightened her shorts, and began pacing around the small area in front of the fireplace.

"Oh, yeah," Penelope said. When Theo looked at her, she seemed suddenly very focused on a knothole in the wooden table, her finger tracing it, around and around. Whatever Ivy was about to say was a secret belonging to both of them. And he expected the secret would have something to do with the manila envelope on the table.

Ivy faced him head on. "Mr. Theo, there's the matter of Alice."

"Alice?" Theo's heart lurched. He had grown extremely attached to Alice. He didn't want to find out she had been used as a pawn.

"The truth is, she didn't randomly show up at your house. We found her near our apartment on Leverett. Penelope had always wanted a dog and, at the time, I thought we had a future with Derrick, a bit of security. Anyway, when everything went south, we couldn't keep Alice in the motel with us. I left her in your backyard one afternoon, hoping you might take to her. I had seen you there when I was cleaning Gloria's apartment for her, and you looked so lonely sitting on that bench underneath the oak tree. And it worked. Alice took to you, and you let her stay, and when that happened, I thought…maybe Penelope and I could eventually get to know you too."

Theo swallowed and croaked out, "I see." He was worried there was more to Ivy's story.

"I'm really sorry for everything."

"Are you saying you want your dog back now, because I don't think—"

"Oh, no! You and Alice belong to each other. She's exactly where she needs to be, with a new home and stability. I just wanted you to know the entire truth." She placed a hand on top of the envelope he'd almost forgotten about. "I brought this for you, but I think it would be better if you opened it after we've left."

Suddenly he knew what he would find inside—the documentation that had led Ivy to him.

"Mr. Theo, I know things have changed, but I hope you'll still let me come to your house and visit Alice sometimes. I promise not to bother you." Penelope began to cry softly.

"Of course, kiddo. You are always welcome. Anytime." A kind of shyness came over him. Theo squeezed his hands together and stared at his knees. He couldn't look either of them in the eyes. The late afternoon sun was shining directly through the back window, and the cabin had become unbearable stuffy. He thought of Annie. She had been gracious, and kind, and always knew what to say. He wished, so badly, that she was there with him, to whisper the right words into his ear. But then, if she had been, none of this would be happening. Everything would have been so, so different.

Eventually, Theo found his voice. "I think you have it all wrong, Ivy." He stood up.

At his words, Penelope's whimpering grew louder, and Ivy seemed to sag back into the sofa. He had to rush the words out. "*I'm* the one who should be apologizing. I should be asking you and Penelope to forgive me. My behavior on the afternoon of Penelope's reading was deplorable. I won't make excuses, other than to say it has been a long time since I've had anything resembling a family. And Penelope, you're absolutely right. Fear has been controlling me. But the past week and a half has been just what I needed. With plenty of quiet time to think, I've worked through a few things. And I've made a decision—right now, I mean, right this very minute, I've decided something." A spark of energy seemed to be traveling from his brain into his heart, and then settling in his belly. Tears burned his eyes. "I may be fearful over the chances I take, but I refuse to stand by and not take them."

His words seemed to strengthen Ivy; her back straightened again and she sat forward. He could actually see her eyes brighten with hope. "So you're saying—"

"I'm saying please accept my apology. Thank you for finding me and dropping Alice off in my yard, thank you for checking on me today, and thank you for everything in between. Alice is one of the best things that has happened to me in a long time. I don't deserve her, and I surely don't deserve you and Penelope."

"Yes, you do!" Penelope jumped from her chair and began cheering wildly.

Gladness and relief filled him. Trust Penelope to break the tension at exactly the right time, and inject some humor into the situation. "Ivy, I don't know what comes next for any of us, but if it's alright with you, I think we should start over, in a way. Spend some time getting to know each other better when we get home."

Penelope leaped across the room to him. "This is the best day ever!" She hugged Theo with such intensity that he almost lost his balance.

"Well, don't hurt him," Ivy said, laughing through the tears beginning to spill from her eyes.

"Can we go find Ms. Nita and tell her everything? Please, please, please?" Penelope was frenetic with energy. Alice had begun barking and running in circles.

Theo smacked his forehead; he had forgotten all about Nita. "Yes, kiddo, let's go find her. And then maybe we could all go down to the lake for a while. It's cooler there. Besides, someone I know needs to burn off some energy," he teased.

"Who? Me? Or do you mean Alice?"

He was thoroughly enjoying their banter. "Well, who do you think?"

She paused to consider this. "Um…Alice. For sure."

Theo wished he could bottle the lightness he was feeling. "Penelope, if you plan to keep hanging out with me, there's something important I need to teach you when we get down to the lake."

"Oh, I do, Mr. Theo. And I promise to learn whatever it is *fast*."

Twenty-Nine

Alice began whining well before Theo turned onto his street, her tail thumping rhythmically against the seat. "You know we're almost there, don't you, girl?" He reached over and patted her head, thinking about the powerful tug of home. He'd once read that a lost dog could find its way back home, even from miles away, because every street corner, every yard, emanated a different scent. It certainly seemed to be true of Alice. She was utterly frenzied by the time he pulled into the driveway. Theo opened the door and she leaped out, sprinting to the front porch and barking to be let in. Despite her loud ruckus, he paused to take in the familiar surroundings. The grass desperately needed cutting, and the clumps of flowers bordering the front bed—coneflowers, salvia, and a patch of black-eyed Susans—had grown noticeably in the two weeks he'd been gone.

He dropped his duffle in the foyer and inhaled the dusty sweetness that lingered from years of preserving old plants. His time at Devil's Den had been restful, and the unexpected visit from Ivy and Penelope cathartic, and he was glad to be home.

Alice was already in the kitchen, whining at the back door. "Can you give it a rest for even a second?" He let her out. It crossed Theo's mind that maybe Penelope was in the backyard. Perhaps she was the reason for Alice's exuberance. While Alice rolled in the grass, twisting from side to side like she had an itch only the dandelions in her yard could satisfy, Theo went to check the side garden. He was glad the carrot tops had grown lush, but disappointed when he saw that Penelope wasn't there.

He kneeled down and pulled up a clump of chickweed at the garden's edge. Pulling a weed was such a simple, satisfying thing, feeling its roots release and smelling the richness of the soil. He was tempted to spend all afternoon tending to the garden. But he couldn't. There was something more important he needed to do.

Back inside, Theo unpacked the cooler and tossed his clothes in the washing machine. Then, before he could change his mind, he called Nita. He'd spent his first week at Devil's Den calming himself, and the second week contemplating his life. After his unexpected visitors left, Theo had done some deep soul-searching, and devised a plan. But he needed Nita's help to execute it.

"Theo? You're back?" She sounded breathless to him, as though she had misplaced her phone and was searching everywhere for it.

"Yes, I'm home. And I wondered if you could come for lunch? I've been craving a burger from Hugo's."

There was an awkward silence on the line when he proffered the invite. Nita was rarely at a loss for words—she tended to have something to say about most everything—so Theo took her quietness as disinterest, but just as he was about to say as much, she sputtered and said, "Well, sure. I would never turn down Hugo's."

"Oh, good. Thank you! I thought you were going to say no. Also, full disclosure, I have an idea to run by you, and I'll need your help to pull it off."

Forty-five minutes later, she was standing at his front door, offering him a pint of Yarnell's ice cream. "I brought dessert. I hope you like strawberry."

"I do. And I have just the perfect serving dishes too. Come see." Theo invited Nita inside with a sweep of his arm. She followed him into the dining room, where he found the small glass sherbet bowls in the lowermost drawer of the buffet. "These belonged to my grandmother. I've not used them in ages." He handed the stemmed bowls to Nita. Straightening up, Theo noticed the life he'd left waiting on the dining room table—the package of ancient plant specimens and the hat box bursting with childhood toys. All the Cracker Jack trinkets and army men belonged to his past, to the time when his brother and parents were central to his life. His passion for plants, fresh or preserved, would never wane, but going forward, he was determined to stop merely existing, in the here and now, with no real aspirations for tomorrow.

She studied the bottom of one of the glasses. "These are Fostoria. They're so pretty."

"I don't know one cut glass bowl from the next, but these were special to my grandmother. She used them only to serve homemade ice cream during family birthday celebrations."

Theo felt a bit self-conscious, sharing his personal history with Nita. By the look on her face, she was delighted to learn this tidbit from his past. And he'd decided that was what he wanted—to be more communicative, more accessible. Walking back to the kitchen, he felt unexpectedly buoyant.

Nita followed him, carrying the bowls and the pint of Yarnell's. "Theo, I have to say I was surprised by your phone call. I take it you're feeling okay about everything? Showing up the way we did…I was very hesitant to do that. You seemed alright when we all walked down to the lake, though, and on the ride home, Ivy said it was the most relieved she'd felt "since forever"—I think those were her words. Even so, I worried we'd misread you. You were so distraught after Penelope's reading."

"No, no, coming to check on me was a good thing. My reaction to Penelope's story was visceral, that's true, although it's sort of a blur now, but I've spent a lot of time thinking over everything that's happened—you know, teaching Penelope, and then basically taking her in when Ivy was in the hospital, hearing so much disturbing news about coronavirus, and then, Winn… I'm not trying to make excuses for my behavior, or maybe I am, but the truth is that I was bursting with angst."

"It was a lot. I agree."

Theo took the ice cream from Nita and put it in the freezer. Lunch was waiting for them on the counter, in a carryout bag. "Nita, I can't remember if I thanked you for driving Ivy and Penelope to see me, so thank you."

Nita grinned. "You're very welcome."

"Seriously, getting away was good for me. I figured out some things. Take my grandmother's bowls, for instance." He took one of the sherbet bowls from Nita's hand, held it by the stem, and twirled it. Bevels of cut glass caught the overhead light, reflecting a diamond pattern on the kitchen wall.

"Sorry? I'm not sure I follow."

"Well, I've decided to stop thinking that there are no good things left to happen. Every day I wake up on this side of the grave is a special occasion. Right?"

"That's very true. It's especially apparent now, with so many people dying from this awful virus. You know, Theo, I've never seen this philosophical side of you. You better be careful—you're sounding downright thoughtful!"

There was that good-humored snark that Theo appreciated. "It's okay if you want to goad me. Lord knows, I deserve it." He plated their burgers and fries and poured water into glasses, wishing he had thought to make a pitcher of iced tea. "Oh, we need napkins." He opened the drawer where he kept random kitchen things and pulled out one of the red polka dot napkins leftover from Penelope's backyard reading. He handed it to Nita just as she slipped into the chair opposite his.

"So, you've changed? Is that what you're saying, Theo Gruene?" Nita dipped a fry into ketchup and ate it.

"I'm ready to move on," Theo continued, feeling rather chatty and altogether unlike himself. He was genuinely glad that she'd come. "I think Ivy feels the same way."

"Well, I have to say, I'm thrilled to hear all of this. I really had no idea what to expect when I came over. You sounded lighter on the phone, if that makes sense, like a load had been lifted from your shoulders. But still, I was apprehensive."

Theo swallowed hard, feeling guilty that he'd made her feel that way. "Listen, Nita, I asked you over so I could apologize. I've not been a very good friend—actually, I've not been a friend at all."

"Agreed." She laughed, and he noticed a sparkle in her eyes. He realized she was thoroughly enjoying seeing him squirm. "You were a real Ebenezer Scrooge before you left. You know that, right?"

"Believe me, I know. I was sick of myself." He laughed and picked up his burger, holding it over his plate while finishing his thought. "I'm going to do better. I realize now how stagnant my life has been since Annie died. Besides Winn, I had closed myself off from most of the world. But...well, being at Devil's Den and having uninterrupted time to think really helped me work through some things. Most particularly, about the time I'd been spending with Penelope. Something...loosened. A person may not be able to change completely in a few weeks, but I realized that I had begun to walk a different path, and it was a good one. And I'm planning on continuing down it." He took the first bite of his burger, reveling in the taste.

Nita squinted at him. Eventually, she spoke. "I'm glad to hear you say all of this, really I am. You're a fortunate man, Theo. I don't know if you realize how fortunate you are. After we visited Devil's Den, I did some soul-searching too. I had decided to come over here and give you a real talking to. I was determined to make you see what was right in front of you."

He didn't know what she was getting at, but knew she was getting riled up. She'd not yet touched her burger. "What do you mean?"

"Theo, sometimes you can be so obtuse. I would give *anything* to have a family appear out of thin air, to have people who truly want to be part of my life. Just like you, I lost my spouse to cancer. When Charlie died, I felt so alone, like I had lost my North Star. Of course, I have my son, Adam, and a granddaughter, Sophia, but I don't get to see either of them often enough. What I'm trying to say, Theo, is that our situations aren't so different."

He nodded. He'd always focused on the differences between them. Nita was sociable and talkative, always enamored of a bit of gossip, while he was solitary and private. But they had both suffered the devastating loss of spouses.

Before he could say anything, she continued, her voice rising. "And then...this fantastic thing practically fell in your lap! Honestly, Theo, I was completely mystified by your reaction." She shook her head.

As a child, Theo hated disappointing anyone—his parents, teachers, even people he barely knew. He had been a sensitive kid, believing wholeheartedly in the golden rule. Nita's words took him back to those childhood days in Midland. He realized he really wanted her to think well of him.

"I don't—"

"Those girls missed you so much while you were away. They are attached to you in an extraordinary way—I hope you know that."

"Yes, and—"

"I'm happy to hear you say that you want to move forward, really, I am. But I hope that path you plan to continue down is the one with Ivy and Penelope on it."

He remembered the flood of text messages Penelope had sent him, and Ivy's words. *We just wanted to know you.* "Nita, I mean all of it. My grandmother always said you have to be a friend to make a friend. I'm going to do a better job at that. With Ivy and Penelope, and with you. You'll see. In fact, I have something exciting planned for Penelope, and I think you'll approve. I was hoping you would help me with it."

Nita smiled. She seemed satisfied, but he knew he still had to tread carefully. Until he proved himself, he would be on shaky ground. After a moment of silence that had Theo worrying she wouldn't help him, she eased forward, picked up her burger and, before biting into it, said, "Absolutely. You know I'll do whatever I can."

A RARE SUMMER SHOWER moved through the area later that afternoon, bringing a much-needed break in the heat. Theo found it relaxing to work while rain pattered against the roof, so he settled down with the specimens he had abandoned for two weeks. First up was a Harperella stem. The delicate wildflower had once thrived in Garland County, but was now endangered. Theo always handled every plant with care, but felt an even greater sense of responsibility with those in peril. He lightly pressed its fragile, quill-like leaves into the glue, picturing what it must have looked like as a young blooming plant growing in an Ouachita Mountain stream in 1921.

A knock at his front door startled him. Then, he laughed. It seemed his plant work was destined to always be interrupted. "Coming, coming," he called, a sense of déjà vu walking with him to the front door. This time, Ivy was standing there. And like Penelope all those months ago, her hair was wet from the rain and her expression was forlorn.

"Ivy, come in. I've been thinking about you and Penelope." It was true. Since his conversation with Nita, he had been thinking about his plan and how he would implement it.

She didn't move, just kept standing there on his doorstep.

"What's wrong?"

"I didn't know what else to do. You were the only person I could think to tell." Her pale eyes shimmered with tears. "Gloria passed away. She took a nap after lunch and never woke up. I was the one who found her. Thank goodness Pea wasn't there. She had just walked over to Nita's house. They were going to the library." A tear rolled down her cheek.

"Oh, honey, come inside." Theo urged her in and wrapped an afghan around her damp shoulders. "Can I make you a cup of tea?"

Ivy shook her head and collapsed onto the sofa. "I don't need anything." Making herself as small as possible, she wrapped her arms around her knees and rocked back and forth. Theo felt inadequate, helpless to comfort her. So he simply sat beside her and tried to absorb the distressing news. After decades of living only a stone's throw away, breathing the same air, and watching the same storm clouds blow over the neighborhood, he had only just connected with Gloria himself.

"I called for an ambulance and held her hand until the paramedics came. And while I waited, I thought about all the things that have happened lately. I realized all I really wanted to do was talk to you." An elongated sob escaped Ivy's throat.

"It's okay. I'm right here." Before he could pat her arm or hug her, Ivy jumped to her feet and began pacing. Like a caged animal, she couldn't seem to be still. "I can't breathe. I need some air. Can we go outside?"

The rain had stopped, and with dusk coming on, the air had cooled. Theo dried the chairs, and for some time, they sat out back in silence, listening to the trilling of cicadas and watching the lightning bugs. The rooftop of Gloria's home practically loomed over them through the branches of the oak tree. "Should we move to the front porch?" Theo suddenly regretted his decision to sit on the back deck. What had Nita called him? Obtuse?

Ivy smiled sadly and shook her head, her damp hair spiraling freely around her shoulders. "No, I like the view from here. You know, it's interesting how things work out. I didn't know Ms. Rice all that long, and before I knew her, I completely disrespected her by moving into her apartment without permission. Still, she forgave me, befriended me, and even helped me financially. If angels exist, that lady already has her wings." Ivy's damp eyes glittered in the day's fading light.

"It's hard to believe she's gone. She seemed to be doing well the last time I saw her." Aware of his woefully inadequate response, he added, "Ivy, you deserved her kindness. She saw something special in you from the beginning."

"Thanks for saying that. It's like she made the conscious decision to be my family. Like she sensed I'd never really had one."

"But now you have me." Five small words popped out. And now that they were hanging in the air, he didn't want to take them back. He had said what had needed to be said for some time.

Confusion flashed across Ivy's face, and she quickly looked away from him. When she spoke, the sincerity in her voice grabbed hold of his heart and tugged. "Please don't say that if you don't really mean it. I can't handle more disappointment, especially right now."

Ivy had suffered so much disappointment through the years that she automatically expected the same from him. He might be obtuse, but he was also patient, and willing to work harder to fully gain Ivy's trust. "I do mean it. And I understand your skepticism. I'm only just beginning to comprehend what a wall I'd built around myself."

"So what are you really saying? That we might be a…family someday?" She was staring intently at him now, as though dissecting his every word.

"Do you want to be?" He recognized his mistake immediately. Answering a question with another question was a copout. "Sorry, what I meant to say is…yes, I would like to be there for you and Penelope. I want to be the person you come to depend on. Ivy, after you left Devil's Den, I stayed awake half the night poring over the documents you left me in that envelope. What a gift that was." His eyes teared. Ivy had left him the letters Annie had written to Crystal, five letters, each one a time capsule. Annie had shared the dreams they had for their future child so lovingly it made him ache. There had been a baby book in the envelope too. Most of it was blank, but Crystal had affixed a photo of Ivy as a newborn, along with her inked footprints and the tiny hospital bracelet that once looped her wrist. The last thing he'd found in the envelope had been a yellowed newspaper clipping—Annie's obituary from the *Arkansas Democrat-Gazette.* Crystal may not have been a good mother in the long run, but she had tried to give her daughter a different destiny. And she'd kept the evidence. That evidence had led Ivy to Theo, and now it was up to him to do something about it. "Here's how I see it, Ivy. If Annie hadn't died, we would have adopted you as a newborn. But she did, and we didn't, and you were raised by your birth mother."

"Raised is not the word I would use."

"I'm truly sorry for that. But, well, think about this: your mother, who evidently didn't or couldn't or wouldn't provide much for you, did give you a wonderful gift. She saved Annie's letters and made sure you received them after her death. She may not have meant to, but she brought us together, eventually. And while I've never believed in fate or destiny, I'm starting to realize this happened exactly as it was supposed to happen." As though on cue, the owl that often visited his backyard offered an opinion. *Hoo-hoo, hoo-hoo.* "Even the wise owl up there agrees with me." Theo's heart seemed to lift in his chest. Discovering this truth and speaking it aloud was healing in a way nothing else had been.

Ivy didn't answer; she was staring forlornly into the distance. Theo thought of Gloria again. He wished he'd expressed his gratitude to her, really thanked her for the recent role she'd played in his life. By forgiving Ivy, and offering her a job and a place to live, Gloria had helped bring Ivy to him. But now it was too late. He imagined Gloria's stately home would be sold. Someone else would be living there by the end of summer. A glum notion struck him—Ivy and Penelope would probably have to move again. Would she return to work at the VA?

"So you think Annie was supposed to get cancer?" Ivy's voice was faint, and she still wasn't looking at him.

"No, cancer never makes sense. But what I do know is that if we had adopted you, you most likely never would have met Penelope's father. That would mean Penelope wouldn't exist. And the world needs Penelope Pie."

Thirty

The big reveal was to begin with a treasure hunt, an idea that had come to Theo in the most vivid of dreams, a farewell gift he'd received on his last night at Devil's Den. Annie had been there, too, so lovely and gentle. If given the choice, Theo would have lived inside that dream forever.

"Shouldn't they be here by now?" Nita was acting like an excited child, peeking out the window as she strained to catch a first glimpse of Ivy and Penelope walking up the sidewalk. Theo had to admit he found her excitement appealing.

"It depends on how fast they walk from tree to tree."

It was the first Sunday in July, and Theo had chosen that particular morning for the treasure hunt after confirming the day was convenient for Ivy. The next day she would be returning to her job at the VA. Like most area hospitals, the VA was short-staffed and in crisis mode, desperately fighting the surging virus with dwindling resources. When Ivy had called to ask for her job back, she had been rehired on the spot. Theo had encouraged Ivy to try and find a different job, possibly a remote position, with less exposure to the sick public, but she wouldn't hear of it. Helping people was her calling, she'd said, and the risks came with the job.

The sun had barely been up when he and Nita walked through the neighborhood, placing gifts in tree hollows and stealthily hanging a canvas tote bag on the door of the guest apartment where Ivy and Penelope still lived. Gloria's daughter had insisted they continue living there until the estate was settled, which was estimated to take several months. She had even offered Ivy a six-month, rent-free lease, saying the property would be more secure with them living there. Theo still chuckled at the irony and liked to imagine Gloria had truly enjoyed having the last word.

"Why am I'm so nervous?" Nita asked, continuing to act as sentry.

"You're just excited." Theo was nervous too. He checked his wristwatch and was surprised to see it was nearly eleven o'clock. Almost an hour had passed since the treasure hunt officially kicked off with his text to Penelope and Ivy: *You're invited to a treasure hunt. If you agree to participate, the fun begins now. Check the bag outside your door for the first clue. Ready, set, GO.*

Penelope had texted back instantly, with a *YAY!* and Ivy had sent a smiley face emoji. Theo had told Ivy a little of what to expect. But only a little. The first clue, written on a pink index card, said: *Inside a unique Boo Radley hole is where you will find your first gift. Remember, a house with a red hobbit door is bound to hold surprises... Text back when you find it.*

Theo could almost feel Penelope's excitement in the vibration of his phone when her text came through. *We found it!* He pictured her taking the tiny plastic compass from the tree hollow and dropping it inside the tote bag.

The second text message clue said: *One block due south, this Boo Radley hole is shaped like a heart.*

Response: *This is the most fun thing ever!* A minute later: *We're ready for the third clue.*

Third clue/text: *The house might be haunted but never fear—brave men keep watch from this safe space.* He had been reluctant to include army men in the treasure hunt, recalling Penelope's aversion to them. But Theo nevertheless viewed those soldiers, at least, as the ultimate protectors, and had placed two on the smooth lip of the tree cavity.

Fourth clue/text: *The tiniest (but mightiest) of all the Boo Radley holes?*

And so the clues continued, guiding Penelope and Ivy through the neighborhood, to seven Boo Radley holes that each held one of Theo's childhood toys. This had been the most straightforward part of his dream—that he would give Penelope the toys he had saved all these years by placing them in her favorite tree holes and guiding her to them. *To him.* The seventh held a single marble and a small piece of paper saying: *Redeem this marble at Theo's house for your next surprise.*

"I see them!" Nita screeched. "Penelope's wearing the bag across her body. They're holding hands and practically skipping down the sidewalk. You've made them so happy, Theo."

A flutter of butterflies filled Theo's belly. Ivy had not been to his house since their heart-to-heart the day Gloria Rice died almost three weeks ago. He'd talked with her on the phone once, to share his idea for a treasure hunt and to get her approval for the overall plan. Keeping Penelope away from the house had been the real challenge, but he'd explained his long absence was due to a new herbarium project, one that required deep concentration and a quick turnaround. He had visited them at the apartment, though, and alluded to a surprise. The kid loved surprises, and wouldn't risk ruining it.

Theo opened the door as Penelope hopped up the porch steps, the pale green tote bag swinging from side to side. *Penelope Pie's Treasures* was embroidered in bright green floss across one side. The other side boasted a tree design appliquéd using fabric scraps in shades of brown, purple, and lime green.

"What a stupendously fun surprise! We found all your toys, wanna see? And I love the bag. Do I get to keep it?"

"Well, kiddo, I don't know anyone else named Penelope Pie. Do you?"

"No. There's no other me."

"Ms. Nita made it, by the way."

"Wow." Penelope ran her fingertips along her name, her eyes wide.

They went inside to greet Nita, who had been watching everything from the window. Penelope ran over to her immediately. "Thank you for the bag, Ms. Nita. It's an exquisite work of art." Her voice quivered.

"You're very welcome, sweetie." Nita hugged Penelope and kept hugging her, until Penelope said, "You're squishing me, Ms. Nita."

Theo swallowed the lump swelling in his throat. What a softie he had become. "The toys are yours too. If you want them."

"Really?" Penelope's voice went high with wonder. "You are giving me a bag *and* all your favorite old toys? My birthday's not for seventy-nine more days."

"Well, if you don't want them, it's okay, I just thought—"

"Oh no, Mr. Theo, of course I want them! I will take excellent care of them and cherish each one until my dying day. Even the little soldiers."

Ivy had been standing by silently, smiling. He turned to her. "It was okay for you, Ivy? Walking through the neighborhood?" Worried about her stamina, he had only selected trees near one another.

"Oh, it was fine. Really, other than my sense of smell, I feel mostly normal. You know, Pea showed me her map of the tree holes a while back, but I had no idea what they were like. It's interesting the things you don't notice until you do, and then it's like the whole world changes! And it never looks the same again. Those tree hollows are like nature's treasure boxes."

Nature's treasure boxes. Theo liked the sound of that.

Penelope began removing the toys from the bag and arranging them on the dining room table. "It's funny, when I first saw these little toys, I thought they were so old-fashioned. Now I think they are sort of cool, like you, Mr. Theo."

"Thank you, I think?" Presumably 'sort of cool' was better than old-fashioned.

She giggled and began moving the trinkets around. "You *are* surprising, Mr. Theo. That's for sure."

He and Nita exchanged glances. "Well, actually, there's one more surprise upstairs," he said.

Penelope, fiddling with the toys, didn't seem to hear him.

"Pea, did you hear Mr. Theo? There's another surprise upstairs."

"I heard him, but I can't handle any more surprises. Mr. Theo, maybe you should save it for tomorrow?"

"No, no, come on. Ms. Nita and I have been working really hard on this. You're gonna love it." He gave her shoulder a little squeeze.

Penelope's answering head nod, so slight, and her faint smile, reminded Theo that his wasn't the only fragile heart in the room.

They all trooped upstairs together, then Ivy and Penelope waited in the hallway while he and Nita went into the bedroom to survey the space one final time. There was nothing left to do, really. He simply needed a minute to gather himself. It had been Penelope's bedroom while Ivy was in the hospital, and before that, the nursery for the baby he and Annie never did adopt.

Nita touched his forearm and whispered, "She will adore this. It's extraordinary, Theo."

"Okay, it's showtime," Theo whispered to Nita, who cracked open the bedroom door and motioned for them to come inside.

Penelope and Ivy stepped into the room hesitantly. As they took it in, their eyes filled with awe. Ivy was the first to speak. "Oh my goodness, Theo, I had no idea. This is incredible."

Penelope placed her hand on the bed knob, as though steadying herself. The bed was the same vintage maple bed he and Annie had purchased at a yard sale years ago, but it looked completely different. After Theo polished the wood, Nita had freshened the bedding with pale green gingham sheets, a matching duvet, and piles of soft pillows. But the most significant transformation was the room's color. Soon after returning from Devil's Den, Theo found Penelope's paint swatch, still tucked away in the buffet drawer. He'd purchased a quart of paint in every color on the swatch and gone to work. The palest green, *Mischievous*, now covered the walls. Behind the bed's headboard, he had painted an arch using the other shades, *Good Luck*, *Folk Tale*, and *End of the Rainbow*.

"There's a green rainbow," Penelope whispered. "And the bed covers are worthy of a fairy princess."

It truly was better to give than receive; Theo felt it in every cell of his body. As Penelope bounced around the room, noticing one change after another, her excitement amplified his own happiness. It was still hard for him to wrap his mind around the fact that when he'd first painted this room, decades ago, it had been for Ivy. Theo had never been a father, much less a grandfather, but he knew now that he wanted to be present for Ivy and Penelope in whatever capacity they needed.

"Is this the same desk?" Penelope pulled out the wooden chair and sat, touching her fingertips to the single dandelion he had placed in a jar on the corner of the desktop.

"It is." Theo had painted it Penelope's favorite color—*Good Luck*. "There's a stack of new journals too. I thought you could write your next book there." Bringing up her writing raised the memory of her backyard reading, which made him uneasy, but Penelope seemed to harbor no ill feelings. She giggled, opening the desk drawer and running her fingers along the pens and pencils stored there.

Nita had helped declutter the bookshelf to make room for their nature school supplies—containers of markers, spiral notebooks and stacks of index cards, construction paper and drawing pads. And Theo had hung the white slick board on the wall beside the desk. Their last nature vocabulary words were still faintly visible: *Phenology, Ecosystem, Biodiversity, Aril, Corm.*

"This is the most amazing thing I've ever seen. Mom, did you know about this?"

Ivy gazed around the room. "I had no idea how beautiful it would be."

"Am I going to live here? Like forever?"

"No, honey, Mr. Theo isn't saying that."

"Why not?" Tears filled her eyes.

Theo sat down on the corner of the bed and patted the space beside him. She plopped down and hunched her shoulders. "Penelope, I want you to have your own bedroom here. It will be your room whenever you need it, and you can stay anytime your mom says it's okay. You can come after school and do your homework, or when your mom is working late."

"But I want to stay here *all* the time—with you, Alice, and Mom—all of us. We should be a real family."

Penelope's reaction to the bedroom, and the effortless way she expressed her needs, touched Theo's heart. At the same time, he felt slightly apprehensive that the solitude he had valued for so long was slipping away. He had missed her chirpy presence, and he was glad they were all on solid ground again, but he hadn't meant for the bedroom he had created for her to provide a permanent living arrangement. "Here's the thing, Pea…we are still navigating this…um…our relationship. But while we do that, this room can be whatever you want. You and your mom will still live in the apartment—I think Ms. Rice would want that—

but you can leave some of your things here, work on your art projects, whatever. It can change as we figure things out."

"Can it be my Room of Requirement?" she whispered.

Theo had read the first Harry Potter book, and enjoyed it thoroughly; he'd even checked out the next three in the series from the library. He had been on a new schedule: working on plant specimens in the morning; transforming Penelope's bedroom in the afternoons; and devouring Harry Potter books at night. Because of this recent immersion in the wizarding world, he understood exactly what Penelope meant. "Exactly. Penelope's Room of Requirement."

"Well, I'll warn you right now, I have a lot of requirements." Her voice had turned thoughtful.

"That's okay," Theo said. "It's a pretty big room."

"There's even a closet," she whispered. "My very own closet…"

There was a hitch in his stomach, that Penelope viewed a small closet with such esteem. "I need to tell both of you something," Theo said. Nervous excitement was swarming through him. He looked first to Ivy and then to Penelope. "I have realized that I truly don't care how you found me. Whether it was carefully planned, or a divine miracle, I know now that the day you knocked on my door was one of the best days of my life."

As Penelope leaped on him and hugged him with all her might, and he breathed in the aroma of her strawberry shampoo, Theo felt his future open up before him.

"Mr. Theo, can I say something now?"

"Please. I wish someone would."

"I know you don't believe in magic, but look at this room. This room *is* magic. It's the end of the rainbow, plain and simple, and as real as anything. And *you* made it happen."

Thirty-One

Theo's time with Penelope and Ivy had been different since the treasure hunt, like the loose-fitting puzzle pieces of their lives had finally begun locking together. Penelope stayed over on weekends when Ivy was working, and visited most days after school—after all, there was Alice to walk, and he still made the best cheese sandwiches. Pizza night was a regular thing, too, every Thursday, when Eureka Pizza offered a two-dollar-off coupon.

As Theo wheeled the Weber grill to the backyard, he regarded the bright crescent moon rising above the garage apartment. Gloria Rice's graveside service had been held in Evergreen Cemetery, for family only, and a city-wide memorial service would be scheduled later when crowds could once again safely gather. The Fayetteville city council had already begun discussing ways to honor Gloria's generous bequest—three million dollars designated for affordable housing for single parents. Theo thought it was strange to miss someone he barely knew, but he was learning to acknowledge his feelings rather than question or ignore them.

He situated the grill near the deck and went back inside to join the festivities. After weeks of counting down to Penelope's ninth birthday, and talking about it incessantly, September the fourteenth had finally arrived. There had been much contemplation and discussion of theme and menu before Penelope had decided on a "sophisticated party" with candles, fancy finger foods, and S'mores for dessert. When Ivy asked Penelope if she wanted to invite any of her fifth-grade classmates, she said, "Absolutely not. No children will be allowed." So, as had become customary since Theo's return from Devil's Den, the guests around his dining room table that evening included only Ivy, Penelope, and Nita, with Alice trolling the floor for fallen nibbles.

"Hurry, Mr. Theo! We're waiting on you, and I can barely control my excitement!" Penelope was bouncing in her chair.

He wished he'd thought to ready the grill before anyone arrived. "Okay, kiddo, I'm here." Seeing her so excited was a gift—to him.

She cheered as Nita handed her the first gift. It was no bigger than a box of matches, and Penelope unwrapped it slowly, taking care not to tear the silver paper. Inside, a simple cross hung from a dainty silver chain.

"Oh, Ms. Nita, it's perfect!" Penelope swept her hair aside, and Nita fastened the necklace around her neck. She covered the cross with her hand, pressing it into her heart.

"Mine next," Ivy said, handing over a large rectangular box tied with a magnificent purple bow. Inside were the all the things listed on Penelope's very detailed birthday wish list: 1) a pair of wide-legged retro jeans (*vintage is a-okay*), 2) black and white checkered Vans (*new ones that fit, please*), and 3) claw clips (*assorted colors would be awesome*). Theo had wondered what on earth those were; now he understood.

"Alright, ladies, how about we take this party outside and start cooking those S'mores?" Theo didn't much care for S'mores himself, nor did he think graham crackers and gooey marshmallow represented sophistication, but he was entirely on board with accommodating Penelope's every birthday request. He had been shocked to learn that she'd never been the guest of honor at a real party.

"Mr. Theo, didn't you get me anything?" Her face was long, despite the jewelry sparkling at her neck and the glittery claw clip now taming her hair.

Ivy shook her head. "Penelope! What kind of question is that?"

"It's a legit question. I mean, you certainly didn't *need* to get me anything, Mr. Theo. You've given me so much that I don't really expect anything for the rest of my life. But I thought I should ask, just in case you forgot. You know?"

"Oh, gosh, yes. Thanks for reminding me." Theo pressed his hand against his forehead, making a great show of pretending to only just remember what had, in truth, consumed his mind for six weeks.

She flashed a broad, Cheshire cat grin at him, and then looked at Ivy, mouthing, "See?"

"Hmmm, now where did I put it?" Theo rifled through the top buffet drawer, which had become somewhat of a catchall for papers and other miscellany.

Nita took the opportunity to refill their wine glasses with bubbly ginger ale.

"Pea, how was school today?" Ivy asked. "What did you learn?"

Theo smiled, recognizing the delaying tactic for what it was. Magnificent moments were meant to be stretched out and enjoyed, after all.

As she answered her mother's question, Penelope's eyes followed him while he pretended to search through every drawer and cabinet in the buffet for her gift. "It was okay. Sort of boring, really. A bunch of teachers are out with Covid. Mom, you might want to consider pulling me out of that place and re-enrolling me in Mr. Theo's nature school."

Public schools in Arkansas had reopened for in-person classes at the end of August, and although Theo did worry about Penelope contracting coronavirus, he believed the return to normalcy was a good thing.

Theo finally retrieved the accordion folder where he stored receipts, and other important papers. He began combing through the pages, turning each sheet over with excruciating slowness. "And are you all wearing masks?"

"Oh yes, of course. And you know, I believed in scrubbing my hands long before Dr. Fauci got involved. Mr. Theo, why have you turned into a sloth!?" She dropped her head into her hands.

He smiled. "I have no idea what you mean."

"You're stalling. You're pretending you can't find whatever it is you got me, and I don't understand why. You shouldn't worry. I will love whatever it is."

SOON AFTER he had returned from Devil's Den, after the treasure hunt and bedroom reveal, Theo paid a visit to Winn's wife, Julie. Never good with small talk, he had gotten straight to the point of his visit, describing the recent developments with Ivy and Penelope, and telling her about Annie's letters. He'd explained to Julie that Ivy had almost been his daughter, and that he wanted to help her, maybe put some money aside in her name, to help with Penelope's future education, or change his will.

Julie had been visibly relieved. She had assumed the worst had happened, and that Theo was seeking her advice because of an embezzlement or scam. "Sure, Theo, you can address your wishes in your will, but that's not always foolproof. Unexpected complications often come up. This may sound crazy, but if you really want to protect Ivy, you should consider adopting her. Arkansas is one of the few states that allows adult adoption."

Adult adoption? "Well, you're right, that sounds crazy."

"The process is straightforward and quick. In your situation, it's the best way to secure inheritance rights for Ivy." Julie gave him the name of an attorney who specialized in such matters.

Adoption was an option Theo had never considered, but once Julie suggested it, he became fixated on the idea. He had grown fond of Penelope very quickly, and even though his relationship with Ivy had taken longer to develop, he had realized during her convalescence just how much he had come to care for her, too. Time and again, he had witnessed how she resolutely faced every problem, whether it was scrambling to make last-minute childcare arrangements or pushing to regain her strength after her hospitalization. Most of all, Theo admired her thoughtfulness, and the way she always put Penelope first. After visiting with Julie, he went directly to Ivy's apartment, intent on talking with her before contacting the legal specialist, and before he could start second-guessing himself.

Ivy had answered the door wearing a pale lavender apron, looking relaxed. The unmistakable aroma of baking drifted out from behind her, the marvelous smell fueling Theo's already heightened senses. He knew he was interrupting, but it couldn't be helped; his elation couldn't be contained another moment. Every detail of the world around him had intensified—the sky was a livelier blue, the tree canopy more verdant than ever before. His eyes began to fill and his breathing was ragged. For a moment he was incapable of speaking and wondered if he might be dying.

"Mr. Theo? Are you okay?" Ivy's quizzical expression had morphed into one of alarm.

Taking a gulp of oxygen, Theo calmed himself and focused on the purpose of his visit. "Yes, yes, I'm great, but I need to talk to you. To ask you something. In private." He glanced over Ivy's shoulder, suddenly wishing he had called first. The question he needed to ask wasn't for Penelope's ears.

"Penelope's at Nita's. You want to come inside?"

"I think I should," he said, not completely sure his feet would move from the apartment stoop.

Afterwards, Theo couldn't have said how long the conversation lasted; time had felt immaterial. His heart directed his words, and with each phrase, each sentiment, he moved closer to a future that had been inconceivable only weeks before. Ivy's reaction, her grateful acceptance, had been instantaneous. She had laughed and cried, told him that she'd hoped for this in some way without daring to articulate it to herself, and Theo knew, right then and there—even after the death of his family all those years ago, and after losing his beloved Annie—that love endured.

PENELOPE MOANED dramatically as Theo continued searching painstakingly through the file for her birthday gift. "Oh, here it is, kiddo. Sorry, it's not wrapped." He handed over an Amazon mailer re-sealed with Scotch tape.

"That's okay, Mr. Theo." She snatched it from his hands, flipped it over, and beamed. "Good things come from Amazon."

Theo and Ivy exchanged eager glances. He sat down at the table, his heart racing wildly.

Penelope peeled away the tape and peeked into the envelope as though it were a mailbox. "You've really got my mind going. Should I try to guess?"

"If you want to."

"Taylor Swift concert tickets?"

"Nope."

"Opera tickets?"

"No…"

"A trip to Hollywood?"

Five days had passed since the court had entered the order, and it had been nearly impossible for Theo to keep quiet about it. Now, his leg jiggled, and his fingers drummed the tabletop. Penelope's guessing game was excruciating! "Pea, just look already!"

"Okay, okay. I'm just having some fun because, as you know, birthdays are rare. My next one won't come around for, let's see, eight thousand seven hundred and sixty hours!"

Theo held his breath as Penelope retrieved the single sheet of paper from inside the mailer.

"In the District Court of Washington County, State of Arkansas. In the matter of Ivy Lillian Palmer, an adult." Penelope paused, frowned, and looked at the envelope again. "I don't think this came from Amazon."

For the first time since Theo met Penelope, he wondered if her mind had actually failed to grasp something printed plain as could be on the document in her hands.

She gripped the edges and continued reading, deliberately pausing between each word. "Final… Order… for… Adoption… of… an… Adult…" She looked up at him, gaping. "Is this…does this mean…Mr. Theo?"

Theo was a balloon pumped full of joy. He sprang from his chair and began pacing the length of the table. "It means your mom is now legally my daughter. And, that means you, Penelope Pie, are officially my granddaughter."

Penelope sat still. She looked frozen in place. "Are you for real right now?"

"It's true, Pea." Ivy was wiping tears from her cheeks.

Ever so slowly, Penelope's expression transformed from bewildered to enlightened.

Theo found it almost unbearable, experiencing the raw truth of this moment. He thought he might burst.

"I can't believe this is really happening. It's truly, absolutely, mind-blowing. You get a billion points! No, a zillion! You won our game for sure! There's no way to ever top this. Can I tell you a secret, Mr. Theo?"

"Of course."

"You know my memoir, the one you had a meltdown over?"

"How could I forget?"

"Well, if you'll recall, you skipped out during Act Two and never heard the ending. Guess what? This *is* the ending. Act Three ended with us being a real family." Penelope hopped from her chair and began clapping her hands and cheering. Alice began howling, caught up in the ruckus. "Am I a great writer, or what?" she added before exploding into tears.

Eventually, after they had all calmed down, the party continued outside. The days were getting noticeably shorter, and only a few lightning bugs flickered around the abelia bushes. One day soon, their season would end. Here and then gone. It always happened quickly. Nearby, a tree frog chanted *puuuu-reeek, puuuu-reeek*. A slight hint of autumn stirred in the breeze. It was much too warm for a fire, but Theo built a small one on the grill, anyway. He gave Penelope and Ivy roasting sticks purchased just for the occasion.

Penelope waved a roasting stick through the flame and marveled as the marshmallow began to bubble. Theo caught a glimpse of future-Penelope, older, even braver and more brilliant, *his granddaughter*. Ivy offered a S'more to Theo, thick and gooey and already sticky on his fingers.

He had a daughter.

A family.

"Oh, it's delicious!" Penelope announced with her first mouthful. "Why aren't you eating yours, Grandpa T?"

The name came so quickly to her tongue. Theo was warmed, not by the fire, but by the thought that she must have been considering it for weeks.

He bit into the corner of his S'more. "Actually, it's pretty good." Did he really think it was tasty, or was everything about the night delicious? He honestly couldn't tell.

Hoo-hoo. Hoo-hoo.

"Hey! Our owl is here." Penelope stared into the overhead branches and then began walking the circumference of the tree, placing one foot directly in front of the next, heel toe, heel toe. Theo looked for the bird, but couldn't spot him in the yawning twilight.

"Oh my gosh, there he is," Ivy whispered, and pointed. The barred owl was perched, motionless, on the peak of the roof of Gloria's garage apartment. "I think he wants to be part of our family too," she said. For a while, they all stared at it, mesmerized.

"Do you think his nest is in your thinking tree?" Penelope asked.

"I don't think so." Theo appreciated the owl's visits and had noticed they were becoming more regular. "He seems to like us though. Maybe we should build him a nesting box and install it high up in the tree." He had some leftover wood stored in the shed he could use.

"Yes! Maybe he would visit more often," Penelope said, her eyes wide with excitement.

Nita had been cleaning up inside, but eventually she joined them. Penelope turned her focus to roasting another marshmallow and assembling a final S'more for her.

"It's been a wonderful night. Thanks for including me," Nita said. "I feel a bit like I'm intruding on this special family moment though."

"Don't be ridiculous," Theo said. "You're family, too." He had no notion of anything romantic ever blooming between them, but he had learned a valuable lesson—friends could be family too. And, they were to be cherished, because life truly was fragile and fleeting.

Penelope was playing with her S'more, mushing the melted marshmallow between the graham crackers. "I don't want this night to ever end. Let's sleep out here, all of us," she said dreamily, lying back on the grass and resting her head against Alice's body. "You know, I just thought of something, Mr., um, I mean, Grandpa T." Moonlight illuminated her eyeglasses as she looked at Theo. "You still haven't taught me to play marbles."

"Tomorrow. We'll do that tomorrow," he said, barely recognizing his voice, it sounded so relaxed. "Penelope, I've been meaning to ask you something."

"Yeah?"

"You know that day you first showed up at my door? When it was raining?"

"Yeah."

"Did you really miss your bus?"

"Yeah, I really did. It was all my fault, because I had walked almost to the corner when I realized I had forgotten my protectability cloak, and I went back to get it because I could tell it was going to rain, but by the time I made it back to the corner, the bus was way down the street, almost out of sight. Since I'd already been left behind, and it was storming by then, I figured I might as well meet Alice's new owner. Your house was closer than ours, and it was all part of my brilliant plan anyway."

"Interesting. I imagined you had skipped school on purpose."

"Nope. But I did have the apartment key in my pocket," she admitted.

He laughed, glee filling him. "Ah, so you *could* have gotten back inside if you'd wanted to."

"And missed all this fun? No way."

In the distance, a train passed through downtown, its whistle a familiar refrain. Theo suspected sorrow would find him again someday—that was the reality of life. But that night, sitting with his family beneath the waning crescent moon, under the generous canopy of his favorite white oak and the watchful eye of a sociable barred owl, gratitude and contentment filled Theo to overflowing. The world was brimming with both wonder and worry. He smiled, closed his eyes, and savored the magic.

Talya Tate Boerner is the author of four books and numerous short stories and essays that have published in multiple journals and anthologies, including *Arkansas Review*, *Writer's Digest*, and *Reminiscence Magazine*. She blogs at Grace Grits and Gardening and writes a regular "Delta Child" column for *Front Porch* magazine. Talya lives in Fayetteville, Arkansas, with her husband and two miniature schnauzers. She is always on the lookout for magic in the ordinary.

If you enjoyed this story, please consider posting a short review to **Amazon** and **Goodreads**. In the sea of new books being released every day, reviews are instrumental in book discoverability.

For book club questions and more information, visit the author's website at talyatateboerner.com or scan the QR code.

Made in the USA
Middletown, DE
11 July 2025